By the Blood of Rowans

Xan van Rooyen

For every reader who feels the wild magic tangled in their soul
For Louise, who believed even when I couldn't
And for Mark, with love always

Rowan

MY SISTERS danced in the waves as I bled on the shore.

Their hair unspooled in the wind; their hands lifted toward the moon hanging like a scythe above the black ocean. They raised their voices, the spell harmonized in four parts, and I felt its pull.

The ghosts within me joined in the chorus, every soul shard ululating to the bruised night and fading stars. I let them sing; I was powerless to stop them. Instead, I closed my eyes, feeling the familiar thrum of the departed within my bones as my sisters chanted in the old tongue, the language of the tamed gods from whom we claimed our power.

Salt stung the wounds cut across my forearms by each of my sisters' blades. Four fresh lines gouged between old scars. I knelt on the sand turning red beneath my knees and let the water take what it would of me.

My sisters' song rose in pitch and volume, their voices straining, beseeching the waves to accept this offering from my veins. Ribbons of light rippled through the foam, darting toward their naked bodies as they spun and splashed.

The waves lapped hungrily at my blood, soaking my

jeans, icy fingers in my skin. A final pull, as if I were being dragged below by a rip current, swallowed by the sea, and my sisters gasped as one.

My ghosts fell silent, spent.

Dawn slashed its talons across the horizon, sending gold and vermilion bleeding through the shredded clouds, and in the light, my sisters' hair turned to flames, each an inferno circling a delicate face.

The spell complete, they dragged limbs made heavy with renewed power from the waves and pulled clothes over sticky skin.

"Thank you," Iona said as she removed bandages from her satchel. She bound my arms as the others toweled their hair and gathered their blades. "See you back at the house?"

I nodded.

"You'll be all right?" She cast a glance toward the cliffs at my back, their shadow receding from the sand but never from my heart, or what was left of it.

"Aye, I'll be fine. Just need a minute."

Iona patted my shoulder as I gingerly rolled down my sleeves.

I heard them leave, clambering along the pebble-strewn path that zig-zagged up the cliffs, but kept my gaze on the ocean. The tide was coming in, the waves thundering against the rocky arms extending in a deadly embrace from either side of the cove.

Cold and drained, I retreated from the waves racing higher along the beach and dusted the sand from my jeans, stiff with salt.

Having pulled on my boots, I started the steep climb, my legs weak, and my arms still numb from the spell. With my sisters gone and their magic dissipating, the birds returned, screeching their greetings to the dawn as they whirled above the black rock.

At the top of the cliff, I whistled for Auryn. She came

at once, trotting through the meadow with a mouthful of dewy grass. She followed me as I traced a path along the edge of the cliff. I couldn't help it, as if an invisible hook had caught within my sinews, reeling me back to this same spot every time I drew near.

Years of storms had washed the stone clean, but I didn't need to see the stain to know the place my heart had beat its last. The breath caught in my lungs like wool tangled in a brier. Auryn nudged my shoulder, huffing sweet breath in my face.

Taking hold of her mane, I leapt onto her back, letting her carry me away from memories of death as it began to rain.

The town on Inisliath had no name. It clung like a barnacle to the ragged shore on the south-eastern lee of the island, lonely, decaying. Here, the waves rolled gently into the bay instead of beating at the rocks. Here, the Kilduffs and O'Donnells made their homes in white-washed cottages with shingled roofs and stone-hemmed gardens. And it was here that we Sheehys had never been welcome.

An unwanted visitor in the nameless town, I kept my business brief. Leaving Auryn grazing among the crumbling graves of the few Christians who'd attempted to lay claim to the island hundreds of years ago, I jogged through the rain to the general store. It would be quiet this early in the morning, not yet bustling with islanders who shunned me and my family. Few tourists ever came to the store, preferring the rustic village market open on Sundays and filled with home-made island novelties like my sisters' candles and jewelry.

I hurried, taking fewer than fifteen minutes to fill the basket with the list of things we could neither grow nor make at home, like pine tar and tampons. Still, I could feel gazes raking against my skin. The ghosts within me quivered, their fingers pushing through my flesh as if they could reach through the prison of my skin and take a hold of their descendants, thereby renewing their grip on life.

In my haste to get to the cashier, I rounded a display and clipped the shoulder of the girl stacking boxes of muesli, scattering several.

"Hey, watch it!"

"Sorry." I held up my hands in apology, hoping she'd let it go, hoping she wouldn't notice me at all. Her nacreous eyes narrowed, her exquisite face twisting into a snarl. The shards of the Kilduffs I carried flexed and juddered: like calling to like across the divide of death for which I was the threshold. Could Lucy hear her ancestors rattling behind the cage of my ribs like moths desperate for the flame?

"Rowan Sheehy." She turned every syllable of my name into an accusation. "You're making a mess on my floor."

I thought she meant the cereal, but blood had seeped through the bandage on my left wrist and soaked through the threadbare cuff of my sweater. Beads dripped from my fingers and were splattering the pristine floor. "I'm sorry."

"Oh, you will be." She pressed her heel onto a box of muesli, then another, kicking the crushed contents toward me. If I reached for her, dared to touch her, she'd scream, and the rest of the Kilduff clan would come running. These days, they were armed with more than pitchforks, dividing their time between the store and police station.

"I said I was sorry." I gritted my teeth and wrapped my right hand around the gash on my arm, hoping to stem the bleeding.

"That'll be—" She studied the carnage at her feet. "About forty bucks' worth of damage. I should charge you for the inconvenience of mopping up after you, too. It's quite disgusting."

Forty. That was almost double how much the contents of my basket would cost, already more than we could afford this week. We would never be able to make enough, not to keep our horses from starving through the winter nor stop us from losing our home.

"Please, don't do this," I said, trying to keep my emotions in check. I didn't want to feed her a moment of fear or anger. My ghosts writhed, their voices shouting inside my skull.

Lucy lifted her foot and brought it down on yet another box. "Shall I keep going?" she asked. "Do you want me to call the manager?"

She'd inherited her hatred for me from every Kilduff who'd come before her, her entire lineage soaked in bitter animosity. It went back centuries, a constant in all the memories I'd inherited from the Rowans before me. The Kilduff hatred was steadfast, as unshakable as it was misguided, but I wasn't going to undo generations of prejudice over shards of cereal.

"I can't pay for this," I said.

"You're going to have to. One way or another." Her eyes widened, trapping me in her stare. She unleashed her magic, her power surging across my skin in an incinerating wave. The ghosts inside me screamed as the wards spelled into my skin flared, the tattoos on my arms and chest burning as they battled against her assault. Her magic couldn't bend me to her will as it did others. She knew all it did was hurt me.

Lucy smiled as my fear trickled toward her. All the lives I'd seen, all the memories that haunted me, and still I didn't understand how someone so beautiful could be so ugly.

5

"Stop it." Teagan approached, her torn fishnets at odds with the yellow store-uniform T-shirt.

"Just a little fun. Ma won't mind," Lucy said, pretending she wasn't out of breath from the effort she'd exerted on me. Unlikely she fed on me either, then.

"Ma *will* mind if you don't get this cleaned up." Teagan didn't even look at me as she tossed a box of Band-aids in my direction. "She's off to meet the new O'Donnell with Gran. Ferry comes in at nine. Also, we've got to close up shop tonight and take inventory."

"Speaking of which..." Lucy folded her arms and looked at me expectantly.

"I told you I can't pay."

"Gods, leave him be, Luce."

"What's got your knickers in a twist?" Lucy glared at her sister.

"This is just—it's childish. It's beneath you," Teagan said with a flick of her raven hair.

"Fine, off you scuttle, Sheehy, back to the dung heap you crawled out of," Lucy said with a cold smile. "And you'll pay. Maybe not today, but someday soon. Trust me, you'll see. Things are going to change around here."

I rushed through the check-out and paused beneath the eaves to swap wet bandages for fresh Band-aids. They wouldn't contain the wounds for long. This morning, my sisters had carved deeper than usual.

My ghosts calmed as well, retreating into the quiet residence they kept between my bones. The rain had eased a little, but it would still be a soaking trek home through the fields. Auryn huffed at me, her amber gaze one of reproach.

I rubbed her white face with my knuckles before I swung up onto her back and took handfuls of her shaggy mane. We headed off along the coast road, climbing out of town onto the gentle escarpment leading north and eventually west around the headland. The vantage point gave me a clear view of the bay where the McNamaras stowed their fishing fleet and tourist boats, where the dock awaited the arriving ferry. The Kilduff women were part of the welcoming party, standing in conversation beneath large umbrellas with Martha O'Donnell, clan matriarch and sovereign of the island.

New O'Donnell, Teagan had said. There couldn't be a *new* O'Donnell, which meant someone was returning. All the island families had lost kin to the mainland; none of us had ever had family return.

We stood in the drizzle, Auryn shaking her head and swishing her tail, as I watched the few occupants disembark, only one group of three taking their time where other tourist groups rushed to escape the rain. The three were wrapped up against the weather, the shortest wearing an arm sling and eye-searing orange jacket, a neon flare against the grey wash of Inisliath.

The ghosts within me stirred, curious as they sensed the foreign yet familiar presence, blood calling to blood across the threads of magic stitching all the founding families into the tapestry of the island.

Martha O'Donnell swept down the dock, arms extended, and pulled the arrival—stooped and dressed in a black trench coat—into an embrace. The long-lost O'Donnell, then.

Lucy's words echoed in my ears, taken up by the chorus of ghosts in my head, a terrifying refrain, repeating over and over, a promise and a threat.

Things were going to change.

FUCK THIS place. Seriously. It hadn't stopped raining since we'd arrived. My Doc Martens were soaked. The cracked leather was used to traipsing around a city, not navigating the quagmires passing for gravel drives in this shithole.

"Be a doll," Mum said, as if that would make me more inclined to get off my ass. We both sat for a few more seconds, the wipers running sprints across the windshield as sheets of more grey poured out of the sky. An ornate gate blocked our way. *Ros Tearmann.* The name had been welded in giant, Gothic letters across the top like something out of a Victorian horror movie.

Finally, in answer, I lifted my left arm dangling in its sling, and tapped my wrist. The hollow sound of the cast was still audible despite the various layers I'd worn in the hopes of surviving the island's persistent precipitation.

Mum didn't look at me. She never could when there were bruises on my face. I think she felt guilty even though it wasn't her fists that had done the damage. I felt the same when it was her with a split lip or black eye. With a sigh, she opened the door and swung her legs out of the car. Her heels, sensible as they were, disappeared into the gravel. She hobbled over to the gate, the metal grating on the ancient hinges as she swung them open to admit the equally ancient station wagon we'd recently bought.

"You should've done that for her," Granddad piped up from the backseat.

"She's not the one with a broken arm." It shut him up as I knew it would. I'm not sure what I expected him to do, wizened and creaky as he was, but I wanted him to do more than watch the bruises bloom and fade across our faces.

Mum tripped her way back to the car and sloshed behind the wheel. She was shivering. I turned up the heat, and she hit the accelerator, the tires spitting up dirt as we pulled into the grounds of the retirement home.

I knew what to expect. We'd spent enough time Googling the place to know the "estate" was massive and old and regal, like the mansions in all those period dramas on telly. But a photo on the Internet couldn't capture the grandeur. Of course, all the photos online had come with blue sky and sunshine in the background, not rain falling like bullets.

Mum rushed indoors, leaving me to gather my granddad. He'd been tall once, but now he hunched as if the weight of the years had become too much. Maybe it was the three bouts of lymphoma he'd had to fight, or maybe it was the guilt of never helping Mum leave the abusive asshole he'd been so keen on her marrying.

"It'll be all right now," Granddad said. "We're home."

Home.

The word hit me harder than my father's right hook. Home didn't exist anymore. Not for me. Everything there

9

belonged to *him*, and we were done with *him*. Mum had promised.

Granddad leaned on me, his weight tugging at the partially torn ligaments around my subluxated collarbone. Partially *ruptured*, the doctor had said. Ruptured was a better word. It described my whole fucking life.

Granddad clutched a battered umbrella in his other hand, letting the rain waterfall onto my shoulder. I was drenched by the time we made it up the steps, while Granddad's wisps of white hair remained waxed in perfect place, clinging like spider webs to his shriveled head. The steps had to be marble—weren't all houses like this cut from marble? The stones of this one were grey, too, blending into the surroundings as if the whole damn place had metastasized from the ground up. I hated it. I wouldn't want to die here, but Granddad said this was where he wanted to be, where he was *supposed* to be, whatever the hell that meant.

I was meant to be starting my final year of school. One more year until I could get away from my parents: my father, the colonel and monster; and my mum, who seemed trapped by his side for reasons I didn't get. Was it embarrassment? She was a police officer, for fuck's sake, which only made it worse. Maybe trying to be "one of the boys" at work meant she couldn't admit to getting her ass kicked at home. If only my father could respect her badge as much as she seemed to respect all his medals. The bruises faded from Mum's skin, but I knew the scar tissue went deeper, knotting up her insides.

If I'd known all it took was a broken arm to finally get her to dump him, I would've let him do it ages ago. At least that's what I told myself as I shuffled my granddad through the doors. He would die here, and part of me was jealous he was getting his wish when none of mine had ever come true.

The imposing doors swung shut behind us, sealing us in a brightly lit foyer, which smelled like a flower shop and not at all like the antiseptic reek of Granddad's previous care home. The décor was drab though, the carpets clean but worn, the furniture outdated. Despite that, the place felt more like a holiday resort and less like one stop from the mortuary, except for the fact it was silent. No geriatric shuffling, no muffled voices from a distant TV, no sounds of human habitation at all, besides us.

Granddad straightened his spine and regained some of his former height. He smiled, and his eyes brightened, even the one gone milky with blindness. I hated him even more. It wasn't fair.

"What do you mean there's been a mistake?" Mum asked the person behind the reception desk. The name badge pinned to their chest read "Siobhan."

Sha-*vaun*, I mouthed quietly, reminding myself how not to say the "b." Traditionally, a girl's name, but I try not to gender people based on superficial stuff like outfits or hairstyles, or the generally accepted gender of a name.

"I sorted this all out online," Mum continued.

"I'm sorry," Siobhan said, their pale cheeks turning pink. "It's just—there's been an error. We don't have a room for you." They gave me and Granddad the once-over with shrewd green eyes. They'd raked their curly hair back into a braid so severe I feared for their hair follicles. They wore a grey-blue dress that looked homemade, and their wrists were ringed with an assortment of leather bracelets. They even had dainty seashells dangling from their ears to complete the local islander look.

"Really? You're full up, are you?" Mum's tone was creeping dangerously close to the one she used when in detective mode.

"We—well..." Siobhan looked down.

"Are you the manager of this establishment?" Mum

had gone full detective inspector now.

"I am, but—"

Another person approached us, scuffed boots silent on the heavy rug in the foyer.

"There a problem?" The newcomer rolled grey sleeves down over bandaged, tattooed arms. Grey was clearly the uniform around here. I felt rather conspicuous in my orange Arc'teryx jacket. Okay, I lied when I said none of my wishes had been granted. I always got what I wanted, if it was something the colonel's money could buy.

"My brother, Rowan," Siobhan said, with a tight smile, introducing the guy with tattoos. They had the same pointy chin and auburn hair. I gave Rowan a closer inspection. He could've been my age or a bit older, judging by the scruff on his jaw. His gaze lingered on me, a shadow momentarily dimming his eyes as he flicked curly hair off of his face. Looked like he'd gone dumpster diving for his clothes, as his jeans were ripped more than was fashionable and his sweater was ratty.

"They're O'Donnells," Siobhan continued, and Rowan's eyes widened. "Could you get Mother, please."

"I don't see how there's been a complication." Mum tapped her fingers on the counter, her lips pursed in annoyance.

Rowan disappeared through a door marked "Private," leaving us all looking at each other for several awkward minutes. Siobhan seemed particularly keen on glaring at Granddad, hawk-gaze boring holes through him. What the hell was the problem? I was about to ask, when a person around Mum's age breezed into reception, dress billowing and long hair hanging loose to the waist. Seashells had been knotted into the tresses.

"I'm Ms. Sheehy, proprietor of Ros Tearmann." She addressed Mum. The numerous bracelets on her wrists tinkled as she moved.

"My God, you look just like your mother," Granddad said, gawking.

"You're too kind." She gave Granddad a smile that didn't touch her eyes.

"I'm Detective Inspector Walsh," Mum said. "Sabrina," she added, trying to be a little more polite. "My father, Brian, and this is Ash."

I held my breath, waiting for one of the Sheehys to ask if I was a son or a daughter.

"Nice to meet you, Ash," Ms. Sheehy said, and I exhaled. "So, I believe there's been a misunderstanding?" She raised a skeptical eyebrow.

"This is Brian *O'Donnell*." Siobhan gestured to my granddad.

"Is that so?" Ms. Sheehy exchanged a look with Siobhan, which made it obvious none of them was excited about having Granddad stay.

"I paid the deposit," Mum said. "And submitted all the forms online as required." Mum was nothing if not a fiend for paperwork. Her case files were always immaculate—the one thing she had actual control over in her life.

"It's just, well—" Ms. Sheehy stabbed at the outdated computer on the desk, not bothering to finish her sentence. "I think I know what the problem is. Our software doesn't know whether to file the name under O or D. Look, here it is. I'm sorry about the confusion." She gave Mum another forced smile. Mum blinked an *oh really?* at Ms. Sheehy's obvious bullshit.

"Mother, are you—" Siobhan didn't finish their sentence either.

"Room thirty-seven. Rowan, could you escort Mr. O'Donnell?" Ms. Sheehy said. "I'm sure our new tenant would like to settle in as soon as possible."

"Nice to meet you, son," Granddad said, offering Rowan his hand to shake over the desk.

Rowan hesitated before briefly shaking my Granddad's hand as if he were afraid of touching the arthritic fingers.

"I'll see you upstairs, then." His accent was all burrs

and island drawl, his eyes dark and guarded. There was something weird about them, but he turned away before I could figure it out. There was a weirdness about this whole place, like it was holding its breath, waiting for something. I didn't like it one bit, even if it did smell like a summer meadow.

"Your family will be up as soon as the paperwork is signed," Ms. Sheehy added. "Do you have a bag?"

"In the car," Granddad said. "Ash can get it." He nodded at me. Was my sling invisible? The doctor had told me not to lift heavy things for at least six weeks, not that anyone seemed to care.

"Nah, you're grand," Rowan said. "I'll get it." Was that pity? I didn't need some strange guy doing me any favors.

I watched Rowan lead my granddad out of the foyer to an elevator. That couldn't have been part of the original design of the place.

"Mum, are you sure about this?" I whispered.

"We've paid for it," she said. "I'm glad the issue has been resolved." She turned to Ms. Sheehy and accepted a sheaf of papers from a scowling Siobhan.

I headed back outside, leaving Mum to sort out particulars. The rain was falling even harder, the drops stinging as they hit the bruises on my face. I tilted my head back, eyes closed, and let them hurt me.

Before I could drown where I stood, I headed for the car and gingerly pried open the boot. Granddad hadn't brought much, just the one large suitcase Mum had used on her honeymoon to Morocco, and then never again.

The case was a bitch to maneuver with only one hand. It had been two weeks, but everything still hurt. My shoulder muscles ached from inactivity, not that I'd be getting back on the wall anytime soon. Amazing how everyone believed the injuries were a result of a climbing accident, same way they believed Mum's were from pushing too hard in the boxing ring. Sometimes I think

14

that's the reason the colonel first took me climbing. He'd said it would be a good bonding activity, and it was at first, until it became an even better way to explain away the bruises.

"Fuck!" I dropped the handle of the bag and pressed my right hand against my clavicle.

"I said I'd get it." Rowan materialized out of the rain like some kind of ghost.

"I can manage." I reached back in for the handle, but his hand was already on it and my fingers brushed his in a moment of awkwardness.

"You're injured," he said.

"So are you." I cut my gaze to the bandage visible through the holes of his sweater.

"Nothing broken," he said, "and I'm happy to help." So polite and decent and irritating.

"Whatever," I said, my glare turning into an inadvertent study of his profile as he leaned past me. His hair was plastered to the back of his neck where black tendrils of a tattoo disappeared beneath his sweater. The guy was seriously inked up. Not what I'd been expecting of an islander, but then what the hell did I know about the people stuck living out here on this rock? He smelled good, at least, like grass and something like licorice, only spicier. I inhaled deeply as he pulled the suitcase out of the car.

"So, you're an O'Donnell," he said with a hint of derision.

"Technically, I'm a Walsh. On account of the colonel— my father," I added.

Rowan seemed perplexed by that, his frown deepening. I braced myself for the inevitable 'are you a boy or a girl?' "Still got enough O'Donnell blood in you," he said instead.

"Enough for what?"

"For the island to want you," he said all mysterious, as

if it would make me intrigued instead of pissed off. I bit back my reply as he lugged the suitcase into the house, his biceps molded by the soggy sweater. I followed, studying his arms and trying to guess his ape index. He had the right build for a climber, lean and lanky. Not me. I'd always been too stocky, constantly waging a war between getting stronger and becoming too heavy.

Inside, Mum was using a towel to dry her hair and wasn't wearing her coat anymore. I was leaving puddles on the floor, but no one noticed, except Rowan. He frowned at the dirty footprints I'd walked through the foyer but didn't say anything. I ground my heels into the carpet, hoping I left a stain.

Together, we all rode the elevator up to Granddad's new digs in a silence so tense I could've sliced it like a pizza. Rowan seemed determined to become one with the walls, pressed tightly into a corner and using Granddad's bag like a shield.

An eternity later, we stepped out of the elevator and trudged down a long corridor until we reached a spacious en suite. Granddad sat at the bay window holding a mug of tea, clearly oblivious to whatever unpleasantness his arrival had caused. He smiled as he stared at the drenched landscape outside. Wet, grey, miserable. On a clear day, you might see the ocean beyond the stretch of fields dotted with twisted trees.

"Here you go, Mr. O'Donnell." Rowan dropped the suitcase on the floor.

I had stopped leaving puddles, but now I was starting to sweat in my jacket. It wasn't worth the effort of taking off my sling, though, if we were going to head out again soon.

"Rowan, how about you give Ash a tour of the place while we get Mr. O'Donnell unpacked," Ms. Sheehy said.

"How long will you be?" I asked Mum.

She pursed her lips. "As long as needs be. You'll just have to be patient."

That's not why I asked, but I didn't bother explaining. I wasn't sure how someone so good at being a detective could be so clueless when it came to their own kid. Instead, I left the room, heading back to the elevator with my face burning from more than just overheating in my jacket.

Rowan stepped in beside me, again pressed as far away from me as possible. We rode down in another uncomfortable silence. Back in the foyer, I wrestled with my sling, gritting my teeth against pain, until I could loosen the Velcro and release my arm made extra massive by the cast on my wrist.

"Need help?" he asked in a tone which said he hoped not. I didn't answer, and let him watch as I struggled out of my jacket and dumped it onto one of the settees that looked purely ornamental. Then I wrestled my sling back on. He looked away, but not before I saw a grin cracking the corner of his mouth and a flash of crooked teeth. At least I was entertaining, I guess.

"Let the tour begin," I said when I was done.

He looked as if he was about to say something, when his whole body went rigid.

"You okay?"

He pressed a hand to his throat and sucked in a breath, his face turning corpse-pale, lips already blue.

"What's wrong?"

"I'll be...fine," he muttered. "Just...stay here." He staggered from the foyer, shoving open the door marked "Private."

"Hey! You sure you okay?"

No answer. Siobhan wasn't at reception anymore, and there was no one else around. I hesitated before following. It was none of my business, but I had a habit of not doing what I was told.

The door wasn't locked, so I pushed it open and headed down a much darker corridor. It was colder here, too, the air misting as I exhaled a shaky breath. There was a small lounge off the corridor, dark with the curtains drawn and no lights on. I turned to leave but caught the sound of a whimper. I peered into the gloom. What the hell? Rowan lay curled in a fetal position beside the couch, clutching at his throat. My heartbeat tripled as I took a tentative step across the threshold.

"Dude, are you—"

"You're not supposed to be here," a person said as they shoved past me, bashing my shoulder and sending a jolt through my collarbone. They reached for the door to the lounge and slammed it shut in my face.

"Hey, I think he needs—"

"He's fine, O'Donnell. You should mind your own business," they said as they folded their arms across their chest. They looked fourteen-ish, maybe younger. They must've been another Sheehy, given the red curls avalanching down their shoulders.

"He could be dying in there," I said.

They laughed, eyes sparking with something I didn't understand. "Trust me, my brother will be fine. Was he giving you the tour?"

I nodded, baffled by this kid's attitude and half-wanting to batter down the door just because I'd had it slammed in my face.

"Come on then, O'Donnell."

"Stop calling me that," I said instead.

"What? O'Donnell? It's your name isn't it?"

"Not really."

"You people, you always forget the important stuff." They took my hand, and I let them steer me back to the foyer, to where it was warm and bright. "I'm Deirdre, by the way. I'm the youngest Sheehy." After a pause, they cocked their head to the side and said, "I'm a she, and I'm not sure if it's nice to meet you yet." The jewelry she wore around her wrists and ankles—more seashells and other brightly colored baubles—made pleasant tinklings as she moved, as she started talking about sunrooms and summer verandas. I tried to tune out, but every time I attempted to bring my thoughts back to Rowan, they exploded inside my head—not like a bomb, more like when you blow too hard on a dandelion. Trying to focus on anything but Deirdre made my head feel thick and fuzzy.

There was mud on the hem of her dress, which was yellow with purple beetles crawling all over it. I blinked, but yeah, the bugs were actually wriggling.

I'd read about certain types of mold causing hallucinations. This building was ancient. Who knew what kind of spores were being excreted by the walls to fuck up my brain.

"If you were a girl, it would probably be different." Deirdre ushered me away from the room.

"What?" I was feeling decidedly weird and disorientated, floating along behind her as she skipped in front. Like, literally skipped.

"Girls have more power here. You'll see. You could probably still decide to be one of us. Well, an O'Donnell, I mean, if not a girl." Her gaze flicked me up and down, and it felt like getting doused with a pot of boiling water.

I couldn't breathe as I tried to process what she'd said. Before I could come up with a response, we were back in the lobby with our mums.

As confusion slowly gave way to irritation, I hugged my granddad goodbye, ignoring the pain in my shoulder, then clambered back into the car like I was on autopilot. Deirdre gave me a wave and a grin, and the fuzzy hold on my mind finally released. Had she really told me being a girl would be better? That I should *choose* to be something I thought I made perfectly clear I wasn't? Fuck that.

It was only when we reached the gates I remembered Rowan and searched the windows for any sign of him.

But the rain came down again, and I slumped back in my seat.

"Dad'll be happy there," Mum said even though she white-knuckled the steering wheel. "*We'll* be happy here. We have to be."

Rowan

FEWER THAN two miles from Ros Tearmann, Andy Kilduff dug his fingers into wet earth, his screams choked short by the silver blade severing skin and tendon, muscle and vein. Blood flooded his hands as he grappled at the rent in his flesh, life pouring out of him in viscous ribbons to stain the churned ground beneath his feet. His attacker stood behind him, but when Andy tried to turn, to face his murderer, their fingers knotted in his hair and dragged his head back, allowing more blood to fountain from the gash across his throat. The softest tinkling of bells accompanied his dying gurgles.

I clutched at my own throat. Pain burned across my skin where the blade had cut the Kilduff. I gasped for breath as he did, the panic rising within me an echo of his as I hurried away from Ash O'Donnell in search of a safe place to leave my body.

There was no evading the summons to join a dying islander. The pain intensified, and I gritted my teeth against it. The world pulsed black and purple, the shadows curling their fingers around my ankles, sending skitters of ice across my skin.

Finally, I let go as Andy sagged, a slow wilt of twitching limbs, and let his death wash through me, dragging me into the Otherworld.

In shadow form, I walked across the clifftop, leaving luminescent footprints behind me. Below, waves thundered, every splash sending stars shivering up to the sky, the music of the crashing ocean reeling away in fronds of foamy light. The moon of the Otherworld was huge, the shadows of butterflies flitting across its surface; the shards of souls sent beyond the veil.

Andy Kilduff appeared on the cliff-top, hands still clutching at his throat. He hadn't seen his attacker. He thought he'd been alone on the meadow path, the same path he walked every afternoon.

He'd taken a moment to catch his breath and observe a ring of flowers in the grass when hands had grabbed him from behind, a blade kissing his skin before he could react. He'd fallen face first into the mud at the foot of a lone hawthorn. All he knew of his murderer was the touch of their fingers in his hair and a scent like potpourri.

Now, Andy crested the rise, his soul no longer weighed down by his arthritic body. I greeted him with a wave and perfunctory smile.

"No, not like this," Andy said. Some people fought the inevitable, but once they were on the clifftop, it was over. No adrenaline to the heart, no defibrillation or prayer could bring them back to life.

"This is the way," I said, gently. "Even for you and your kind."

"Who?" he asked with tears on his face.

"I don't know."

"My family. You'll tell them, won't you?"

"I'll make sure you're found," I said.

Andy let his hands drop away from his throat. Wisps of starlight still seeped from the wound, silver droplets skittering across the swirling shadows.

"I don't want to die," he said.

"No one ever does," I said. This was the worst part, the battle every soul fought on the cliffs. None of the souls I'd met had actually wanted to die. Not even suicides, and I'd seen five in as many years. Some were relieved at the end, tired of fighting daily battles against their demons. More were angry. Very few were ever truly ready to let go.

"This shouldn't have happened," he said.

"I know. I'm sorry." I offered him my hand, a ripple of darkness against the stark light of this in-between.

Andy's lips peeled away from his teeth, sharp canines flashing.

I should've known it would be like this. As soon as I carved my mark upon his forehead he would be mine and safe from becoming one of the wandering sluagh. He ran and I moved with the power of a thought to step in front of him and slow his charge.

"Don't touch me!" he screamed, his voice shattering into sparks as he beat me with his fists. I was stronger—I had to be—and managed to pin his flailing arms to his sides before dragging him down in a tangle of curses.

I used my legs to hold him and placed the mark upon his forehead, a single line with two more hanging perpendicular to it. It would ease his passing and protect him from the prowling threat of the restless. "Death in Life, and Life in Death," I said.

"No," Andy cried. "I wasn't ready. Not like this!"

I let him rage, let him sob and hurl fistfuls of dirt into the air. Then he curled onto his side and clutched at me, rage replaced by grief. I held him as he wept. Island deaths were usually gentle, the aged passing peacefully in their sleep, content to take my hand and follow me beyond the veil. Murder wasn't entirely new to me. My first journey across the Otherworld had been the result of violence.

When Andy stilled, I rose and offered him my hand. This time, he accepted it, and I helped him to his feet. His eyes pulsed electric blue in the shadows, an effect of the magic imbuing the Kilduff clan, lingering even after death.

"There was a time we couldn't die," he said. "The Sheehys changed that. You've ruined my family."

He was wrong, of course. The four families were all touched by magic, a magic inherited from our ancestors. Our power had diminished, but the Sheehys had nothing to do with failing Kilduff allure or the McNamaras no longer being able to shed their human skins. Yet, Andy— like most of the islanders—believed my family was to blame for all their ills.

"You'll be where you want to be soon," I said.

"Where I want to be is home, heart still beating." He glowered. "Some bastard murdered me. Was it one of you?" he asked, hands on his throat again. "Was it your hand on the blade?"

"None of mine could've done this. I promise there'll be justice."

"Justice," he snarled the word. "What does a filthy Sheehy know of justice?"

Indeed, considering very little had been shown to us. The O'Donnells and Kilduffs had hurt us in numerous ways over the years and no one had held them accountability for the destruction they'd wrought.

Still, a murder on the island wouldn't go unpunished. The Kilduffs wouldn't rest until they knew who had killed one of their own.

My skin prickled. The Sheehys would be the first suspects. The dread tiptoeing across my skin burrowed deeper, settling in my center like a stone. There was a murderer on our island.

Andy said nothing more as we walked inland, across the rolling hillocks of the Otherworld garbed in tendrils of mist. As we meandered through the ephemeral, memories from his life flitted past us. Some were butterflies with the softest touch as they passed through me; others came with teeth and claws ready to maul. I received them all, grateful when a gentle one lingered.

Andy having his first kiss in a meadow with Sarah McNamara. He'd ended up marrying her against her family's wishes and fathering several children. He hadn't wanted to believe their families' warnings, that the love of a Kilduff was toxic, that they'd siphon the life from their lover until nothing but a hollow shell remained, that Andy and Sarah's union could only end in heartache.

The memories I carried from the other Rowans faded as Andy's own memories became more vivid even as they darkened, kisses and joy replaced by hospital waiting rooms, blood, and despair. The memories tore through me, and I had no way to defend myself from their attack. The pain of losing a child was a special kind of agony. I braced for it, but it still left me doubled over. My hands balled into fists as Andy's grief wound its thorns around my soul, every barb tearing fresh wounds.

It would pass as long as I had the strength to endure.

"You Sheehys did that," Andy said, breathless. "You cursed my wife's womb. You took my babies. My sons and daughters. You!" He pointed a finger at me, tears leaving silver trails down his cheeks.

More memories assailed me, memories of finding butterfly wings beneath the unused crib, of my grandmother painting invisible runes in the air behind Andy's back, of my great-uncle smiling in the cove when Andy's first child burned on the pyre. Andy's memories infected my own, his hatred and despair rubbing my insides raw.

Soon he would be in the river, and his pain would leave him. He could think me and my family the villains a few moments longer—trying to change his mind wouldn't ease his hurt.

Andy was fading faster now, letting go of the life he'd known. Together, we wound our way down the path through the forest of rowan trees stretching along the river, which cut the Otherworld east to west. Everything here felt flimsy and insubstantial, mere echoes of their true forms. Except the trees. Their bark was warm to the touch, power thrumming through their green veins and swelling their blood-red berries. I pressed my hand to the first tree, honoring the spirit that moved within it.

The trees were more than my namesake; they were bound to my lineage just as I was bound by blood to them. One day, I would join their ranks along the river, yet another rowan. It was my fate, my curse. I would live my life on Inisliath ferrying the dead until it became too much, one way or another, and I remained in the Otherworld for good.

Together we walked down the lane, the trees knitting closed behind us.

"Truth be, I'm scared," Andy said without bitterness.

"You needn't be. They're waiting for you."

"I'll not thank you," Andy said.

"I don't expect you to."

Andy went easily then, happily even, splashing up to his knees as he forged through the shallows, his soul shredding to purple wisps when he passed beyond the veil into the waiting arms of his loved ones. He had been granted release in death. No turbulent current had sucked at his legs or dragged him into perpetual darkness.

I shivered as the rowans surrounded me, their branches tangling in my hair and about my limbs. It was always a fight back to the realm of the living. The dead wanted me. They'd wanted me that night on the cliffs, the ritual performed in a hurry so that I might lead my uncle's soul to the river.

I'd found him waiting on the clifftop for me, and together we'd traversed the Otherworld. He left me at the river, his remnants twisting into soil and air to become one of the many rowans flanking the shore. He left me to ford the river alone. That part had been easy enough, but to assume my duty I had to cross back and pierce the veil a second time. The current had sucked at my legs, the voices of the dead singing to me of sweet release. I'd been so close to letting the currents take me.

Not then. And not today.

I'd done this so many times it was no longer frightening, only exhausting. I pushed against the branches, trying gently to disentangle my limbs. Usually, sheer will was power enough, and the trees surrendered. This time, they didn't let go. The hairs on the back of my neck rose in warning at the sound of the whispers.

I hadn't heard the voices of the dead since the night of my own trial. They never spoke to me, only my charges. I shouldn't have been at risk of their spells, of their menace, and yet the trees tightened their grip and pulled me deeper into their ranks. A branch slid around my throat, and though I needed no air to breathe in this realm, I reached for my dagger, panicked. My fingers fumbled at the hilt, unable to grasp it.

The voices were sharp and shrill, and belonged to the sluagh. Something had disturbed them, and they were hungry, but the trees weren't theirs to command. I relaxed in their grip, and the rowans eased their hold, keeping me hidden and protected.

The whispers grew louder, screeches of claw on slate. Then came a rasping like the slow shift of scales. The trees pressed closer. Between their branches I could see a coiling black smoke moving down the river. The rowans withdrew from the presence as it charged for the shore. A deafening roar accompanied it, emanating from the thickening cloud.

The darkness furled and danced in the air, finally forking into fingers—talons—reaching from the river. Where the fingers grazed the nearest trees, they blackened and withered.

I could feel their suffering, the fear burning through the trees, spreading from bough to bough. The same fear ignited in me, my chest scorched from the inside out. I looked down at my incorporeal form. Light poured from the wound, flames licking at my skin in the interlocking ovals of a triquetra above my heart.

My family were calling me home, and the Rowans released me. The smoke writhed, its screams of rage ringing in my ears as I tore free from the Otherworld.

Ash

I'D WARNED Mum that any time a realtor called a property "quaint," what you were really getting was some shitty hovel in desperate need of demolition. Mum liked the sound of "quaint" and signed the rental agreement without even bothering to see the place in person.

"Well, it's not quite how they described," Mum said as we stood in the narrow driveway, looking at our new home. No shit. I've never hated being right so much.

I'm pretty sure the online description had read, "quaint two-bedroom cottage with rustic furnishings and sea-views." It hadn't said the thatched roof was lopsided or that there were clear signs of damp rising up the walls. We went inside anyway because where else were we going to go? And it was raining again. Of course.

"Oh, this is...this is charming," Mum forced through her teeth as she took in the tiny kitchen. The couches in the lounge looked as if they were a moment away from collapse, and the carpets were threadbare. The place stank, courtesy of the perpetually damp thatch, probably. I inspected first one bedroom, then the other.

"We'll have to share a bathroom," I said. Urgh, gross.

"We'll make do," Mum said as she deposited her bags in the room with a sliver of sea-view out of a grimy window.

I claimed the other, and I approached the bed warily before I put my weight on it. It groaned and creaked heavily as I moved up and down. There'd be zero privacy in this house with a bed announcing to the world every time I rolled over.

"This sucks." I hadn't meant to say it out loud, and I didn't just mean the bed, or the house, or the fact that we'd been forced to move to the ass-end of the world into a crap cottage that was all we could afford on Mum's salary. Not like cops in the city earned bucket loads, but her salary here was going to be even less.

"I know it does, but at least here we're..." Mum's eyes focused on mine for just a moment before she darted her gaze to the window.

At least here we're safe, I finished for her. Mum was a police officer. We should've been safe no matter where we went. Despite the tough-as-nails act she put on in her department, around the colonel she'd always been weak. She'd never had the guts to lay charges or file for divorce before. I could've pressed charges, too, I guess, but Mum was the one who'd told the doctors I'd had another climbing accident before I'd had the chance to say otherwise.

Now we were here. Mum said she'd left him for good, that he knew about it, and had accepted it. This was something I doubted considering he'd gone on some or other peace-keeping mission the day after he broke my arm.

"I'm sorry, sweetheart." Mum perched on the edge of the moaning bed. "Truly, I am. But things will get better.

This will be good for us." She patted my right hand where it rested on the torn knee of my damp jeans.

"How long will we be here?" I asked.

"Forever, Ash. I told you. It's for good this time."

"You've said that before."

Mum didn't respond, but her hand slipped away from mine as I stomped all over the momentary spike of regret. This was all her fault. Twice before she'd tried to leave him, once when I was just a baby, and again when I was eleven, right after the first time he hit me. We'd only been gone three nights before he'd come up with an apology so good she'd believed him, and we'd gone back. It had taken less than a month for him to forget we weren't punching bags. The thoughts left acid burns on my brain, but I kept my mouth clamped shut and tried my best to bury my doubt. Part of me wanted to believe her.

"You must be tired," she said. "You stay here and settle in. I'm going to check in at the station." She gave my hand a squeeze before she left. The station where Mum's Aunt Martha worked, Aunt Martha who'd been our lifeline and means of getting to Inisliath. She'd seemed decent enough down at the dock, but I wasn't looking forward to further introductions. The rest of our relatives here were probably all inbred, given the island's staggering population of 256. Make that 259 now.

I waited until I heard the front door shut and the car tires churn up gravel before I fought my way free of my sling. It was only then I realized I'd left my jacket at the retirement home. My new, expensive, awesome jacket.

"Fuck," I whispered, then said it louder and louder until I was yelling the single syllable at the top of my lungs, until it hurt my partially ruptured ligaments. I'd have to go back to get the jacket, which meant possibly seeing Rowan again. The thought didn't repulse me. I was kind of curious about what might've left him curled in a ball on the floor.

Alone, I stood in the center of my tiny bedroom and ran through the isometric exercises the Internet recommended for subluxation rehab. I was supposed to be seeing a physiotherapist starting next week, but I doubted Inisliath possessed something so sophisticated.

My mobile *beeped*, and I grabbed for it, realizing too late I'd instinctively reached for it with my left hand. I hadn't had reception all day, but now two glorious bars appeared in the top right corner of the screen. A text message waited for my attention, a message from the colonel.

The colonel: Keep trying to call but can't get through. Please reply asap. Love, Dad.

And another and another appeared, all sweet and caring, sent four, six, seven hours earlier. My vision blurred, and I didn't dare blink until a new message popped up. Sent 1 minute ago.

The colonel: Can't get hold of your mother either. Really concerned. Please respond.

No "love, Dad" at the end of that one. My thumb hovered over the screen, tempted to reply with *We're fine. FUCK YOU! We're better now we're far away from you. I HATE YOU! Sorry I was always such a disappointment. WHY CAN'T YOU LOVE ME? We're afraid of you, afraid of what you might break next.*

Instead, I deleted the thread with trembling fingers. Mum hadn't put in for an official transfer—she'd simply said she needed time to take care of Granddad, and they'd believed her. Mum hadn't told anyone where we were going—she didn't have anybody to tell, the colonel had seen to that—and I hadn't said a word to any of my friends.

They weren't real friends, anyway. They were the kind of people I met up with at the climbing gym in winter and hitched rides with to crags in the summer. They let me take photos of them doing impressive dynos or bat-hangs and followed me on social media like vultures waiting for me to upload cool pics they could tag and like and share. While they liked to tease me about how I always seemed to get injured when they weren't around, they never bothered to take it further. I don't think they wanted to know. They only ever wanted to talk climbing beta, not real life. As for school friends—yeah, I didn't have any of those.

I turned off my phone. Without Internet, the thing was pretty much useless anyway. I returned to the exercises instead. I needed to heal. I needed to get strong. This was the last time I'd let him or anyone hurt me. It was a promise I repeated to myself as I completed rep after rep, until I was sweating and sucking in lungfuls of breath, until I'd convinced myself the pain in my chest was because of the injury and nothing else.

Rowan

I WOKE ON the kitchen table, my chest on fire and my thoughts still swirling in black smoke. My mother and sisters gathered around me wearing concerned expressions. The triquetra smoldered on my bare chest where they'd worked their spell to pull me from the Otherworld.

"Are you with us?" Siobhan asked.

I nodded, hand on my throat, before sitting up and shuffling my legs off the table. Iona immediately wrapped a blanket around my shoulders. It smelled of sage, rosemary, and several other cleansing herbs. It itched and stung the scratches the grappling rowans had inflicted. My head spun, and I gripped the edge of the table.

Candles illuminated the kitchen, their pungent aromas only contributing to my nausea. Ginger and orange, cardamom and angelica, rose, bay, and myrrh. Neasa and Deirdre had hand-crafted each one with specific purpose, although I doubted burning them all at once was having the intended effect.

I heaved and Iona produced a bucket as I coughed up remnants of the Otherworld.

"You're here?" I asked and wiped my mouth. She should've been working at McDuff's tattoo shop in town; her part-time hours at the old sailor's parlor were the only way we managed to pay the bills of Ros Tearmann.

"Of course," she said, giving my shoulder a squeeze through the protective layer of wool before getting rid of the bucket and returning to her seat.

"Drink this. It'll help." Deirdre pushed a mug of tea into my hands as I slumped into a chair. Agrimony and burdock with sweet basil and a pinch of chamomile for good measure; herbs for purifying and exorcising.

I sipped and waited for the dizziness to pass while Iona rubbed a salve of lavender and yarrow into the bruises on my arms. I watched her hands, calmed by the deft yet gentle movements of her fingers, each capped by a nail painted a different rainbow color. She worked quickly, not wanting to touch me longer than she had to while remains of the Otherworld still clung to my skin. She checked the dressings on the cuts, but they were clean. The blade wounds had finally stopped bleeding.

"Who was it?" Mother asked, pen poised above her notebook full of the names of the dead.

"Andy Kilduff," I said, and Mother's pen scratched the paper, gouging deep.

"Good riddance," Deirdre mumbled, still bitter about the ax Andy had taken to our grove two years ago.

"He was murdered."

Mother stopped writing. "Murdered? Are you sure?"

"Someone slit his throat and left him to die in a ring of gentians. The killer used a silver blade." As I spoke the words out loud, my family stopped their fidgeting and turned their wide, surprised gazes on me.

"Silver? A *faery* ring? Think it's a tourist playing at rituals?" Mother asked.

"Perhaps," I conceded when no one else answered. Mother glanced at me with incredulity but didn't argue. It was easier for all of us to think the murderer an outsider and not one of our own.

"But why?" Siobhan asked. "And who could do such a thing?"

"Andy never saw his attacker's face," I said.

"And there was nothing to explain it in his memories?" Neasa asked, folding her arms.

"How about letting him catch his breath?" Iona interjected, always ready to defend me. "You know how overwhelming it can be."

"Sarah's mother never did like Andy," Mother answered. "Perhaps the McNamaras finally decided to avenge their lost daughter."

Sarah had died more than twenty years ago. It seemed unlikely the McNamaras' grief had only now become a desire for vengeance. If only Sarah's family could've known how much Andy had loved her, how much he'd genuinely believed his love for her would conquer the incompatibility of the magic in their blood.

"This is going to be a problem," Siobhan said. "How long until the Kilduffs come banging on our door?"

"It is what it is," Mother said. "Nothing we can do. We'll have to let the police handle it."

"Oh yes, the O'Donnells and Kilduffs with badges, the epitome of justice." Neasa knocked her fist against the table.

"Did he go easy?" Deirdre asked, letting her fingers brush mine where they lay on the table.

"As easy as anyone taken before their time," I said without offering details. She looked down and didn't ask more.

"We haven't had to pull you back since you first

started," Siobhan said. "You're lucky Iona checked on you. What happened?"

"The trees always try to stop me leaving. This time they were trying to protect me," I said while giving Iona a nod of gratitude. "I think maybe...to hide me." My hand trembled, and I set the cup back in its saucer. Mother poured more tea.

"From what?" Deirdre asked, warily.

"Can't be sure. I heard voices. I thought they were the sluagh at first, but then this black smoke..." I paused, trying to gather my memories while Andy's still writhed within me. "The sound of claws, of rasping scales."

"Smoke?" Siobhan raised an eyebrow and tugged at the cuffs of her dress.

"A cloud, a shadow. It was hard to tell."

My sisters and mother exchanged worried glances before turning five identical sets of hazel eyes back on me.

"Was it the murder?" Deirdre continued. "Is that why you almost got stuck?"

"Did Andy do something?" Siobhan asked. "Was it that Kilduff magic?"

"Did *you* do something?" Neasa asked with a petulant tilt of her head, her lips smeared black to match the thick lines circling her eyes.

"No," I said, meeting her gaze. "I don't think so." My mind reeled, but the tea and herbs drifting off the blanket helped to keep my thoughts my own. "Maybe the murder upset the balance in the Otherworld."

"Maybe you just can't handle a tough death?" Neasa said.

"Remember the tourist bus that crushed during the storm a couple years back?" I asked and she swallowed, dropping her gaze to the table. Thirty-three people died in that crash, their bodies twisted in the wreckage. They'd died screaming in pain and terror as their bus plunged through a railing and off the cliffs. I'd had my skull split open, a face full of glass, my organs punctured by steel, and I'd drowned. Seventeen times I'd drowned, cold water like knives flaying my skin, brine burning my throat and filling my lungs.

Four days I'd spent in the Otherworld. Four days of dying and ferrying souls to the river, my body left unconscious for my sisters to tend. Twelve of the passengers on that bus had been children. I still dream their memories.

"Come back to us," Iona said, her hand tapping mine, drawing me back to the present.

"We almost lost you," Siobhan said. "Whatever it was, it was powerful."

"Think it has anything to do with these O'Donnells returning?" Neasa asked.

"They were here when Andy died," I said. "They didn't kill him."

"I know. Had to work a little magic on the young one." Deirdre flexed her fingers and earned a scowl from Siobhan.

"Does Gran know?" Iona asked. "It is her Brian, isn't it?"

"*Her* Brian?" I asked, not sure I was following. Andy's life flitted behind my eyes, disturbing the other strange memories roosting in the shadowed corners of my mind. I drank more tea, unable to wash the taste of copper from my tongue.

"Brian O'Donnell broke our gran's heart. They were promised and everything, weren't they?" Iona said.

"It's complicated," Mother said with a sigh. "It's been complicated between us and the O'Donnells for generations, but what Brian did...that was the final straw."

"How can one of them even be allowed to stay here?" Neasa's lip curled in disgust.

"I doubt he'll be here for long," Mother said, giving me a pointed look. I knew why she'd asked me to escort the old man to his room. Even though Death lingered about me like a second shadow, I didn't choose who made the journey to the Otherworld. A weak heart might stutter at my touch, an aneurysm biding its time might burst at my passing, but those souls were already marked by Death, a mark I couldn't—wouldn't—give on my own.

"You'll need to take greater precautions when you're in the Otherworld," Iona said. "Though that should help." She pointed at my chest where the spell was fading, leaving another scar to add to my collection.

"Thank you," I said and traced the sensitive flesh. "But I'd be more worried about living. There's a murderer out there."

"Can you remember anything else?" Siobhan asked.

I swallowed another mouthful of tea: the fear burning through the trees, the cloying smoke curling around my body, the heat of Andy's blood seeping through his fingers. Purple-black wings beneath an unused crib, the taste of his wife's kisses, her hands and fingers...

"The trees withered where the smoke touched them," I said and shook my head to banish the borrowed memory. "Their bark turned black. I think they were afraid."

Five pairs of eyes widened. Siobhan clenched her jaw. Iona tugged on a dreadlock. Neasa laid her clammy hands flat on the tabletop, caught me looking at the newest ring adorning her finger and quickly hid her fingers in her lap. Deirdre chewed on her bottom lip. Mother drew in a breath, letting it whistle through the gap between her front teeth.

"We'll have to think on this," she said, which meant perform magic rituals in which I could have no part. It was the women in the Sheehy family who had the real power, the men were merely bellhops for the dead.

"You should take it easy," Deirdre said. "You look a

39

little corpse-like yourself."

"Having one foot permanently on the other side will do that to you," Siobhan said, unable to find humor in Deirdre's teasing. Deirdre rolled her eyes and snatched away my teacup.

"Back to work then," Siobhan said.

"I promised Andy he'd be found," I said.

"They'll find him when they think to look. I don't want us getting any more involved in this," Mother said. "We have our own concerns." She gave Siobhan a pointed look, one that said there should've been a mewling babe in the house by now. A look that said Riona McNamara and Maire O'Donnell both had infants on their hips, *so what's wrong with you?*

Siobhan responded with a sigh and turned away from Mother's gaze, a gaze which landed on Iona next before alighting on Neasa. Neasa was only seventeen, Mother couldn't possibly expect—and yet she had been barely twenty when she'd brought Siobhan into the world.

"It'll be dinner time soon," Mother said, a command of dismissal.

Neasa left the kitchen, headed back into the main house to help with food preparations. Iona paused to dust a kiss across my forehead, while Siobhan gave me a last disapproving look before she followed Mother.

"You really okay?" Deirdre asked, hands in the pockets of her dress spotted with dried wax from candle-making.

"Andy remembered Gran cursing his wife. She was drawing simple blessing runes, but Andy was convinced. He found butterfly wings. He thought our uncle enjoyed watching his babies burn." I struggled for breath, just as Andy's children had, tiny lungs malformed, little hearts thudding out of time. I pressed the heel of my hand to my chest.

"They're all addled," Deirdre said. "Take no note."

"You didn't feel what I felt." I dug my fingers into the

lump of scar tissue filling up the rent in my heart. "Their hatred, they burn with it. It consumes them. Hatred and fear and—"

"Maybe he deserved—"

"No," I said. "No one deserves that. Not even the Kilduffs."

"Rowan, it's okay." Deirdre took my hand and pulled it away from my chest where I'd left nail marks in the keloid. "It's not your fault. You know who you are, what we are. Also, Ash O'Donnell left a jacket here." She gestured to the violently orange garment hanging in the mudroom before she scooted out of the kitchen to do whatever Deirdre did when she wasn't riding Comet, making candles, or entertaining the elderly. We were all shackled to fate, one way or another.

With a sigh, I got up from the table and stretched. My skin felt too tight, my bones too heavy as they always did after a jaunt in the Otherworld. I pulled my shirt and sweater back on before heading to the mudroom. I needed to see the horses settled for the night. Gooseflesh flared across my skin even as I donned my boots.

The hawthorn. The blood. The flower ring and silver blade. And in the wake of Andy's murder, something from beyond the veil had reached for me, something capable of damaging the rowans and stirring the sluagh.

Outside, I closed my eyes and let the sorrow of the island wash through me, the fingers of wind in my hair as cold as the hands of the ghosts within me. Both buried themselves in my lungs, an inescapable burden I felt with every breath. Inisliath mourned the loss of their own, the skies weeping and thunder rolling from the sea as if even the ocean sobbed for the passing of Andy Kilduff.

Halfway to the horses, I slipped my phone from my pocket and stared at the screen. Guilt, rage, regret. I couldn't be sure if the feelings were mine or echoes of Andy's. His life simmered behind my eyes, his pain still so vivid, his hatred and distrust of us a bitter black presence. I'd promised him this much. It was the least I could do. I keyed in the number for the Inisliath police station and held my breath, letting the ghosts within me knot together into resolve. An unexpected voice answered my call:

"This is Detective Inspector Walsh. How can I help you?"

I doubted she could, but I told her where to find Andy's body.

Ash

SLEEP WASN'T happening. I couldn't remember the last time I slept through the night, and this collarbone thing made getting comfortable a total bitch. It wasn't quite 3AM. The world beyond my window was black. No sodium glare from streetlights, no halo of light spit up from the city, no flashing sirens or neon adverts. Not even a damn porch light on this cottage.

I tested the rickety window. It opened more easily than I expected, letting in a draught of air way too cold for August. Back on the mainland it was still summer. Here, the breeze smelled of wet soil and sea salt. Not entirely unpleasant. There must've still been clouds, because I searched the sky and didn't see a single star, but I did I hear what sounded like a drum.

Doom, ba-da-ba-da doom.

The rhythm repeated. It was definitely a drum. It sounded far away, though it was hard to judge distances here. The wind could've carried the sound from town or maybe from one of the beaches below the cliffs. A gust blew stronger, and I caught a snatch of singing.

Inisliath didn't strike me as the type of place to host all-night raves, but maybe that was what people were into here: dropping lots of acid and getting their grind on to tribal trance. It didn't sound bad. Half the people I climbed with back home were into rainbow gatherings and hallucinogenics, not that I'd ever been allowed to go to one of the tie-dyed festivals. The colonel liked to keep me close to home with a 9PM curfew, the fact I was seventeen having clearly escaped him.

The wind gusted again, rattling the window in my hand. I pulled it shut and ducked under the covers, trying to stop the shivers from tearing the rest of my damaged body apart.

I guess I fell asleep, because the next sound I heard was the clip-clop of hooves on gravel. Sunlight the color of boiled oats spilled through my window. It was still cloudy, but there was a hint of blue on the horizon. Miraculously, it wasn't raining.

7AM.

I rubbed my hands over my face and carefully rolled my left shoulder before scrounging in the duffel bag I hadn't bothered unpacking yet for a clean shirt. There was a knock on the door before I'd managed to pull on my jeans. I didn't bother with my sling.

"Who the hell comes 'round so early?" Mum asked blearily as she staggered from her bedroom in pajamas. She'd come home super late—apparently her first day on the job had been more exciting than anticipated.

"I've got this. Go back to bed," I said before making a quick stop by the bathroom to brush my teeth while I peed. Both needs taken care of, I approached the door. No peephole and no one visible through the kitchen or lounge windows, either.

My heart thumped behind my ribs. What if it was the

colonel? Taking a calming breath, I opened the door to
see Rowan swinging a leg over the back of a large, stocky
horse with a patchwork coat.

"Thought you were still asleep," he said, every word
made round and burred by his accent. I didn't hate it one
bit.

"I was."

"Sorry to bother you." He dragged a hand through
his hair, giving himself a crooked halo. "Just wanted to
return that." He pointed to my jacket, which he'd hung
from a nail in the wall beside the door.

"Thanks," I said as I retrieved it. What else was I
supposed to say? I hadn't had caffeine yet, so my brain
was firing on half cylinders. It didn't help that Rowan
looked pretty good on horseback and not at all like the
whimpering kid curled on the floor. I'm not usually into
the whole country-boy aesthetic. I prefer my guys in
combat boots and skinny jeans when they're not climbing
walls.

"You're welcome," Rowan said. "I'll be off then."

"Want some coffee?" I asked before I'd thought it
through. "I mean, it's the least I can do since you came
out all this way." It might also be a good opportunity to
figure out what the hell happened to him yesterday, I
guess.

Rowan frowned and studied his hands.

"I'm making anyway. Come in or don't. Whatever,
dude." I shrugged, hoping it came off as nonchalant.

Rowan stared off into space for a moment. "Actually,
coffee would be grand."

His reluctance almost made me regret the invitation,
but then he gave his horse's muscular neck a pat and
dismounted. I may have taken the moment to check out
his ass. He unclipped the lead from whatever that thing
is that goes over the horse's head and clicked his tongue.
The horse snorted before moving off into the nearest

field, nose already in the grass.

"Won't it get lost?" I asked.

"She'll come when I call her." He hung the lead up on the nail where my jacket had been, then paused at the door to run his hands along opposing jambs as if he were feeling for something.

"There a problem?"

"Don't think so," he said, although he still took a tentative step across the threshold before leaving his muddy boots at the door. He smelled more like horse this morning, and I didn't entirely hate that either.

"Shit, I don't even know if we have coffee." I began a search of the cupboards while Rowan sat stiffly at the table.

"Tea will do."

"Here, we've got some." A small tin of cheap-ass instant stuff, but it was better than nothing. There was milk in the fridge, and a bag of sugar on the counter, alongside a loaf of soda bread.

"Want some breakfast?" I asked as I set a mug of coffee in front of Rowan. I had to make individual trips to the counter for milk, then sugar.

"If you let me help," he said, coming to stand at the counter.

"I'm not a total invalid." I brandished the bread knife for emphasis.

"I can see that," he said. "Only trying to be polite."

I was about to say something nasty, when I remembered I was the one who'd invited him in.

"Fine, get slicing." I let the knife clatter onto the counter.

"I take it you're not a morning person," he said as he scraped the tangles of hair off his neck and into a knot at the back of his head, securing it with a hair tie from his wrist. He wore several leather bracelets. Some were decorated with seashells, others had engraved metal charms on them. There were gauze dressings taped on his wrists instead of bandages now. I didn't ask what happened—it was none of my business—and if whatever it was had been self-inflicted, my nosiness wasn't going to help at all.

"I'm a little cranky before coffee," I said instead.

"Never would've known." There was a hint of a smile on his lips.

"It is seven on a Saturday," I said as I caught a glimpse of the tattoo peeking out of the gauze on the inside of his left wrist, just three black lines, two perpendicular to the other. His arms were heavily speckled with freckles, as were the backs of his hands.

"I get up before five every morning," he said.

"Why the fuck so early? You doing penance for something?" I'd meant it as a joke, but he wasn't smiling as he answered.

"Just tending the horses." He glanced at me with seriously intense eyes. The right one was more brown than green, with a dark band around the iris. I'd never met anyone with heterochromia before. I was about to say as much but went to the fridge in search of cheese instead.

When I returned to the counter, he cocked his head and said, "You're not wearing the sling today."

"Don't need it unless I'm likely to get bashed or do something silly because I've forgotten I'm injured." I knew what was coming next, and I wasn't sure how to answer.

"How could you forget?" He pointed at my cast with the knife in his hand.

"The sling isn't for that. I subluxated my collarbone," I added, braced for interrogation.

"Sounds unpleasant," he said.

I studied his face, noting the freckles on his upper lip. "About as unpleasant as what happened to you yesterday. Are you okay?"

Rowan broke eye contact and took the cheese from me. He ditched the bread knife and pulled an impressive blade out of a sheath clipped to his belt. I hadn't noticed it before. It was clearly more than just a utility tool. The handle was all decorative twists of metal, and the edge looked sharp as he gave it a quick wash in the sink before using it on the cheese. Is that what he'd used on his arms?

He cleared his throat and might've been about to answer, but never got the chance.

"Oh, I didn't realize we had a guest," Mum said as she shuffled into the kitchen. "Is everything okay with my dad?" Her brow furrowed.

"Aye, he's grand. Nothing to worry about Mrs. Walsh," Rowan said.

"I forgot my jacket. Rowan brought it back. He came all this way. Thought I'd offer him breakfast."

"Of course," Mum said tight-lipped. Money was even tighter, and I knew she was probably doing mental arithmetic, working out how much having Rowan over was going to cost us. *It's just bread and cheese!* I wanted to yell, instead I gritted my teeth and started the kettle boiling for another cup of coffee.

"Did you walk here?" Mum asked.

"Rode my horse, why?"

"You might want to stick to the roads, avoid the fields."

"Mum, you're doing the cryptic cop thing," I said, and Rowan carefully folded away his knife.

"Seems Inisliath isn't quite as dull as I'd hoped," she said.

"You found the body?" Rowan asked.

"Whoa, a body?" *Seriously?*

"How did you know about that?" Mum was suddenly awake and morphing into detective mode.

"News travels." Rowan shrugged stiff shoulders and concentrated on the cheese.

"I'll bet," Mum said.

I didn't want her joining us, but she planted herself at

the kitchen table and waited for me to make her coffee. I only put half a sugar in it. That was the game we played. I knew I was in trouble on the mornings Mum put burnt toast on my plate, or the days she "forgot" to do my laundry, but managed to pick hers and the colonel's out of the basket. I wasn't sure which was worse: Mum's passive-aggressive tendencies, or the colonel's brutal aggression.

We joined Mum at the table, and Rowan sat opposite, his arms folded across his chest. Mum would've called that defensive posture, indicating a suspect might have something to hide.

"Do you have any leads?" he asked.

"Why so interested?" Mum asked.

"Murder isn't exactly common 'round here."

"I didn't say anything about a murder."

Murder? Holy shit. I'd lived in the city. I knew my mum dealt with all kinds of fucked-up stuff there, but to land a murder case on day one here? This place really was like something out of a horror movie. Then I remembered Rowan's wicked-looking knife and how he hadn't let Mum see it.

Rowan squirmed, his gaze flicking up for a moment before settling back on the table.

"From what I heard…" He cleared his throat. "Do you think it was an accident?"

"Do you?" She had the most annoying way of turning questions around on the person asking them. Something she'd learned in How to be a Detective 101, no doubt. "You know, we found the body thanks to an anonymous tip," Mum said as she straightened her shoulders and stared at Rowan's bowed head. "You wouldn't happen to know anything about that, would you?"

"No, Ma'am," he said.

Mum seemed to be studying her coffee, but I followed her gaze where it rested squarely on the tattoo on Rowan's wrist and the edges of the gauze. He dragged the tattered sleeves of his shirt over his fingers.

"You going to school here?" Rowan asked me before taking a bite of toast, this change of topic releasing the tension hanging over the table like a guillotine.

"That's the plan," I said. "Did you go to the school in town?" The island only had one school, kindergarten through grade 12.

"I didn't have much use for it," he said. "Home schooling, mostly," he added when Mum started frowning. "Finished all that in May."

"And you're still here?" Mum asked.

"Inisliath is my home. I'll never leave. My sister Neasa goes to the town school, though. She'll be starting her final year."

"So is Ash. It'll be nice to know someone, won't it?" Mum nudged my arm a little too enthusiastically, and I winced. "Sorry, I forget when you're not wearing your sling. They had a bit of a climbing accident," Mum said before taking a sip of coffee. This time *she* winced, and I felt bad. She'd managed to use the correct pronoun. She deserved a little sweetness for that.

"You climb?" Rowan narrowed his eyes, as if he could see through Mum's bullshit.

"I'm guessing there isn't a gym here."

"No, not a gym, but there are plenty of crags," Rowan said. "Deep water solo, too, if you can stand the cold. Do you prefer sport or trad?"

Wow, the dude was speaking my language.

"Sport and bouldering mostly."

"Plenty of both here. When the weather is good," he added.

"*When?* You mean it doesn't rain all the time?"

"Not raining right now, is it?" Rowan said with the tiniest grin.

"Maybe you can show me some time, give me a tour

of the island or something?" I asked, very aware this conversation was happening in front of my mum and how extremely uncomfortable that made me feel.

"Maybe that's not such a great idea," Mum said. "Not until—just don't go wandering." She cocked her head a little to the right, which was her way of saying she meant it.

Right. Because not only had someone been murdered, but Mum was looking at Rowan more and more like he was a suspect. Typical. First friendly person I'd had over in like, ever, and now he might be a murderer. Sometimes Mum could be as bad as the colonel. I concentrated on my breakfast, keeping my mouth full so I couldn't say something to earn me burnt toast for the rest of the week.

"I heard Mr. O'Donnell was born on the island," Rowan asked. "Were you?"

"I wasn't," Mum said. "My parents moved to the mainland soon after they met."

"Why?" I asked, leaking crumbs and hoping Rowan didn't notice.

"Not a lot of work on the island," Mum said. "And it wasn't easy in those days for your grandparents. Inisliath isn't particularly welcoming to outsiders." She shot Rowan a dark look.

"Not much has changed it seems," I said.

"Ash," Mum used her warning tone.

"What? We hardly got a warm welcome yesterday, did we? Seems outsiders still aren't welcome."

"Aye," Rowan said. "Things change slowly here, and the elders don't want them to."

"What about the younger generation?" Mum asked. "I bet a lot of the young people leave."

"Those that can." He shrugged. "But it's not easy with island blood in the veins."

"Do I have island blood?" I asked.

"A bit." Again, a flicker of an almost smile hooked Rowan's upper lip.

"What have the Sheehys got against the O'Donnells anyway?" I asked.

"It's complicated," he said. "There's a long and not always pleasant history between our families." He took a bite of toast, and we fell into an awkward silence, Mum sipping away at her bitter coffee and staring off into the distance. I doubt she knew anything, but I made a mental note to ask her later about our family history. I bet it had something to do with my Brummie grandma and the fact she'd stolen the heart of an island boy.

I'd never met my grandma, never even been to Birmingham. She died long before I was born, when Mum was only a teenager herself. And if Mum had ever been in touch with that side of the family, she'd never said anything. It felt like a missed opportunity, like a huge part of me wasn't just missing, but had never even been there to begin with. A bit like this island and all it might mean in terms of my heritage, too. Really, I didn't have a bloody clue who I was, and Rowan knew it.

The not-too-distant ringing of church bells shattered the quiet.

"Thanks for breakfast," he said, "but I should be going. I've got a funeral to attend."

"Funeral?" Mum asked. "You mean—"

"We don't like to let the dead linger," Rowan said.

"But we weren't done with the body. There hasn't even been an autopsy yet. You're saying they're burying him already?" Mum reached for her phone.

"No, they're burning him," he said softly.

Mum's eyebrows shot up before she stabbed at her phone. She strode out of the kitchen in search of better signal, muttering a string of expletives.

"Thank you for bringing my jacket," I said.

"It was nothing." He headed for the door.

Mum stayed inside, yelling at someone over the phone about procedure and paperwork, leaving me alone with Rowan as we crossed the yard to the edge of the field.

He whistled a long, high note, and a moment later, the horse came prancing up to him. She was beautiful and terrifying, and would make a pretty cool photo subject, especially with all that mane and tail billowing in the wind. Her rider wouldn't make a bad model, either.

She pushed her nose against Rowan's shoulder, and he stroked her face before clipping the lead back on.

"Are you going to stay out of the fields?" I asked.

"No reason to," he said. "Don't think the murderer is after me."

"How can you be so sure?"

He seemed about to respond, but shook his head and patted his horse instead.

"You never answered my question, you know," I said before it was too late.

"And which one was that?" He looked past me, frowning at a large butterfly flitting about the yard. Its wings were so deeply purple they looked almost black. I'd never seen one like it and chalked it up to strange island fauna.

"About what happened to you yesterday," I said. "If you're okay?"

He fiddled with the lead, running his hand along the horse's shoulder before he answered. "I'm okay, Ash. Are you?"

I was about to respond with some smartass comment until I saw the look on his face, lips set in a grim line and eyes intense as if he genuinely cared about the answer. Which was stupid, considering we'd known each other all of five seconds.

I stood there staring at him, not knowing what the hell to say, emotions rising in a suffocating swell inside my chest. God, he needed to stop looking at me like that, like he understood or wanted to.

"Don't you need a saddle or something?" I asked, the words sticking to my teeth and coming out half-chewed.

"Not with Auryn." Rowan grabbed a handful of mane and jumped onto his horse's back in one lithe motion that made me more than a little jealous of his long legs. "Do you ride?"

"Never tried," I answered.

"Maybe when your arm's better that's something we might remedy," he said, and this time the twitch of his lips lingered long enough to be considered a smile.

"Even though I'm an outsider and an O'Donnell?"

"One of those things we can fix." He turned the horse toward the fields. "Thank you for breakfast."

"You're welcome, any time—preferably after I've had some coffee."

"Aye, fair enough. Well, we know where to find each other," he said, and with that he trotted out into the meadow beneath a sky starting to look a little less grey.

Rowan

AURYN GALLOPED across the field, churning up sod with heavy hooves, and I resisted the urge to glance back at Ash.

The mist had fanned her skirts, ruffling her frayed garments out over the sea where the occasional ray of sunshine spangled the ocean. The water lay calm beneath the black cliffs, gulls riding the gusts and casting shadows across the sands. Squinting against the glare, I searched the road coming from town. The procession painted a dark smear against the green of the fields.

I felt sorry for Ash's mother. Whatever had happened to Andy Kilduff wasn't going to be solved with DNA evidence and big city detective work. No autopsy would reveal the ritual in which he'd been sacrificed, or the spell woven by his blood. His assailant had been sure to keep out of sight even when Andy's death was guaranteed. Maybe they didn't want Andy to see them in his final moments, or perhaps they knew I'd witness the death and recognize them as the killer.

We took the longer, wider trail down to the cove this time, wending our way among the rocks with scalpel edges and long grasses grasping like dead fingers until we came to the beach. I eyed the sheer cliffs rising behind me, my gaze drifting to the same spot every time as my heart stuttered in my chest as if it too remembered the bite of the blade. My thoughts drifted to Ash again, to bruises and twisted bones, and sad grey eyes.

A small part of me envied Ash: a life in the city, the freedom to travel the world. I'd never been allowed to leave the island for fear that crossing a body of water would diminish what power the Sheehys had managed to maintain over the years. And so I remained on Inisliath, my life's purpose already ordained, my fate chiseled in stone. I was a part of the island, my blood running through the bedrock, my flesh netted in the roots tangling the soil. I was...a prisoner. The thought rose unwelcome in my mind, but I tamped it down with a grind of my teeth.

At the sound of the drums, I turned to face the funeral procession making its way slowly across the beach.

Orlagh, the Kilduff matriarch and Andy's sister, led the group, the wrapped body borne on the shoulders of her sons and grandsons. The rest of the family followed behind, while one of her granddaughters playing the bodhran, the drum's beat slow and solemn. The wind tugged at their black lace cuffs and headscarves. The McNamaras and O'Donnells brought up the rear of the procession, showing their solidarity in sorrow and righteous anger—anger directed at me and my family.

The procession continued along the beach until they reached the cove where I waited. They glared through their tears. I didn't blame people for disliking me. It was hard for them to see me and not bleed through the stitches on their loss, as if I'd been the one to cause the wound. Perhaps it would appease them to know every death hurt me, too, that their memories—good and bad—haunted my every waking moment.

Not the Kilduffs. Their hatred for me was palpable, a sentiment I couldn't return. It was hard to hate a person once you'd felt their joy and despair, lived their hopes and fears.

I waited until Andy's kin had said their goodbyes, until they were ready to surrender the body to the pyre. Their eyes blazed from deepest black to azure as pale as winter stars. Their magic slicking the air made my skin tingle and sweat turn icy. I dismounted and strode across the sand to place two rune stones on Andy's shrouded face in the hollows of each eye. My mother had engraved the stones, one for pine and the other for yew, symbols to ease the passing of a loved one.

"That'll do," Conall Kilduff said as he and the others lifted the body and elbowed me out of their way. He didn't spare me a second glance.

"Filthy *fetch*," Lucy spat as I returned to my horse.

I tried not to flinch. Fetch. Lucy and her family weren't the only ones who saw me as an ill-omen and harbinger of tragedy.

"You won't be happy until we're all cinders in the sea," she shouted after me. "Did you enjoy cutting his throat?"

"It wasn't my doing," I said.

"So you say, fetch," she said, punctuating her sentence with a spitball that landed a foot away from me. "Did you even take him to rest, or did you leave him wandering in the void?"

"I did my duty," I said, jaw clenched. Auryn threw her head, tugging the lead through my fingers.

"Inisliath is ours, too, you know," Lucy said, and Cillian McNamara looped his arm through hers as if to hold her back. "You're killing this island. Don't think we won't fight back. You can't take all the magic for yourselves."

"You think it's our doing?" I asked. "You think we want to stop the McNamaras slipping their skins or take any power from you?" By the looks on their faces, they believed my family responsible for the waning magic of the island, that we were capable of robbing the other founding families of their birthright. "Let's not forget who desecrates sacred sites on this island," I said instead and Lucy's eyes turned lambent and deadly. She hadn't been there that day in the grove, but she knew what her family had done.

"You all carry blades," Lucy said, eyes burning bitter blue. "Which one slit Andy's throat?"

"Not mine."

"That's enough, Luce. Let's go," Cillian said, easing her away.

"He was all carved up, too," she added, pointing at my wrist. "This crap. Why'd you have to do that to him?"

"What?" My gaze flicked from Lucy to Cillian, who'd turned paler than usual, his eyes catching mine for a moment before looking away.

"He was butchered," Lucy said, her words a sharp hiss through gritted teeth.

"I'm sorry, I didn't know." It must've happened after Andy died. I hadn't felt the cuts on him, and he'd had no memory of being wounded when I was called to his death. Such markings only confirmed my suspicion. His death had been part of a ritual or a spell. The why and who evaded me. No Sheehy could've done it, that much I knew. My family were herbalists, not killers.

"Screw you," Lucy said. "Fergus O'Donnell had the right idea. Pity he only stopped after putting one Sheehy in the sea."

I mounted Auryn and nudged her flanks. My presence was no longer required, and I had no desire to stay, even less now that Ash's mom was striding across the sand, her blue jacket conspicuous among all the black. I left the beach and escaped the detective's questions, Lucy's glare, Cillian's disdain, and the gasoline fumes as Andy Kilduff turned to ash. But the guilt followed me, a thing with teeth burrowing beneath my skin to gnaw on the parts I'd tried and failed to harden against the pain of death.

By lunch, I'd replaced several broken slats in the paddock fence, weeded the vegetable patch, tended my sisters' herb garden, and spent more than an hour in the greenhouse maintaining the more sensitive plants and grooming the mushroom logs. It was an endless process of planting, gathering, drying, and storing, but one I'd come to accept, if not enjoy. It also kept me away from the elderly while they still lived.

My sisters had spelled wards into my skin to prevent the fingers of the Otherworld reaching through me to take a soul prematurely from the land of the living, but they could only suppress what I was so much without compromising my ability to ferry the dead altogether.

Leaving Auryn, my mother's gelding Solas, and Deirdre's pony Comet to graze, I took my thermos of soup to a corner of the paddock and stepped beneath the spreading boughs of a hawthorn. Perhaps it was seeing the tree, the tapestry of the branches above me, the smell of rich earth and flowers, that ignited the memory.

One moment I was myself, the next I clutched at my throat, the gout of blood hot between my fingers as I relived Andy's death, as I struggled against the pain of severed skin, against the fear of imminent demise, and the fire in my chest. Panic knotted the breath in my lungs, and my vision blurred in a swath of green and brown as the ground rushed to meet me. I dropped the thermos, and the contact it made with my big toe sliced through the fug of borrowed memory.

It wasn't this hawthorn; it wasn't my throat slit by silver.

Once I recovered my lunch and sanity, I sat beneath the tree and leaned into the trunk. I let the bark dig into my shoulders, let it remind me I was alive until my hands had stopped shaking. When the last tremors had passed from my fingers, I unscrewed the lid of the thermos. The black lines of my tattoos showed in stark contrast against my pale skin. If only I'd seen the runes cut into Andy, perhaps I'd understand what they meant, why he'd died, and who'd opened his throat.

"I was just thinking those could use a touch-up," Iona said, startling me with her sudden appearance. She drifted like a breeze through the grass, her sandaled feet barely making a sound. She was wearing the T-shirt she'd made for last year's Pride parade on the mainland, all rainbows and unicorns. It was the one event she risked Mother's wrath to attend. I would go, too, if it wouldn't risk my ability as a deathwalker.

"Shouldn't you be at the shop?" I shifted to make space for her.

"McDuff let me take the day off." She settled beside me, less cautious in my presence today.

"How is the old man?"

"Too stubborn to die." She smiled. "But this week he did his last tattoo. His hands shake too much now, says he's ready to retire to his hut and watch the sea until Death comes for him." She jostled my shoulder, but it wasn't comforting. I wasn't Death itself, just a conduit for souls—a distinction rarely made even by my family.

"What'll happen to the shop?" I asked.

"He offered it to me," she said. "It's mine if I want it."

"Do you?"

Iona plucked a blade of grass from between her feet and parted the stem with dexterous fingers. "Not while all I know how to do are runes and anchors. I've had two offers for apprenticeship, though, both with great artists."

Both on the mainland. My heart seized, my stomach tightening. "Have you told—"

"No." Iona shredded the blade of grass and tossed the remnants to the ground. "Not until I've figured out a way to make it happen."

"You'd risk it?" I asked. "Knowing what happened to Eileen and Brighid, you'd still go?"

"Not forever," she said, "and maybe that's the difference. Besides, how do we know for sure they've suffered so much?"

"Mother wouldn't lie about that."

"Wouldn't she?" Iona said, leaving the question unanswered. We'd all heard the stories of our aunts, of their lives turned wretched the moment they abandoned the island for a life on the mainland. The misfortunes they'd suffered, the unhappiness and illness, and yet, they'd never chosen to return. No one had, except Brian O'Donnell.

"If it's truly what you want—"

"You know it is," she said, crushing another frond of grass in her fist.

"Is there some way I can help?"

"If there is, I'll let you know, little brother." Iona gave me a sad smile, and I didn't ask how she planned to slip this past our mother. I didn't want to be the one to leave my sister's dreams in ashes. She took my arm and dragged a finger over the ink, peeling away tape and gauze to inspect the gashes on my arms. Like usual, they had healed quickly—the magic in my veins sealing the wounds with stripes of silver-pink. She removed the dressings from my others wrist, too, the cuts there thicker and still an angry red.

"Siobhan and Neasa should know better," she said

kissing her fingers and pressing them to the scars before tapping the green-tinged ink. "Pop 'round the shop sometime, and I'll redo these for you. No charge, of course," she added with a wink.

"Andy was marked with runes, too," I said.

"Like yours?" Her finger lingered on the ink at my wrist.

"Don't know. I never saw them. Heard it from Lucy and Cillian."

"Ah," she said, a muscle twitching along her jaw. "Not the most credible sources, then."

"Even without the runes, his murder had purpose. Who could do something like that?"

"We're all capable of great and terrible things," she said. "Why does anybody do what they do, Ro? Because they want something. We all want something, don't we? You should know. You've seen dozens of lives. Must've seen hundreds of wants." She removed a joint from her pocket, and I watched her fingers work the ends to a tapered point, trying not to let her words excavate the memories I'd worked so hard to bury.

"Is being a tattoo artist all you want?" I asked.

"No." She lit up, the acrid-sweet scent of weed filling the space between us. "I want things to be better, for me and for our sisters, for all the women of this island. We should be free to live our own lives." She took a slow drag before she passed the joint to me. "You know, Mother actually told me I better start thinking about getting pregnant, in case Siobhan can't."

Can't, because Siobhan choosing not to have children was a concept our mother failed to fathom.

"Do you even want children?" I asked.

"Maybe one day with a guy I actually care about. Not now. Besides, being forced to do something sucks all the joy out of it. Hence Mother getting angsty." Iona spat into the dirt between her feet. "Nothing is more important than breeding the next generation of Sheehy witches."

"And a rowan."

"That, too." She nudged my shoulder with her own again. "Pity you can't help with that."

A fact which left me feeling relieved and grateful that magic flowed only through the women in our family. My sisters were expected to become mothers. My only duty was to the dead.

"What if you had a son? Do you think you could do it?" I asked, not able to ask her outright if she could do what Mother had done to me.

She remained silent so long, I didn't think she'd answer. I was about to apologize for asking when she took a deep breath.

"No, I don't think I could, but it's not like I'd get much of a choice, is it?" She sucked on the joint.

"Is Mother worried something will happen to me without a rowan to take my place?" I asked. "Or is she worried about losing power if we don't produce more Sheehys?"

"Both, probably, but I'm not sure I believe it, you know," Iona said. "I know Gran had a freak attack when Eileen and Brighid left, but I think it's old-timer superstition."

"Our entire lives are based on superstition," I interjected. "We're all beings of myth."

"Gods, listen to you. 'Beings of myth.'" She giggled, the weed clearly taking effect. "But I don't buy that our power has anything to do with how many of us there are." Uncharacteristic bitterness tainted Iona's words. "And I don't believe half the crap Mother says has actually happened to our aunts."

Iona offered me the joint again, and I accepted, inhaling deeply, holding in the smoke for several heartbeats before releasing it. We stayed like that for a while, wrapped in darkness despite the sunshine, passing the joint back and forth as we watched the horses flick the flies away with their tails and butterflies scud among the flowers. Red admirals, fritillaries, and the large purple-black ones, which had no name.

The world's ragged edges softened, the colors washing into shades of pastel, my limbs growing heavier, and my thoughts slowing. I finished the joint and stubbed out the last ember.

"I have to know why." The words were heavy on my tongue. "Why Andy, why silver, why the tree?"

"Did it hurt?" Iona asked gently as if she hadn't heard me.

"It always does." My hand rose involuntarily to my throat, but she caught my fingers and brought them down to rest on the ripped knee of her acid-wash jeans. Every death hurt, and the hurt lingered, easily relived every time I closed my eyes—sometimes I didn't even need to do that to be washed away in the riptide of ghosts within me.

"You scared us," Iona said. "I don't want to lose you. We need you."

"I know." I drew my knees to my chest. What I wanted...the memories swirled through me, a maelstrom of lives, of love, regret, loss, guilt, pleasure, hope, need, want... I wanted their voices to stop, for the shades of their memories to cease haunting me, to be my own person unencumbered by the souls I carried into the void.

It was a burden some rowans before me had been unable to bear, seeking to end their suffering with a noose around their neck, a black barrel between their teeth, a slow plunge to the rocks below the cliff. No rowan had ever lived long enough to grow old, and I could still feel those rough fibers of rope against my throat, taste the bitter steel against my tongue.

"Think these new O'Donnells are up to something?"

Iona's question cleaved through my memories.

"Maybe," I said as I gathered my unraveled thoughts through the weed-smog hanging like a pall behind my eyes. "But murder doesn't seem like the work of druids."

"The McNamaras, then?"

"I don't think they're capable of it."

"You never know what a person is truly capable of when pushed to their limits," she said, her words heavy, clotting the air between us. "There's not much I wouldn't do to protect my family."

"Is that what Andy's murder was about?"

"Don't know, but if it was, I think I'd understand."

Despite what the Kilduffs might've thought, we Sheehys weren't immune to the waning magic, either. Once, Ros Tearmann had been overflowing with residents, the happy elderly content to live out the remainder of their days in our home. Now, our house was sepulchral, inhabited only by the memories of those who'd passed through its walls. We hadn't had more than five residents at a time in the past two years. Without Iona's income, such as it was, we wouldn't have survived this long.

Still, the McNamaras had lost the most. Their magic had been the first to erode. Once, they'd all been able to slip their skins and dance beneath the waves or soar across the skies. Now only the oldest of their clan could shift and only for the shortest duration. Their livelihood had been hardest hit, too.

Perhaps they were growing desperate—desperate enough to take the life of a Kilduff, but to what end?

"The new O'Donnell woman, Brian's daughter, she's a cop," I said. "A detective inspector."

"We know."

"Is she going to be a problem?"

"Aren't all O'Donnells?" Iona said. "At least Ash is cute, right?" She nudged my elbow.

Ash's face rose unbidden in my mind. Grey eyes and

dark hair, a sly smile and filthy mouth.

"I knew it!" Iona laughed, and my cheeks burned. I hadn't realized I'd been smiling. "First crush?" she asked.

I'd experienced crushes, the first stirrings of nascent love. I'd experienced the kindling of lust, of fire-in-the-veins desire. I'd experienced solid, everlasting companionship built on foundations of trust and understanding, a love unconditional. I'd experienced all of it second-hand, borrowed moments lived by others.

"I don't know," I said. "I've never really felt..." What did I even feel?

"Attraction?" she asked. "Ash *is* pretty."

"So is every single Kilduff." A memory of watching Conall climb, shirtless and sun-kissed, rose from the depths of my own memories. "And the McNamara twins are beautiful, too."

"Do you prefer Rian or Riona?" Iona asked.

"Based just on looks? Neither. Both. Do I have to choose?"

"No, you can be bi."

"It's just... I don't know the twins. You like people just because of their looks?"

"Sometimes," Iona answered with a shrug.

"But with Ash... I'm starting to know them. It's different." I struggled to articulate what I was feeling. Perhaps the weed was to blame. I'd known Conall too, once, and never experienced the off-balance sensation I did when I was around Ash.

Iona patted my hand and gave me her know-it-all, big sister smile. "You'll figure it out, and we'll still love you no matter where you end up on the rainbow." She rose to her feet, not bothering to dust the mud and grass from her jeans. "But Ro, I actually came out here because Mother sent me to tell you—" She bit her bottom lip.

"What?" I squinted against the frail sunlight streaming through the branches, trying to see her eyes.

"Eamonn Davidson wants the horses," she said. "You

remember him, friend of our father's?"

"And our mother's."

Davidson had visited the island often, back when Mother still kept our father around in case she needed another baby. She'd finally released him back to his mainland life when Deirdre turned five, but Eamonn Davidson had returned at least once a year for several years after that. We rarely saw him, Mother preferring to keep him company at the hotel in town.

"Well, he's coming to see Solas and Auryn this week. Might be willing to take Comet, too."

"But, your job, my art—the candles. I thought we were doing enough."

"Not nearly," Iona said.

"What about my designs at your shop?"

"Ro, your stuff is brilliant, but it's dark. Most people coming to our shop want traditional knots or maritime stuff, not your nightmare creatures."

"I could draw something else," I said without conviction.

"I'm sorry," she said. "I know how much you love her, but we have to let her go."

I clicked my fingers and Auryn responded. She nuzzled against me, and I rubbed her nose, combing my fingers through her forelock. My chest ached at the thought of losing her. She'd been my only friend since the summer I turned seven, the only one who saw me as something other than the magic in my veins and my duty to the dead.

"Deidre's going to be devastated."

"She is." Iona paused, as if gathering her thoughts. She sighed, then twirled a dreadlock between her fingers before she drifted across the meadow, the trinkets in her hair tinkling as she moved. They reminded me of the chiming bells I'd heard through Andy's ears when the blade split his flesh.

Ash

IT HADN'T taken much to settle in, but somehow it had still been the better part of a week before I finally had my things unpacked. Because of one-handedness, and definitely not apathy.

I threw my clothes into the warped wardrobe, caring only about my camera and climbing gear. Briefly, I thumbed through the photos on my Canon EOS-1D X Mark II—a Christmas present from the colonel. Seeing pics of my climbing buddies sending routes I was months away from even attempting made my muscles seize with envy—it was even worse seeing the few pics I'd let them take of me. Every image added fuel to the fire of hatred burning in the pit of my stomach.

I dropped my camera on the bed and studied my room. The paint on the walls had maybe been off-white once. Now it was seriously *off*-white, speckled with mold and stains I didn't want to know the origins of. They all disappeared—slowly, because one-handedness sucks—

beneath my posters of Squamish and Joshua Tree, Fountainbleu, and Rocklands. Distant places I vowed I'd climb my fingers bloody one day, where I'd take amazing photos of even more amazing climbers that would get my name into *Rock and Ice*.

And...that was it. Decorating complete. It was all Mum had let me pack. No Xbox, no PC, no big-screen TV, no Wi-Fi, no climbing gyms. I was bored already, had been bored ever since we arrived.

"I'm heading to work," Mum said from where she stood in my doorway, surveying my bedroom walls. She seemed satisfied I'd made an effort. I didn't bother asking her why she was working on a Sunday. I knew the drill—work came first, especially when there was a fresh body in the morgue. Well, had been until they'd burned all Mum's evidence.

"How's the case going?" I asked.

"What case?" She huffed. "They don't seem to believe in due process out here."

"Got any leads?" It was the question I always asked even though I knew she could never actually answer.

"Maybe," she said, and I couldn't help but wonder how high up on the suspect list Rowan had made it. "Want to see the town?"

"The buzzing metropolis of Inisliath? Count me in." I picked up my camera.

"I know this isn't what you're used to, Ash," Mum said in a tone that meant a lecture was coming, "but like it or not, this is where your family is from."

"Half of it." A quarter, really.

A muscle twitched in Mum's jaw, but she didn't argue. As much as island blood ran in my veins, so did my father's, and that was something I'd have to live with.

"I'm leaving in five minutes. Your choice." She left me to hurriedly pull on my sling, mostly unnecessary now, but I didn't want people accidentally bumping into me or touching me in general. The sling was like armor, and it would hopefully get people to respect my personal space. Since it wasn't raining, I left my jacket by the door, hoping my hoodie would be enough. It was supposed to be summer, not that the island had noticed.

The car trundled down lanes so narrow I feared for the side mirrors as they raked against thorny hedgerows and dry-stone walls carving up the farmland. We arrived in town without incident.

Town was a generous term. It had an old stone building I assumed was a church despite the cross missing from its spire, and an equally ancient-looking pub, which was all a town needed, I guess. It also had a store that appeared to sell everything, and a library that shared a building with the police station.

Mum parked and headed for the station, telling me to go explore. That would take all of ten minutes, but I spotted a bunch of teenagers smoking cigarettes while sitting on a low wall. I didn't want my first impression on potential school mates to be one of me hanging out with mummy. Besides, walking was exercise, which I desperately needed.

One of the kids was dressed all in black, their blond roots starting to show against the dye-job. Weird. I hadn't expected to find goths on the island. An image of Rowan's tattoos flashed through my mind. Hell, someone had been murdered. Maybe I'd misread this place entirely.

With my curiosity somewhat piqued, I wandered about. The town was larger than I thought, with a maze of tiny side-streets spider-webbing away from the main road where the church was. There was a surprising number of tourist offices, signs in their windows offering horse-back tours, bicycle rental, kayaking, spelunking, and climbing. Most of them were closed, and some looked as if they hadn't been open all season. I'd be back to check them out during the week.

The cafés were open, offering an array of local baked goods, and surprisingly, they were full of people speaking French, Spanish, German, and Chinese. It was too loud, too many people crammed into too tight a space. Struggling with sudden claustrophobia, I scuttled back outside, sucking in a lungful of air. Just because I couldn't climb didn't mean I couldn't get more exercise, and an inviting path snaked along the cliffs.

It wasn't raining, but Inisliath clearly struggled with the concept of summer. The wind off the sea was fucking freezing, poking frigid fingers through my hoodie. Wishing I'd brought my jacket, I continued along the path, determined to take my camera for a stroll.

At least the wind kept the tourists away from the cliff, which left me alone to contemplate my grey surroundings, trying to get used to the idea of this place being "home."

A few brave souls were out in kayaks, their paddles stabbing furiously at the choppy waves as they rounded the headland, fighting their way back toward the bay. I raised my camera and snapped a few photos before following the path, pausing occasionally to take pictures of the gulls as they dipped and weaved through the air. Nothing super exciting, but it felt good to be outdoors and doing something.

In the distance I spotted two horses, one larger with a patchwork coat, the other small and dark. *Click.* My heart beat faster. It looked like Rowan's horse. I scanned the meadow but didn't spot any redheads. Stupid. The horses had probably just wandered off to graze.

The path split, the right fork leading down toward a beach more rock than sand. I headed right, treading carefully on the muddy trail. The beach was empty except for two figures walking at the water line. Their hair was a fiery flare against the grey of the rock, grey of the water, grey of the whole damn world. *Click.* I followed my feet down the path, blood booming in my ears, hoping Rowan

71

wouldn't object to my presence.

He looked up as I skidded onto the beach, the soles of my Docs struggling to get traction on the slick pebbles. So graceful, balletic really. Well done me.

"Hey, you all right?" Rowan called and took a couple of steps toward me.

"Yeah, fine. Thanks," I called back, deciding to rest my butt against a boulder and not risk further embarrassment by trying to get any closer.

He returned to whatever he'd been doing, saying something to Deirdre I couldn't catch because of the wind. I was content to watch. The view was pretty good. Rowan wore the same ratty sweater he'd been in the day I met him. His hair was tied up at the back of his neck, though several curls had come free, whirling behind him like flaming noodles. He wore his jeans rolled up to the knees, which gave me a view of his calves. Both of them had seven concentric bands tattooed across their middles of gradually increasing thickness.

Deirdre waved to me, her long hair writhing like snakes about her head. I blinked. No not actual snakes. That was impossible. It must've been the wind in my eyes, the tears making my vision blurry. The butterflies on her dress couldn't possibly be moving, either. There were real butterflies, too, purple-black ones, clinging to the rocks nearest Rowan as he picked his way along the tideline, bending every now and then to collect something he dropped into the bucket in his left hand.

After fifteen minutes of sitting in the wind, I was pretty sure hypothermia had set in, my teeth chattering and bones screaming at me to get somewhere warm. How the hell were Rowan and Deidre walking through the water barefoot?

Deirdre bounded over to me, all smiles and happiness. "Look what I found!" She shoved her open hand toward me, a single perfect shell sitting on her sandy palm. "Isn't it beautiful? Thank you, Mrs. Snail for losing your home so I can make something pretty." She stroked the shell with a grubby finger. "Do you like it?"

"Yeah, it's—colorful," I said, feeling just as off-balance in her presence as before.

"I'll make you something. Like this." She shook her wrist at me, her many bracelets jangling.

"Dee, I'm going to take a break." Rowan handed her the bucket before perching beside me. I might've inhaled a little deeper when he got closer. "You should check the pools before the tide comes in."

Deirdre snatched up the bucket and skipped away, butterflies crawling off her dress and flitting from her shoulders only to vanish in a gust of a wind. Clearly, I'd been imagining it. The hypothermia was making me hallucinate.

"Aren't you cold?" I looked down at Rowan's bare feet.

"I'm used to it," he said, squinting sideways at me. "We do this at least once a week."

"And what is this? Toe torture?"

He scraped away a curl stuck to his lips. "I help Deirdre collect sea glass and shells. She makes jewelry." He showed me his wrist, the leather bracelets sitting over the ink I'd noticed before. No gauze today, just bright pink scars cut in neat striations. I focused on the bracelets instead. Some were decorated with metal charms, others had seashells. Most of those were cracked and chipped. "She and Neasa sell them at the tourist market," he continued. "And at the tattoo shop in town, too."

"That's very entrepreneurial."

"We try," he said, a sour note creeping into his voice. "So, you're a photographer?" He gestured to the camera in my lap.

"Yeah. No. Sort of." God, brain—tongue, work please. "I mean, I took some photos of you—and your sister. I hope you don't mind. I can delete them if you want."

73

"Only if they're awful," he said with that almost smile. "Can I see?"

My hands were trembling because of the cold, not nerves, as I handed over the camera, telling him to swipe left.

For a moment he stared at the photos in silence, and I wrapped my hand around my stomach to keep it from audibly churning.

"If you don't like them, just delete them," I said. "I should've asked before taking photos of you. Sorry."

"No, it's—" He glanced up at me for a moment. "These are great. You're really good."

A fire burned in each cheek, my chest ready to explode. Mum sometimes told me I was good, but she had zero eye for the artistic, and all the colonel ever offered was criticism. What Rowan thought shouldn't have mattered to me at all, but his smile as he looked at the photos gave me an attack of the warm fuzzies.

"Thanks," I managed when he handed back the camera. He hadn't deleted a single photo. I must've been doing something right.

"So, are these the climbing crags?" I pointed to the cliffs behind us, a sheet of black rock sweeping along the beach.

"They can be climbed," Rowan said, "but they're not the safest. Wind gets them too wet most of the year." The ocean grumbled, a gust blasting spray at us as if to emphasize his words. "These aren't even bolted," he added. "The best crags are south of the harbor."

"Do you climb a lot?" I asked.

"No," he said. "Not anymore. I used to, though. I've done most of the easier sport routes on the island." He dug his toe into a patch of sand, drawing spirals. "But that was years ago back when my uncle was alive. He used to belay me."

The way he said it made it sound like there was a scab

74

on a wound. I wasn't going to be the one to pick at it.

"Yeah, I'd need someone to belay me once I start climbing again," I said.

"I might be a bit rusty, but I think I'd manage," Rowan said.

"ATC or grigri?"

"I'm old school," he said. "Only ever used an ATC. That okay?"

"If that's what you're most comfortable with. I'll be putting my life in your hands, you know," I said, my words sinking slowly into the space between us.

"I know." Rowan stared down at his hands, cracked a knuckle, then wiped his sandy palms down his long, lean thighs. "Just let me know when you're ready to go. We'll figure out the rest."

"Thanks. That would be great," I said, my gaze still on his fingers where they rested on his legs. I would literally be putting my life in his hands, trusting him to hold on to the rope while I was suspended thirty meters above the ground. There were very few people I'd trusted back home not to fuck that up, but somehow, I didn't think Rowan was the type to get distracted by chatting or fiddling with their phone when they were supposed to be taking up slack.

"You should go," Rowan said, looking out over the sea. "That storm'll be here in less than twenty minutes."

Thick black clouds barreled toward the island, a low rumble I'd thought was the crash of waves, now so obviously thunder. Twenty minutes gave me just enough time to haul ass back to town.

"What about you?" I asked as I got up and dusted myself off. "Aren't you coming?"

"I'll wait with my sister. She loves storms," he said, like it should've been obvious. I looked over at Deirdre where she was dancing knee-deep in the waves, hands twirling in the air above her.

"Okay, be safe," I said, for some unknown idiotic reason. The thought of Rowan getting struck by lightning or washed out into a tempestuous sea wasn't exactly high up on my "Things I Wanted" list. I clamped my teeth on my bottom lip, waiting for him to make some snarky comment, but he didn't.

"Same to you, Ash," he said instead, his voice soft and genuine as he pushed off the rock. "Hope to see you around," he added before jogging toward his sister. She greeted him with a splash, which he returned and made her squeal.

I picked my way back up the path, pausing to snap a couple more photos of Rowan and Deidre playing on the beach, black clouds providing a ferocious background to their bright hair. I wanted to stay, to watch, maybe even to join in, but the storm was coming. Another vicious blast of wind sent me scurrying up the path as thunder shook the ground beneath me. It was definitely not my knees jellifying at the thought of going climbing with Rowan Sheehy.

Rowan

THE STORM had raged all night and doused the island in heavy rain most of the day, too. Now, the sun sank low in the west, unfurling pink and red streamers across the lingering clouds, staining the ocean similar shades. My thoughts turned to Ash, to the promise I'd made for a climbing expedition, for the memories that conjured, memories of happier times before I'd understood the full weight of the mantle I'd inherit. A time before I'd truly comprehended mortality.

Inisliath still mourned for Andy, sorrow seeping up through the soil, bowing the heads of the summer flowers dotting the meadow, dripping from the branches above me, the hawthorn's leaves falling like tears around the police tape demarcating the murder site. Not that I needed blue-and-white tape to know where Andy's throat had been slit.

The grass had been trampled in intricate circles around fractal blood splatters spiraling outwards from a larger, darker smear. The ring of gentians was gone, scuffed into oblivion by police who knew better but didn't care. Or maybe someone wearing those boots wanted to cover evidence, to obscure the real reason a Kilduff had been sacrificed.

The memory of his death stalked toward me and, this time, I let it sink its claws in, reliving the moments of pain and panic. Gasping, I placed a hand against the hawthorn, trawling the memory for some secret clue.

The tinkling sound of bells lost in gurgles as Andy choked.

The scent of lavender, or maybe geranium, obliterated by the copper tang of blood.

Andy's memories whispered through my mind, tangling with the fifty-two others already there. The ghosts stirred, a choir of the departed. For a moment I let their lives slither through my veins and shudder through my bones, then I tamped it down. It was too easy to lose myself in the joy experienced by others, too easy to become mired in borrowed misery.

The rumble of an engine erased the voices, and I squeezed my eyes shut and slipped back into my own skin. The rough scrape of bark against my palm, the salt in the wind lifting the hair from my sweaty neck. A battered station wagon fumbled over the dips and rolls of the meadow, drawing inexorably closer.

I whistled for Auryn, not wanting Detective Inspector Walsh to find me trespassing at her crime scene. If I wasn't already on her list of suspects, I would be soon.

"Hey!" Ash's mom shouted through her open window, still far away. She opened her door, and I swung up onto my horse's back. With a squeeze of my knees, we were off, the detective's shouted orders for me to wait fading beneath the thunder of Auryn's hooves.

A peppering of stars had spilled across the sky when I finally saw the horses settled for the night and went in search of dinner for myself. I found Siobhan sitting at the kitchen table with yarrow leaves pressed against her eyes, a bowl of water infused with bay leaves before her, and several clary sage candles burning on the table, each decorated with seashells and bits of sea glass.

"Don't you need to see to scry?" I asked.

"And you would know?" She let the leaves drop and stared into the water instead, stirring it counterclockwise with a piece of dried bracken root. From the frown creasing her face and the fierce concentration with which she glared at the water, she wasn't having much success.

"Nothing," she said, massaging her temples where the hair strained at her skin, desperate to be released from the severe braid imprisoning her curls.

"Is that because the magic is lacking or because there's nothing to be found?" I asked.

"Don't be clever, Rowan. We still have plenty of power."

"Aye, thanks to my blood." I showed her the protruding strip of keloid her blade had left on my wrist.

"We've tried everything," Siobhan said, ignoring the mark she'd left on me. "Still don't know what it was you think you saw in the Otherworld."

Her doubt in me was as expected as it was corrosive. There was no way to prove what I'd seen without taking her to the river.

"What about Andy?" I asked.

"Not our concern. The Kilduffs can deal with it."

"What if it's connected to what I saw? What if whoever killed Andy is responsible?" I sat opposite her with the plate of dinner Deirdre had put aside for me. "If someone murdered Andy to release the entity at the river, we should investigate."

Siobhan pursed her lips, still stirring the water, but

now her gaze was fixed on me as I tucked into the bowl of lentil stew.

"If I could get to the river without having to ferry someone, then—"

"No," Siobhan said. "Last time we struggled to pull you out. Now you want to cross over and risk yourself for one of *them*?"

"For myself. I want to know what I'm facing without the weight of a soul to bear, otherwise next time maybe you won't be able to bring me home."

She pondered my words, drumming her fingers on the table.

"It's the wrong time of year," she said. "The solstice has come and gone, and if it were Samhain, maybe, but now?" She shook her head. "You need to leave this alone, Rowan." She hadn't raised her voice, but the vehemence of her tone made me lower my spoon all the same. "I don't care what you saw, what you felt when that Kilduff died, what he's whispering in your head right now. This is not our problem." Siobhan rose abruptly from the table and swept the bowl into her hands. She dumped its contents in the sink, crushed the bay leaves in her fist, then tossed them in the compost bucket. She did the same with the bracken root and yarrow leaves. "Make sure you wash up after yourself," she said before striding out of the kitchen.

She hadn't always been so angry or cruel with words. Once, she'd known how to smile, to laugh. Once, when she'd had dreams. Dreams of a life on the mainland, of going to medical school and melding our ancient herb lore with modern practices. She'd studied herself into a stupor, taking the entrance exam without telling Mother, willing to risk misfortune and leave the island.

She'd been accepted, too, but Mother had set fire to the letter of acceptance, leaving Siobhan crying over the ashes of her dream, a reminder that my sisters also

80

had a role to fulfill and, as the eldest, Siobhan's first responsibility was to continue the Sheehy line, regardless of what she actually wanted.

After that, my sister was never the same. A cloud had settled over her, a fog of bitter acceptance, her crushed dream like a stone in her shoe, forever chafing.

It took almost an hour to wash and dry the dishes, including the sink-full my sisters had left for me to do. The house was quiet, bereft of the eerie ambient music Iona liked to listen to when she was home. An hour alone with my thoughts, the chorus of dead whispers in my head all echoing my fear that Andy was only the first.

THE TOWN seemed more alive today. Many shops were still closed, though, windows sporting spider webs and months of grime, I guess meant they hadn't opened their doors all summer. The few tour shops in operation were packed with noisy tourists. I wasn't going to risk getting jostled by over-exuberant backpackers. There was no point, anyway. Not like I'd be kayaking or climbing any time soon. Thanks, Dad. And when I was ready to hit the rock again, I'd have my own personal guide. If Rowan had meant what he said. If he still felt the same way weeks from now when my arm was healed.

Escaping the tourists, I traipsed down a skinny alley between buildings leaning toward each other, blocking my view of the sky. There didn't appear to be much here, just painted doorways leading to dingy apartments. There was one shop, though, and I froze mid-step when I saw it.

The sign read *O'Donnell's Antiquarian* embellished with curling knot-work.

The windows sported displays of second-hand books on fishing or farming or similarly dull pursuits. I went in anyway. What I'd learned that breakfast with Rowan was almost everything I knew about my family. Granddad had been born here. When he was nineteen, he'd met a student from Birmingham and fallen in love. They'd moved away before Mum was born, and Granddad had never been back until now.

The bell chimed as I opened the door, and the must of old books slapped me in the face. There was a sickly sweet smell, too, as if someone had overdone it with the incense sticks. The shop was a lot larger than it appeared from the street but no less cramped. The stacks overflowed with books of all sizes and shapes. Someone had taped hand-written labels to the shelves. Sporting. Cooking. General non-fiction. History. And so they continued as I wound my way through the chaos, too wary of creating a domino effect to take a closer look at anything.

Inisliath.

I paused at the shelf, scanning the titles. A couple of outdated Lonely Planets, several guides to island bird watching, a book on island mythology—could be interesting—and a last battered tome called *A Brief History of Inisliath: Volume 3*. Brief my ass.

"You doing okay then, lad?" A deep voice sounded behind my shoulder, causing me to startle and sending a shock of ache through my collarbone. *Lad.* Guess I did look more boyish today in camo cargos and an over-sized hoodie. Most days I aimed for androgynous and did a half-decent job of it.

"Just looking around," I said.

"You must be Sabrina's kid, I heard old man O'Donnell was back," the store owner said with a lift of bushy eyebrows. You'd need a weed-hacker to trim them, the beard, too, which was a mass of black and white growing like tree moss down a barrel chest.

"You know my family?"

"As I should. I'm your granddad's uncle—no, second cousin, which makes me your cousin, let's see..." The person, a man presumably, tapped his chin and grinned. "That'll make me your third cousin once removed."

I wasn't going to argue.

"I've only met Martha," I said.

"Now you've met me, Fergus," he said. "There are a bunch of us O'Donnells; you'd be the youngest if Maire hadn't just had a bairn," Fergus added while his gaze did a quick, if unsubtle, sweep of my body.

"Actually, I'm a Walsh on account of my dad," I said.

"*Tch*," he made the disapproving sound at the back of his throat. "You're at least half an O'Donnell." He clapped me on the back, making me wince. I squirmed away from his grasp, about to tell him his genetic math was wrong, when the bell above the door chimed.

It was the goth I'd noticed the other day, the one dressed in black, with someone who looked like an older sibling. The younger one wore a lace concoction, while the older one had jeans tucked into boots and a dark red sweater slipping off broad shoulders. Blond hair hung in a dead-straight curtain down their face, the fringe an asymmetrical slash across their left eye. The two of them had nearly identical faces: high cheekbones, wide mouths, narrow noses, big eyes, and skin so white it was almost translucent.

They were both so beautiful it hurt to look at them, but look I did. I couldn't help it. They must've been wearing contact lenses. No one had eyes that blue. The older one caught me staring and slid a smirk onto their perfect lips that did nothing to diminish their prettiness.

It was impossible to look away, kind of like when you pass a car accident and don't want to see the carnage, but can't stop looking for dismembered body parts, either.

"This'll be the long-lost O'Donnell, then," the older

one said.

"Aye, indeed." Fergus smiled.

"It's Ashlee, right?" The younger one stepped forward and offered me a delicate, gloved hand.

"Ash, yeah." I took their hand and gave it a gentle shake.

"I'm Teagan. This is my sister, Lucy. We're the youngest Kilduff girls," Teagan said like it should mean something to me.

"We hear your grandda is staying at Ros Tearmann," Lucy said, her lips twisting on the name as if it tasted bad. "Why there?"

"Why not?" I tentatively leaned against the stacks, hoping it made me look cool and not like a total dork given the sling on one arm and camera slung over my good shoulder. God, I must've looked like such a tourist, and these Kilduffs made me feel so uncomfortable, claustrophobic in my own skin. I didn't want to look at them but couldn't tear my eyes away.

"It's run by that Sheehy clan," Teagan said. "I'm surprised they'd let an O'Donnell under their roof. Or why the O'Donnells would allow it."

"Special circumstances," Fergus answered. "Sabrina and her da have been away a while."

"So it's all forgiven, then?" Lucy asked.

"What's forgiven?" I asked.

"Don't you know?" She turned to me. "The O'Donnells and Sheehys have a history of bad blood. They're not the sort you want to mix with, anyway."

"Really?" I raised an eyebrow, too late realizing it was a thing my mum did whenever she thought I was lying. "I met Rowan," I continued. "He seemed nice." More than nice in more than many ways, but I didn't think they'd appreciate the details.

"He's the worst of the lot," Lucy said, all trace of the smile wiped from her face.

"Wouldn't want a new arrival getting in with the wrong crowd, is all," Teagan added with a shrug.

"And you'd be the right crowd?" I asked, eyebrow inching back up my forehead.

"Only thought you should know his family are a bunch of quacks," Lucy said. "Fancy themselves witches, they do. Strange, the lot of them."

"And Rowan, with all those scars and tattoos," Teagan added. "It's just not right. He's into the dark arts, you know." She waggled her fingers and her delicately plucked eyebrows.

"The dark arts?" I asked.

"Why do you think they run an old age home?" Lucy fixed her cerulean gaze on me. "They're into death magic."

"Seriously?" I tried and failed to stifle a laugh.

"You heard about what happened in the meadow, right?" Teagan asked.

"A man was murdered," I said, trying to keep my voice even.

"Our uncle Andy. Had his throat slit and was all carved up in symbols just like Rowan has inked," Lucy said.

My expression must've told her how much I didn't believe her.

"Truly. It's in the official files," she continued. "Our cousin Claire works at the station. She shares all the details."

An involuntarily shudder rippled down my spine. I hoped the Kilduffs didn't notice. It definitely grossed me out thinking about someone cutting random symbols into a murder victim, but it mostly made me more curious about Rowan. I blame it on growing up with a detective for a parent.

"Still don't see a connection to the 'dark arts' there," I said, using air quotes and all in case they missed how idiotic I thought they sounded.

"Fine, don't believe us. But your grandda could be next," Lucy said.

Fergus interrupted with a gruff, "That's enough now."

"Come on, Fergus. Don't you think Ash should know the truth about this island?" she said.

"Aye, the truth and not rumor." He laid a meaty hand on Lucy's shoulder. "I am sorry to hear about your uncle, though. Andy was a good man, a good man indeed."

Teagan seemed about to say something when her phone started ringing. She moved away to answer, and Fergus became busy with books two stacks over, leaving me alone with Lucy.

She stepped closer and lowered her voice. "Seriously, Ash. For your own good, stay away from Rowan. He's not what you think." Her gaze was unnervingly earnest. It felt like I was falling, drawn into those mesmerizing eyes, the doubt about Rowan seeping out of me to be replaced by a fear that didn't quite fit.

"What are you doing?" I stammered. "Stop." I blinked and turned away from her. The fear evaporated, leaving behind a wake of irritation. Fuck this girl thinking she could get inside my head with her too-blue eyes and stupid smile.

"Trust me," Lucy said, sounding equally annoyed. "The Sheehys are bad news. You don't want to get mixed up with them. There's a reason the Kilduffs and O'Donnells have stuck together. We all loathe the Sheehys. You'll understand in time." She rested her hand on my arm, the contact causing my skin to tingle.

"I doubt it." I pulled away, and Lucy's eyes widened as if surprised anyone could resist her proximity.

"That was Ma," Teagan said. "Let's go."

"Right, hope to see you around, O'Donnell." Lucy stepped away and replaced her frown with a smile, the expression banishing the gloomy mood her previous words had conjured.

"We'll be in touch," Teagan said. "Actually, here's my number." She scrawled her digits on a sticky note she produced from the depths of her bag, handing it to me before she and her sister swept out of the bookstore. I watched them sashay down the street, not knowing what the hell to think. The farther they walked from the store, the more normal I felt, as if their presence had given me vertigo, and now I was staggering away from the precipice.

"Ah, those two are quite a pair," Fergus said beside me, making me jump.

"Who are they?" I asked as I pocketed the note. "I mean, I know they're Kilduffs but—"

"The Kilduffs and O'Donnells run the island."

"And the Sheehys? What's so bad about them?"

"There's a lot to love about this island," Fergus said, "but it can be a bitter place. Old wounds are rarely forgotten or forgiven. Best you keep away from them Sheehys."

"Hard to do when Granddad's at Ros Tearmann." And with everyone telling me to stay away, the opposite was exactly what I planned on doing.

"Aye, but we're going to remedy that," Fergus said. "Don't you worry. No Sheehy will hurt an O'Donnell, not while I be breathing."

I was about to tell him it was none of his damn business and nothing needing a "remedy," but his final words had sent icy tingles pricking up my spine.

"It's naught for you to worry about, yet," Fergus said. "I've got just the thing for you." He turned to the shelf marked Inisliath and reached for a title above my head. "Here we are." He handed me a beat-up copy of *A Brief History of Inisliath: Volume 2*. It was at least 400 pages. "On the house. Hope it helps."

"Thanks," I said and was about to ask about volume one when the bell chimed again as a couple of German tourists came in. Fergus hurried off to help them. I shifted the book in my arms and cracked open the spine to the contents page. There we were. *Chapter Four: O'Donnells*, sandwiched between *Chapter Three: Kilduffs* and *Chapter Five: Sheehys*. A chapter on the McNamaras completed a section titled *Founding Families*.

With the book held awkwardly under my good arm, I shoved open the door and stepped into drizzle. I flipped up my hood then hurried back toward the main street and the sanctuary of a coffee shop. Mum would probably be hours, which gave me time for caffeine and a history lesson. I'd hated history at school, so tedious and dull, but this wasn't about foreign kings invading places I didn't care about. This was my own history. Maybe I'd learn something to explain the mess of my life.

Rowan

NEASA'S CAT, white-furred but named Onyx out of my sister's constant need to be contrary, lay on my bed, her tail twitching as she watched the ever-present butterflies flitting around my desk lamp. Night had wrapped its arms around the island, her breath wafting in milky tendrils off the sea. Mist seeped into the courtyard, billowing cool air through my window and across my bare back. The butterflies cast darting shadows over my drawing, but I didn't mind. Night was my time, the only hours free of chores and sisters.

Having renewed the strip of duct-tape holding the frame of my glasses together, I double-checked the specs on the commission and got to work. If only I had less to do during the day, I might finish more drawings and be able to make a more meaningful financial contribution. "Entrepreneurial," Ash had called us, but it wasn't nearly enough. I'd have to complete ten commissions a week, every week, just to feed Auryn through the winter. I was lucky if I received a commission a month. And selling prints online didn't provide much income, nor did the sale of my sisters' jewelry and candles, while Iona's paycheck barely kept enough food on the table.

I paused, listening beyond the scratch of charcoal on paper and the flutter of gossamer wings. I thought I'd heard voices, real ones, but only mist and darkness lay beyond my window.

I scratched at the triquetra on my chest. The scar was raised, as were many others dotting my body: the twin knots on my shoulders binding me to the realm of the living, lines marking my forearms restraining the essence of the Otherworld that moved through me like living threads, a constant writhing presence. Resentment stirred within me. I pressed my fingers into the scar on my chest, my nails drawing fresh blood.

There, a snatch of laughter and a boot heel on cobbles.

I switched off my lamp and took off my glasses, blinking as my eyes adjusted to the darkness. Peering into the courtyard, I watched figures emerge from the mist. Neasa stood in the arms of a Kilduff, their mouths locked together. The Kilduff's eyes flashed ethereal blue against the night, and my blood turned glacial, a slow-spreading dread shearing ice through my veins.

Still, I watched them, part of me wondering what it would be like to kiss Ash. In unwelcome response, the ghosts within me seethed, assaulting me with borrowed memories of others' kisses. In the beginning, absorbing the memories of the dead had left me in an existential quandary, not knowing where those other souls ended and I began. In the beginning, I'd been muddled up, confusing which memories were my own. It took me the better part of a year to learn how to navigate the tangled tapestry the dead had woven inside my skin. Would I ever get to make such memories of my own?

I turned away from the window and blinked away the deluge, then I waited until feet smacked across kitchen tiles, until Neasa tiptoed down the corridor, her seashell and safety-pin jewelry tinkling in the quiet.

"Have a good evening?" I asked as she approached, trying to keep the anger from incinerating my words.

"What do you care?" she snapped, her face flushed and hair disheveled.

"Teagan Kilduff? Neasa, what are you doing?"

"None of your fucking business." She glowered and shoved her hands into the voluminous sleeves of her black lace dress.

"They swapped Claddagh rings, didn't you know?" Deirdre added softly, her head peeking out of her room next to mine.

"You stay out of this," Neasa shot at Deirdre as I shook my head. "What? You think you get to have an opinion?" Neasa glared back at me.

Even in the dark corridor, I could see the anger burning in her eyes. "But you know what they do. You know what happens to anyone who gets close to them."

"Is that what happened with you and Conall?" she asked, folding her arms.

"We were only ever friends, and look how that turned out," I said, bitterness blackening the edges of my words.

"It's different with me," she said.

"How can you believe that?" My heart ached for her. "Knowing what they are."

"*Were*," Neasa said. "Teagan wants nothing to do with her family's history."

"She *is* her family's history. Whether she wants to drain you or not, she will. She won't be able to stop herself."

Neasa rolled her eyes. "We're taking precautions," she said. "There are protection spells and herbs to counteract Kilduff magic."

"What if it's not enough?"

"It won't matter, because Teagan's not like that anyway."

"It's not something she can choose," I said, softly, remembering all the times the spells in my skin had saved me from Conall.

My sister bristled at that. "Well, she can choose whether or not to stay on this damn rock," she said. "And she's leaving for college next month. Next year, I'll join her."

There was no college on Inisliath. Even if Teagan had intentions of leaving the island, of risking the island's wrath, she and Lucy were the favored heirs apparent to the Kilduff legacy—they'd never be allowed to leave Inisliath. Teagan must be toying with my sister for some other twisted purpose, maybe to consume her vitality and leave her a living wraith out of spite.

"You can't be serious," I said. "You know what happened to Sarah. And how can you leave knowing what happened to Eileen and—"

"I don't care," Neasa said. "Rather any of that than living here."

"You think Mother will allow it?" I lowered my voice.

"I'm not staying here just to breed more of you," she snapped, her words like barbs slipping into my skin.

Neasa clenched her jaw while Deirdre stared at her, eyes wide and lower lip trembling. Deirdre would never willingly leave Inisliath, not because she was spell-bound like me, but rather because she couldn't imagine living anywhere else. My youngest sister was pure like that, a true daughter of the island.

"What's Onyx doing in here?" Neasa pointed at the cat now rubbing herself against my legs. "She's mine." She scooped up her pet, and Onyx meowed in protest.

"Tell me, Ness, is it only kisses and rings you've exchanged with Teagan or have you already given her something more?" I asked. "Would you even know if she was depleting you?"

Neasa balled her left fist, magic flickering in her eyes. I'd pushed her too far. I should've known better. She opened her hands, and the drawing on my desk ignited with silver flame. More than six hours of work began to burn. I lunged for her, wanting only to stun the spell from her fingers and save my drawing. Instead, she turned the magic on me. The scars on my shoulders and forearms flared as my knees buckled.

Her rage crashed over me like storm-tormented waves. Her magic ignited in my skin, making my eyes water and breathing increasingly difficult as she activated the binding spell. Had I been in the Otherworld, it would've been a tether, reeling me back to the living, but here it was suffocating, an agony compressing my ribs and constricting my veins. A pall descended over my vision, purple and black, a curtain of shadow and mist. The walls of my bedroom retracted, and I was falling, my flesh sloughing away as the shadows welcomed me beyond the veil.

"Stop! You're hurting him!" Deirdre screamed, her voice far away.

Neasa's hold on me snapped abruptly, knocking me to the floor. Onyx hissed, scratched at Neasa's face, and bolted down the corridor. I lay gasping, the pain blurring my vision with images of the Otherworld.

"Stay out my business!" She stood over me, her left hand curled like a talon, and her eyes alight with the power of Sheehy magic.

"Mother will hear of this," Deirdre said as she crouched beside me. "All of it."

"Urgh, I hate you!" Neasa said before thudding down the hall to her bedroom. I knew how much restraint it must've taken her not to slam her door.

"You're all right," Deirdre said, as if her words could make it so.

My body still shook from the assault, my skin tingling, and my mind reeling. I knew how to access the Otherworld now. I didn't have to wait for someone to die or for my sisters to allow the crossing. All it took was sufficient pain.

Ash

IT MUST'VE been some kind of miracle. After nothing but rain for the past forever, a gash of blue sky was leaking sunshine. I tilted my face into the warmth, letting what passed for heat around here wash over me. A breeze fanned the back of my neck, and for a moment I could imagine being on a tropical island sipping a fancy drink with a little umbrella in it. Then my chair wobbled, the back leg caught between cobbles, and I came crashing back to reality.

Once again, I found myself sat outside The Copper Kettle on their idea of a terrace. It was really just a strip of sidewalk where the café had squeezed in a few outdoor chairs and rickety tables. It was better than staying indoors, and at least here, the lattes kept on coming with zero effort from me. Mum would be pissed at how much I was spending, but I didn't care. I missed being able to use the credit card the colonel had given me, but the card came attached to the person, and I'd rather be poor than anywhere near the man.

The Copper Kettle also had relatively decent Wi-Fi, allowing me to look up horsey terminology I never would've thought I'd want to know. I guess chestnut and bay, saddle and bridle and all the rest of the terms were as foreign to me as grigri or quickdraw would be to a non-climber. Thanks to a new sim card, I was safe from messages from the colonel. So far, only Mum had my number.

After twenty minutes, I'd learned enough about horses and focused again on the open book in front of me. I'd already read the chapters on the founding families, and the chapter on the O'Donnells several times. Three things I knew for sure:

1. It read more like mythology than history.
2. Our families were seriously fucked up.
3. There was absolutely nothing brief about any of this.

"Can I get you anything?" a waiter asked. They weren't the one who'd served me before. Shifts must've changed as morning became afternoon. My stomach rumbled, reminding me to ingest something other than caffeine.

"Yeah, can I get the chicken salad and another latte," I said, looking up at the person whose nametag read Cillian. They had deep brown skin and thick, dark hair with the longest eyelashes I'd ever seen.

"You want bread with that?" they mumbled from beneath a floppy fringe. I declined, and they drifted away as I returned to the book.

Most of it was boring. I'd skimmed past the screeds on genealogical studies tracing the founding families to the original clans who'd conquered the island in some god-awful pre-soap and sanitation era, sticking to the pages with clear-cut paragraphs instead of walls of text.

I was engrossed in a bit about druidism when the waiter shoved the latte at me, spilling froth onto the page

I was reading.

"Shit, watch it."

"It's a load of bollocks anyway," Cillian said, and dumped the salad on the table. I barely had time to swipe the book away before it got doused in dressing as well.

"You've read it?" I asked.

"Don't need to. I'm a McNamara," they said as if they couldn't decide whether it was something to be proud of or embarrassed by. They jutted out their chin, staring at me with eyes bordering on violet.

"So, you don't turn into a seal at sunset?"

"No."

"How about a bat, then? A fox? A hawk?" I rattled off all the animals the book had listed.

"Screw you," they said with more venom than I thought I deserved, glaring at me from behind horn-rimmed specs.

"Sorry," I said reflexively. "It's just that the book says—"

"I know what the book says." They folded their arms. Wow, I'd stood it in good and proper. To their credit, they hadn't raised their voice, which meant we weren't getting too many stares from the other customers.

"Well—" I might've given them a more genuine apology if they'd let me finish.

"You O'Donnells," Cillian snapped. "You're all the same."

"And how's that?" I asked, genuinely ignorant of how my island genetics dictated my personality traits.

"Think you know everything just because you used to."

"But I thought the book was wrong, and we aren't druids," I said, and they rolled their eyes. "So that bit about faeries, then?"

"You mean the fey." They frowned down at me. "Aye, we've all got fey blood on this island. Best not to forget

97

it."

"Not all bollocks then, is it?" I tapped the book, trying not to smile. "So, you believe in faeries?"

"The *fey*," they corrected me again with a twitch of their head, flicking dark hair off their frown-creased forehead. "You really should learn something about your ancestors."

"I was trying to." I flipped open the book again and sipped my latte, hoping they'd take the hint and bugger off.

Cillian lingered. I tried to ignore them, but it was kind of hard to focus on the book with them standing over me.

"God, what?" I asked without looking up.

"Is your mum investigating the Kilduff murder?" they asked.

"She is a detective," I said.

"She got any suspects?"

"Why, do you?" I asked, annoyance starting to itch under my skin. I glared up at them. If they said another word, they sure as shit weren't getting a tip.

"Forget it," Cillian said with a shrug as they turned away from the table. Someone inside was yelling their name, and they yelled back, "Coming!" as they navigated a path between the crowded tables.

Between mouthfuls of salad, I flipped to the back of the book where the family trees had been sketched in black and sepia. There they were: Cillian McNamara, sibling to Saoirse, progeny of Rose—no second parent listed—and grandkid to Patrick—no other grandparent listed. Cillian's aunt had been Sarah, married to none other than the recently murdered Andy Kilduff.

I flipped past the Kilduffs to the Sheehys. According to the book, it was a matrilineal family with the Sheehy name passed down through daughters. The family went back generations, several hundred years in fact. Several names reoccurred, but there was one that appeared without fail in every new generation: Rowan. Right down to the current generation: Siobhan, Iona, Rowan, Neasa, Deirdre.

I checked for a publication date on the volume but couldn't find one. The book seemed ancient, but it couldn't have been printed more than six months ago if the newest addition to the O'Donnell clan was listed. Weirder still was the lack of partner names. It didn't say who Rowan's dad was, or who any of the non-familial fathers or mothers were, for that matter. Was there some racist bullshit going on? It also looked as if entire branches had somehow been erased. I could just make out pale grey text saying Brighid and another saying Eileen. They were or had been Rowan's aunts. Many other names had faded to a dull sepia.

I turned to the O'Donnell family tree next and almost dropped the book in the remains of my salad.

When I'd first looked at the family trees—like, a day ago!—I'd been disappointed but not surprised to see my grandfather's name in pale grey ink and no mention of my mum or me. Of course not. I'd assumed the book had been published decades ago. But now, there we were in bright, black ink as if the text had been freshly printed, except it had us listed as Sabrina and Ash O'Donnell. There was no mention of my father, and none of my grandmother, either.

With a shudder, I shut the book and closed my eyes. After several deep breaths, I opened the book again and there was my name, just as before. How the hell had changes been made?

"Something wrong?" Cillian materialized beside me, making me jump, the movement tugging painfully at my collarbone. They picked up my dirty plate and cocked their head, waiting.

"Just—It's nothing." I took a sip of air and waited for the awkward moment to scuttle off.

"Didn't look like nothing." Cillian lingered again and the awkwardness did, too.

"Well..." I swallowed. "Could've sworn my name wasn't on this family tree two days ago. Now it is." I pressed open the page and tapped my name.

"Druids." Cillian's nose wrinkled as if they'd gotten a whiff of something gross. "This is why you can't trust them to keep our histories. Always changing things to suit themselves."

"But—"

"You'll learn," they said. "You're an O'Donnell. Doubt it'll take you long to figure it out. Welcome to Inisliath," they added before breezing off again with my plate and only half-finished latte.

I looked back at the book. My name stared up at me, my *preferred* name, too. Whoever had added me had at least taken the time to find out that much about me. Couldn't be mad at that. But—but it was all a fantasy anyway. Someone's poetic interpretation of how settlers had come to the island. Sure, there were neolithic monuments on Inisliath, but those hadn't been built by faeries. Faeries didn't exist, no matter how many myths and superstitions might suggest otherwise. I highly doubted the McNamaras could shape-shift into wild animals, that the Kilduffs were supposed to be some sort of vampire capable of seducing the unsuspecting, or that the Sheehys were witches. Actually, the bit about the Kilduffs could be true—not that Teagan and Lucy needed to be vampires to seduce anyone.

But why did everyone think the Sheehys capable of murder?

If Cillian was right, and the book wasn't to be trusted, then no one was. If I wanted to figure out why everyone had warned me away from the Sheehys, I needed to go to the source. I needed to talk to a Sheehy. I may have had a particular one in mind.

I walked across the fields and didn't die.

Not sure how Mum expected me to get around when I didn't have my own wheels and wouldn't have been able to drive or bike anyway with my arm still buggered. So, I walked across the fields, taking the most direct route I could to Ros Tearmann. Besides, I was armed. If anyone jumped me, I'd be sure to bash them with *A Brief History of Inisliath: Volume 2*. It could probably crack a skull.

I paused now and then to snap a few photos when the sun managed to crack open the cloud cover. Landscapes weren't my thing, but the island could be pretty when it wasn't being grey.

I didn't mean to find the crime scene, but there it was. A tree stood by itself in the middle of a muddy field all wrapped up in police tape. My feet decided before my brain, leading me over the squelchy grass to ground zero. There wasn't much to see.

Crushed flowers lying in an approximation of a circle beneath the tree and blood, lots and lots of blood splashed across the trunk in ruddy-brown streaks. And butterflies, a whole horde of those odd purply-black ones. Their wings snapped open and closed as they sucked on the spilled gore. I didn't know butterflies did the whole carrion thing.

It was beautiful and creepy, and I approached slowly, camera at the ready. My presence sent them spiraling up into the trees, and I managed to capture several photos of the bloodsuckers in flight, their wings reflecting the sunlight. Then the clouds closed up and the butterflies flew out of range, just dark little specks in the view finder.

I crouched beside the stain and reached a tentative finger to touch a blackened blade of grass. I couldn't quite bring myself to do it. Someone's life had ended here.

Violently. My stomach lurched, leaving me gulping down air, praying I didn't puke and ruin any evidence still on the ground. How did you take the life of another person? Had the killer found it easy, or were they wracked by guilt?

Guilt was temporary. At least it was for the colonel. He had no problem hurting us. He blamed it on stress, on trauma, on alcohol, on a fucked-up childhood, and a father who used to beat him senseless for the smallest infraction.

He always said he was sorry afterward, too. Sorry for losing his temper, for losing control, for hurting us, but I knew it was a lie. I'd looked him in the eyes one too many times before his fists started flying. If the guilt was real, he'd have done it once and never again. I knew deep down he *wanted* to hurt us. Something inside him got off on leaving us bruised.

Maybe that was how this killer felt. Maybe they enjoyed the rush of taking a life.

I closed my eyes, unexpected tears tumbling down my cheeks. I didn't want to think about this. I didn't want to understand it.

Maybe that was Mum's problem. She understood violence, saw it every day. She dealt with monsters on the street for a living and had to get inside their heads to catch them. Maybe by understanding the monsters on the street, she'd started understanding the monster at home. Maybe that's why she always forgave him.

Not me. I didn't understand Mum or the colonel, and I didn't want to. I didn't want to forgive them. I couldn't, wouldn't. No way. Fuck that.

Is this who you want to be? A lazy good-for-nothing who squanders their potential? His words ricocheted inside my head. Apparently skipping a day of summer school was a sign of failure, the summer school I hadn't wanted to attend in the first place. I'd scraped a pass last semester, my grades nothing great but enough to get me into my final year. It wasn't good enough. It never was. Even when I'd been trying hard and scoring As, the colonel had always found a reason to call me a disappointment. Why bother, then? If I was going to be a failure and fuck-up anyway, might as well not waste my time studying for it.

Same went for climbing. When I started, it wasn't enough to do it for fun—he wanted me to compete and win. When I started getting interested in photography, he wanted me to submit my photos to competitions and magazines, and almost succeeded in sucking all the joy out of that, too. I hated him for it, hated how he twisted everything I did into a contest, one I'd never be able to win.

I probably shouldn't have told him as much, though. I winced at the memory of his anger, of the disgust flashing in his eyes as he balled his fists. Who knew, maybe I deserved what came next.

After I turned away from the crime scene, I continued through the fields, almost disappointed when I arrived at Ros Tearmann having had no brush with a blade-wielding psycho. There was no one at reception or in any of the downstairs areas. *Private* beckoned, and I was tempted to try my luck, but a more rational part of me led me to the elevator. I trudged along the corridor, angry for not better preparing myself for the possibility of coming all this way and not finding a Sheehy to talk to.

"Granddad, you decent?" I knocked on his door.

"Come in, kiddo," he said.

Kiddo? He hadn't called me that in years. I turned the knob and found him sitting on the window seat, panes open and sunshine spilling across the floor.

"You smell that?" He took a deep breath, puffing out his whiskery cheeks.

"Your old socks?" I was rewarded with one of

Granddad's rare smiles.

"The sea. The soil. The whole island." He closed his eyes and leaned back his head. He looked good. His face wasn't quite as sallow, his eyes a little less murky—even the mostly blind one seemed brighter. He was dressed, too, not lounging around in pajamas like he did back in the city. The toll his battle against cancer had taken seemed to be disappearing.

"You up for a chat?" I asked.

"Depends on the topic." He shifted so there was space for me on the cushioned seat.

"Do you like it here?" I eased myself into the corner gently, very aware of how easy it would be to topple out of the open window and go splat in the courtyard below. "Do you feel...safe?"

"Of course I feel safe. Who've you been talking to?" He frowned, his tufty eyebrows drawing together to form a caterpillar across his face.

"Just with the murder, I mean."

"Aye, bad business that, but I'm safe as houses here."

"Even if the Sheehys are witches?"

Granddad chuckled. I hadn't heard him do so in a good long while, the sound warming me inside out. Back on the mainland, people would've laughed at anyone who believed in witches and druids. Bullshit, all of it. Obviously.

"What have you got there?" Granddad asked.

"Got this from a bookshop in town. I met our cousin Fergus, too. Shop was called O'Donnell's Antiquarian. Large guy with a big beard."

"So, it's Fergus been filling your head with nonsense, is it? What did he give you?"

I showed Granddad, and the brightness in his eyes dimmed.

"Tedious read," he said, leaving the book untouched on the spot between us.

"That's what Cillian McNamara said."

"Cillian? Patrick's son?"

"Grandkid. I was hoping you could tell me more, about all of this."

"Like if the Sheehys are a bunch of feral wildlings into the occult?" Granddad asked, all traces of his good mood evaporating.

"Well, yeah." I felt bad admitting it.

"Utter poppycock," he said with a harrumph.

"I met Lucy and Teagan Kilduff, too. No one seems to like the Sheehys much."

"You steer clear of the Kilduffs," Granddad said, back to his usual bitterness.

"Because they're vampires?" I asked. Granddad grumbled something incoherent before clearing his throat.

"There's more history than what can be written in books," he said. "You've a brain on your shoulders. Use it."

"So, the O'Donnells aren't druids."

"Maybe. Long ago," Granddad said wistfully, "but that's ancient history."

If the O'Donnells were druids, I wasn't sure why Sheehys couldn't be witches—or Kilduffs vampires, for that matter—but the scowl on Granddad's face said I was better off not saying as much.

"Why all this Sheehy hatred?" I asked. "I mean, everyone but you seems to think they're dangerous." I drummed my fingers on the book's weathered cover.

"Ah, would you look at that?" Granddad pointed out the window. I resisted the urge to turn my head. I wanted to know about our history. There had to be more to it than some ancient grudge involving a land dispute as the book claimed.

"Reminds me of when I was a young man here," Granddad said.

"When you were in love with a Sheehy?"

"What I wouldn't give to go riding again," he said. "But with these old bones..." His words faded as I followed his gaze out the window.

Rowan was riding in the paddock beyond the courtyard on the patchwork horse. The horse was a "gypsy vanner"—according to the website I'd studied this morning.

For a good long while, all I could do was stare, my fingers automatically picking up my camera. Rowan rode without even the lead rope this time, and yet the horse responded, changing direction, slowing down and speeding up at some hidden command. *Click.* Rowan's hair caught the afternoon sun, giving him a corona of copper fire. *Click.* Another person watched from the fence where they stood with Siobhan. They seemed deep in conversation, the stranger nodding and Siobhan smiling. The stranger gave Rowan a wave before following Siobhan away from the paddock. Rowan brought the horse to a halt and stared after them. *Click*, I snapped another photo.

"Ash!" Granddad tapped my knee, making me jump.

"Sorry, what?"

"I said, why don't you go and bother someone else with your questions," Granddad said. "It's time for my nap."

"Are you trying to get rid of me?"

"Desperately," he said with a smile. "I think some fresh air will do a city kid the world of good." He tried to wave me away, but I leaned in to kiss his wrinkled cheek anyway. Got to hand it to the old man. He tried really hard and mostly succeeded at not misgendering me.

Nestling the book in the crook of my bad arm, camera slung over my good one, I hustled down the stairs and out the front door. My heart pounded, and Cillian's words echoed inside my skull. Watching him be so gentle with his horse, it was impossible to believe Rowan capable of murder.

With a deep breath, I rounded the corner of the building and strode toward the paddock where he was trotting his horse in looping serpentines. Trot, canter, saddle, bridle—I did a quick run-through of my recently acquired terminology, hoping I didn't mess up and sound ridiculous.

Content to watch, I stayed at the fence, taking photos and listening to the way he clicked his tongue. He whispered soft words in another language to his horse, all throaty crackles and slip-sliding vowels. Not going to lie, it did seem a little like magic.

This was also the first time I'd seen him in a T-shirt, giving me an unimpeded view of his arms. *Click.* The tattoo on his wrist wasn't the only one. In fact, he had several in a similar style on both his forearms. The same sort of marks had been left on the murder victim, if Teagan was to be believed. Ink wasn't all he had. There were scars, too. A lot of them, all of varying thickness. Four looked more recent than the rest. My heart twisted in my chest thinking about what might cause him to cut himself like that.

Rowan completed a circuit of the paddock before the horse slowed, coming to a stop at the fence where I stood. *Click.*

"Come for a ride?" he asked as he raked his hair away from his sweaty brow and tugged it into a knot at the back of his neck.

"I'm still broken," I said as he dismounted. I meant it literally, but the hidden truth of my words made me swallow hard, harder still when Rowan frowned as if he'd understood.

"Not sure it's a good idea," I added, finding it hard to breathe.

"Auryn is gentle. I'll walk her for you," he said, a

cautious smile tweaking at his lips. "Been taking more photos?"

"Of you—your horse, I mean. A couple, yeah. Want to see?" My traitor body was doing this weird trembling thing as I handed over the camera.

"Of course." He hooked an arm over the fence and accepted my offering.

"Wow, you really do take amazing photos." His words caused another physical assault of warm-fuzzies on my insides. Then his expression darkened. "You've been to the crime scene."

"Shit, sorry. I should've warned you."

"It's all right." He continued swiping through the photos, then paused and stared at a picture for an eternity and a half in total silence. "This is incredible." Finally, he tilted the camera, showing me the one I'd taken of the butterflies in flight. "You're really talented," he said, and I was pretty sure I would spontaneously combust on the spot.

"Thanks." I took back the camera. "It was an accident, really. Didn't mean to find the crime scene. The butterflies were creepy but kinda beautiful."

"Yes, they are." He headed for the gate without saying anything else, and I kept pace with him on my side of the fence.

"What are you reading?" he asked.

"A book my cousin Fergus gave me." I dumped it in the grass and placed my camera gently on top. "I was hoping I'd learn more here about the founding families."

"I'm sure any O'Donnell will gladly fill your ear." Rowan shifted a few paces closer to me as his horse used him as a scratching post.

"Oh, I've heard plenty. All dreadful," I said with a grin I only had to partially force.

"And yet you're still here."

"I don't like being told what to do," I said. "I prefer

making up my own mind."

"Glad to hear it," he said.

"The Kilduff sisters sure had a lot to say, though," I said. "I met them in the bookstore the other day."

"Aye, I'll bet." Rowan reached around me to close the gate. I inhaled and caught a whiff of rosemary and sage along with horse. Tentatively, I stroked Auryn's nose. That much I'd done at a petting zoo as a kid. I was a little afraid of her. Her shoulder was as tall as my head, her feet massive and fluffy, and there were plenty of teeth in her mouth.

"Nothing to say about the Kilduffs?" I asked.

"Thought you liked making up your own mind?" Rowan said, teasing and totally not making me blush. Dammit. I kept my head down and followed him as he led the horse to a wooden block at the far end of the paddock.

"The book is full of stuff about druids and faeries and magic, but none of that stuff is real. I was hoping my granddad, or a Sheehy, would be a more credible source."

"Real." Rowan blinked at me as if he was struggling to make sense of what I'd said.

"I was hoping someone could tell me why our families are supposed to hate each other so much," I added more gently.

"Ah, well, people hate what they fear, and they fear what they don't understand," he said with a shrug, as if that explained everything and didn't fire off another volley of questions inside my skull.

"Can you take your sling off?" he asked. "It'll be better for balance without it."

"Um, sure." Usually, it wasn't hard removing the straps but now, for some reason, it was proving impossible.

"Want some help?" he asked.

I nodded and turned, feeling his breath tickle the back of my neck as his fingers peeled away Velcro. I didn't hate a single bit of it, even if I couldn't tell if the goosebumps were a result of Rowan's proximity or the echo of Lucy's warning hammering at my brain.

Rowan draped my sling over the fence and held Auryn by her halter.

"I hope you don't mind me asking this," he said, meeting my gaze. "But I wasn't sure I heard your mom right and didn't want to just assume. Do you use he, she, they, or something else?"

It wasn't the question I'd expected him to ask. Ever. Most people were happier to make assumptions even after I corrected them. He didn't break eye contact, not even once. Generally, people looked away, embarrassed and awkward, pretending their gaze wasn't resting on my chest trying to figure out whether I had boobs. It was even worse when their gaze fell lower.

"I'm sorry if I offended you. I just—" He clamped his upper teeth on his bottom lip, looking delightfully bashful.

"I'm not offended, just surprised you'd even think to ask."

"I live on a rock," he said. "Not under one."

"Well, thanks for asking. I use they." I bit back the *if you don't mind* or *if that's okay with you*, resolved to stop apologizing for who I was. "No one else has asked me here." Though I was sure they'd all been wondering.

"That's because you've been hanging out with the wrong crowd," he said.

"Teagan doesn't seem so bad."

"I wouldn't trust any of them. You should keep your distance."

"They said the same about you."

Rowan laughed, the sound dry and brittle. "Up you go, then," he said and gestured to the wooden block, which was really just a couple of packing crates stacked precariously together. "One leg over each side, hands in her mane. I'll be right here." He patted Auryn's neck and whispered something soft and gentle, reassuring me, too. With sweat making swamps of my armpits, I stepped onto the crates and swung my leg over Auryn's broad back in a way I hoped didn't make me look like a seal on land.

"Ready?" he asked, looking up at me with those damn intense eyes of his.

"Your eyes are different colors," I blurted.

"I know. This is one lets me see into the Otherworld." He pointed to his left eye, the one with the dark band circling the hazel iris.

"The Otherworld?"

"You know, where the faeries live," he said with a grin I couldn't help but return.

He clicked his tongue, and Auryn shifted beneath me, her muscles bunching and flexing, making me realize just how much horse was between my legs and how easily it could kill me.

We'd walked halfway around the paddock before he asked me, "Doing okay?"

"You tell me?"

"You're looking good."

My insides snap-crackle-popped as his gaze swept over me.

"Try not to look down," he said. "Shoulders back, there you go. You're a natural."

"Hah, I bet you say that to everyone," I said, trying my best to keep my back straight and not freak out about how far away the ground was.

"No, he doesn't," Deirdre said from the fence. Her presence reminded me how little I knew about this guy or why he'd ended up in a fetal position on the floor. She looked as if she'd been crying.

"Dee, what's wrong?" Rowan asked, bringing Auryn to a stop.

"You didn't tell me we were selling Comet." She glowered, tears trickling down her cheeks.

"I thought Iona told you."

"She didn't, and now he's sold. They all are. Davidson's coming to get them next week." She failed to stifle a sob and my own heart lurched.

"I'm sorry, I thought—"

She raised her hand, and Rowan tensed as if bracing for something. My stomach clenched, too.

"I hate you. I hate all of you." Deirdre ran back to the house, her daisy-print dress swishing about her knees as she went. I'm pretty sure I saw it shedding petals as she ran, but I blinked, and she was gone, a trail of shriveling yellow in her wake.

"That's the second sister to say that to me this week," Rowan said, still staring after her.

"She doesn't mean it. Siblings say dumb stuff all the time."

"You don't have siblings." He squinted up at me.

"If I did, I bet I'd yell shit like that at them twice a *day*," I said, hoping it would help.

Rowan didn't respond and didn't seem convinced.

"Who's Comet?" I asked.

"Her pony. We have to sell the horses. All of them." He rubbed a hand down Auryn's wide face, a sad smile on his lips before he kissed her nose. "Keeping them through the winter is getting too expensive. Better to sell them than let them starve."

"Oh dude, that sucks. I'm sorry." I studied Rowan, noting his torn clothes and disheveled hair, the crude leather jewelry he wore around his neck and wrists. No wonder the furnishings of the retirement home were so drab.

"Nothing to be done about it," he said, and I squirmed in my clothes, hoping Rowan wouldn't notice the brand names as he led us back to the crates.

"Not so bad, was it?" he asked.

"I didn't die, so that's good."

"Indeed," he said, a cloud momentarily passing across his face and dimming his eyes. He'd been about to offer me his hand, but let it drop to his side, leaving me to clamber off the horse by myself with all the grace of a newborn giraffe.

"Thanks for that," I said. "I'm glad I got to do it before..." *Before your beloved horse got sold off*, yeah, well done, me. Rowan bit his bottom lip and rubbed Auryn's face. I couldn't stop staring at his arms. I pictured him using his knife like he'd done with the cheese, the image searing my retinas. Thanks, brain.

"Hey, what do your tattoos mean?" I asked, pointing at the three-lined symbol exposed on his wrist. "If you don't mind me asking."

"That's the rune for Rowan," he said.

"Your name?"

"The tree, which is the same." There was a catch in his voice.

"Ash is a type of tree, too," I said. "Does it have a symbol like that?"

"It does. It's one of the three sacred trees. Oak, Ash, and Hawthorn."

"Sacred trees?"

"Aye, it's an old belief," he said. "That those trees grow together to mark the entrance to the Otherworld. Where the faeries live," he added, eyes sparking.

"I'll have to look out for that, then." I didn't want to admit I had no idea how to tell an ash from an oak. Acorns, maybe, unless ash trees also had acorns. My knowledge of botany was worse than my knowledge of horses. "What does the ash symbol look like?"

"Like this." He tapped a tattoo farther up his forearm. It was similar to the one for rowan, but had five parallel lines perpendicular to a single, thicker one.

"Andy Kilduff had marks like those cut into his body," I said, not sure why I felt the sudden need to blurt that out.

"Did your mom tell you that?"

"No," I admitted, making a mental note to fact-check with Mum as soon as possible. "Do you know why someone would do that to a person?"

"I thought your mom was the detective?" Rowan's tone had turned flinty.

"At the crime scene," I said. "There was so much blood. I just—"

"It wasn't one of us. Despite what the Kilduffs might be saying. I'm sure your mom will figure out who did it, but it wasn't a Sheehy." He looked down, giving me the opportunity to note the freckles splashed across his face.

"Are you okay?" I couldn't help asking it. He looked so...burdened, as if a weight had been dropped onto his shoulders, crushing his smile, and extinguishing the light in his eyes.

"You going to ask me that every time you see me?"

"Only until you give me an answer." God, where did I get off being so bold?

"Inisliath is a complicated place," he said, and handed me my sling.

"I've got time to figure it out." I was unashamedly flirting, but Rowan didn't seem to notice. Instead, he shook his head, a single curl tumbling loose over his ear.

"I doubt it," he said with the same sad smile he'd given Auryn, as if he was destined to lose the things he loved or something equally poetic and tragic. "Sorry, Ash, I've got chores to do," he continued before I could ask him to explain. "Think you'll be fine on your own?" He was already walking away, clicking his tongue at Auryn, who dutifully followed.

"Yeah, sure. Thank you," I called after him. He waved as he led his horse out of the paddock.

I gave him a head start before following, stopping to pick up my camera and book. There was a single, purple-black butterfly wing on the front cover, right above the author's name. Fionnula O'Donnell.

There was no such thing as objective truth. Everyone always had a different perspective, and everyone thought their version was the absolute truth. The O'Donnell who wrote this book probably thought they'd gotten it right. What if they hadn't? What if the Sheehys weren't the ones everyone should be afraid of?

My thoughts led me on a dark meander to my father. Maybe in his version of the truth, I was a smart-ass little shit who deserved a slap. Maybe in his version of the story, it was my own clumsiness that sent me spinning into the glass-topped coffee table and not his fist. In his version, maybe he'd tried to grab me at the last minute to stop me from falling through the glass and that was how he'd broken my wrist, or he'd tried to stop me putting my hand out and dislocating my collarbone. Maybe he hadn't been about to clock me again.

Maybe I remembered it all wrong.

Maybe *I* was wrong.

Maybe, *maybe*, in his version of the truth, he loved me.

I brushed the wing off the book and traipsed inside, pretending I didn't glance toward the stables, pretending I wasn't hurt...that I wasn't starting to get used to feeling this way all the time.

Rowan

THE GRASS bent in the wind singing off the sea as afternoon slouched toward twilight. Ash's gaze burned into my back, but Ash O'Donnell was a complication I did not need, as much as I enjoyed their company. They were...refreshing, unencumbered by their history and island prejudice. Although, it probably wouldn't take long for that to change.

Already the Kilduffs and O'Donnells had started poisoning Ash's opinion of me and my family. And for some inexplicable reason, that bothered me. What Ash thought shouldn't have mattered—just another O'Donnell despising the Sheehys—but there was something about them...something that made me want them not to hate me.

Thoughts of Ash followed me to the stables even as I tried to banish them. Tree runes carved into Andy. Until I knew which ones, there was no way of knowing why anyone would mark him other than to make me look guilty. Regardless of the enmity between our families, I doubted even a Kilduff would murder one of their own only to frame me for the crime. There were easier ways to be rid of me, if that was what they desired.

Back at the house, I found my mother and my younger sisters sitting at the kitchen table.

"What's this?" I asked.

Mother stared at Neasa, who sat slumped with her chin in her hands, glaring at the table with a particularly bilious expression. Deirdre's face was still tear-stained, her eyes puffy and red-rimmed from crying. She wouldn't look at me.

"Your sister has something she wants to say to you," Mother prompted. Deirdre gave Neasa a kick under the table, which earned her Neasa's middle finger.

Mother sighed and smoothed a hand over her hair. Unlike the rest of us, hers was straight and hung in a gold-red sheet past her shoulders. We'd inherited waves and curls from our father.

"Well?" Mother raised an eyebrow.

"I'm sorry," Neasa said as if it physically pained her. "I'm sorry for using magic on you like that."

"She's not sorry about sucking face with Teagan Kilduff, though," Deirdre added, unhelpfully.

"I accept your apology." It was the right thing to say, and Mother expected it. They'd all hurt me before. They would again, making me dance to their magic whenever they deemed it necessary. Perhaps I should've been thanking Neasa for showing me a way to use what little power the Otherworld had imbued me with.

"As for this Kilduff," Mother said. "Neasa knows what's expected of her. I trust she will conduct herself with the maturity and propriety befitting a Sheehy, especially at a time like this."

"Gods, you're impossible!" Neasa beat her fists on the table. "Teagan had nothing to do with the murder! Why would she?"

"We don't know why Andy was killed, but it stirred something in the Otherworld," I said. They turned their gazes on me: Neasa's cold and Mother's surprised, as if she'd forgotten I was present.

"As if they'd kill their own," Neasa said. "As if they have the power to mess beyond the veil. They're so weak, they're practically human."

"Not quite, though," I said. "And why is it the McNamaras have lost their ability to transform? That the Kilduffs no longer lure hoards to the island like they used to? That the O'Donnells can't practice their arts anymore? And yet we've retained power?"

"Have we?" Deidre asked, chipping a splinter from the edge of the wooden table with her thumb nail.

I looked to Mother, who sat stiff and straight in her chair, her fingers teasing the rune-painted charms of the bracelet on her wrist.

"We keep to the old ways and don't destroy sacred groves. We respect our history and complete the necessary rituals." Her gaze dropped to the scars on my arms. "And, because the others, unlike the Sheehys, have forgotten their duties to their families," Mother said.

"It can't be because of numbers," I said. The Sheehys were down to seven while the Kilduffs numbered thirty, the McNamaras forty, and the O'Donnells were up to twenty-six, counting the three recent additions.

"We are as we're meant to be," Mother said. "The world changes. Inisliath isn't immune to that. Old ways die, new ways are forged, but the Sheehys will endure. We always have."

"Even if we start snogging Kilduffs?" Deirdre asked, without looking up.

"Neasa will put an end to that," Mother said. "This infatuation is like an infection and can be treated accordingly. I'll see your sister cured." Mother gave Neasa a pointed look and Neasa seethed, her fingers turned to claws against the tabletop.

"It's not—you wouldn't—" She clenched her jaw, and my heart ached for my sister, for the life she wanted and could never have. "She's leaving, anyway," Neasa managed to say through gritted teeth. "Teagan's going to university on the mainland. That'll make you happy won't it, Mother? One less Kilduff for you to hate."

"Considering Claire's state, I doubt very much Orlagh would see her granddaughters stray to the mainland," Mother said. "Besides, you know what becomes of those who do."

Claire's "state" being the inability to get pregnant, and not for the lack of trying these past four years. Perhaps Mother could've helped her had the Kilduffs trusted our herbs. A mainland doctor could've helped her even more, but islanders shunned modern medicine. So that left Lucy and Teagan the responsibility of bringing more Kilduffs into the world. Their male cousins could breed, but the Kilduff magic would only be strengthened if they had daughters.

"Yes, she will!" Neasa shoved her chair away from the table and stomped to her feet. "Teagan is leaving, and as soon as I can, I'll be joining her."

"You will not." Mother said, her voice soft and deadly. "And I'll not hear more talk of the mainland, not from you, nor from any of my children. Do you want to end up like Eileen and Brighid?" Her words crackled in the air like lightning. "We are Sheehys, and this island is our home. You should show more respect."

"Oh, I'll show you." Neasa fled the kitchen before the tears in her eyes could betray her true feelings and spill down her cheeks. My sister's pain stirred the memories within me of so many others who'd lived and loved and lost on this island. How easily Mother destroyed, how easily she smothered without flinching.

One way or another, we were fated and bound to the

rock. Condemned to it. The whispers grew louder in my mind, whispers of freedom, a freedom found only in death. Eileen and Brighid had risked the wrath of the island in deserting it, and they had been punished for it.

"Is there a spell for moodiness?" Deirdre asked in Neasa's wake, earning a shake of Mother's head.

"We need to tread carefully," she added after a moment. "The Kilduffs are an influential family on the island. They have the O'Donnells in their pockets, and with this new detective, we don't know what lengths they may go to to destroy us."

"What about the McNamaras?" I asked.

"They're devastated by the loss of their magic," Mother answered. "It won't take much for the Kilduffs to convince them we're to blame."

"Are we?" My question was met with a withering glare from Mother.

"So what?" Deirdre asked, ignoring my question. "It's not like they have magic enough to hurt us."

"Not only magic can hurt you," I said softly.

"Don't forget it was a gun that killed your uncle," Mother said. "Best we mind ourselves."

"Why don't we just spell them all and have done with it?" Deirdre asked.

"Because that's not—"

"The Sheehy way," Deirdre completed Mother's sentence with a sigh.

"You'd rather prove them right about us?" I asked, and Deirdre's face twisted into a sour frown before she stuck her tongue out at me. She was leaving a puddle of petals beneath the table, the flowers wilting on her dress and sloughing into the pile at her feet.

"We'll just have to..." Mother started, but I wasn't listening. I couldn't. My body was rigid, my nerves on fire. The world swept sideways into shades of violet and black.

"It's happening again," I managed to spit between my

By the Blood of Rowans

clenched teeth as the ghost of a blade whispered across my skin.

Patrick McNamara toppled from the cliff-top, clutching at his severed throat. The beach rushed up to meet him, a fist of earth splintering the old man's spine and crushing his skull.

For several heartbeats, I remained paralyzed, lying in his dying body. As the last breath trickled from Patrick's lips, I struggled to my feet on the familiar cliff in the Otherworld. Slowly, I unfurled my spine, the pain of Patrick's death still vibrating through my bones.

He'd been alone, sitting quietly observing the sunset, dreaming of a time he could slip his skin and sink beneath the waves. He'd been attacked from behind same as Andy, the blade taking him by surprise.

Gentle fingers in his hair. A soft tinkling of bells. The scent of potpourri.

Hands on his shoulders, wrestling him to the ground. Four hands. There'd been two people on the cliff with him. Patrick was a big man, much larger than Andy Kilduff, whose life had been snuffed out by ten fingers. Patrick had turned, smacking his shoulder into soft flesh as he fought back. Someone had kneed him in the back of the legs, and he'd gone down harder than expected, his weight sending him toppling over the edge.

The ocean below was calm. Unnaturally so. No waves crashed stars into the sky.

Silence.

I took cautious steps into the shadows and fumbled over a crumpled body. A large butterfly, her wings like ragged sails. She wasn't the only one. There were several mangled corpses scattered on the clifftop. All butterflies, all dead.

A shimmer in the shadows announced Patrick's

approach. The darkness was thicker without stars to illuminate the clifftop, my footprints lackluster as I strode toward the wandering soul.

Voices shrieked above me, guttural cries and a rush of air as if something swarmed above me. The sluagh shouldn't have been able to leave the river. The rowans were there to hold them back, to protect souls until they forged the stream to face judgment.

"Patrick!" His name tore from my throat as I sprinted toward him. I reached for his insubstantial hand, the hollows of his eyes yawning wide. The cloud above me cinched closed around us, a swirling tumult of screams.

I reached at emptiness as the sluagh spirited Patrick over the edge of the cliff. He grappled for the edge, his fingers catching at the rock. I dove across the shale, skinning my arms as I grabbed his hands.

"Don't let them take me," he said, and I wouldn't. For more than a century, no Rowan had ever lost a soul to the sluagh, to that flock of condemned souls haunting the Otherworld.

"I've got you. Hold on." I clutched at his fingers, his wrists, his arms, hauling him over the edge. But the sluagh were relentless, battering against me and tugging on Patrick.

I screamed as his body was wrenched from my grasp. The sluagh ripped him apart, shredding his body into ribbons as they carried him across the black fathoms. I tore rocks from the cliff, hurling them after the sluagh as if I could knock them from the sky and draw Patrick's soul back where it belonged.

It was too late. He was gone. Lost. It was my fault, my failing. The ghosts within me wailed in a chorus of chastisement, of mourning, of disbelief. My own voice joined them, the wind of the Otherworld shattering my cries.

"This is not the way of it," I yelled into the indifferent

darkness, not expecting an answer.

I stared after them, chest heaving, blood pounding in my ears, body shaking. Then I ran, tripping over more butterfly corpses and skinning my palms on sharp pebbles.

When I reached the grove of rowans, I fell to my knees and sent up a puff of cinders. It had been a foolish hope to think I'd find Patrick waiting when I'd seen the restless dead devour him. Here at least, the skies were silent. Only the river rattled past, as if bones churned beneath the surface, beating moribund rhythms against the rocks in its path. And the trees—Gods, the trees.

My chest constricted, my eyes staring unblinking at the impossibility of what I was seeing.

The rowans were dead. Those still standing were black and withered, their berries rotten and leaking foul ichor, their bark pockmarked and peeling.

This couldn't be. It went against the order of life and death, against everything I thought I understood. When my ancestors had first been delivered to these shores, we'd assumed a sacred duty, subduing the wild gods and bringing balance to the island. It was those gods from whom we took our power.

I sucked in a mouthful of air, its acrid taint burning my throat. The nearest tree crumbled, collapsing into a pile of ash made slimy with ichor. My trembling hands were greased in the blood of my ancestors. It soaked through my knees, seeping beneath my skin and sinking into my bones. I clawed at my arms, tearing away wisps of my Otherworld body. Still, I could feel the corruption spreading.

A rasp cut through the stillness as if some large serpent shifted its sinuous body, scale against scale, and the water lapping the shore became an arcane music calling me to the deep. I peered toward the river and gathered my legs beneath me, taking one shaky step at a time despite the chorus of voices in my head telling me to run.

My feet hit the mud, my toes squelching in the mulch of dead rowans where the trees were being reclaimed by the stream. Desperate to wash the muck from my fingers, I plunged my hands into the water, but the river had become an oil slick, and my hands dripped black.

The shadows laughed, reaching for me. I felt their caress, their hot breath, and questing fingers. Time seemed to slow, and my ghosts hushed. A hundred questions, a thousand possibilities assaulted my mind. All my fear, my hopes, and a gnawing truth I wasn't ready to face. Did I do this? Was it my own selfish desire for a life of my own that had caused this destruction and cost Patrick eternal rest?

I snatched back my hand and turned to run. The laughter became a screech of rage as silver light pierced the darkness. It radiated from my chest, from the triquetra seared into my skin. I let my body follow the pull, the power drawing me back to life.

Having extracted Patrick's name from me, my mother and sisters left me to sleep off the effects of the Otherworld. I woke to the sound of Deirdre coming down the passage. Her footsteps were light and quick as if she were ever about to start skipping. Neasa stomped and Iona wafted, while even Siobhan's footsteps were no-nonsense and sensibly measured. Mother strutted, her very presence creating a pressure wave through the world.

"You're awake? Good." Deirdre handed me a cup of tea, more agrimony and burdock, then proceeded to light the valerian and lavender candles on my desk. "Listen, I'm sorry," she said. "I didn't mean it when I said I hated you. I was just so angry about Comet." She sniffed. "I don't hate you. You're my brother, how could I? I don't want you to die."

"It's okay, Dee. We all say things we don't mean sometimes." I hoped the same was true for thoughts.

"I don't want anyone else to have Comet." She flopped onto the bed beside me, ladybugs emerging from the embroidered flowers on her hem to buzz out the open window. "Siobhan said Davidson wanted Comet for his kid," she continued. "Auryn and Solas for him and his wife. He has a family now."

It explained why Davidson had stopped visiting Mother a few years ago. Even though the man was hardly a stranger, I clenched my teeth, my grip tightening on the teacup at the thought of someone else riding my horse.

"I'm sure they'll be well looked after," I forced the words off my tongue and took a sip of tea.

"If I find out they're not, I'll put a hex on his whole family."

"If only we were those kinds of witches." I might've mussed her hair the way I used to when we were younger, before I became a deathwalker, before my touch after a stint in the Otherworld became so dangerous. Instead, I kept my hands at my sides, afraid to infect anyone with the darkness.

"I asked Siobhan if Eamonn said anything about Dad. Said he hasn't heard from Dad in years, that he's gone to work on the mines in Australia." Only Deirdre referred to him as Dad.

Of course, Mother would've wanted him as far away as possible lest he meddle by trying to parent. He'd been a tall, quiet man, bending to Mother's will as we all did, and frequently away for work on the mainland, barely a person at all to us let alone a father. I didn't even miss him—I'd never really known him beyond polite conversation twice a year at the dinner table.

"Guess it could've been worse," Deirdre said, her

gaze on the drawings tacked to my wall. "Neasa could've burned the zombie owls or the—what exactly are those?" She pointed at the contorted figures of wolves, one grey— one black, twisted together in a morass of limbs as they feasted on each other's hearts.

"It is what it is," I said, sitting beside her, tamping down the ember of resentment smoldering within me. Neasa's revenge seemed petty and meaningless in light of what had happened in the Otherworld, the loss of my drawing ultimately meaningless.

"Dee, I need to tell you something," I said.

"I'll get Mother."

"No, wait. Please." I almost took her hand, but she edged away from me, and I balled my outstretched fingers into a fist instead. I glimpsed the rowan rune on my wrist, partially obscured by the chunky sweater my sisters had put me in despite the warmth of the summer evening. The ink in my skin glared back.

I knew what I was. I'd always known. I'd been told since before I could talk. It was a story that shaped my childhood, that made me think I was special and magical and destined for greatness. I was destined to die, twice, and turn into a tree. Now, the ink only made me realize how my family possessed me. I was a tool, conceived and born for a singular purpose. The marks in my skin were chains binding me, every spell-scar shortening the leash they kept on me.

No, *no*—those weren't my thoughts. They were born from the darkness, from whatever lurked beyond the river. I shuddered and drew my knees to my chest.

"It's something bad, isn't it?" Deidre asked. "Something in the Otherworld?" Her features settled in the stern, old-soul look she reserved for serious occasions. "Rowan, you can tell me."

I exhaled the breath I'd been holding and told her about the trees.

"Gone?" Her bottom lip trembled.

"Just cinders and mulch," I said, my voice oddly even considering how my insides roiled. "The few that remained were empty, hollow."

"The spirits," she said. "What happened to the spirits?"

I shook my head as if I could dislodge the thoughts taking root in my mind. Thoughts of freedom and relief. I shivered and tucked the folds of the sweater closer.

"What else?" Deirdre demanded, sounding surprisingly like our Mother.

"There were dead butterflies. Dozens of them. Their bodies broken. It was so dark. There were no stars in the sky, just shadows."

"But Patrick managed to cross the river?"

I didn't answer. I couldn't. Mother had asked for the name of the departed, as she always did, and I'd told her, admitting another person had had their throat slit. I hadn't admitted to losing Patrick's soul. Losing a soul like that was unspeakable, unconscionable. It didn't happen, it couldn't, and yet I'd seen Patrick disappear into the darkness.

"Tell me," Deirdre said. "Please don't make me force you." She raised a hand, and a tingle began in the scars on my shoulders. Even my baby sister, the one I'd always thought myself closest to, the one I'd always thought compassionate and kind, even she would hurt me to get what she wanted.

"Patrick is lost. He was taken."

Now Deirdre trembled, goosebumps standing up on her arms as she slid to her feet.

"No, oh no." Her face creased, making her look so much older than fifteen. "This isn't meant to happen." She clutched at her hair, her body visibly shaking, threads from her dress weaving into the air like angry serpents, twisting and knotting together.

"I'm sorry. I tried, but the Otherworld is changing."

"Do you know how or why?" she asked.

I shook my head, and she hugged herself.

"I'm sorry," I said again, the word a whisper—inside my head it was a shout, a scream. I was begging for forgiveness. Not for the dead trees, or even for Patrick, but for the moment of relief I felt seeing the rowans were gone and maybe my fate with them.

She looked up with eyes made glassy by unshed tears. "It's not your fault," she said, and I wished I could believe her, the doubt a knife twist in my chest.

"Whoever is doing this, we have to figure out why. We have to stop them," I said. It was the least I could do.

"It's not our place," Deirdre said. "Mother doesn't want us involved."

Involved. I choked on my response, my nails cutting crescents into my palms again. My throat still smarted where the blade had sliced Patrick's throat. My body still shuddered with his fear as he plunged to his death. I was inextricably *involved*, and I'd made a promise to Andy— one I intended to keep.

"It'll be fine, Ro. You'll see. It'll all be all right in the end," Deirdre said, "but now, you should get some sleep. You look more than a little corpse-like this time." She draped a blanket over my shoulders and blew me a kiss before leaving me alone, thinking I'd shared all my secrets with her. All but one.

Carefully, I peeled the sweater up my arm past the runes supposed to protect me from the things lurking in the dark, past the scars supposed to protect me from myself. There, above the crook of my left elbow, were two jagged lines, as if I'd been clawed by a large house-cat, except these scratches were black and smoldered at the edges where the thing in the shadows had reached for me across the void. It had touched me, infected me, and the gashes weren't healing. I could feel it, its presence spreading up my arm, through my veins, and seeping into my heart.

WE HADN'T been here two weeks yet, and we'd already gotten dead guy number two. Mum almost seemed excited when she got the call about the body on the beach. Apparently, it had been found by a kayaking tourist group. What a shitty ending to a day out. Or maybe not. According to Mum, local police were working overtime to get the assholes to take down their dozen social media posts about it. People did weird things when confronted by death, I guess.

"They won't be able to quash the investigation now," Mum said as she gathered her things from the kitchen table. "This time we'll get an autopsy. They'll have to take proper action. Same MO as last time. We've got the makings of a serial killer on our hands."

"Did this one have runes cut into them, too?" I asked.

"How did you know about that?" Mum paused at the door.

"Teagan told me. She said—" I bit back the words that had been about to drop out of my mouth.

"What is it, Ash? What did she tell you?"

"Mum, I—Teagan said the runes were like Rowan's."

"Rowan has runes cut into him?"

"Tattoos. Scars, too, but not like that." Damn, I was talking way too much. "Anyway, I asked him about them. He said they're symbols for trees."

"Trees," Mum repeated as if she derived some greater meaning from the single syllable. "You lock this door, and don't leave the house until I get home."

"Mum."

"I mean it, Ash. There might be some crazed maniac on the loose. I don't want you out there. Promise me." She pointed her car keys at me.

"I promise. I'm going back to bed anyway. See you later." I stifled a yawn, but Mum stood outside the door and made sure I'd latched it before letting me go back to my room. As soon as I lay down, I was wide awake.

Another victim. Another person with their throat slit, the beach turned red, and ocean foam a frothy pink. I love how the images you least want to see are the ones your imagination sears into your brain.

I'd seen Rowan's knife. It wouldn't have any problem opening someone's carotid or whittling runes into flesh. I seriously hated the images my mind conjured, but it was a deluge I couldn't stop.

I might've messaged Rowan if I'd had his number, but I didn't, and I needed to talk to someone or I was going to explode. Curiosity burned holes in my thoughts like a welding torch. I went in search of Teagan's Post-it note. I stabbed at my screen and hit send on the message before I could second guess the decision.

It took her less than thirty seconds to respond.

Rowan

THE BUZZ of Iona's tattoo machine lulled me, the sound like bees in a meadow, the lingering scent of McDuff's cherry tobacco adding sweetness to the tang of disinfectant. I leaned back in the chair, relaxing as Iona traced fresh ink over old lines. The faint burn in my skin was almost pleasant as she wove protection spells into the rune, whispering the incantation softly as she worked.

McDuff's tattoo shop was never busy, with only a handful of bookings a week during tourist season. Most of their clientele were walk-ins deciding on a whim to mark their bodies with anchors or triskeles.

A walk-in waited in the reception area, a German backpacker with strands of his blond hair dyed neon blue. I watched him over the low partition separating the waiting area from the sterile zone as he flipped through the catalog containing prints of my work.

"These are quite good," he said, and a small balloon of pride inflated inside my chest before he pushed the catalog inside and asked, "So how much for a compass?"

I sighed as Iona gave the man a quote based on size and placement.

"Done," she said, spraying my skin with a solution of witch hazel before wrapping it in plastic. "Next arm."

"It's okay, we can be done for the day."

"Ro, he can wait. It'll take me twenty minutes to finish you up."

I hesitated, not wanting her to see the gashes above my elbow, not wanting her to know I'd been tainted by a shadow in the Otherworld.

"Would be easier if you just took it off," she said, gesturing to my sweater. But then she'd see, and I wasn't ready for her concern or pity, anger or admonishment.

I pulled up my left sleeve, and she rolled her eyes before cleaning my arm and getting to work. Maybe it was the magic she was working into the ink, maybe it was the bite of the needle and prickle of pain, but the wound above my elbow began to ache, then throb, weeping black, which seeped through my T-shirt and stained my sweater. I closed my eyes and gritted my teeth, praying Iona was too concentrated on what she was doing to notice, praying it would be over soon.

"Oh damn, did I do that?"

My eyes snapped open. She dabbed at the spreading black stain as if it were ink. Her touch only aggravated the wound beneath, black looping down my arm as sweat trickled down my back.

"What is that?" She set down her machine.

"It's nothing, I'm fine." I started rolling down my sleeve, but she held my arm with her gloved hands. Even through the layer of latex, her magic singed my skin in warning. My gaze flicked to the German guy. He was on his phone, paying no attention to us, and that was how it needed to stay.

"Don't you have a customer?" I asked.

"Show me your arm, then," Iona said, suddenly more like Mother than she'd care to know.

"It's just a scratch." I peeled back my sweater.

"A scratch?" She sucked a breath in through her teeth. "Gods, you've been mauled. Why aren't you healing?" She immediately sprayed the wound with antiseptic, which raised plumes of smoke from the ragged edges of skin. Iona wrinkled her nose at the charred licorice scent. "This happened in the Otherworld?"

"From the trees," I lied, hoping she wouldn't notice when I turned away, unable to meet her gaze.

"Really?" she asked, and I couldn't answer. "Rowan, what aren't you telling me?" Her fingers curled around my forearm, her magic prickling along my skin again, making me flinch.

"I told you about the creature in the shadows," I whispered.

"And it did *this* to you?" she asked, eyes wide and eyebrows arched toward her hairline. "It hurt you. Oh Gods, I'm—you think it's because of the murders?"

"Never seen anything like it until now," I said. "Seems the two are connected."

"I'm sorry you got hurt," she said. "It's not fair."

"None of this is fair, is it?" I hadn't always thought this way, but when the smoke had risen in the Otherworld, so too had the dark thoughts buried in my mind.

For nineteen years, I'd done what I thought I had to. I'd been the son my mother wanted, the brother my sisters needed, and the deathwalker the island didn't even know they needed. But beneath it all, beneath the smiles and nods, there was a well of resentment, and it scared me. It terrified me not knowing whether the hatred starting to erode the love I'd always had for my family was a result of borrowed sentiment, or a feeling all of my own. One I'd buried, one that wounded so deeply no scab or scar could keep it from festering. And now that infection had turned to poison, seeping into my veins.

Iona said nothing more, instead swabbing the wound and pressing fresh gauze over the grazes. It burned, the witch hazel setting fire to my flesh, but I didn't complain. The sooner she was done, the sooner I could escape and evade further questioning.

"How much longer?" the German asked as he drifted toward the stand at the counter laden with the jewelry made by Neasa and Deirdre.

"Five minutes," I answered.

Iona's lips twisted as she secured the dressing over the gash in my arm with surgical tape. Without another word, she returned to the runes at my wrist, pressing harder than necessary for a minute before she sighed and lightened her touch.

"You need to be more careful," she said as she wrapped the fresh ink.

"I didn't deliberately get hurt," I said, wondering if that were entirely true. The shadow had reached for me, and maybe I could have done more to avoid its touch.

"I know." She tousled my hair as I tugged down my sleeve. "Sorry. It's just—we don't want anything to happen to you. We need you."

As if I could forget, the responsibility a weight on my chest.

She gave me a rueful smile and pulled off her gloves. "You know the drill." She nodded at my arms. "And take care of that, too." She fingered my stained sweater. "You should probably get Siobhan to take a look. It might need stitching."

"Aye, I will if it doesn't heal."

"Promise?"

"Promise," I said, avoiding her gaze again. "Thanks for the ink. Mind if I take back the prints? If you can't use them here, maybe I can sell them."

"Of course," she said, her attention already on the

German as she handed him the disclaimer form. They haggled over the price, Iona finally agreeing to do the tattoo for less if the guy threw in a baggie of weed as well.

Arm still burning, I picked up the catalog, flipped up my hood, and stepped out of the shop, narrowly avoiding a collision with Ash O'Donnell. The catalog ended up on the soaking sidewalk.

"Shit, sorry." Ash scooped up the binder and was about to hand it back to me, when the pages fell open. Their eyes widened, mouth forming a perfect circle. They weren't wearing their sling today.

"Whoa, that's some serious artwork." They gazed up at me through the dark forks of their fringe, rain dripping off the hood of their garish jacket. They stepped beneath the eaves of McDuff's, taking shelter from the persistent downpour. I followed, leaving my left arm in the rain, the drops managing to soak through my sweater and dressings somehow soothing and alleviating the burn.

I wasn't sure what to say. Last time I'd seen them, things had ended awkwardly. For now, I was content to watch their face as they continued their concentrated study of my artwork. Fingers flipped slowly through the pages, teeth worrying their bottom lip, and a slight frown pulled their eyebrows together.

"You thinking about getting one of these?" Ash asked.

"No," I said. "I was hoping others might consider getting them, but apparently all the tourists want are knots and anchors."

"How boring. Wait, *you* drew these?" Ash turned their full attention on me, and I trembled under their scrutiny. Having them see my drawings made me feel naked, stripped bare, and afraid of their judgment. Not because they were an O'Donnell—although looking into Ash's grey eyes it was impossible to forget their lineage—but because I inexplicably wanted Ash to like me, to see me not as a despicable Sheehy, not as a backward islander, but just for me. I couldn't explain it, the sensation as unfamiliar as it was frightening.

I managed to nod at Ash as the ghosts in my head began to whisper. Memories fluttered unhelpfully behind my eyes while I tried to make sense of what I was feeling, holding my breath, still waiting for Ash's reaction.

"These are fucking incredible," they said. "This one"—they tapped the image of the entangled wolves—"it's like that Cherokee proverb, right? About how we all have two wolves inside us, good and evil, light and dark, and they're constantly fighting, but the one that wins is the one you feed."

"Aye," I said, a slow shudder working its way from my toes up to my head, every hair standing on end as Ash glanced between me and my drawing.

"But in this, you're saying something like—they're feeding on each other?" Big eyes stared up at me out of a chiseled face, strong jaw, dimpled chin, mottled bruising still fading from their eye and cheek. Somehow, they'd understood, and I was finding it hard to breathe as I nodded.

"This is super dark, dude, but pretty damn awesome, too." They smiled, and the shudder still rattling my bones turned to a pervasive heat warming me inside and out as I met their gaze.

"Thank you," I said, even though I wanted to say so much more.

"Seriously, this would make a wicked cool tattoo." They looked down at the drawing, tapping it thoughtfully.

"You can have it if you want," I said, the warmth inside me spreading up my neck and spilling across my face. "The print. If you like it, you can keep it."

"Are you sure?" Ash asked.

"Of course. Here, let me." I took the binder from them, our hands momentarily brushing together, and I almost dropped the catalog again as my fingers struggled to release the clasps and extract the plastic sleeve containing the print. When I looked at Ash, I didn't want to stop studying the angles of their face, the way their hair caught on their lashes, the quiver of their lips.

I handed the drawing to Ash, and they took it from my fingers with a reverence I didn't think my work deserved even as that balloon of pride inside my chest inflated once more.

"Thank you. This is so going up on my wall," Ash said. "I mean, with other posters. Of climbing mostly. Posters of Joshua Tree and stuff."

"None of your own photos?" I asked. "Because your photos should be in a gallery."

"So should your drawings."

We stared at each other for a moment, a moment which stretched beyond the limits of discomfort. Perhaps we'd both glimpsed slices of each other's soul now, Ash's photos—my drawings, and neither of us knew quite what do with the seemingly intimate knowledge of each other. I would protect what I knew of Ash, how they saw beauty in the world even if their mouth and demeanor suggested otherwise. I could only hope they'd protect what they knew of me.

"Um, I'm meeting a friend. I should go," Ash said, "but thanks for the drawing, and it was really nice seeing you." They swallowed hard as they looked up at me again.

"I'd like to see more of your photos sometime," I said. *And more of you*, but I couldn't say that out loud.

"I could give you my number. If you have a phone. I mean, not to imply you don't or wouldn't because—shit. Sorry."

I laughed, the sound shattering the tension in the air between us, and Ash smiled, too, their eyes lighting up silver, flecked with blue and green.

"On a rock, not under one, remember?" I pulled my phone out of my pocket, the device extremely basic and uncomplicated but serving its purpose. We swapped numbers, and as I hit save on Ash's name, I wished I could hit save on this moment and store it in my head as a perfect memory. My mind was a fractured kaleidoscope, a muddle of recollections that made it challenging to retrieve the ones that were entirely my own.

"Okay, I really should go. But thank you, and yeah, let's do this again," Ash said as they carefully tucked my drawing into their pocket.

I watched them go, walking through the rain, their orange jacket the brightest part of the day, disappearing as they rounded the corner. I was still staring after them when a shoulder bashed against mine, sending pain singing down my left arm, and a spitball narrowly missed my foot.

"Fuckin' fetch," Oisin McNamara said, even as he led a group of tourists past me, bound for the kayak shed at the western corner of the harbor where tours were now being escorted far from the beach-turned-crime-scene. "You working off a list?" Oisin asked under his breath. "Or maybe it'll be you next." He pointed his fingers at me as if he held a gun and pulled the trigger.

Just like that, my moment with Ash disintegrated, the island reminding me of what I was. Once, Rowans had been revered, their role as soul-bearers understood and appreciated by the islanders. Like so many things about our history, that understanding had been corrupted until now I was seen as Death itself.

With the gashes in my arm burning, I walked away from town, striking out on foot for the crime scene, having left Auryn warm and dry in her stall today. I needed to know what to make of the smoke creature beyond the river, but more so, who was murdering islanders, and why.

The grass was trampled, the rocks stained, though most of the blood had been washed away, pouring over the precipice to the sliver of beach below. Butterflies hovered, their purple wings sheened with Otherworld iridescence. They offered no further insight into who might've stolen Patrick's life.

I knelt and pressed my hand to the cold stone. The island's sorrow oozed up through the dirt, slicking the rocks with grief. The wind howled in agony, the sea a tumult of white-capped waves. The ghosts within me shifted, resonating in time to the ache within the heart of Inisliath.

I pulled my gritty fingers away.

The scar on my chest throbbed, the one cleaving my heart. This wasn't where it had happened, but it must've looked a lot like this. Only, my body had stayed on the cliff, kept from toppling by my sisters' hands.

I stared over the edge, the wind cutting its teeth on my bones as I studied the beach. More police tape, ugly and out of place, a blemish of the modern world on ancient, sacred ground.

Fewer than fifty meters from the cliff, a huddled copse of trees rose from the grass, their trunks bent and twisted by the winds off the sea. Among them stood an ash. That was where they'd wanted to take him. I cut a path through the grass, following a trail of flattened stalks toward the tree. Blood had been daubed on the trunk and splashed over the exposed roots at its base. Whoever had killed Patrick had made sure to consecrate the ash. The carpet of wildflowers stretching long necks toward the copse had been equally speckled, ritual complete, if imperfect. I headed away from the trees, sliding and climbing down the treacherous path to the beach.

Patrick had fallen below the high tide mark. His body would've been claimed by the sea had he not been found so early. I stepped across the tape and crouched where he'd fallen, where I'd felt his skull—my skull—burst like an egg against the stones. Pressing my hand to the bloodied earth, I let the memories of his death wash through me. There hadn't been time for him to share the memories of his life with me before the sluagh bore him away. Those memories were lost now, unraveled across the fathoms of the Otherworld.

Patrick had been murdered before I'd had time to test my theory and attempt to cross into the Otherworld without a death to guide me. And now, now I was afraid of what lurked beyond the river.

Tentatively, I wrapped my fingers around my injured arm where my T-shirt stuck to the seeping wound. I didn't want to face the entity of smoke and rot, not without knowing what else it could do. Cold trickled through my veins, a saturating sense of dread, as I tightened my grip on the wound and gritted my teeth against the pain.

Not yet. Not until I was ready.

Slowly, I released my arm and gazed across the water instead. The sea writhed like rippling steel beneath an aluminum sky. Three seals raised their heads above the swell. They were unnaturally still, all looking at me. Waves broke against the shore, the ebb and flow in time with my heartbeat as I returned their accusatory stares. They couldn't know I'd lost Patrick to the sluagh, but that didn't stop the guilt from gnawing on my insides.

"I'm sorry," I shouted into the wind, hoping it would carry my words to McNamara ears.

"For what?" an all-too-human voice startled me. I turned to find Ash's mom skidding the last of the way down the narrow path, her hand on her hip where her weapon rested. "You know, criminals don't always return to the crime scene," she said, her eyes dark and unreadable. "But it's always a mistake when they do."

"Am I a suspect now?" My grip tightened on the binder in my hand.

"Should you be?" she asked.

"When Patrick was killed, I was at home with my family. Ask them."

"How can you be sure?" DI Walsh asked. "How do you know when the victim died?"

I turned to leave, but she grabbed my arm, pulling up my sleeve to reveal the fresh tattoos visible through their plastic wrappings, the scars cut deftly by my sisters, which were always misunderstood by others. Her fingers dug into the smarting wounds on my biceps, and I winced, biting my tongue to stifle a cry. She eased her grip.

"The same markings were on both bodies," she said.

"Everyone here knows what these mean."

"And the scars? Did you do that to yourself?" she asked, with a hint of pity in her voice. "Or is someone hurting you?"

I pulled away from her. She wouldn't believe me if I said no. She wouldn't understand if I told her every scar on my body had been inflicted by my family.

"Oddly ritualistic how both bodies wind up with the same symbols you've got all over your arms."

"The killers could've found them on the Internet or in any of the souvenir shops."

"Killers?" Her eyes widened, her hand drifting toward her weapon, and I knew I'd said too much. "You said killers. Plural. There's only one way you could've known that."

"Islanders talk. It's nothing that's not in your files," I said, hoping she didn't know the Sheehys had no friends in the local police force.

"It wasn't in my files," she said. "It was just a theory I had, and now I'm very keen to know why you thought the same."

I didn't think, I *knew*, but telling her so would only make things worse for me.

"I didn't do this," I said.

"Then you'll have no trouble coming down to the station and making a statement."

"Are you arresting me?"

"Do I need to?"

I scuffed my toe across the pebbles. There was a smear of blood along the tip of my boot. Butterfly wings flickered in the corner of my eye. "I know you're only doing your job and what you think is right, but you're making a mistake."

"That remains to be seen. Let's go," she said. "My car's parked up the path."

"Do I have a choice?"

"With or without cuffs," she said. "I just want to talk more about these symbols." Her tone was suddenly placating. "Think you can help me?"

"I'll need to see pictures of the runes on the bodies."

She hesitated before nodding and gestured for me to walk ahead of her. With my heart hammering against my ribs, I let my feet lead me up the path.

With every scrambling step, I fought the urge to run from her prejudice, her accusations, from the steel cuffs I knew would inevitably end up on my wrists. It didn't matter if I told the truth—if Ash's mom even believed it—the Kilduffs had long ago condemned me. They'd just been waiting for the opportunity to finally, *legally*, justify their desire to purge the island of my family.

MY THOUGHTS were as jumbled as my feelings as I walked away from Rowan. Being around him felt like putting my brain through a spin cycle. I pressed my hand to the drawing tucked safely beneath my jacket. I wanted to put it up on my wall, but something told me Mum wouldn't like it, and I'd be better off keeping it stashed somewhere secret where only I could find it.

His drawings were all so damn good, and so damn dark. Teagan and the others might not be completely wrong about him, but they'd probably never bothered to get to know him either. I wasn't going to make that same mistake.

Anyway, thanks to my stellar ability to navigate island back-roads and the encounter with Rowan, I now stood almost an hour late and utterly bedraggled outside The Copper Kettle, eyeing the titular teapot hanging precariously above the door.

If Mum found out, I'd no doubt be in trouble, but when Mum was working a case, I pretty much ceased to exist.

I pushed open the door, greeted by the aroma of coffee and cake. Given the shitty weather, the café was packed, and I was about to pull a 180 to escape the crowd when Teagan waved from a corner table. She was hard to miss in her black and red—clothes, make-up, and nail polish—looking conspicuously punk-rock in the otherwise quaint establishment. Lucy was with her, looking decidedly less punk-rock.

Having decided it was too late to back out, I forced my feet over to their table. "Sorry I'm late. I got lost."

"You're here now," Teagan said. "Sit, they'll take your order at the table." She gestured to the chair opposite her.

I sat, feeling super awkward and wishing I hadn't come, hanging up my jacket and making sure the drawing was neatly secreted in one of its many pockets.

"Hi." I nodded at Lucy, who glanced up at me for a second before returning to the arduous task of peeling the label from her soda bottle. Her gaze slid past me, and I followed where she looked, surprised to see her watching Cillian McNamara as they bussed tables. If McNamaras were some magical creature capable of shape-shifting, I couldn't tell. But then, what was I supposed to look for? Whiskers and a furry tail? All Cillian had was floppy hair and an unflattering apron.

"That's Cillian," Teagan said. "He'll be finishing school with us this year. He's also Lucy's crush. It's all very Romeo and Juliet if Romeo had been two years younger."

Lucy responded by giving her sister the middle finger.

"Yeah, I know him," I said. "I was in here the other day."

"Great." Lucy's smile might've been dazzling if it were genuine. I was saved from having to respond by the arrival of the waiter—sadly not Cillian. Lucy's face crumpled with disappointment.

"I strongly recommend a cappuccino," Teagan said, sipping from her mug. "Unless you like things darker?"

"Latte is fine, thanks," I said to the waiter, not sure what Teagan was getting at. This was feeling more and more like a colossal mistake.

"I hear you're into horse riding," Lucy said.

What the actual fuck? I'd been alone with Rowan in the paddock. Except for Deirdre, and something told me it wasn't her who'd run tattletale to the Kilduffs.

"Actually, I'm into climbing," I said, trying to play it cool and ignore Teagan's knowing grin.

"That how you broke your arm?" Lucy asked.

"Accidents happen." I shrugged. "It's a dangerous sport."

"You'll have to take us sometime," Teagan said. "I've always wanted to try it."

I highly doubted that considering the length of her nails, but I kept the thought to myself.

"What's the school here like?" I asked instead.

"Dull, but enough for the leaver's certificate. I'm sure it'll only be a disappointment to someone from the city." Lucy's words all had sharp edges.

"How come you don't do home-schooling?" I asked.

"You mean like the Sheehys?" Lucy snorted her derision. "Oh please, we're not all backwards here. Some of us even have plans to leave, right, Teagan?"

Teagan pressed her lips into a straight line, suddenly very interested in destroying her napkin. She looked up at me with her electric blue eyes rimmed with thick, black liner. My skin prickled a warning. There was something predatory in her stare, something as threatening as it was enticing. I wasn't really into girls, but damn, Teagan was take-your-breath-away beautiful, and she knew it. A slow smile tugged at her mouth, and I wanted to look away, but I couldn't. I was paralyzed, entranced.

Then Teagan blinked. I sucked in a breath and wiped

my cold, sweaty hands on my jeans.

What the hell? My skin tingled—not in a good way—same as that time with Lucy in the bookshop. Maybe there was some truth to all that about Kilduffs being masterful seducers. Vampires, that's what the book had alluded to, but neither Teagan nor Lucy had overly large canines. Too bad I didn't have any garlic on me to test the theory.

"You want to leave the island?" I asked, trying to pretend the moment of weirdness hadn't happened.

"To study on the mainland," Teagan said.

"As if you'd be allowed to," Lucy added.

"Allowed to?" I glanced from one to the other.

"You don't know how lucky you are," Lucy said. "You didn't grow up here. You don't know how difficult it is to leave this place. How the family makes you feel like you owe them something—everything. And then there are all the horror stories about what happens to the people who leave."

"My grandfather left. He's fine."

Lucy and Teagan exchanged a look I couldn't read, which made me think of the loss and hardship Granddad had endured. Could it really all have been some bizarre punishment for leaving Inisliath?

"It's harder for the girls," Lucy said after a moment. "We're meant to stay here and make babies so we can continue our family traditions."

"I read about how the family 'power'"—I used my fingers for air quotes in case they thought I actually believed in magic—"seems to favor the women here," I said, which was some seriously sexist bullshit and also clearly the wrong thing to say because Lucy's face shriveled into a look of sheer revulsion.

"Favor? Are you serious?" Her eyes were huge, a muscle ticking along her jaw.

"But isn't having magic supposed to be cool?" I asked.

"It's a curse," Teagan said softly. "One we didn't even ask for. One we definitely don't want."

"There's nothing *cool* about being be forced to breed the next generation with people we can't even love, a new generation that never achieves anything except to continue dying traditions," Lucy said. "That's the only value our lives have."

"That can't be—"

"Trust me, Ash. If your kitchen came with an oven, they'll expect you to put a bun in it," Lucy said as her gaze swept me up and down. I didn't even know where to begin unpacking that.

"Lucy! Calm down." Teagan placed a hand on her sister's arm, but Lucy wrenched it away.

"Oh please," she snapped. "You know it's true. What value do we have beyond our ability to breed? We're not allowed to study, to travel, to even love who we choose." Her gaze flicked again to Cillian, who caught her eye and gave her a tiny smile. "The old ways are dying. The McNamaras have lost almost all their power. Our family is barely hanging on," she said. "All I want is a normal life. Is that too much to ask for?"

We sat in stunned silence after her outburst. Several tourists had turned in our direction, then discreetly turned away as if they hadn't overheard everything Lucy had said.

"We all want the same thing," Teagan said in a harsh whisper.

"It seems only some of us are willing to do anything about it, though." Lucy chugged the last of whatever she'd been drinking and picked up her bag. I had no idea what had just happened or why Lucy was so angry.

"Come on, Luce," Teagan said. "Don't go. Please."

"You going to stop me?" Lucy asked as she stood up from the table. Teagan looked away.

"You'll see, Ash." Lucy gave me a vicious smile. "You're

going to wish you'd never come here." She marched out of the café, and the door slammed shut behind her.

"I'm sorry about that," Teagan said. "What she said—just ignore it."

"Not sure I can." I wrapped my hands around my stomach, suddenly, horribly aware of my body—what it was and what it was not. It never ceased to freak me out how people could look at me and wonder about the configuration of my sex organs. Most days, it hardly mattered. Then someone like Lucy would come along and smack me upside the head with the fact that being non-binary and genderqueer meant I was often nothing more than a puzzle others felt compelled to solve. Well, fuck them, and fuck Lucy Kilduff.

"She's going through a lot right now," Teagan said. "It's not like our family approves." She jerked her head toward Cillian. "And it was his grandda they found on the beach. Lucy is taking it all kinds of hard."

"The first victim was related to you, right?"

"Yeah, my great-uncle," she said flatly. "I really need a cigarette." She gathered her things, leaving a crumpled bill under her saucer. I downed my latte and did the same, making sure Rowan's drawing was carefully stowed before I followed her out of the café. The rain had turned into a fine drizzle. I flipped up my hood as she lit up and took a deep drag. She offered me one, but I refused. Mum would skin me alive if she caught me smoking again, besides, it did nothing for climbing.

"You have college plans?" she asked as we walked.

"Not sure, yet." Part of me wanted to go to art school and study photography. The better part of me knew it would only give the colonel another means to control me. I could just imagine him threatening not to pay tuition if I wasn't top of the class. Or telling me it was all pointless and that my "talents" would be wasted on something like that.

"What do you want to be?" she asked, and my mouth opened on its own.

"A sports photographer," I said.

"Sounds awesome. You have a camera yet?"

"Yeah."

"I'm not sporty, but any time you want a model, I'd be happy to oblige." She winked at me, and I mumbled something like a maybe as we continued our amble along the street toward the church. The grounds were neatly manicured, all trimmed hedges and tidy flower beds. A massive Celtic cross stood to the right of the church, the stone ancient and slimed with moss.

"I'm surprised there's a church here," I said. "I mean, everyone keeps going on about the old ways and things."

"Centuries ago they tried to bring religion to the island. It didn't end well, but we got a church and we've kept it for the tourists. It used to be in high demand as a wedding venue."

"What changed?" I asked.

"Nothing. Everything," she said with a sigh as she crushed the butt of her cigarette beneath her boot. "People keep leaving. No one new chooses to move to the island."

"Is life really so bad here?"

"Lucy makes it sound like we're just brood mares. We're not," Teagan said, "but we do have obligations to our families and that can be...stifling. It's complicated."

"I've been hearing that a lot lately."

"You're part of something so much bigger than you realize," she said. "It's not really my place to explain."

"No one seems willing to explain anything. Fergus just gave me a stupid book."

"Which one?"

"*A Brief History of Inisliath* by Fionnula O'Donnell. It talks about druids and shape-shifters, makes your family sound like vampires."

"You don't believe it?" she asked.

"Should I?" Back home, I'd been a proud atheist, not believing in any of the religious mumbo jumbo spouted at school. Mum didn't much care what I believed, while the colonel was the sort of Catholic who only went to mass on Christmas and Easter.

So why the hell would I think any of this supernatural stuff was true? Somehow, I found myself straying precariously close to believing it all.

"I haven't read it, so I can't say for sure," Teagan said, "but I know Fionnula was a well-respected druid. What? She was," she said when I rolled my eyes. "Fionnula was a historian, too. I would be inclined to believe what she's written."

"She says the McNamaras can turn into wild animals."

"Not anymore," Teagan said sadly. "That's what Lucy was talking about. Only the oldest of the McNamaras can shift these days, and not for long. No one under fifty can change at all. The McNamaras have lost their magic."

I laughed so hard I hurt my collarbone.

"Do you want to know the truth or not?" Teagan glared, her gaze shutting me up instantly. "You can't ask for answers and then pull that face when they're given to you."

"Sorry." I rearranged my face to show I was taking her seriously. "So, the McNamaras have lost their power."

"We all have," Teagan said. "Well, the power is fading. The magic is leaving Inisliath. It's been leaching away more and more every year. Our families are diminishing."

"Because people are leaving the island?"

"That's one theory," Teagan said, "but Brighid and Eileen Sheehy left, too, and the Sheehys are stronger than ever." Her eyes were a darker shade of blue now, as if the resentment in her words were staining her irises. "They're the only family who still has their magic while the rest of us are hemorrhaging it."

"Is that why everyone hates them?"

"One of the reasons. They've always kept to themselves, as if they're better than everyone else," she said.

"Are they?" I asked carefully, keeping my gaze on the ground.

"They're witches. They're the only ones who can do spells and craft potions and things. They're the only ones with proper magic, I guess, so maybe they are," she said with a hint of envy.

"I don't get it," I said. "You talk about leaving and how much you hate it here, so wouldn't losing your magic be a good thing?"

"Not like this. This is killing us," she said. "And what I want is a normal life, not to walk around like a half-starved ghoul."

"What kind of magic do you even have?" I asked, the jury still out on whether I was buying any of this.

"Not the wands and pointy-hat kind," Teagan said. "Our magic comes in many forms, like the McNamaras being able to shape-shift or the O'Donnells with their ability to curate history."

I had no idea what that meant, but I had a more pressing question. "So, you're a vampire, then?"

"We don't like that word. It misrepresents our heritage. People hear vampire and think Bram Stoker or Anne Rice. We're neither of those. We don't drink blood."

"That's a relief," I said with a chuckle. Clearly, she was having me on.

"But we're very good at getting what we want." The look she gave me liquefied my bones and turned my blood to lava. The sensation was intense and blinding, making me pant in fear of what she was doing to me, and in even greater fear she'd stop whatever she was doing. I couldn't help but stare at her with a longing so intense I would've gladly stopped breathing if she'd asked me to.

No, this wasn't right. I didn't want Teagan—she was

beautiful, but—the image of Rowan on horseback stole into my mind, and I managed to tear my gaze away from her.

"Huh, guess the O'Donnells aren't as weak as we thought."

"What did you do to me?"

"Demanded attention." She shrugged. "Consumed a moment of your emotions."

"Consumed?"

"It's what we survive on, the emotions of others projected in our direction. Envy, anger, hatred, fear, love." She choked on the last part.

"Sounds like a healthy, balanced diet," I said, which only earned me a sneer. "But how is this useful?" I managed to exhale as my body regained equilibrium. I leaned against the cross for support, wondering how much of me she'd slurped up.

"How do you think we maintain the tourist industry here?" She gestured to the town. "We lure in the crowds and they fall in love with Inisliath, which nourishes us, too. Some of those tourists end up staying, providing the island with new blood and fresh souls. But that's nothing." She waved a hand dismissively. "We used to be able to do so much more. Now...now only the Sheehys have real magic. The other families resent that, but their hatred toward us is nourishing, too. It's only indifference we can't stomach."

"The Sheehys I've met seem nice enough."

"Deirdre is sweet if odd, and Neasa—" Teagan swallowed and lit another cigarette. "Suffice it to say, the Sheehy women aren't the problem."

"You're talking about Rowan," I said, blood slamming in my ears. Must've been an after-effect of whatever Teagan had done to me. She took a drag on her cigarette without answering.

"Fionnula's book didn't say much about the

152

Sheehys except call them witches. Apparently, they're practitioners of death magic—whatever the hell that is," I said, hoping Teagan would elaborate. Her lips parted as if she were about to say anything. Instead, she exhaled a smoke ring.

"Oh!" She startled, her phone screeching from the bag beside her. "Hold on, it's Lucy." She answered, and her cheeks grew even rosier. She turned toward me, her eyes brightening before she hung up.

"Well, fancy that," she said with a curl of her lip.

"What is it?" I asked, my mouth dry and heart kicking against my ribs.

"Your mother," Teagan said. "She arrested Rowan."

Rowan

THE POLICE station looked innocuous from the street: a shabby building—run down courtesy of O'Donnell neglect—that most wouldn't have recognized as a police station save for the single blue lantern bearing the force's crest mounted above the door. I hesitated at that door, feeling along its edges for wards meant to keep the likes of me out. Nothing. Perhaps they wanted to be able to incarcerate us more than they wanted to avoid our presence.

Steeling myself for the scorn I'd meet on the inside, I followed Detective Inspector Walsh into the station. The last time I'd been here was the day my uncle was murdered, when my mother tried to convince Martha O'Donnell her son had killed my predecessor in cold blood. Martha had asked for proof, and Mother had pushed me forward, a trembling thirteen-year-old still recovering from his first death walk.

I'd seen Fergus through my uncle's eyes, seen the hateful expression on his face as he'd pulled the trigger and riddled my uncle's body with deer shot. It had been in retribution; Fergus incapable of believing his wife had chosen to step off the cliff and drown beneath the waves. He'd blamed my uncle as every islander blamed my family and all the Rowans before me for wielding the scythe.

Of course, Martha and the rest had responded with derision and considered my testimony inadmissible even as my flesh itched for weeks, peppered with the memory of my uncle's death. When they found my uncle's body, they'd called it a hunting accident. They hadn't shown any remorse. Instead, they'd looked at us with even more disgust, satisfaction, too, as if they were glad to have culled our numbers. If only I could show them how the Rowans had once been respected, deliverers of souls, defending the deceased from the grips of the sluagh. That had all changed when the magic began to seep from the others.

Now, O'Donnell and Kilduff animosity pulsed through the air, battering rams against my skin.

"Well, well, isn't this a sight." Martha grinned at me. "Rowan Sheehy, can't say I'm at all surprised to see you here."

I didn't respond. If anyone should be a suspect, it should be Martha. She and Orlagh Kilduff owned Inisliath. Nothing happened on the island without their blessing. Hard to imagine Orlagh condoning the death of her son, though, unless the Kilduffs stood to gain something significant from Andy's death. My mind spun, a storm of possibilities. The Kilduffs wanted power more than anything, but I didn't want to believe they'd sacrifice one of their own to get it. I'd know more once I saw the runes.

DI Walsh ushered me down a short corridor and sat me at a tidy desk I guessed belonged to her.

"You should put him in holding," Claire Kilduff

said, standing in the doorway. She looked so much like Lucy, sharing her cousin's exquisite perfection and incandescent eyes, although Claire had the umber skin and black hair of her Ghanaian father making her all the more striking.

"He's not under arrest."

"He should be." She glared at me, her eyes electric. "Him and his whole family. I bet they did it together. Tell me, who held the blade? Was it you?" Her magic uncoiled, a serpent energy slithering across the distance separating us, snaking around my limbs and tightening in suffocating bands about my chest as the wards burned in my skin. I stared back, hoping the pain of her magic wouldn't send me slipping into the Otherworld. She winced, pressed a hand to her temple, and shook her head. Her magic released me, dissipating like tendrils of mist flayed apart by the dawn.

"Don't you have paperwork to file?" Ash's mom said before shutting the door in Claire's face. "Sorry about that, the Kilduffs are all a little raw after Andy's death."

"I know."

"Of course you do," she said with a perfunctory smile. "Is there anything you don't know about the island?"

"Why they continue to hate us," I said before I'd thought better of it, which wasn't the truth, either. I knew why they hated. I'd seen the false perceptions and misconceptions in Andy's memories, I only wished they'd take the time to understand us better.

"Rest assured, I don't hate you," DI Walsh said as she settled opposite me and steepled her fingers. She had Ash's nose and perfect cheekbones, but her eyes were several shades darker. "This may be personal for others," she continued, "but you should know that's not the case for me. I'm simply following leads, looking at the evidence, and—"

"I understand," I said, and I did. Were I in her shoes,

surrounded by O'Donnells and Kilduffs, I'd probably suspect the Sheehys, too.

"What do you have there?" She gestured to the binder I still clutched.

"Drawings. Just designs for McDuff's tattoo shop."

"Can I see?" She extended her open hand, and I didn't think she'd give me the option to refuse. I handed over the binder, and she flipped through the pages, her gaze narrowing.

"This is some pretty dark stuff," she said, and already I could feel her judgment pouring into the space between us as she closed the catalog and pushed it back across the table.

"You like horror?" she asked. "Gore, death, that kind of thing? Do you find it beautiful, fascinating?"

Gods, if she only she knew. I folded my arms and tried to keep my voice even. "They're just tattoo designs."

She eyed me warily for a moment before she took a file off the top of a short stack to her right. "We were going to talk about the runes," she said. "These pictures are a little gruesome, but I don't think you'll mind." She removed several photographs and laid them out in front of me. I had to lean back to make out the details. Inadvertently, I pressed my fingers to my throat as I looked at Andy. His shirt had been torn open and runes carved into his chest. Runes so much like my own, unmistakable despite being slightly out of focus.

"I looked it up," DI Walsh said. "I think it's an old symbol for a thorn tree."

"Hawthorn." Although the work was crude, as if whoever had done it had been in a hurry, or nervous, their hand shaking as they dragged the blade through dead flesh. "He died at the base of a hawthorn, too," I added.

"Does that mean something?"

"It might." I turned my attention to Patrick, ignoring

the mess of his skull, focusing on the runes also carved into his chest. These were done with an even shakier hand. Perhaps the person responsible had felt regret—revulsion—at what they were doing.

"That's the symbol for Ash," I said and tugged my sleeves down, twisting their torn hems between my fingers.

"Ash?" She startled, her dark eyes widening.

"Aye, there's an ash tree near the cliff. It's covered in blood, probably Patrick's," I said.

"We didn't find—" She scrawled in the file. "So, ash trees. What's so significant about them?"

"Ash trees are sacred to some. As are hawthorns. They're part of a sacred trinity," I said, the knowledge scratching at the back of my mind along with memories of Kilduffs and O'Donnells destroying our grove.

"What's the third?"

"Oak," I said, wondering if I should be saying anything at all. "Their significance varies according to beliefs, but—" I pushed the photos away, no longer wanting to look at the grotesque shapes that had once been people.

"But?" she pressed.

Some people believed the place where these three trees grew marked the entrance to the Otherworld, a way to cross the threshold without being like me. It was myth, supposition, and yet myth was made flesh on Inisliath, so maybe opening a doorway to the Otherworld was exactly what the murderers were hoping to achieve. If not, then I had no idea what their motivation might've been. There'd been nothing in Andy's memories to suggest someone wanted to kill him, and what I knew of Patrick suggested he was similarly innocent.

Regardless, the pattern seemed clear. Hawthorn was the tree of the Kilduffs, and Andy had died beneath one. The Ash belonged to the McNamaras. The Oak was the tree of druids and a symbol of the O'Donnells. An

158

O'Donnell would die next.

The trees of the founding families, families who'd settled on the island after the wild gods had been tamed by the Sheehys. I closed my eyes, scouring the annals of memory, searching for something I knew I should remember, something that eluded my grasp even as I reached for it. I carried the memories of my ancestors with me, but the further back I reached, the fainter they became, eroded by the passing generations.

"Rowan, care to continue?" DI Walsh looked at me expectantly.

"Some people believe these trees are connected to old power." I chose my words carefully, trying to untangle the threads of suspicion from what I knew to be true. "Magic." There was no avoiding it, and sooner or later she was going to have to face the truth about this island and her heritage.

"Magic?" She didn't manage to suppress her snort of disbelief. "So, these murders are rituals?"

I shrugged.

"What would these deaths achieve?" she asked.

"I don't know. Honestly," I added when I saw her frown of incredulity.

The Kilduffs might be desperate enough to consider tapping into Otherworld power, but it was poor folly. The McNamaras might see a passage to the Otherworld as a route to their animal forms, a risk worth taking even if it meant they could never return to the realm of humans. The O'Donnells, too, might risk meddling with the darkness to rekindle their druidic powers, but they knew best of all the entities of the Otherworld weren't to be trusted.

As for the Sheehys, we had no reason to cut a doorway to the Otherworld when I could already walk between the realms. And we had little to gain. Our magic had not yet diminished so significantly. And yet...

Three trees, three families—by their blood—a seal, a doorway.

A borrowed memory, knowledge stolen from one who had passed, a seed of something important sewn into the tapestry of recollection in my mind bubbled to the surface.

"What size shoe do you wear?" DI Walsh asked, tearing me from my thoughts.

"You found a print?"

"Answer the question."

"Eight and a half."

"And why did you think there was more than one person on the cliff with Patrick McNamara?" she asked.

"The runes don't look like they've been done by the same person," I said.

"You wouldn't have known that without seeing the bodies," she said. "Have you seen them before?"

"No."

"Then how did you know?"

"I didn't. I guessed."

"You're lying."

I dragged my hands through my hair, resting my fingers at the back of my neck.

"Were you on the cliff? Did you see something?" she asked.

"I was home with my family, I told you."

"Then how—unless you were one of the people who killed Patrick. Did you do it?"

"No."

"I'm trying to help you."

"You're trying to solve your case without knowing the first thing about any of this." I folded my arms, leaned back in the chair, and pressed my knuckles into the wound on my arm, savoring the spike of pain.

"I know we've got two ritualistic killings performed for supposedly arcane purposes, and I know the rumors surrounding your family," she said. "You can see how my suspicion might flow in your direction."

"I do, but you're wrong about me."

"What about the rest of your family? You have four sisters, don't you? I hear one of them is the tattooist who did your runes. Could any of them be involved?"

"No," I said. *It's not one of us. It can't be.*

The sound of bells. The smell of flowers. The runes.

Memories swarmed my mind, more and more rising from the murk. The voices of the dead chattered, a chorus of words mostly insensible, but some taunted, echoing the detective. I recognized Andy's voice, a roar of indignation as he repeated the question, his words beating against the walls of my mind with angry fists.

"Stop, please stop." I dug my fingers into my temples and closed my eyes. I hadn't felt this overwhelmed by the ghosts for well over a year. I had thought I was past this, past the surge of terror and regret, of guilt and fear as the dead clamored to be heard.

"Are you all right? Can I get you some water?" The detective's voice sounded far away, drowned out by the maelstrom within me.

"You can't do this!" A raised voice echoed down the corridor, and at first I didn't recognize it, then I felt it, that familiar pressure in the air as if the very atoms were afraid of my mother.

The voices in my head quietened, and I sat up straight again.

"Don't you dare touch me," my mother snarled from outside the door. "You know what I can do."

A moment later my mother flung open the door. "Out. Now," she said, and I obeyed without hesitation, never so grateful for her presence.

"We weren't done." DI Walsh rose to her feet and stepped around the desk, as if her being taller would somehow intimidate my mother.

"Is he under arrest?"

"No, but I had questions and he's an adult and—"

"You're done." Mother jerked her head, and I didn't need to be told twice.

Their sneers and judgmental gazes followed us down the corridor and out of the police station. DI Walsh accompanied us out of the building, all the while pleading with my mother for more time, her tone vacillating between placating and threatening. Neither achieved the desired result as we approached Auryn and Solas.

"The next time you want to speak to a member of my family, you better have grounds to arrest them," Mother said, swinging onto the broad back of the grey. We left Ash's mom staring after us, angry and thwarted.

We rode hard until we were about a mile out of town, Auryn struggling to keep pace with Solas's long-legged canter. Mother hauled on the reins, bringing Solas to an abrupt stop as she turned toward me. Her hand met my face before Auryn could dance out of reach.

"You went to the crime scene!" Mother said. "Of all the foolish things to do. What were you thinking?"

Any answer would only earn me more scorn, so I gritted my teeth while knotting my fingers in Auryn's mane to keep from rubbing at my smarting cheek.

"Well, what did that woman want to know?" Mother asked, as commanding as ever.

"There were runes carved into the bodies," I said. "Hawthorn on Andy, Ash on Patrick."

"What did you tell her?" Mother asked, her expression grim.

"Nothing she couldn't have discovered for herself."

"Do they have any suspects?"

"Other than us, I don't think so," I said quietly, not wanting to risk stoking her ire.

"We need to be smart, Rowan. We can't afford to lose you. Not now, not to them."

"And what about the creature in the Otherworld?"

"If it's a threat, we'll take care of it," Mother said.

"If? It destroyed the rowans, it—" I bit my tongue, resisting the urge to wrap my fingers around the wound in my arm.

"Our ancestors defeated the wild gods," Mother said. "Some disgruntled fey is no match for us." With that, Mother dug her heels into Solas's side. Auryn tossed her head, resentful of being left behind. I laid my left hand against her neck to calm her, but she shivered and shied away. Again, I gently splayed my fingers against her shoulder. Her skin rippled, and she whipped her tail, her ears flattened as she tossed her head and danced several steps to the right. She quietened as soon as I removed the offending fingers. Then I released my grip on Auryn's mane, letting her run in the gelding's wake.

We, my mother had said. *We'll take care of it.*

But there was no "we" in the Otherworld. I walked that darkness alone and would have to face whatever haunted the shadows on my own as well.

Ash

WELL, THAT didn't last long. Here we were, once again pulling up the drive to Ros Tearmann. This time we'd come to rescue Granddad from the clutches of the Sheehys. Or so Martha O'Donnell had convinced my mum. It meant Granddad would have to live with us for a while. I'd been booted out of my room and onto the moth-eaten couch.

I'd messaged Rowan to give him a heads-up, but he hadn't responded. I wasn't sure what to think. What if he hated me now after what Mum had done, or what if I'd gotten his number wrong? My stomach cramped painfully, my hands a little sweaty.

"What if Granddad doesn't want to leave?" I asked as the tires of our station wagon churned through gravel and came to a halt.

"Not his decision, I'm afraid," Mum said and stepped out of the car.

"You really think the Sheehys are responsible for the murders?"

"I don't know, Ash, and until I do, I'll not have my dad at risk here. And I don't want you hanging around them, either."

Without further argument, I followed Mum inside, braced for inevitable confrontation. Siobhan was behind the counter again.

"Morning Mrs. Walsh, here to see your father?"

"Detective Inspector," Mum corrected in her best I'm-with-the-law voice. "And I'm here to fetch my father. He won't be staying at this establishment anymore."

The smile plastered on Siobhan's face fell away immediately. "I see." Her eyes narrowed. "You'll still be charged for the rest of the month and due to early termination of the contract, you'll lose the deposit as well, I'm afraid."

Mum glowered. It must've been a struggle, but she managed a surly "fine" and Siobhan started the paperwork.

"We'll need Mr. O'Donnell's signature as well," Siobhan said.

"As you wish." Mum snatched up the papers and marched toward the elevator. I followed, glancing around for Rowan, surprised by how disappointed I was when I didn't see him.

Granddad sat at the window with a cup of flowery tea. His room smelled like one of those trendy bath bombs with a pretentious name like marmalade mojito. It must've been the candles. I counted at least seven, all different colors and offensive fragrances.

"I'm not leaving," Granddad said.

"Come on, Dad. We talked about this," Mum said as she sagged on the edge of Granddad's bed. "We agreed—"

"No, you decided, but this is my decision. This is where I want to die."

"Don't say things like that. We've got a lovely place nearer town. Don't we, Ash?"

I kept my mouth shut and looked down so I wouldn't have to see the expression on my granddad's face.

"I thought you were better than all this," Granddad said. "That you wouldn't let childish superstition cloud your judgment and influence your opinions."

"For Christ's sake, Dad. This whole family are suspects in a murder investigation. And..."

And I inched my way toward the door as Mum continued. The argument was only going to escalate, and I didn't want to be around when it did. Granddad turned to Mum and took her hands. While she was distracted, I slipped out of the door and hurried toward the elevator. I didn't want to hear any of it. Not about Granddad dying or how awful the Sheehys were.

"Hear the old man's leaving," Deirdre said when the elevator doors opened. I almost peed my pants getting ambushed by the girl. She was dressed in mismatched stripy socks and a poofy skirt with bouquets of flowers on it. Her bumblebee shirt was splattered with what looked like oil or wax.

"Mum's trying to convince him. Think it'll take a while."

"Is it because she thinks one of us is the murderer?" she asked.

"I don't know," I lied. "Everyone is on edge."

"My gran likes to say prejudice is contagious. Guess she's right." Deirdre scuffed her bare toe through the hole in her sock. I didn't know what to say to that. Part of me wanted to believe Mum was better than that, stronger somehow, but I knew she wasn't. If she was any kind of strong, she would've left my father years ago.

"Do you like jasmine?" Deirdre asked as a strange buzzing seemed to emanate from her shirt. I must've been imagining the bees' wings moving, and the buzzing must've been tinnitus.

"Um, not sure I have an opinion." Although now

that she'd asked, I realized that was what I could smell. Jasmine and lilac and a dozen other fragrances I couldn't name, as if somehow the flowers on her skirt were real, too.

"Okay, well, here." She held up a leather bracelet sporting one of the chipped shells she'd shown me that day on the beach. "As promised." She fastened the band around my right wrist. "You're one of us, now the island knows it. Also, he's in the stables," she said, looking up at me with eyes like her brother's, except hers were identical where his were mismatched.

"W-what?" I stammered, struggling to process her words.

"Rowan." She grinned before scampering away. It took me a moment to get a grip. So far, every encounter I'd had with Deirdre left me feeling disorientated and confused. Guess my feet weren't, though, since they were already headed toward the stables before my mind had fully caught up.

Outside, the air was muggy, and thick grey clouds were rolling in from the sea. I headed to the stables, following the unmistakable farmyard smell of animals. My breath caught at the back of my throat, my whole body tingled at the sight of Rowan in the yard. He was brushing Auryn, her coat already gleaming. He was gleaming, too, his auburn hair burnished by the sun. I'd be lying if I said that was the first thing I noticed, though.

What I noticed first was how he didn't have a shirt on.

Second, the mass of ink sprawled across his back: a tangle of trees and runes and traditional knot-work.

Third, how the muscles contracted and released beneath his freckled skin as he worked the brush over the horse.

Fourth, how he had a black-stained rag tied around his left biceps.

Fifth, his chest—scarred and inked and lean.

Oh, how my fingers ached for the camera left at home on my desk. I'd never enjoyed shooting portraits, but damn, I was ready to make an exception.

Regretfully, I noticed last how he'd stopped brushing his horse and turned to look at me while I continued to stare.

"Ash," he said my name and it was like being struck by lightning.

"Sorry, I—Deirdre said—I mean..." For fuck's sake, I didn't know where to look or what to say, words suddenly a confusion of syllables I couldn't parse.

"Are you okay?" he asked.

"Don't steal my line."

He smiled, flashing a slice of delightfully crooked teeth. "Give me a minute," he said, and I was content to watch him lead Auryn back into her stable. The other two horses must've already been groomed. One had a coat like liquid silver, the other so dark brown it was almost black except for the spattering of white on its face. I hadn't meant to follow him, but there I was standing outside the stall.

"Did you get my text this morning?" I asked around the lump in my throat.

"Yeah, but only about ten minutes ago. Figured I'd get to see you soon anyway, so didn't reply."

Okay, no biggie, I've just been dying a slow and painful death staring at a blank screen, but it's fine, dude, really, no worries.

"I've been with the horses all morning. They're leaving soon," he continued.

"I'm sorry," I answered automatically, even though it was a pointless thing to say.

He didn't say anything back, just kept looking at Auryn. God, what I wouldn't give for someone to look at me the way Rowan looked at his horse.

"You must love her."

"She's been my best friend for almost ten years," he

said softly before grabbing a shirt on a hook in the wall. Ink and scars disappeared beneath cotton. It was easier to make eye contact with him now.

"My granddad's leaving," I said.

"I didn't think he'd stay, not after yesterday." He took a step into the yard, looked up at the sky, and stepped back beneath the eaves as the first drops of rain began to fall. A low rumble of thunder rolled across the island, and I huddled deeper into my hoodie, aware of the bracelet on my wrist where rough leather made contact with skin.

"There's tea in the tack room," Rowan said, and I followed him past a couple of empty stalls to a small storage room that doubled as an office. It smelled of leather and oil and chamomile.

"Did my mum really arrest you?" I asked as he filled the kettle.

"Only took me in for questioning," he said, busy with mugs and tea leaves. "Although I'm sure the Kilduffs are saying something different."

"Teagan did seem quite excited by the prospect of you in handcuffs."

Rowan let out a short staccato laugh, and my cheeks burst into flame when I realized what I'd said.

"Um, yeah—I didn't mean..." *Just stop talking already.* I zipped my mouth shut and Rowan handed me a mug of tea with bits of green floating on its surface. Then our fingers touched, and I no longer minded if I was going to have to chew my way through the beverage.

"From Deirdre?" His index finger brushed the shell in the bracelet.

"Apparently now the island knows I'm one of you, or something."

"Aye, for better or worse."

His words weren't even remotely reassuring. Neither was the gulp of tea I took that left me eating bitter bits of foliage.

"It's a pity your mom thinks it's me, though." Rowan

169

studied the contents of his mug, his butt resting on the desk opposite me.

"Is there a reason beyond the obvious?" I sank into the musty couch behind me.

"It's a waste of time." He looked up at me with those mismatched eyes, and I nearly choked on my mouthful of tea. "Your mom is wasting resources investigating me when she should be trying to find the real murderer."

"She's good at her job," I said, more defensively than expected.

"I don't doubt that, but she's working in a department full of people who hate my family."

"I've been wondering about that. I mean, I read that book Fergus gave me. I've spoken to Teagan, and Cillian. They all say you and your family are dangerous. That you're witches."

He seemed to consider my words for a moment, tapping his fingers on his mug, his jaw clenching. "We are. Well, the women are," he said.

"What about you?"

"I'm a rowan," he said, and the rain drummed harder on the tiles above us, water pouring off the eaves.

"They had family trees in that book. I saw yours. Seems to be a Rowan in every generation."

"Aye, there is."

"Just a naming tradition, or something else?"

"Are you sure you want to know?" he asked.

"You're not some kind of fey creature, are you?"

"What would you say if I was?" Rowan asked.

Now it was my turn to pause and consider. I squinted at him, trying to imagine him sprouting wings or horns, which was how I all fey creatures looked, right?

"Part of me wouldn't believe it," I said.

"The Walsh part."

"Another part of me wouldn't be surprised."

"That's the O'Donnell in you. Your blood knows the truth," he said, and I wanted to believe it. If Teagan was really a kind of vampire, and Rowan was some sort of magical creature, then maybe what the book had said about my ancestors was true, too. The idea of being at least partly related to powerful druids was actually pretty cool.

"Okay, let's say I believe you. Why does everyone think you're the murderer?"

"Because it's easy to believe." He ran long fingers through his hair, snagging on a curl. I'd seen his drawings. There was definitely a dark side to the guy, but that didn't mean he was a psycho.

"The book mentioned death magic."

"I bet it did," he said, "but they don't understand. They don't even try...because if I'm not the murderer, they'll have to look a little closer to home and admit maybe one of their own is responsible."

"Who do you think did it?" I asked.

"I don't know, yet," he said slowly. "Not without seeing more evidence from the crime scenes." He held my gaze, and I knew what he was going to ask.

I'd never had any reason to go snooping before. Why would I? Mum's cases had never had any personal connection to me, but this was different.

"I don't think I can help you."

"They found a footprint, or shoe print, maybe more."

"No, I can't." I couldn't betray Mum's trust. Not like this.

"I need to know exactly what they found."

"If there were other suspects, Mum would've taken them in already."

"You think the O'Donnells and Kilduffs on the force would let your mom arrest one of theirs? They're going to twist the evidence and convince her it was one of us."

What if it is one of you? Thankfully, I kept the thought to myself.

"I'm not asking you to do anything you're uncomfortable with," Rowan continued before I could say no again, "but people are dying, brutally, for reasons I—" He ran a hand over his face before looking at me. "I'm scared, Ash," he said in his slow and measured way, which sent a rash of prickles scurrying over my skin.

"Scared of what?" I whispered.

"Of what they're trying to do, of what they'll unleash if they succeed. Of not being able to stop them before— Ow, f—" He dropped his mug and grabbed at his arm where the rag was tied. Something thick and dark welled up between his fingers.

"Holy shit, is that blood? Are you hurt?" Shards of mug crunched beneath my boot as I stepped toward him.

"Don't touch me." He pulled away.

"I'm just trying to help."

"I know—but—" The breath hitched in his throat. "Please, don't touch me."

The fear in his voice made me back up a few steps as he leaned against the desk, gasping for air.

"Should I get someone? Deirdre, your mum?"

"Don't. I'm fine." He tried to straighten and succeeded only in wincing. Sweat beaded his forehead, and more blood welled between his fingers. A few drops splattered the floor and curled into thin streamers of black smoke upon impact.

I blinked, then rubbed my eyes. Nope. This was real. This was happening. Rowan was bleeding red-black gunk that turned into smoke.

"I don't think that's normal."

"I just need—" Rowan pushed away from the desk and staggered out into the storm. He released his arm and peeled away the filthy bandage, letting the rain wash the ooze from his skin. It gave me a pretty clear view of the injury: two gruesome rips through his skin as if he'd been side-swiped by a grizzly.

"What the fuck happened? Did someone do that to you?" My hands were already clenched into fists.

He looked over his shoulder at me, bedraggled hair

framing his eyes, T-shirt sticking to his shoulders and chest. "I need your help, Ash," he said. "Whoever's doing this, there's magic involved. Dark magic. We don't know what it is, but it's reaching from the Otherworld."

Otherworld. Guess he hadn't been joking about his mismatched eyes.

"That's what hurt you?" I asked, not that it meant I believed in any of this magic stuff.

He nodded. "I have to stop it. I have to stop the people doing this. What they could release in the Otherworld, on the living—it puts us all in danger." He bit his lip, staying in the rain until the wound ran red and the drops falling into the mud no longer turned to smoke.

"Rowan, I can't."

"An O'Donnell will be next," he said, his words making me hold my breath.

"Are you sure?"

"I wish I wasn't, but the symbols, the trees—oak is the third and that's the tree of the O'Donnells."

"My Granddad?" I asked between my teeth as I exhaled a shaky breath.

"He would be an easy target," Rowan said. "I don't know for sure but—but no O'Donnell is safe right now."

"What about half-O'Donnells?" I asked.

Slowly, he shook his head.

Well fuck me sideways. I wasn't prepared for this. We'd come here to escape my father's fists, not get caught up in island hocus-pocus. Now I was being told my granddad could be the target of some sadistic, ritualistic serial killer.

"Will you help me?" he asked.

How could I say no to a guy bleeding black smoke in the rain? To the guy who'd just told me I could have a bull's eye on my back?

I don't believe in magic. I don't—I don't—but what if, what if it's real, and Rowan is right, and everything the book said is true, and my family is in danger?

173

"Yes," I said before I could over-think it. "But—shit—I have to go."

"Ash! What the hell are you doing?" Mum yelled from where she stood beneath the dripping corner of the house.

Rowan tugged the sleeve of his T-shirt over the cuts on his arm, but I was pretty sure Mum had already seen.

"Everything okay?" she shouted over the ordnance of the storm.

"I'm coming," I yelled back. "Two minutes."

Rowan walked back into the stables, pausing when he reached me beneath the eaves. He lowered his voice, his breath against my neck. "Helping me could be dangerous. Are you okay with that?"

"I'm not sure."

"Then think about it. Let me know what you decide. You know where to find me," he said before trudging back to the tack room.

Mum was yelling at me, threatening me with all manner of punishments if I didn't haul ass immediately.

I obeyed, rain stinging my head. I wished it would pour inside my skull and wash away all the doubt.

"What the hell were you doing with him?" Mum grabbed my good arm and spun me around to face her.

"Having a quick shag, proposing marriage. God, what do you think?"

"Don't, Ash." Her grip tightened for a moment before she released me, holding up her hands. "Granddad's waiting in the car. Let's go." She frog-marched me away from the stables toward the parking lot. I looked back, hoping to catch a glimpse of Rowan. Instead, I saw dozens of purple-black butterflies fluttering above the stables, seemingly unaffected by the rain.

You know shit's messed up when magic is the most logical explanation.

Rowan

WHAT I'D asked of Ash wasn't fair, but it was all I had.

Hawthorn. Ash. Only oak remained to complete the ritual. An O'Donnell would die next, unless I stopped it, unless I confronted the shadow creature trying to claw its way into the realm of the living. Ash was an unlikely victim, given the previous two, but they were still an O'Donnell, and that made them vulnerable. I didn't want to dwell on Ash, on what they must now think of me.

The rain continued to hammer against the roof, the island still lamenting the loss of Andy and Patrick, its sorrow soaking into my bones and sousing my veins. The ghosts screamed inside my head, a singular voice begging me to make it stop.

Three trees. Three sacrifices. Blood.

Blood spilled, soaking into earth, through stone, down into the bedrock of the island.

A spell, a ritual.

The knowledge was buried within the borrowed memories, if only I could burrow deep enough into my own mind to retrieve the answer.

The wound in my arm brought me back to the present. It was already starting to blacken and smolder again. The cleansing effect of the rain offered a temporary reprieve from the magic infecting my flesh. Now black tendrils reached toward my shoulder, skirting the wards, sending questing fingers down my back. Resolved, I quickly gathered what I thought might aid me in the Otherworld, and perhaps provide a tether to the living realm, a lifeline home should I fail to defeat the shadow.

From the drying shack, I gathered agrimony and burdock, sage, chamomile, and a preparation of belladonna in case pain alone was insufficient for me to bridge the worlds. I lit my sisters' candles, the scent of ginger and thyme, orange, valerian, and cinnamon filling the storage room as I shut the door. I filled my pockets with the herbs and hoped it would be enough. Without any magic of my own, what I knew of rites and rituals had been gleaned only through wary observation. I knew no incantations, no spells, or sigils.

As ready as I could be, I pressed a piece of old saddle leather between my teeth, rolled up my sleeve, and held my knife in my right hand, fingers squeezing the hilt. A single deep breath made my head swim with the dizzying fragrance of herbs, quietening the multitude within me. I closed my eyes and pressed the blade against my arm, silver parting skin.

It wasn't enough.

Even when my blood soaked the straw-strewn floor, even when I twisted the blade and thought I'd snap my teeth as I screamed against the leather—it still wasn't enough.

With trembling fingers, I reached for the bottle of belladonna, a preparation reserved for rites of transcendence. Perhaps it would aid me now, allowing me to slip into the Otherworld.

The potion tasted bitter on my tongue, and I waited until the edges of my vision grew dark and hazy before picking up my knife again. This time, the pain bore me like a wave, sweeping me far away from myself toward a comforting blackness. But it wasn't the familiar purple shadow of the Otherworld, and I lost my grip on the knife as the darkness became smothering, as the ghost-memories leached from ferried souls became a suffocating mist in my lungs.

Then I was falling, flailing, as I plummeted towards a gaping void, vaguely aware of my hand knocking over a candle, of the straw on the floor, and a hundred purple butterflies beating their wings to fan the flames.

Ash

WE DROVE home in a silence so angry I could practically see the atoms sparking between us. Granddad was pissed at Mum, Mum was pissed at me, and I sat pissed at everything. I was glad Granddad was safe with us if what Rowan had said was true and an O'Donnell could be next.

"Mum, Rowan—" I tried but didn't get very far.

"You're grounded," she snapped.

"What? Why?"

"I told you to stay away. I told you I didn't want you talking to him."

"Actually, I'm pretty sure you said none of those things."

"He's a murder suspect!"

"Was it his shoe print you found?" I asked.

Mum pressed her lips together. So, it hadn't been a match for Rowan. If it had been, Mum wouldn't have let him go so easy.

"If it wasn't his, you must have other suspects. If there's a list of people I'm not allowed to talk to, I'd like to know."

"Don't get smart." Mum's words drilled holes through me. Those were the words my father usually said right before his fists started flying. I huddled against the passenger door, pressed as far away from her as I could before I responded.

"Why? You going to start hitting me, too?" I asked.

"Enough. Both of you," Granddad piped up from the back. "Ash, you're not grounded. And you—" He tapped Mum's shoulder. "You let the Sheehys be."

"This is *my* murder investigation." Mum slapped the steering wheel with the heel of her hand. "Don't tell me how to do my job. And don't you dare tell me how to raise my kid."

"Because you've done such an excellent job so far." I went for the jugular.

Mum white-knuckled the steering wheel, her jaw clenched so hard I could almost hear her teeth grinding. I was in for burnt toast for at least two weeks now, but I didn't give a fuck. She didn't get a monopoly on anger.

As soon as the car rolled to a stop outside our cottage, I bolted out the door and started running.

"Ashlee, you get back here right now!" Mum yelled after me. Maybe if she'd used my proper name, I would've slowed down, but she didn't, so I pumped my legs harder, kicking up wet stones as I hurtled through the rain.

I didn't look back and didn't stop, tearing across fields and clambering over walls and stiles, not caring where I was going.

Somehow, I ended up behind the church, wheezing, sweating, and clutching at my collarbone. I took a moment to compose myself, shaking the rain from my hair beneath an arch, surveying the battened-down town. The deluge had eased up, but the wind still howled, tearing at awnings and skidding chairs across sidewalks.

I didn't really feel like talking to Teagan or her sister, but it wasn't like I could waltz into the police station and demand to see Mum's case files either. There was only one way I could think of to get what Rowan needed, a way that meant I wouldn't be completely betraying Mum. Not that she deserved my loyalty right now.

Teagan responded to my text within a minute, agreeing to meet me during her lunch break. I had an hour to get myself to the general store, an hour to plan exactly how I was going to wheedle information out of her without raising any suspicion.

The general store was easily the biggest building on the island, taking up a large chunk of real estate on the bluff above the harbor where the ferry had spat us out just a couple of weeks ago. I checked the time and did a mental run-through of what I planned to say before I shook the rain from my hood and stepped into the store.

Lucy found me first, sashaying over to me as if the ugly, mustard shirt she wore bore some designer label instead of the store's logo.

"Hi there, little O'Donnell," she said. "You coming to the funeral Wednesday?"

"Funeral?" I asked, hating how she'd caught me off guard. Hating how off-guard I felt with her laser eyes boring into me. Even in the hideous shirt, she was still beautiful and breathtaking.

"Patrick's. It would be good for you to see how things are done around here. Besides, we should show our support. Founding family solidarity and all." Her words were acerbic, laced with a bitterness I didn't get.

"Ah, sure. My mum will probably want to be there."

"It'll be a true introduction to island life for you, show

you who that Rowan really is."

Her words sent a thrill through me, equal parts excitement and fear.

"Is Teagan around? We're having lunch," I asked.

"She's in the back. Follow aisle 37 and head through the 'Staff Only' doors. Break room is on the right. Tell her I'm clocking out, will you?" With that, she sauntered past me, all smiles and ice-cold eyes.

I hustled down aisle 37 and pushed through the doors as described. Teagan was talking on the phone to someone, hushed and punctuated with little gasps. I hung about outside, wondering if I should leave, but we had an arrangement, and I needed info. I knocked on the door before I stepped inside. Teagan's eyes flashed with irritation, her frown fading when she saw it was me. She beckoned me inside.

"Okay, Ness, I gotta go. I'll call you later." She hung up and turned to face me. "Sorry about that." Her cheeks were flushed as she smoothed back her dark bangs, her previously blond roots now the same shiny black as the rest of her hair.

"Everything okay?" I asked, pulling up a chair.

"Yes. No. I mean—that was Neasa Sheehy," she whispered as she closed the door and sat at the battered table. "Apparently, Rowan's sick. He's got some sort of infection."

The mark on his arm, the black gunk pouring down his skin.

"A magical one." She held my gaze, daring me to laugh or maybe trying to mind-trick me into believing her. She needn't have bothered.

"I believe you," I said. "Mum and I were at the Sheehys this morning to get my granddad. I saw Rowan."

"Did you see his arm? Neasa said it's really gross, like gangrene or something."

"Well, I didn't get too close," I said, remembering the

shape of Rowan's biceps and the tattoos on his back, the muscles lean and chiseled, and the look on his face when he begged me for help. Gross was the last adjective that came to mind, even with all that black stuff dripping down his fingers.

"That's probably for the best. Feels like none of us are safe anymore." She scratched varnish off her nail.

"That's why I'm here. I think…" The lie burned my tongue. I forced it out anyway. "I think maybe Rowan might be the murderer."

"Really?" She cocked an eyebrow at me. "What makes you think that?" she said, her words and gaze turning sharp.

"Just a hunch."

"Did your mom say something?"

"I know she has evidence, but she won't say what, and it's not enough for an arrest. She needs more before she can take him into custody. I want to help."

Teagan studied her hands, chipping more black polish off a finger with her thumb. "There was a shoe print," she said. "They're still trying to figure out the make. The size wasn't a match for Rowan, but that doesn't mean he didn't do it."

"Do you know the size?"

"You're awfully interested all of a sudden."

"Trying to help." I shrugged, as if it the answer didn't matter.

She seemed to consider, scraping away more polish and chewing at her bottom lip.

"My mum will never find out you told me anything, promise."

"No, it's not that…" It's a women's size six, men's six and a half. Tread from a trainer," she said. "Not that that's much help. Lucy and I are both sixes. So are a dozen others."

"Me, too." I admitted. "Is that all they've got?"

"Come on, there must be something else making Rowan a suspect. Is he their only suspect?"

"Has your mom said anything about suspecting others?" Teagan paused in the demolition of her manicure.

"Not to me," I said.

"There was one more thing Claire mentioned," Teagan said with a breathy exhalation. "Apparently, they found traces of wormwood and rue at both murder sites."

"What's that?"

"They're plants," Teagan said as if it was something I should've known. "Herbs used in spells by witches."

"More evidence against Rowan," I said, heart sinking.

"I'm telling you, Ash. He's dangerous. You should stay away from him."

"Do you know what those herbs are used for?"

"Why the hell would I know?" she snapped. "My family isn't into that kind of thing."

Rowan would know. This was exactly the kind of info he needed. My fingers itched to message him, to let him know straight away what I'd found out. Part of me wanted to jump up and run right back to Ros Tearmann, but another part of me started doubting... I'd seen the wound on his arm and knew the history of his family, albeit according to Fionnula O'Donnell. Maybe Rowan wasn't the one behind the murders, but that didn't mean another Sheehy couldn't be responsible, which lead me to another question burning in my brain.

"Why were you talking to Neasa?" I asked.

Teagan pursed her lips and spread her fingers on the table. They were festooned with silver rings. She rubbed at one fashioned to look like a pair of hands cradling a crowned heart. A Claddagh ring.

"Are you *with* her?"

She sucked in a breath.

"Holy shit, you are, aren't you?"

"You can't tell anyone." Teagan looked up at me with tears making her eyes all the more electric. "My mom would kill me if she knew. You don't know what it's like here being...being—"

"Lesbian? I think I can sort of relate."

She jerked her head up at that, like she was seeing me for the first time despite what Lucy had said to me at the Copper Kettle. "Yeah, we've been wondering if you're a boy or a girl."

"Both. Neither." I took a deep breath. "I use they."

"Good to know." She gave me a smile. "But, no. Being gay isn't the problem. Being a Kilduff in love with a Sheehy—that's the real issue." She let out a laugh that was more-than-half a sob. "I've never even said that aloud, you know. That I love her. Other times, I thought maybe I was in love." She twirled the ring on her finger. "But now I know, I never was. It was just infatuation maybe, me getting swept up in their adoration. It's kind of addictive, this thing we do." She batted her eyelids at me, and I gave her a nod, not that I really understood what she meant. All I could think about was how I'd always figured love was a scale from crush to soulmate, which left me wondering where my feelings for Rowan currently sat, if they were even on the scale at all.

"Anyway," Teagan continued. "My family isn't exactly thrilled about me being gay, because progeny and all, you know, but being with a Sheehy would be incomprehensible to them. They'd disown me. And that's not all—"

I let her suck in a few breaths. Clearly, the words were a struggle.

"We—loving someone—being loved—we absorb it," she said. "Even if we try not to, even if we don't want to. We eat it all up. All of it. Until there's nothing left." There were tears in her eyes.

"Eat it? Like, you mean you suck all the love out of a

184

person until what? They die?"

"Not just the love. We take it all—everything the person feels, their emotions, their vitality. But they don't die. They're just empty after we've—done our thing," she said, a single tear rolling dramatically down her cheek trailing black mascara in its wake.

"Wow, that's epically goth." I tried not to think too hard about how many hapless tourists might be wandering around mostly dead because they'd fallen for a Kilduff.

With a quiver of laughter, Teagan dabbed away her tears. "What Lucy said about our responsibility to the family, she's not wrong, even though I wish she were. My uncle Andy, he married a McNamara, and that was bad. It almost tore the families apart with what happened to Sarah and all their kids."

"Even the kids died?" I asked.

"Sarah had half a dozen miscarriages, and the few babies she did carry to term never survived."

"Shit, that's terrible." I couldn't even begin to imagine that kind of loss.

"Andy blamed the Sheehys for what happened. He didn't want to believe it was his own fault," she said.

"So aren't you taking a huge risk being with Neasa?"

"Yes, but she knows some spells, and there are sigils for protection as well. We're taking precautions," she said. "But with Lucy and Cillian. Cillian doesn't have the benefit of witchery. There's nothing protecting him from my sister."

"But she's still with him?"

"No, she isn't, but they want to be together."

God, it was all so tragic.

"I probably shouldn't have told you any of this." Her tears were gone now, replaced by a cool detachment as she regarded me. "Me and Neasa, it's a secret. It has to be, and one I could *make* you keep, but I'd prefer it if we were friends and could trust each other."

"I won't tell anyone. I swear."

"Thank you, Ash." She exhaled, her shoulders drooping a little as if she were relieved she wouldn't have to work her vampire magic on me. I was relieved, too. "It's exhausting," she said. "I hate this, hate knowing I could hurt her."

"Sounds terrible." Brutal. If I were in Teagan's shoes, I'd be furious and want nothing to do with my family and its sick, twisted magic. I couldn't imagine having lived my whole life on this stifling little island with my family cinched around me like a straitjacket. Maybe Lucy was right, and coming here was a mistake. Maybe getting away from my father wasn't worth getting involved in all this. But—but—a tiny thought wriggled through my brain, reminding me of a boy with copper hair and mismatched eyes.

"I should get back to work." Teagan ran two fingers under her eyes to wipe away smudged make-up.

"You didn't eat lunch," I said.

"I'll be fine. I'm a vampire, remember?" She smiled, showing me a sliver of canine no pointier than my own.

"Will you let me know if they find anything else?"

"So you can help your mom catch Rowan, right?"

"Of course." I almost choked. "You said it, no one is safe with the murderer out there. The quicker he's caught, the better."

"And you think you can do what a detective can't?"

"Mum has to follow procedure and protocol. I don't."

"You're a lot more like your ancestors than you realize." She grinned, and I wasn't sure I liked it. Or the comparison. My ancestors seemed like prejudiced assholes determined to pin everything bad that happened on the island on the Sheehys without much justification. Maybe that could change if I helped Rowan figure out who the real murderer was.

Having said goodbye, I left Teagan stocking shelves and cursing Lucy for taking off early. She also made me promise to meet her Wednesday morning so we could go to the funeral together as if it were a shopping expedition and not a mourning ritual.

Outside, the clouds were thinning, and patches of blue sky showed in the east. Finally, I pulled out my phone. I could've just texted Rowan what I knew, but I wanted to see him. I wanted to look him in the eye when I told him about the shoe print and herbs. I also didn't hate the idea of having an excuse to see him again.

I waited and waited, and once again there was no response. My heart hiccoughed behind my ribs. Either Rowan lacked 21st-century communication skills, or maybe that magical infection had made him too sick to answer.

Still holding my phone, hoping for a message, I squinted toward the sun, watching the ferry coast into the harbor and bump into the dock. This boatload of tourists was lucky to be arriving on the tail-end of a storm. Not like us, coming ashore cold, soaked, and seasick.

A fresh wave of visitors disembarked, families with suitcases and a few older couples who hobbled their way along the dock. A single figure brought up the rear. Tall, balding, and dressed in a blue overcoat so much like my father's I couldn't breathe for a moment.

It couldn't be.

The colonel was on a work trip. He'd be busy for at least another week or more. He hadn't known we were coming here. It couldn't be him. It couldn't, and yet the figure far below me had turned to look up at the hill, and I swear he was looking right at me. My neon jacket had caught the sun, that was all. I was a bright spot against a vista of grey. Anyone would pause to stare. Not just anyone had a blue coat like that, though, or a shaved, balding head, or a long-legged stride.

No. I was dreaming. Nightmaring. It was not my father.

I turned away from the dock, balled my hands into fists, and stuffed them into my pockets. It wasn't the colonel. We were safe here—here where a murderer was slitting throats and people got infected with black-pus magic. Here among vampires and shapeshifters, here the colonel couldn't touch us. I needed to believe it, so I walked away without looking over my shoulder, trying to convince myself the only monster I truly feared hadn't just come ashore.

Rowan

VOICES. A choir within me, clamoring, screaming. Warmth licking at my face, a pervasive heat, flickers of light beyond my closed eyelids.

Rowan. A what, not a who. Me. My name a whisper inside my mind, growing louder, a shriek, a shout.

"Rowan!"

"By the Gods, get him out of here."

"The horses! Get the horses!"

"Warm water. Herbs. You know what to do."

A twitch of muscle, a firing of impulse over which I had no control.

The horses. The heat. The caress of flame.

But I couldn't move, my arms sinking into the ground, embedded in the earth like roots. My legs immobile, driftwood, deadwood—my body heavy as stone. Hands sought that body—fingers digging me from the earth, tearing at my clothes, at my skin.

Coolness. Air and rain, and I was drowning even as I kicked toward the surface.

"Rowan, wake up. Wake up!"

Stinging across my face, a blow across my mind, my eyes fought against the weight, fluttering against the shroud encasing me.

"Thank the Gods." Mother stared down at me, her hands fisted in my shirt, her hair snarled by the rain. "Get up, Rowan. You have to get up."

The acrid sent of burning wood, the crackle and spit of fire. Hooves churning through mud, their thunder resonating through the earth and into my bones, jolting me from the ground and onto my knees.

"They're fine," Deirdre said, leading the horses to the paddock. They shouldn't be in the storm. They should be warm and dry in their stables, but the stables burned, clouds of black smoke billowing into the yard, the rain dousing the flames.

"What did you do?" Mother asked, her hands still in my shirt. She shook me, my head snapping back, giving me a glimpse of the black butterflies circling like carrion crows above.

"I had to try," I said, but my voice wasn't working, the words stuck between my teeth, gummed against my tongue as memories trickled through the cracks in my mind.

Pain.

Blood.

Deadly nightshade.

"We have to get you inside. I can't carry you. You have to walk." She gave me another shake. "Do you hear me? Get. Up." Her magic spun through the scars carved into my body, animating my limbs. I heaved onto my feet, the world a dizzy kaleidoscope. I closed my eyes, my hand on her shoulder, and breathed, sucking in a mouthful of rain and bitter ash. I moved like a puppet, my mother controlling the strings.

In the kitchen, I pulled the boots from my feet and

peeled the shirt from my back before collapsing in a chair at the table. My mother's magic drained away, leaving my skin stinging and head pulsing with the fug of magic.

"Gods above, why, Ro?" Deirdre's fingers hovered above my arm. I looked down, observing the damage my blade had wrought as if the limb weren't my own, as if the wounds hadn't been self-inflicted. It had all been in vain, providing no ingress to the Otherworld.

"I'm sorry," I said, the words falling from my lips this time. "I tried—I wanted—"

"You should've come to us," Mother said.

"I'm sorry. I—"

"Shh, it'll be okay," Deirdre said as Siobhan placed a bowl of warm water on the table. The steam rose, redolent with yarrow and burdock. Neasa kept her distance, her gaze glazed.

With firm but gentle fingers, Mother examined the wound in my arm. With a hiss as if she'd been scalded, she snatched her hand away. "Did this happen in the Otherworld?"

I could only nod.

Mother dipped a cloth into the fragrant waters and began bathing my arm, washing away scabs and black blood oozing fresh from the cuts I'd made. I'd dug deep, twisting the blade, thinking pain could bridge the worlds, but now the marks seemed shallow, only the skin rent.

"You're healing, even faster than usual." Mother said. "But not here." She touched the gash across my biceps. "You let it touch you. The creature beyond the river. You let it touch you!" It was an accusation not a question.

"I didn't *let* it do anything."

"You let it fester." Mother said.

"It looks like a tree," Deirdre whispered through the fingers pressed against her lips. "Like a rowan. A dead one."

I almost laughed at that. Sometimes my little sister

was as astute as she was innocent in her observations.

"And what did you hope to achieve with this?" Mother held up my knife stained black and burgundy. "An excision?"

I didn't answer, already cowering from the fury on her face.

"It's spreading," Siobhan said. "Look!" She pointed at my shoulder where black veins spread like ivy through my skin, reaching past the wards and stretching a questing tendril down my back. I felt the slither and twist of the magic as it searched my skin and found its tether. The trees inked on my back: Hawthorn, Ash, Oak, and Rowan. The magic spread across their boughs and down the knotted trunks.

"We have to stop it," Deirdre said through a sob. "We have to do something."

"There's a cleansing ritual," Mother said. "But this will not be pleasant, and without all of us—"

"Please..." I said. It was all I could manage through my chattering teeth, my hands trembling and skin awash in cold sweat.

"Siobhan, Neasa, bind him. Deirdre, get candles."

My sisters hurried to do as Mother commanded, helping me lie down on the kitchen table. Deirdre put a towel under my head. Siobhan apologized as she bound my wrists, ankles, knees, and waist to the kitchen table with rope from the stables. Neasa tied her knots in silence, never once meeting my eye. Mother prepared more herbs, and Deirdre lit several candles, until the air became choked with aromatic scent.

"It'll be okay." Deirdre stroked my hair, which only added to the nerves already broiling in my belly. I inhaled, the acrid taste of burning sage catching at the back of my throat. Mother placed smaller bowls of water on either side of my head then placed more bundles of cleansing herbs at my feet as Siobhan set an ancient talisman bearing the sign for rowan on one side and our family insignia on the other in the center of my chest. It nestled in the scar above my heart, sitting snug in one of the lobes of the triquetra.

The talisman was cold and heavy, no larger than an acorn, yet its presence was crushing. The weight of its power made my skin prickle with goosebumps, every hair standing on end as my family gathered around the table and raised their blades.

Mother lead the incantation, singing softly in the ancient tongue to guide the ceremony. Four blades were raised and passed through the sage smoke. Four blades were lowered. I was thirteen again, terrified, and about to die on the clifftop.

The cuts were superficial, mere whispers across old scars. I barely felt them, but I felt the magic.

The threads of darkness embroidered in my flesh rose to the call, writhing through my veins. My arm burned, the gashes oozing. The infection retreated, the tendrils recoiled. It felt like hooks being dragged through my skin. I was sweating and shaking, fists clenched and nails digging into my palms. The world blinked in and out of shadow. One moment I was in the kitchen, the next I was in the Otherworld.

This is what I'd wanted. Finally.

"Is it working?" Deirdre asked, her voice distant and distorted.

"Slowly, but yes," Mother answered, and the incantation continued, the inexorable withdrawal of the smoke creature's presence an agony I struggled to bear.

Mother pressed her hand to my forehead. I tried to pull away, to avoid the scent of vanilla assailing me, but she increased the pressure, holding me still, just like she had that night on the cliff.

Darkness swamped my vision. I tried to blink away the Otherworld, but the darkness congealed, solidifying behind my eyelids. The burning in my arm turned cold, the magic of what my mother had made me sinking away from the surface, a slow ebb of familiar power to be replaced by something else entirely.

An insidious ripple beneath my skin. Branches and roots once more began to take hold. I must've screamed, but I couldn't hear anything beyond the blood pounding in my ears—the thunder of waves crashing against ragged rock.

I opened my eyes in the Otherworld and it seethed, myriad colors chasing each other across the sky in an infernal race. Spirits wailed, others laughed—a cacophony I couldn't protect myself from.

A single butterfly circled above me, its wings torn, yet somehow it remained aloft. It fluttered against my face and then farther away, drawing me along the cliffs, our path snaking ever south. The sea grew wilder, as if the waves were determined to obliterate the very rock we stood on. Eventually, the butterfly turned away from the sea, its path leading us inland and up a hill I didn't recognize.

The butterfly flitted out of sight beyond the rise, and I hurried after it. Above me, the sluagh screamed through the air, the vengeful spirits dancing in the gelid wind, dipping and weaving but remaining far out of reach.

Below me, a vast ring of stone and tangled vine encircled two large trees. These trees were grotesque approximations of their living cousins, spawned from ground darkened with blood. Andy's and Patrick's. The Hawthorn was gnarled and gaunt, its branches a snarled canopy. The Ash had a monstrous trunk, black and suppurating, its branches rising like spears.

The butterfly circled above the trees, and tentatively, I made my way down the hill. I stopped at the ring of stones, some instinct warning me not to breach that threshold. Smoke rose from the ground, writhing as it assumed the vague shape of two more trees. One appeared to be an oak, the other was unmistakably a rowan.

The shadows contorted, the darkness coalescing into blue flame rippling like water. The rowan burned in icy fire, and I pressed my right hand to the scar in my chest. My body ignited, a freezing agony burning through my chest and permeating every capillary.

Before me, the smoke began to solidify, assuming the shape of a rowan tree, my tree. Berries burst from naked branches, only to weep red as they rotted on the bough. My tree was bleeding, and so was I. Ichor leaked between my fingers as I began to change, my knees buckling and toes elongating into roots.

Trees. Blood. A spell, ancient and powerful. A pact, a binding. The ghosts within me danced to the chaotic throbbing of my heart. The darkness shivered as understanding crawled from the deepest recess of borrowed memory.

A spell to bind; paid in blood—broken in blood.

It would be so easy to remain rooted in this soil, to wait for the circle's completion, to become what I was destined to be, but—

I tore my hand from my chest, the inferno engulfing me. I screamed as I struggled to my feet, tearing my body from the soil of the Otherworld.

"No!" This time I heard my voice, the raw desperation ripping from my throat.

Blades clattered to the floor. Siobhan, Neasa, and Deirdre all staggered back, tears and sweat streaking their faces. Mother simply stared at me, aghast.

I raised my hands, my limbs free from their bonds. The rope lay in charred piles beneath the table. The talisman that had been on my chest had shattered, the pieces skittering across the floor.

"What the hell just happened?" Neasa asked, retrieving her blade.

I stared at my hands, at my left elbow where the infection faded, the fronds of black already turning grey beneath my skin smeared with blood. They'd tried to cut it out and failed. They'd plunged a dagger into my heart and taken my life once. Once was enough. Their blades would never touch me again.

"Four trees," I said, though my voice sounded strange to my ears, distant and hollow. "Four trees in a sacred circle growing from consecrated ground. The sacrifices—" I paused to swallow. I swung my legs over the edge of the table and picked up an end of charred rope. I'd done that. I stared at my hands, studying each finger as if they might ignite any moment. Just pink skin and freckles. The leather bracelets on my wrists had survived when the rope had burned, the knots merely singed from whatever eldritch force had allowed my fingers to wield fire.

My family all stared at me with expressions ranging from fear to disgust.

"What are you?" Mother asked.

Looking first at my mother, then at my sisters, I tightened my grip on the rope, turning it to ash between my fingers. "I am precisely what you made me."

Ash

IT ONLY took him twenty-three hours and forty-two minutes, but my phone finally beeped with Rowan's reply during breakfast.

Sorry, things have been complicated. Patrick's funeral is this morning. Are you going? he asked.

Yip. See you there? I tried to play it super cool.

We can meet afterwards. I'll find you.

My heart may have kicked up a gear at that, even though I only sent back a thumbs up. I'd never been so excited to go to a funeral. Scratch that. I'd never been to a funeral at all. Maybe that was weird. Not like I got a say in the matter. Somehow, I'd managed to make it through seventeen years of life without having to do this.

Mum had been up and out of the house by 6AM, chasing down leads and doing other detective stuff. She said she'd meet me at the church. Granddad was staying home.

Again, I walked to town and didn't die. Whoever was offing islanders clearly wasn't interested in me. I met

Teagan at the church where I'd expected the whole thing to take place. She stood with her sister and Cillian, a little apart from the larger group of people gathered outside the ancient building. They all seemed oblivious to the tourists snapping photos. Everyone was clad in black. I should've known, but I only had one jacket and the wind off the ocean was damn cold today, the clouds thick with the threat and promise of rain. I searched for Mum but didn't find her.

"We're not going in?" I asked Teagan.

"No," Cillian answered, looking forlorn in his over-sized black suit.

"Ours isn't the Nailed God," Lucy said with a wry grin, looking as exquisite as ever with white-blond hair framing her icy eyes.

"I should join my family." Cillian gave Lucy's hand a squeeze, before drifting off to join the McNamaras. They didn't really share any features—not like how the Kilduffs all had nuclear eyes regardless of their color—but there was something about the McNamaras that made it clear they all shared a common ancestor. An awkwardness to their movements, maybe, as if their skins fit like borrowed clothes.

Then came the O'Donnells, an equal mash-up of features and racial ancestry. It reminded me how much of my father was in my veins, how I'd inherited my mom's dark hair and thick eyebrows, but my father's pale skin. I recognized Martha, the old lady sporting long, grey braids who'd met us the day we arrived. She waved at me, and I gave her a quick smile.

"Don't you want to join your family?" Lucy said, gesturing to those walking with the McNamaras. I shook my head, preferring to walk beside Teagan than make nice with a bunch of strangers wearing tear-stained faces. Were these people even truly family? All of them were strangers despite our shared DNA.

Same for relatives on the colonel's side, really. All I knew was his parents had been loaded. Considering how severe and totalitarian his father was, I'm glad he died when I was a toddler. The colonel's mum was now in a care home with dementia, hardly recognizing my father even on a good day. We rarely visited her. She'd never liked my mum and had apparently been pretty vocal about how her son was marrying "down" when they'd gotten engaged. Surely "family" should mean more than a few matching alleles.

"Where are the Sheehys?" I asked, searching for red hair.

"Wait and see." Lucy grinned again.

The church bells started ringing, drawing even more tourists to stand and gawk. Someone beat a drum, and we started walking.

It was a long, unpleasant trek along the cliffs, the wind whipping water in our faces and making Teagan's mascara run. The sea below us was all foam and choppy waves. I hoped the deep-water solo Rowan had mentioned wasn't off this violent coast. I paused and slipped the camera out of my jacket, snapping some pics of the ocean.

"Where are we going?" I asked.

"To the cove," she said, as if that explained everything.

"They bury people there?"

"No, they burn them."

"Um..." I somehow doubted there was a crematorium on the beach.

"On a pyre," she added.

Right. Of course they did. I don't know why I expected anything on this island to be normal. I kept my head bowed against the drizzle and followed Teagan as we wound our way down the cliffs. Maybe if Fergus had given me *Volume I,* a lot of this would make more sense.

Our feet hit the slick pebbles of the beach. The drums stopped, and I squinted through the rain at the cliffs, involuntarily mapping crimps and pinches across the rock, before scanning the crowd on the beach. Surprisingly, Granddad was there, his umbrella fighting a losing battle against the weather as he joined the procession with Fergus's support.

Granddad saw me and paused in his hobbling until I caught up.

"Thought you weren't coming, Granddad."

"Fergus didn't give me much choice," he grumped.

"You all right?" I asked.

"Right as I can be with all this nonsense." Granddad's face wore its usual expression of unimpressed. "Ah, Martha." He stepped away from Fergus to embrace his sister.

"Ash, nice to see you again, though I'd prefer more pleasant circumstances." Martha pulled me into a hug before I could protest. Since it had been several weeks now, I'd ditched my sling, but getting crushed by old ladies was still on the list of things to avoid. She gave me a lingering look I wasn't sure how to interpret. It could've meant: "Are you a girl or a boy? You really should be one or the other." Then again, it might've just meant "What possessed you to wear neon orange to a funeral?"

"You do have the look of your father about you," she said. "But those are O'Donnell eyes." She peered intently into my face, making me feel super awkward.

"Thanks, I guess," I said, which earned me a smile.

"I'm needed up front," she said and drifted toward the—oh God, it was a body wrapped in fabric, burlap maybe, being carried by six people of varying ages. It was completely mummified, the layers of fabric thankfully hiding any gruesomeness. Left behind with Granddad and Fergus, I could only stare.

"Aye, this must all seem a wee bit strange," Fergus said with a wave toward the body.

"A bit." Understatement of the year. "Actually, I was

thinking maybe I could come by the bookshop and get an earlier volume," I said, wrenching my gaze from the corpse. "I'd like to know more about the island."

"I'll bet," he said, "and I think you're ready for it."

"Don't go filling Ash's head with nonsense now," Granddad said gruffly. Fergus made no comment but gave me a wink behind Granddad's back.

Not wanting to start an argument, I searched for the Sheehys again and spotted Rowan's sisters standing in a tight knot higher up the beach, separate from the rest of the families, marked as *other* by their red hair and the abundance of leather jewelry they all wore. I lifted my camera, wanting to capture the fire of their hair against the black cliff. The wind cooperated, sending the girls' hair billowing as I snapped a couple of frames.

Then we all pressed forward, drawing closer to some sort of scaffolding made from driftwood. The pyre. *Click.*

And then there was Rowan, standing beside the pyre in a grey sweater and black jacket. He had the hood drawn up and his gaze on the sea. I followed where he was looking, surprised to see a seal staring at the beach. *Click.*

"Etain McNamara," Teagan said, still beside me. "She's Patrick's mother, Cillian's great-grandmother. She's one of the only ones who can change these days."

I stared at the seal, trying to convince myself it was a little old lady, trying to convince myself I wasn't losing my mind starting to believe in all this magic stuff.

I turned my attention back to Rowan.

He met the men carrying the body, and I pressed closer, hoping to hear what he said as they struggled to get the corpse up the scaffolding. The wind stole his words, and after a minute or two, Rowan climbed up the pyre to leave what looked like two stripy pebbles on the dead man's face. *Click.* This was as macabre as it was fascinating. There was a sort of beauty in it, if you didn't think too hard about the cut throat and carved runes hidden by the burlap.

"What's he doing?" I asked.

"Death magic," Teagan said with a visible shudder. "He supposedly takes the souls to the Otherworld, like the Grim fucking Reaper. He gives me the creeps."

Easy to see why, given his hood looked like a cowl. He was only missing a scythe. Even so, Rowan had never made me feel uncomfortable, not like Teagan and Lucy had with their ability to seduce and paralyze someone while amping up their horniness.

That aside, if the islanders believed Rowan was some sort of Grim Reaper, no wonder they thought him capable of murder.

Behind me the drum began to play again as the rest of the McNamaras poured gasoline onto the damp timbers before lighting it. The flames struggled against the rain but burned just the same, giving off putrid, greasy smoke.

I watched, awed and repulsed. As the body burned, the drum beat a solemn rhythm and the crowd, led by Orlagh Kilduff, began a strange and eerie keening in the same odd language Rowan had used with his horse. *Click. Click. Click.*

For several long minutes, we stood in the drizzle, watching the flames lick up the scaffolding and start on the body. As the fire raged, the song faded and Martha returned to stand beside Granddad. The roar and pop of the pyre was punctuated by raised voices.

Lucy and Cillian were yelling at Rowan, their words inaudible thanks to the crackling fire and the wind. Rowan stood his ground, looking stoic as the rain dripped down his face.

"That lot," Martha said with a shake of her head.

"I see nothing's changed. Everyone still loathing the Sheehys for no discernible reason," Granddad said with obvious scorn directed at his sister.

"What did you think you'd achieve by coming back here?" she said, her eyes all but devoured by wrinkles. "Grainne made a life for herself. It does no good to go stirring things up now after all this time. These things have consequences." She gestured to Rowan. "You picked a dangerous time to return, Brian."

"Oh, I don't think anyone plans on slitting my old gizzard," Granddad said, which only earned him a scowl from Martha.

"Your presence stirs old anger."

"Seems there's plenty of that already. I hear Fergus shot a Sheehy dead?" Granddad said, his words making my whole body jerk.

"What?" I asked, shocked that bookish Fergus could be capable of violence.

"Aye," Martha said. "Shot that Rowan dead, and good riddance, too."

"That's—that's not the way," Granddad said.

"What would you know of our ways? You abandoned them."

"Why, Martha? Why?" There were tears in Granddad's eyes.

"Ash, let me be alone with the old man, will you? We've got some more catching up to do." Martha muscled her way between Granddad and me, surprisingly strong for an old lady. I let Granddad go, not sad to have his weight released from my shoulders.

"Is it true?" I asked Teagan.

"That Fergus killed old Rowan? Yeah, of course," she said without a smidgen of sympathy. "Fergus thought the Sheehy bastard killed his wife."

"Thought?"

Teagan shrugged, offering no further explanation.

Shocked and appalled and confused, I turned back to Rowan in time to see Lucy take another threatening step forward, she grabbed for his arm, and Rowan tried to

block her, his hand wrapping around her wrist. Cillian
drew back his arm, and I knew what was coming next,
but was too far away to stop it. Rowan's head snapped
back as Cillian's fist landed against his teeth.

Siobhan stepped forward and raised a single finger as
Cillian grabbed Lucy by the hand. Whatever Siobhan said
clearly had the desired effect. Lucy's shoulders sagged,
and she let Cillian lead her away as Rowan strode off
down the beach, away from his sisters. Away from me.

Teagan stiffened, her gaze locked with a girl who
looked a lot like Deirdre, except an angrier, black-clad
version. Must've been Neasa.

"He disgusts me," Lucy growled as she strode past us.

"We're heading to the wake now," Cillian said, as he
polished the lenses of his specs with his sleeve cuff—as if
he hadn't just used that same damn hand to hurt Rowan.
At least two of his knuckles were red, one starting to
bleed where it must've caught a tooth. Good. I hoped it
hurt.

"You should join us, Ash," Teagan said.

"Sorry, not feeling up to—" My whole body went rigid,
my heart paralyzed, the breath seizing in my lungs as my
gaze swept along the beach and landed on approaching
figures.

The colonel.

My mum.

They walked together across the sand, her face
scrunched in a frown.

What the actual fuck?

Had Mum known he was coming? Had she planned
this? Was this how it ended? A few weeks of freedom on
the island only to have the colonel drag us back home.
I blinked, but the image stayed the same, Mum and the
colonel drawing ever closer.

"Who's that?" Teagan asked, still standing beside me.

I wasn't breathing.

"Is that your dad?" she asked.

My heart thumped against my ribs.

Fight or flight?

I balled my hands into fists as the colonel smiled and gave me a wave.

Fight or flight?

I wanted to fight, to stand my ground, declare myself an O'Donnell and wait for the island to do whatever strange magic it could to stop my father from hurting me. All the island provided was another gust of freezing wind and a pattering of rain on my head.

Fight or flight?

They drew closer, and I still couldn't move. Teagan drifted away, leaving me alone to face the colonel. The bruises had faded from my face, the cast on my arm hidden beneath my jacket. The real damage he'd dealt me was invisible from the outside, anyway.

"Hi, Ash," he said in the growling baritone used to issuing orders and having them obeyed. "I've been looking for you." His words were a grenade detonating in my brain, the shrapnel making minced meat of my insides.

Flight.

My feet came unstuck from the sand. Blood rushed into my legs, and I started running, my heels kicking up clods of damp sand as I raced past the pyre, ignoring the blast of heat and noxious fumes in my face.

Mum shouted after me, but it only made me push harder.

I skidded my way across the pebbles, slip-sliding over rocks, not caring when barnacles cut my palms. My camera bounced painfully against my back, but I ignored it. My foot slipped, and I recovered by gripping the rocks with my left hand. The pain through my shoulder was a blade, reminding me why I was running and what waited for me back on the beach.

Fuck my father.

I ran to the beat of those three words in my head, stomping through tide pools and tripping over ropes of seaweed stranded on the beach. A small cave appeared, a hollow cut into the cliffs providing shelter from the rain if not from the wind. I ducked into the opening. Breathing hard, I rested my hands on my knees, sucking in mouthfuls of salt, from the sea and from the tears pouring down my face.

"Ash," he said my name, and I looked over my shoulder, afraid of what I might find. He was sitting hunched in his coat, bleeding from his split lip, his face streaked with rain and maybe tears, too. I exhaled in relief. For a moment I wouldn't have to pretend I was strong or unafraid.

"Guess I found you," I said.

"Aye, you did." He shifted over on the dry boulder at the back of the cave, making space for me beside him. I joined him, hoping our shoulders or knees might touch, but he kept a careful distance between us, and maybe that was easier.

For several minutes, we sat sharing tears and oxygen, and somehow, I started feeling better. A black butterfly flitted out of the rain and into the cave. It circled once above our heads before landing on Rowan's open hand. Carefully, I pulled my camera around and took the cover off the lens. *Click.*

"What are they?" I asked, my voice croaky from crying.

"Fragments of the Otherworld," he said. Speaking opened the gash in his lip. He closed his eyes and lapped away a fresh bead of blood. I knew what he must be feeling. Split lips stung like hell and the taste of blood, all sticky on your teeth, was enough to make you gag. It wasn't the injury, though, but the intention behind it that did the most damage. Knowing someone had deliberately wanted to hurt you, hurt far more than the bleeding and bruising.

What was Lucy saying? Why did Cillian punch you?

*What did you put on the body? Why do they burn the
dead? Can you do death magic? Did you kill them? Can
you please kill my father?* The questions buzzed inside
my skull.

Rowan licked his lip again, and I couldn't help but be
fascinated by the flash of pink tongue.

"At least he got you in the mouth. Split lips heal faster
than black eyes," I said.

He blew a gentle stream of air against his hand,
sending the butterfly back to flight.

"You didn't get hurt while climbing," he said.

"No." I wanted to say more, but the sudden boulder
lodged in my throat made forming words a little tricky.

"Not your mom, though," he said, turning to look at
me.

"My father." I held my breath, a fresh wave of tears
threatening to spill down my cheeks. No "I'm sorry," no
worthless, platitude like "it's not your fault"—instead...

"It hurts," he said, pressing a hand to his chest. He
closed his eyes for a moment, lashes damp again. "There's
so much pain inside. So much sadness. Joy, too, but the
sadness shouts the loudest. Sometimes it's too much to
bear. To know. To have the weight of their lives inside
me. To carry that." His voice cracked, and he stopped
talking.

"Teagan says you take the souls of the dead to
the Otherworld." Somehow, my words didn't sound
ridiculous.

"Aye, I do. I'm a rowan." His thumb pressed against
the tattoo on his wrist. "Like all the men in my family, all
the rowans that came before. I'm a deathwalker."

"What exactly does a deathwalker do?" All the hair
on the back of my neck stood up. No point pretending I
didn't believe this stuff anymore.

He took a deep breath and looked at me, a penetrating
stare, and I could practically see the gears turning in his
mind.

"Please, Rowan. I want to know. I think I need to," I said as gently as I could.

He nodded, but turned away from me, staring at the sea instead.

"When someone dies on the island," he started, "I meet them in the Otherworld. It's my job to lead them safely to the river. They have to cross the river to pass beyond the veil, to find eternal rest."

"And those are the lives you were talking about?" I pressed. "The joys and sorrows?"

"I experience every death," Rowan said. "I mean, I feel it. I feel what they felt. And then, when I meet the soul in the Otherworld, I experience their lives as they shed their memories on the way to the river. Some of those memories linger, like—like ghosts inside my mind. Like echoes." He pressed two fingers to his temple and winced.

I didn't know what to say to that. My issues seemed so damn trivial by comparison.

"You felt the deaths of the murder victims?"

"Aye, I did," he said quietly, fingers drifting to his throat.

"Wait, you mean you *literally* felt it? Like—"

"As if it were my own throat."

I sucked in a breath. Fucking hell. I tried and failed to imagine what that must be like, to live other people's deaths and then walk through their memories. I couldn't. It was beyond the ability of my imagination. The way it should be, because that was some seriously messed-up shit. Living one life was hard enough without having to carry around other people's baggage. I wanted to hold him, to comfort him—as if a hug could combat any of the stuff he'd been through, but what else did I have to offer?

"How come it's you?" I asked. "Why not one of your sisters?"

"Only the men are rowans. Sheehy women have the true power, we're just—tools," he said with bitterness.

More sexist BS. "So, if you're born a boy, you're a deathwalker? What if you were assigned male at birth, but aren't a boy? Or what if you're assigned female at birth, but aren't a girl? Do you get to keep the magic?"

Rowan turned to look at me, a frown gathering between his eyebrows. "I don't know. I'm not sure it's ever come up. I don't know how that would work."

"Just feels stupid to have this be based on something as fluid as gender."

Rowan smiled, his eyes igniting as he looked at me. Even the one rimmed in darkness seemed brighter. "You're right, but that can be said about a lot that happens on this island."

"Maybe it's time things changed."

"I think they are changing." His smile faded, and the split in his lip wasn't there anymore. Damn, the guy healed fast.

"You mean the murders?"

He nodded. "Now you know why everyone thinks I did it. But I didn't. I was with you when Andy was killed."

"The day at Ros Tearmann?" Understanding dawned on me. "When you were on the floor, that was you—dying?"

"It was Andy dying. I was called to the Otherworld. When I go, I leave my body behind."

"That must get awkward. Or dangerous. What if you're riding or swimming or something when someone dies?"

"Then I fall off my horse or have to trust someone else will keep me from drowning." Rowan tilted his face up to the sky. It had stopped raining, leaving behind a haze just as likely to make you soggy. The mist made the sea a smudge of greys and blues, the water lapping at the mouth of the cave. I took a couple of photos before replacing the lens cap and slinging the camera over my shoulder.

"The tide is coming in," Rowan said. "We should head back."

"The colonel is here," I said, my fingers digging into the damp rock beneath me. "My father, I mean. I saw him on the beach. I can't go back. I just can't. My mum promised she'd leave him this time. She said we'd be safe here." The words rushed out of me. "I wanted to feel safe. And I did, until—"

Rowan's fingers hovered near mine as if he wanted to take my hand. I wished he would, wanting so badly for him to tell me it would be okay. Maybe a hug couldn't fix things, but damn it wouldn't hurt right now to feel his arms around me.

"Can you help?" I asked. "I mean, you're a deathwalker. Your sisters have magic, right? There must be something you can do."

"Ash— I—"

"I found out more about the murders. Please, Rowan. I'll help you if you help me."

"I'll gladly help you, I'm just not sure how to," he said.

"I don't want to live if living means being with my father." The words erupted from the darkest pit inside me and left my tongue bleeding. I wished I could suck them back between my teeth. It was a secret I should've left buried, but I'd said it now, and the truth of it burned in the air around me.

Rowan leaned his shoulder into mine, and the stew of pain-fear-confusion inside me switched from a wild boil to a light simmer.

"It won't come to that," he said. "We'll find a way."

"How?" I whispered.

"I don't know yet, but I don't think magic is your answer. And if it is, I'll help you any way I can," he added softly.

We sat together, his shoulder touching mine, anchoring me to the rock for a few more minutes before he broke the silence.

"We really should go, but you don't have to head home

if you don't want to. I know a place where we won't risk drowning."

"Okay," I said and forced myself to my feet, not wanting things to be awkward between us after my unexpected confession. I offered him my hand, and he reached for it, hesitating a moment before our fingers touched.

"I'm not sure I should touch you," he said.

"Because of your arm? Teagan said you were infected by magic."

Rowan frowned a *how did she know that?* look before his forehead smoothed again. "I guess Neasa tells her everything."

"You know about that?"

"Unfortunately," he said. "And yes, I'm infected with something from the Otherworld. I'm not sure, but best not to risk—contamination."

I let my hand drop, my heart plummeting through my chest to land squelching between my feet. Guess that hug wouldn't be coming any time soon.

He started walking, and I followed. We weren't done talking about any of this, not by a long shot, but it was raining again, and I was sick of the sky pissing on me. I wanted to continue our conversation somewhere warm and dry—and far away from my parents.

"What was Lucy saying to you?" I asked as we retraced our steps across the rocks.

"She's always disliked me," Rowan said. "She's angry about things neither of us have any control over, and she's angry about Andy dying, about the way things are on the island. For some reason, she's decided to blame me for all that. I didn't mean to touch her, I just—no one wants me to touch them," he added. "Hence Cillian's reaction."

God, I wouldn't mind you touching me. I managed not to say that out loud, though.

"Besides, his grandda just died. If punching me helps

him feel better..." Rowan shrugged and licked at his lip.

His words settled into me like lead. The colonel was angry. It seemed to be his default state of being. I didn't want Rowan to be right. I didn't want my father to feel better after hurting me and my mum, but it was probably true.

"I heard my cousin Fergus killed your uncle."

"Aye, he did." He sighed.

"Teagan said your uncle—" I swallowed, not able to say the words.

"Fergus's wife killed herself. After losing someone like that... It makes sense he'd blame my uncle," Rowan said. "Still, it was murder, and everyone knew it, but charges were never filed. Fergus got away with it because no one cares if there's one less Sheehy on this rock, least of all the coppers." He paused and took a breath. "That's the department your mom is a part of now," he continued. "And they'll pin these murders on me unless I can prove someone else did it."

"I spoke to Teagan, asked if she'd heard anything," I admitted as we stalked across the almost empty beach. The pyre was still going, despite the rain. A couple of Kilduffs, or maybe they were O'Donnells, were still on the beach watching the flames. I wondered how long it would take until there was nothing left but cinders.

I checked left and right in case the colonel suddenly appeared. We were alone except for the hunched figures on pyre-duty, noisy seagulls, and the black butterflies circling above us.

"And? Did Teagan share anything useful?" Rowan asked as we started the trek up the cliff path.

"The shoe print was a women's size six. A trainer with a worn sole." I shrugged, knowing it wasn't much. "Apparently they also found wormwood and rue at the crime scenes."

Rowan stopped midstep, right hand clamped on his

left elbow. His eyes were glazed, his breathing quick and shallow.

"What is it? Is someone dying?" I asked, forgetting not to touch him as I placed my right hand on his shoulder.

"No," he said, eyes clearing. "I was just remembering something about wormwood and rue."

"They mean something to you?"

"Maybe," he said, striking out across the cliffs and into the fields with long legs I could only envy.

"No Auryn today?" I asked, not sure which would've been worse: riding or walking.

"Davidson came to get them. She's gone."

"I'm sorry, Rowan," I said, when what I really wanted to do was wrap my arms around him.

"It is what it is," he said and stomped into the field. His rubber boots would have no problem navigating the quagmire. My poor Doc Martens weren't going to survive this abuse much longer, but considering my options were to follow Rowan through a muddy field or go home to the colonel, my boots would just have to accept their fate.

Rowan

BY THE time we arrived at my grandmother's cottage, the fog had drawn its skirts closed over the island, smothering Inisliath in a comforting embrace.

"Looks like ours," Ash said. "Although, you know, not shit." They swung their camera to their eye and took a photo. "This okay?" they asked, and I nodded.

Gran's cottage had known a lifetime of love and care. The outer walls were spotless and decorated with gifts from the ocean. Rustic chandeliers made by Neasa hung from the eaves. The polished sea-glass baubles usually cast rainbows across the white-washed walls in the morning sun but hung dimly now. Driftwood chimes made by Deirdre clinked their music in the breeze, and neatly tended beds—kept so by me—brimmed with flowers and herbs in the surrounding garden.

"I'm a bit nervous," Ash said. "Family history and all. Are you sure I'll be welcome?"

"If my gran bears a grudge, it's toward your grandfather. Not you," I said, and pressed the button at the door, which made the lights flicker inside.

Gran answered a few moments later.

"Hi, Gran," I signed while speaking out loud for Ash.

Without hesitation, she pulled me into a hug. I tried to fend her off, but despite her slight stature and kindling arms, her grip was a vice.

"Gran, this is Ash." I spelled their name for her and added that Ash used 'they'.

"Ash." She signed back by drawing the rune in the air. "Brian O'Donnell's grandchild?"

I nodded, and Gran offered Ash her liver-spotted hands. Warily, Ash accepted, receiving a welcome squeeze from my grandmother. I gave Ash a nod, and they seemed to relax a little.

"You have your grandda's eyes," Gran signed, and I spoke her words out loud. "Islander eyes."

"So I've been told," Ash said with a smile.

I wish it was in my power to give them a reason to smile more often, to rinse the fear and pain from their life. But that was a service I could only render when they died, if they did so on the island.

Gran beckoned us into the warmth of the cottage. We left our boots and soaking jackets in the mudroom. Ash shivered in their thin sweater, wet patches on shoulders and sleeves where the rain had found a way in. My own clothes were wet, too, but I was used to it and welcomed the chill.

"You're soaked, both of you. You know where to find your uncle's clothes. Get dry, I'll make tea," Gran signed in a flurry and turned her back to me when I started to argue.

"What was that about?" Ash asked.

"My gran being stubborn. Want a dry shirt?" I asked, and Ash nodded.

The home was small, just two cramped bedrooms off the living room, which flowed into the kitchen. I led the way into the room, which had once been my uncle's. My gran had kept his bedroom as a space for visiting grandchildren, complete with a closet full of his clothes, clothes that now fit me uncomfortably well.

"The bathroom is across the living room," I said, handing Ash a towel. "Choose whatever you want." I gestured to the wardrobe.

"Whose were these?" they asked as they selected a dark, woolen shirt.

"My uncle's. The one Fergus shot."

Ash gave me an apologetic look before traipsing out of the room, leaving me to rifle through my uncle's things, the memories of his life playing behind my eyes.

His childhood growing up at Ros Tearmann, his first death when his mother and sisters held him down on the cliffs—his experience a mirror of my own, our fear tangling together in my memory, the shared sensation of the blade cleaving our chests and plunging into our hearts.

I took slow, steady breaths, extricating myself from the past and reasserting myself in the now, my fingers knotted in a home-knitted sweater. I peeled the damp shirt from my body, my left arm and shoulder aching when I stretched the skin.

"Holy shit fuck," Ash said from the doorway. I hadn't heard them return and now they stood toweling their hair, staring at my naked back. "Is that new ink? No, wait, is it *moving*?"

"You saw my arm before. Seems to be spreading now."

Ash stepped closer, and it took every ounce of willpower not to back away as they approached me. I didn't want to hurt them, I didn't want them to become tainted by whatever darkness slithered through my skin, and yet, how I longed for the feel of their hand on my shoulder again, for a touch from someone other than my family.

Ash raised their hand, fingers outstretched, and traced the snaking line of black running from my biceps over my collarbone and down my back, a hairsbreadth from my skin. I could feel the warmth radiating from their fingertip.

"It looks like it's part of the tree. Which one is this?" Ash asked.

"The one at the top is Oak, the one to the right is Ash. Hawthorn on the left and Rowan at the bottom."

"Ash." Their hand stopped above the tree to the right of my spine. All the fine hairs on my body rose, an electric sensation as their hand grew closer, closer, until it rested against my ribs, skin to skin, the contact making me shudder.

"Is this okay?" they asked as they pressed their palm over the tree that was their namesake. The heat of their touch soaked through me, igniting a hunger I'd never felt before.

I wanted to say yes, but I could scarcely breathe, let alone form words. I should've said no, that the risk was too great. I should've pulled away. Instead, I leaned into their touch and closed my eyes. A moment of contact couldn't hurt, surely a moment I could have.

"Why the trees? Why all the ink and scars?" Ash asked, their fingers a feather's kiss against my spine where my family's spells had formed a convoluted knot between my shoulders, hemmed in at the four compass points by Iona's inking of the sacred trees.

I forced air into my lungs, then licked my lips and tried to speak—cleared my throat—and tried again. "I'm a doorway to the Otherworld," I heard myself say, although I couldn't focus on anything except the touch of Ash's fingers as they traced the curling keloid. "It's a lot of power to contain. The scars are spells. They stop me from hurting others."

"Hurting others?"

I sifted through my mind for the right words. I didn't want Ash to hate me, to fear me, and yet that seemed inevitable. There were no words to describe what I was, and allow a person to love me.

"The spells bind my power, making it easier for me to be in the realm of the living and to be around those closer to death."

"Like old people at Ros Tearmann?" Ash asked.

"Weaker souls can be vulnerable to my touch. Not just the elderly, but yes. If I'm around someone who's close to death, I can cause them to pass over before their time. It's also a way to keep me tethered to this world, for my family to reel me back if I get overwhelmed in the Otherworld."

"Does that happen often?"

"The forces there don't always like me leaving," I said. It was an oversimplification, but all my brain could manage considering Ash's touch was incinerating my ability to think.

"Can I see more?" they asked, sounding intrigued instead of revolted.

I turned around to show Ash the spells whorled into my shoulders and seared into my chest. They brushed their index finger across the rings tattooed in bands below my right elbow. I had a matching set on my left arm and the same on both legs.

"Is that what these are for as well?" Their fingers traced the neatly carved scars across my forearms.

"All part of spells and rituals."

"And you were born with this deathwalker ability?"

"No, I was made," I said.

"Made?" Their voice caught in their throat, their hand falling away. I missed their touch already.

"To become a deathwalker, you have to die," I said. "Before I could lead anyone to the river, I had to make that journey myself."

"Did you choose it?" they asked.

"I—I was born to do it. It was my fate, my reason for being."

Ash was quiet for a while, their gaze burning a trail across my chest until it came to rest on the scar above my heart.

"How did you die?" they asked.

I didn't want to answer, preferring Ash continue to see me as a *who* and not a *what*. I tugged my uncle's favorite sweater over my head, thereby hiding the marks from Ash's eyes. Still, they stared.

"Sorry, that's super personal. You don't have to tell me." Ash cleared their throat and finished drying their hair, turning to hang the towel on the back of the door. I watched, studying their neck where skin gave way to the shaved stubble of their undercut, the curve of their jaw, the single silver ring piercing the tragus of their right ear, the dry shirt pulled taught over their back and shoulders where muscle strained the fabric.

"So, you died, but you're still alive, right?" Ash turned back to face me. "I mean, you're not like a zombie or something."

"I'm a vegetarian. No eating brains, I promise," I said, my lips tugging into a smile. Impossibly, Ash made me feel less like a monster even when comparing me to creatures out of horror movies.

"Good to know." They stepped toward me again, and I stopped breathing, every part of me vibrating in anticipation of the unknown.

"I'm sorry it hurts you," they said. "It doesn't seem fair, what you have to go through. That you didn't have a choice, and now you're stuck living other peoples' lives, their deaths like that. That's really fucked up."

And how. My family had robbed me of choice, of freedom, of a life of my own. The thought rose unbidden from my corrupted depths. The dark presence rippled beneath my skin.

I bleed, I hurt, I ache. Every death an agony. Every memory—they shred me from the inside out. They burn. Gods, do they burn. But I couldn't say those words, not to Ash, not ever. I couldn't say out loud what I had been taught to keep interred within no matter how the darkness twisted inside me, unlocking memories I'd worked so hard to keep buried.

My family had warned me my first deathwalk would be painful. I'd spent hours with my uncle as a child, learning all I could from him about my destiny. But he'd died too soon, before I could fully grasp what my life—and death—would entail.

It was Deirdre, only nine years old, who'd stayed with me that first night, her tiny body curled around mine when I came back to the realm of the living, sobbing and sweating and wishing I'd cross the river and never return. Mother had said it would get easier. Siobhan had said I'd have to get used to it. Iona had wept quietly as she wrapped me in a sage-soaked blanket. Neasa had made me tea and told me I'd get stronger. They'd all left me, except Deirdre.

But we'd both grown up, and now she rarely shared tears with me. I had grown stronger, I had become more accustomed to it, but Mother was wrong—it never got easier. I just became better at hiding how much it hurt, and how much I resented it.

My thoughts turned darker still, my mind unleashing the floodgates on the harbored memories, my own and others. My family had done this to me, imprisoned me in a life from which the only release was to die and be entombed within a tree.

I hated them for what they'd done.

I hated them for what they'd made me.

I hated—

"Rowan?" Ash waved their hand in front of my face.

"It burns." Those weren't the words I'd meant to say, but it was true. I was burning, and not from a recent deathwalk or residual memories. My arm.

The pain seared, my vision blurring. I tore at the sweater, gnarled fingers snagged at my flesh, hooks through muscle, ripping fire through my nerves, sending ribbons like roots shooting down the backs of my legs.

"Oh my God," Ash said, their breath on my shoulder, their face above mine. I must've fallen. I was on the floor, being dragged into the ground, the roots from my skin twining ever downwards.

My ink split, the rowan on my back coming alive as branches twisted from my body. The wounds were suppurating, oozing viscous black to stain my clothes. And I was being hauled into the Otherworld, Ash's face receding into shadow.

"Dude, what's happening? Please Rowan, shit, tell me what to do?" Ash asked, eyes wide and hands shaking even as they tried to lift me from the floor.

"Gran," I managed to say through clenched teeth, my jaw locking shut while pain tore through my body like a hurricane.

The mist of the Otherworld descended, enveloping me in ropey tendrils, fingers plucking at the threads of my being, pulling me apart. I burned hotter, fire smoldering beneath my skin. I knotted my hands into the fibers of the sweater, wanting to tear it off, to tear away my skin and muscle, to dig into my bones and excise the maggot-magic burrowing within me.

Or I could let go. Let the darkness have me.

Perhaps then I'd be free.

Cool fingers twined around my own. I peeled open my eyes to see Gran's concerned face as she dug her nails into my cheeks, forcing open my jaw. She placed something bitter on my tongue before tipping water into my mouth. I swallowed, desperate for the cold, desperate for the light.

She signed sigils in the air above me and on my skin,

her fingers chill against my clammy skin, drawing magic on my forehead, my cheeks, my chest.

Cold permeated my cells and, gradually, the room came back into focus.

Ash had been holding my hand and now helped me up off the floor and onto the edge of the bed.

Gran smoothed hair off my face and marked more spells against my forehead, the kiss of magic sinking into my skin.

"What happened?" she signed. "What is this?" she pointed to my arm and, sluggish though my gestures were, I signed the story for her, too exhausted to say it out loud as well. Ash watched from the doorway, fear stitched into the corners of their eyes and mouth.

Wormwood and rue, I spelled the names of the herbs for her and she recoiled as if I'd slapped her. "Do you know the ritual? Do you know what they're doing? I keep trying to remember, but I can't—I can't." I let my hands drop into my lap, the last dregs of energy draining from my limbs.

For a while, Gran remained still, contemplative, her fingers tapping her knee.

"Please," I signed. "If you know anything that could help. Is there anything in our Grimoire?"

"I don't think so," Gran signed.

"Can we check?" I asked.

She looked at me, eyes clear and bright, piercing as they held my gaze. "You're changing." She pointed to my face. I'd seen myself in a mirror, I wasn't oblivious to the darkness encroaching on my eye. "There are things in our book you shouldn't see," she signed. "Not while you're like this."

"All the more reason to try and stop it," I said. "Please, Gran. If there's something in the Grimoire about this, we have to try. I don't want to be like this," I signed the last part without speaking out loud for Ash.

Gran's expression softened into one of pity as she rested her hand on my shoulder for a moment and gave it a squeeze. "Stay here. I'll be back soon." Gran beckoned Ash over and patted the bed. Ash acquiesced, sitting beside me, their face still knotted with concern.

"You okay?" Ash asked.

"Not yet, but I hope I will be." Resting my elbows on my knees, I let my head hang forward, and pressed the heels of my hands against my eyes. "I'm sorry you saw that."

"I'm just glad I was here to help," they said. "I think you'll need to change again." Ash nodded at the sweater. Hand-shaped holes had been scorched into the wool, the garment destroyed.

"I thought you said you didn't have any magic," Ash said.

"I don't. Not normally. Not the useful kind, anyway. Did I do this?"

"Dude, your hands were burning, like flames and everything. I thought you were going to set this whole place on fire."

"It's not my doing, it's this power from the Otherworld." My skin was coated in icy perspiration. A moment ago, I'd been on fire, yet now I shivered and cradled my throbbing arm.

"And it's connected to the murders?" Ash asked.

"I think the murders are part of a spell, a spell to unleash whatever this is in the Otherworld. I don't know why, or who would do it. Wormwood and rue are powerful herbs. It's not the sort of magic one does for fun. And it's not the sort just anyone is even capable of."

"Could it be an outsider?" Ash asked.

"I'm certain it's not, which leaves me with a very short list of suspects." A list comprising my siblings' names. No, not Deirdre. She was too gentle, too good, too kind. Siobhan was calculating, meticulous—perhaps given

enough cause she might consider such a spell. Iona—
unlikely—and had she been the one to carve runes into
the bodies, they would've been works of art, not jagged
and unsteady. Neasa was angry and hateful, her judgment
clouded by her proximity to the Kilduff. With Teagan's
help, perhaps she would be capable of executing such a
diabolical ritual. And then there was Mother, who had
more than enough power and expertise to carry out such
a spell, and perhaps motive, too, about to lose everything
she'd worked her whole life to preserve. Mother wore a
size six, though I'd never seen her in trainers.

"You think it could be your family, don't you?"
Ash rested their shoulder against mine. My shivering
subsided, the warmth seeping through my skin from Ash
as strange as it was comforting.

"I do," I admitted.

With a delicate fingertip, Ash traced the rowan rune
on my wrist now bereft of the bracelet Deirdre had made
for me when I turned thirteen. I didn't remember losing
it.

"You really shouldn't touch me, especially not now,"
I said, though I had neither the energy nor the will to
move away from them.

"Because you think touching you could kill me?"

"I'd rather we didn't test the theory."

"I'm still alive," Ash said as they threaded their fingers
through mine, holding fast. They looked up at me with
eyes like small moons framed by long lashes. It was safer
for them to hate me. It would be easier for both of us if
they were disgusted by me and recoiled from my touch,
but I didn't move as Ash inched closer. They smoothed a
curl off my temple, their fingers lingering on my cheek,
their breath on my neck.

I turned toward them, about to list all the reasons
this was wrong and impossible—instead our lips
pressed together. I closed my eyes, melting, dissolving,

disappearing into Ash's kiss as their mouth opened against mine. My heart thundered behind my ribs, the blood a symphony in my ears.

Ash was gentle, their fingers cupping the back of my head, and I did the same, hoping I was doing it right. A dozen memories fluttered in my mind, memories of kisses gleaned from the dead. But this kiss was mine, a memory of my own to be treasured and kept safe from the ghosts clouding my consciousness.

A sharp rap of knuckles against the door frame snapped us apart. Gran strode into the bedroom, hefting our family Grimoire. Instead of admonishment, she signed an apology and shooed Ash over so she could settle her brittle bones between us. I glanced at Ash, who glanced at me, a smile on their lips and cheeks as flushed as my own.

Gran hesitated and signed, "Are you sure?"

I nodded and she handed me my glasses, which she must've retrieved from my coat pocket, before she opened the book to one of the oldest spells at the back. It was written in the old tongue on cracked, stained vellum, a part of it missing, the vellum torn and the rest of it stained. I started reading what was left on the page.

"What does it say?" Ash leaned in closer, and I shoved my glasses up my nose, fingers catching on the duct-tape over the hinge.

"It's a description of a very old ritual." I signed the words as well.

"Ancient," Gran corrected me. "One of the first in the Sheehy collection."

"Is it the right one?" Ash asked.

"Seems this spell is a binding, used to contain a person or power. Think of it like wrapping something up in magical chains," I said.

"Chains that can be broken?" Ash asked, looking nervous.

"So it seems." Although why anyone would want to

undo a binding on a dark Otherworld power remained uncertain.

"Who could do this?" I asked my gran, and she responded with silence, her eyes devoured by wrinkles as she frowned. "Mother?" I signed without speaking my suspicion out loud. "Siobhan?" I signed when Gran didn't answer. "Could someone other than a Sheehy work this spell?" I felt Ash's gaze on me but continued to sign without speaking.

Gran finally answered, "A Kilduff might channel enough power, but they'd need O'Donnell's help with the spell."

"Is this the only copy of it?" I asked.

Gran shrugged a bird-wing shoulder. "Back then, we shared more with the others. The O'Donnells might have a copy."

"A complete one?"

"Impossible to say," Gran signed.

Two people had been responsible for ending Patrick's life. A Kilduff and an O'Donnell—of course. It seemed so obvious, so perfect for them to be the perpetrators and pin it all on my family.

"What are these?" I drew Gran's attention back to the book by pointing at a pair of odd symbols I'd never seen before.

"Wormwood and rue," she signed, and I spoke the words out loud.

"Wormwood, rue, and—" I paused.

"And?" Ash asked.

"Blood," I said, scanning the page again to be sure I'd understood correctly. "The ritual requires the blood of the four founding families."

"But that means an O'Donnell and a Sheehy, too," Ash said and the momentary joy, the momentary spark of hope I'd felt with their lips against mine, their fingers wrapped in my own—it all turned to cinders, crushed beneath the heel of fate.

"Are you in danger?" I asked Gran.

She shook her head.

"How can you be sure?" I asked, and she didn't answer. She didn't have to. Realization dawned slowly, the answer I'd been avoiding now staring me in the face.

"They only kill men," I signed, and tears brimmed in her eyes as she wrapped her gnarled fingers around my wrist, covering the rowan rune.

"What are you saying?" Ash asked, but I shook my head.

"Is there a way to stop it, to undo what's already been done?" I asked Gran.

"I don't know," Gran signed. "I'll try to find out. I have other old books. I'll try to find something to help."

"We have to stop this," I signed, and spoke out loud for Ash, too. "Whatever it takes, we have to stop them unleashing this thing on the world."

Gran removed her hand from my wrist and worried a loose thread from a seam on her dress.

"How long do you think I have?" I asked.

She shook her head, tears trickling over her wizened cheeks. Either she didn't know or didn't want to say.

"Gran, I won't let them do this," I signed to her, my movements sharp and deliberate, showing her my determination. "I'll do whatever it takes to stop this from happening. No more Sheehys will die. That I promise."

She responded by cupping my cheek with her hand and kissing my forehead.

"What, what is it?" Ash asked, their face pale.

Ash didn't need to know. They carried enough hurt as it was. This much I could protect them from. My death would be the last required to seal the ritual, and really, it had already begun—the slow turning of the blood, the binding of the flesh to the Otherworld providing a living tether for the power in the darkness.

That power, partially freed, surged through my veins. Were it not for Ash and the way they were looking at me, the feel of their lips on mine—I might've been relieved knowing my end approached, but now—now I didn't want to die.

Still, if a Sheehy were to be murdered, I could only hope it was me. I would never wish a death like Andy's or Patrick's on another member of my family. It was anathema to even contemplate. If a silver blade were to slit a Sheehy throat, were a Sheehy to be shoved from cliffs and crack open their skull, then I prayed it would be me. But I wasn't going to let that happen. This time the O'Donnells and Kilduffs weren't going to get away with murder.

Ash

ROWAN'S GRAN sat us in the kitchen and plied us with tea, asking me about my granddad, about my life in the city, about everything except ancient blood rituals. Rowan seemed only too happy to translate, although I figured out his gran could read lips, provided I faced her and spoke slowly.

It was hard to imagine this old lady as a teenager in love with my granddad. Even harder to imagine my buckled, half-blind granddad as "handsome" and "strapping" and a "wooer of island girls." Not sure I wanted to imagine that last part at all. She smiled when she talked about him, but I could tell it hurt her from the way her eyes got all misty.

It was odd learning personal things about my granddad's life here from a complete stranger, but I was happy to learn what no one had ever bothered to share with me before. To be honest, I'd never really asked. I would've been even happier to learn about my family history if I knew it wasn't all some ploy to distract me from the murders we should've been talking about. They were keeping something from me, I just wish I knew what.

After three cups of tea, I'd had my full, and it was time to go. I didn't want to leave the cozy little cottage, but I couldn't stay forever. Sooner or later, I'd have to face my own family.

"Lovely to meet you," his gran signed at the door. She signed something else, but Rowan didn't translate.

"Thank you," he said, waving his fingers away from his chin. I copied the gesture and his gran beamed before pulling me into a hug. Her arms were skinny twigs, but they nearly crushed the breath out of me.

"She's pretty awesome," I said when she'd closed the door, leaving us in the murky twilight outside. At least it had stopped raining.

"She is," he said, carefully folding his specs and tucking them into the inside pocket of his jacket. "Where do you want to go now?"

"If I had a choice? As far away as possible."

"You do have a choice."

"Yeah right, I barely have money for a ferry ticket."

"But you can still leave. Perhaps you should, before—" Rowan bit his lip. I couldn't take my eyes off him, my mind still reeling from the weirdness of discovering he was a deathwalker. I had barely begun to parse the reality of the supernatural on this island and then I'd kissed him. I wasn't even sure why.

Liar, I knew exactly why... Because he'd looked so vulnerable, so broken, so in need of something. Maybe the same something I needed, too. Kissing him had seemed like the only way I could tell him he wasn't alone—that neither of us were because we had each other, even though I had no idea what that meant. Words were hard when kisses were somehow easier.

"Before what?" I asked. "Before the ritual is complete?

What does the spell even do?"

"Hard to say for sure. It's written in a language we've mostly forgotten. But it's a binding of some kind."

"Binding what?" A frisson of fear rattled my bones.

"A powerful entity in the Otherworld, I think."

"They need the blood of an O'Donnell and Sheehy to complete it, right?"

"Yes," Rowan said without looking at me.

"Then we have time to stop them, don't we?" I said with a fuckton more bravado than I felt. I wanted to be strong for Rowan. He was already carrying so much.

"We?" He gave me a quizzical look.

"I'm a quarter O'Donnell, right? That has to count for something. You're not in this alone." I offered him my hand, and he regarded it skeptically. "Oh, come on, we've swapped spit. If that didn't get me your Otherworld lurgies, then holding hands certainly won't."

With a smile, Rowan took my left hand in his right, and I clamped my fingers tight, hoping he understood what I was trying to say without making me choke out the words. I needed his hand in mine, needed to feel not alone while I was swimming through my own shit, too.

"Is it okay I kissed you?" I asked, hoping he'd say yes. Hoping he'd answer by pulling me close and pressing his lips to mine.

"I think so," he said.

"No, I didn't mean because of that." I pointed at his injured arm. "I meant... I just want to be sure it was what you wanted." My cheeks were getting warm as I studied our interlaced fingers instead of looking at his face.

"I've never kissed anybody before," he said.

What? Thankfully I managed to bite my tongue.

"Don't think I've ever even wanted to," he added.

"Really? Not a single hot tourist catch your eye?" I guess islanders were out of the question, given how they felt about the Sheehys.

"Never," he said, his grip tightening a little on my hand. "Honestly, I've never really wanted to get closer to someone, close enough to think about kissing them. But I wanted to kiss you."

My heart may have exploded a little, dousing my whole body in a confetti shower of the warm-fuzzies. "Are you demi?" I asked, and Rowan frowned.

"Demi?" he asked, which kind of answered the question.

"It's in the ace spectrum. A person who doesn't really experience um—" My face was burning again. "Sexual attraction to someone until they get to know the person." *Just stop fucking talking already, dammit.* "Or maybe grey ace, someone who doesn't always experience sexual attraction, but can. Sometimes. Depending." *Stop. Just stop.* "It's different for everyone. Lots of different labels." Finally, my mouth got the memo and stopped moving. Nerves always made me spew words.

"Oh. Okay." Rowan cleared his throat, a blush spreading beneath the freckles scattered across his cheeks. At least we matched.

"Look, I'm sorry. That's personal. You really don't have to tell me." I clung to his hand, hoping he wouldn't let go even if I'd stomped my boot into it.

"I would if I knew," he said quietly. "I've just never needed to think about any of this."

"Until me?" Dear God, I'd said that out loud.

"Until you," he said.

I risked glancing at him and caught him smiling. There were a dozen things I could've said, wanted to say, buzzing through my brain, but all of them were based on the presumption he'd want to kiss me again.

"I think I should get back before Mum launches a search party," I said instead, my voice all quavery with jumbled emotion making kebab meat of my insides.

"I can walk you home, if that's where you need to go."

232

He squeezed my hand.

"Thank you." We walked, hand in hand, in pleasant silence for a while before he spoke again.

"How long has it been going on?" Rowan tapped my cast with his thumb.

I'd never told anyone before. For the past six years, I'd kept it a secret, a secret burning me up inside. It would be good to finally release it, to finally admit what I'd been forced to hide and lie about and pretend didn't matter.

"I was eleven the first time he hit me," I said, cold sweat dripping down my spine. "It wasn't so bad at first. The odd slap, squeezing my arms hard enough to leave bruises, but nothing more than that." I paused and sipped at the air, breathing through my mouth. "I was fourteen the first time he punched me. It's been getting worse ever since. And then this." I raised my broken arm.

"But your mom is a cop." Rowan didn't need to say more. I knew exactly what he was thinking because it was same thing I'd been thinking for years. How the hell did a cop put up with it? How the hell did a cop watch her husband beat the crap out of her kid and do nothing? Questions I wish I had the answers to.

"He hits her as well," I said. "Never broke her arm—far as I know—but it got pretty bad."

"Why did he hit you?" Rowan asked.

"Because I was a disappointment. Because I was a lazy smartass. Because I didn't know how good I had it. Because he wished he could knock some sense into me. The list goes on."

"So it was never about who you are?"

It took me a moment, but I realized what he was asking.

"No, never that. Actually, I think my father rather likes having a queer kid. Like he earns brownie points on the 'progressive parenting scale' for never misgendering me." I paused and sucked in a breath. "Maybe I should be more grateful I'm not a statistic, you know. That I'm not another LGBT kid kicked to the curb by asshole parents who can't handle a little rainbow in their black-and-white lives."

"You don't owe him anything," Rowan said, emphatic.

Maybe not, but it sure would've been easier to hate him if he was a total asshole and not supportive of me in any way.

"You ever get hit by your parents?" I asked.

"Nothing more than a slap," he said, "but I don't think it's whether they use a palm or a fist that matters."

Shit. He was going to make me cry. Again. I clung onto his hand, and he let me without flinching, even though I knew my nails must be leaving marks in his skin. Not wanting to add to his collection of scars, I eased up my grip but stayed pressed close to his side.

The mist damped down my hair and any hope I had of a happy life away from the colonel. He wouldn't let us go. Of course he wouldn't. We'd been stupid to think coming here would be some kind of escape. My stomach ached, all of me wound tight and tense, ready to snap. This was how it always felt after a "row" with my father. That's what the colonel called it because, I don't know, I guess having a "row" with your wife or kid sounded better than "punch up."

I concentrated on my breathing and focused on the feel of Rowan's fingers in mine, the heat soaking through his shoulder and into mine. Slowly, my pulse dropped, and the threat of tears stopped prickling behind my eyes.

We took a winding route along the cliffs, the wind blasting us with relentless gusts off the sea, barely visible thanks to the blanket of fog. Abruptly, Rowan stopped, his hand in my mine tugging me to an unexpected halt.

"This is it," he said. "This is where I was made." He scuffed a toe through the loose rocks. "My mother and sisters—they brought me here the day I turned thirteen.

234

They held me down—" He paused, staring out into the mist as he released a low whistle of air, his gaze somewhere far out over the ocean. "My sisters held me down and my mother put her knife through my heart." He pressed his left hand to his chest. I'd seen the scar there, and I thought my mum was awful.

"They held me down until my heart stopped, and I passed into the Otherworld. Then they brought me back. That's how I became a deathwalker." He sounded detached, as if it had happened to someone else. Is that how I sounded talking about my father?

"There was no light at the end of that tunnel, Ash, only shadow. And vanilla. Gods." He turned away from me and squeezed his eyes shut. "My mother's vanilla scented hand-cream." His nose wrinkled. "Every time I smell it, I relive that night. I was so scared, I was—" His voice broke.

I didn't know what to say. Words were hard, but kisses... "Can I kiss you?" I asked, because I needed to be sure he wanted it—wanted me.

He tugged me toward his chest and closed my mouth with his. He tasted of salt and the honey he'd had in his tea. I closed my eyes, wrapping my broken arm around his waist, pulling him even closer until our bodies fit together—hips and chests—all warmth and want. I wanted his hands on me, but he kept the left one away, his right cupping the back of my head inside my hood as his tongue flicked against my teeth.

With a tremor like an earthquake running through his body and passing into mine, he tore his lips away and took a step back, creating a sudden gulf between us.

"We shouldn't," he said with a shaky exhalation.

"I'm not scared," I said. "Whatever it is that's infecting you, I'm not afraid of it."

"I am." He held my gaze with his mismatched eyes. Maybe it was a trick of the darkening evening, but

I could've sworn the black band around his left iris was thicker than before. "Whatever protection your O'Donnell blood gives you, I'm not sure it's enough. I don't want to risk it."

Protection? My mind hurtled back to the time Lucy had tried her mind-tricks on me and what she'd said about O'Donnells not being that weak after all. "Are O'Donnells immune to magic?" I asked.

"Not at all, but O'Donnells aren't always as affected by certain kinds of magic as others. That doesn't mean you're safe with me."

"With you, I think I'm the safest I've ever been," I said.

Rowan took my hand again, his right gently gripping my left, his cold fingers curling against the back of my hand.

"Does the label matter?" he asked. "Does what I am matter to you?"

I don't think he was only talking about his potential ace-ness. "No," I said. "All that matters is whether or not we both want to kiss each other."

He closed his eyes for a moment before nodding. I'd been hoping for another kiss, but without another word, he set off along the cliff path again and I followed, only too happy to walk away from the place where he'd died.

Far too soon, the white-washed cottage loomed out of the darkness, lights blinking in all the windows.

"If he's here, I'll stay. I won't let him hurt you," Rowan said, and I could've kissed him again right there in the front yard with my mum peering at us through the kitchen window. No one had ever said that to me before. No one had known or cared enough to figure out where my bruises came from. And Mum had never said it, knowing it was a promise she couldn't keep.

"Ash, thank God. Are you all right?" Mum stood in the doorway, her eyes ringed black with fatigue, not bruises. Martha O'Donnell joined her, glaring daggers at Rowan. He tried to pull away, but I held onto his hand.

"Is the colonel here?" I asked.

"No, Fergus is taking care of him in town. He won't come here," Martha O'Donnell answered, and I exhaled in relief, muscles aching as I released the tension that had been holding me together.

"I should go," Rowan said, turning to face me. "You'll be okay. The O'Donnells take care of their own. If you need me, let me know."

"Thank you." I stood on my tiptoes and planted a kiss on his lips. "For everything. I'll see you soon," I said as he slowly, painfully released my fingers. I didn't want to let him go, but I did. All of me ached watching him strike out across the fields, the mist swallowing him up. A single black butterfly flitted after him then disappeared into the shadows.

Mum stood with her arms folded, a scowl on her face. She opened her mouth, closed it again, thinking better of whatever she'd been about to say.

"I'll make some tea," Martha said, leaving me alone with Mum as I shucked my jacket and boots.

"You didn't have to run off like that," she said.

"You lied." I looked her right in the eye, eyes so different from my own. "You didn't file for divorce, did you? Did you even tell him we were leaving?" I was irritated and tired, tired of Mum, and so tired of feeling like shit waiting for the next time the colonel's fists got twitchy.

"I thought I told you to stay away from that Sheehy boy. He's a murder suspect," Mum said.

"At least he doesn't slap me around."

Mum sucked in a breath, and I looked up in time to see the tears brimming on her eyelashes before she turned and stalked into the kitchen.

Part of me wanted to apologize, knew I should, because it was a cheap shot I never should've taken. Another part of me wanted her to know how done I was with all of this.

"He's a person of interest, I can't have you compromising my investigation." Her tone was cold and distant.

"Is that all you care about?" I slumped at the kitchen table. "My abusive father makes an appearance, and all you care about is this stupid investigation? You should be filing for divorce, getting a restraining order. Something!"

Mum dropped the mug she'd been holding. It shattered in the sink, making both of us jump. Martha gathered up the shards, saying nothing.

"You think it's that simple?" Mum said.

"It should be. It should've been that simple years ago when he first started hitting you. You're always telling me to stand up for myself, to not take shit from the world for who I am, but it's all bullshit."

"Ash, don't talk to me like that."

"You let him hit you, for years! You let him hit *me*!" The tears were unexpected, burning like battery acid down my face as all the emotion I'd been damming inside suddenly boiled over.

"You provoke him!" Mum yelled back, her words knocking the breath out of me. "Why do you always have to provoke him? This, this is what they do." Mum turned to Martha and waved in my direction. "Always so clever, always so self-righteous. I don't know why you like pushing your father's buttons, but you get what—"

"I get what I deserve?" I said, my voice eerily calm considering the raging storm inside me. I was going to be sick. I was going to break something. Maybe I was my father's kid because all I wanted to do was punch something. Punch it, kick it, break it, until it shattered into smithereens. It. Mum. *Myself.*

"That's not what your mum is saying," Martha said, setting a mug in front of me. I sat on my hands to keep from sending the mug flying into the wall. Not everything could be fixed with a fucking cup of tea!

"Is that why you stayed? Why you let him do this?" I asked. "You think we deserved it?"

Mum stayed at the sink, her back to me. She swatted tears off her cheeks and dragged her fingers through her hair before replying. "I thought he would change." She stared out the window, holding her hand above the sink where blood dribbled from a cut on her thumb. "I thought it was PTSD. I thought he could get help, that he'd want help and want to be better. He was for a while," she said. "After you were born, for years, things were good. I thought being a father had made him realize...but then you got older, and it started again."

"This isn't my fault," I said, not sure I believed it anymore. "You're a cop. You could've done something."

Martha sat beside me, her hand on my arm, but I pulled away.

"You have no idea how hard being a female cop is." Mum turned to face me. "How hard it was to prove myself. How I have to keep proving myself every damn day. I had to be better at everything. I couldn't make a single mistake. I couldn't be seen as weak. If I gave them one reason to doubt me, I never would've made inspector."

"So you let him hurt us for the sake of your career?"

"You don't understand. I was in such a dark place when I met him. He was everything to me. In some ways, he saved my life, and I thought I could save him. We were both—damaged. Neither of us had had a particularly easy time growing up."

"But he hit you." I came to stand beside her, wanting her to look at me, to really look at me and see the damage beyond the fading yellow on my skin, beyond my cast and crooked collarbone.

"I thought if I didn't let him see how much it hurt me—if he thought I was as tough as he was, I thought—" She choked back her words. "I thought if I could keep the peace, if we could keep him happy then it wasn't so bad, but you—I was wrong, Ash, wrong to think he could change. Wrong about everything." She hiccoughed a sob, and I wanted to wrap my arms around her, tell her it was fine, that I forgave her, and everything would be okay, but I didn't want to lie.

"You need to divorce him. You have to tell him we're not going back."

She looked at me, and I think this time she saw me. She cupped my chin in her hand, fresh tears spilling down her face. "If I do that, I could lose you."

"What do you mean?"

"He's here to fight me for custody," Mum said. "He has all the connections. He can pull strings."

Panic gripped my insides. I'd only just turned seventeen. I couldn't live with the colonel. Not for a whole year. Not for a single minute! I wouldn't. I'd meant what I said to Rowan in the cave. I'd sooner jump off a cliff than spend my life dodging his fists.

"On the mainland, maybe. But not here," Martha said. "He has no power on this island. We'll protect you. Don't you worry none, lass."

"I do worry," Mum said.

"But you're a cop, you know judges. Can't you pull strings of your own?" I asked.

"Not like he can."

"But the abuse, there's no way a judge will give him custody."

"Your father is a highly decorated, highly regarded colonel. He'll say *I* hurt you, and we've got no proof to the contrary. If anything—" Mum gulped.

"What is it?" I asked, white-knuckling the sideboard.

"I haven't always been the gentlest cop. There are a few write-ups in my file, excessive force—I was trying to prove myself to the boys, but a judge might see it differently."

"Not here. We'll take care of it," Martha said.

"The way Fergus took care of the old Rowan Sheehy?" I asked.

Martha pressed her lips together in a thin, pale line and folded her jiggly arms. "We're here to help, if you want it," she said. "Your choice."

"Thank you, Martha. Perhaps I should speak to Ash alone, if you wouldn't mind," Mum said.

"I was just thinking it's about time I head out. Ash, I left some books from Fergus for you on the coffee table." She waved toward the lounge. I'll come by tomorrow to check on Brian."

"Is Granddad okay?" I asked, suddenly remembering he lived with us and hadn't shown his face despite the shouting match going on.

"He's fine. Still giving me the silent treatment, is all," Mum said with a jerk of her head toward the closed bedroom door that used to be mine.

"Tomorrow, then." Martha hauled her large body out of the kitchen chair and strode toward the door. Mum went with her, thanking her and promising to see her at work. I squeezed my eyes closed until the door clicked shut and Mum threw the deadbolt.

"So what are you saying?" I asked when she returned to the kitchen. "You can't file for divorce? That we'll have to go back with him?" My voice cracked, hysteria bleeding all over my words. "Mum, we can't live like this."

"We'll figure it out. You heard Martha. We have family here. Support."

"Is that the real reason we came here?" I asked.

"Partly," she admitted, looking not nearly as sheepish as she should've. "And Dad's been talking about it for years. He always said it was a mistake to leave."

"Pity he didn't think it was a mistake for you to marry the colonel."

"Ash, that's enough. Please."

"You're just as bad as him, you know," I said through gritted teeth.

"I'm nothing like your father. I'm r-really not," Mum stammered, her denial hardly convincing.

"Excessive force on the job. Excessive force at home." I shrugged. "What's the difference?"

"I have never hurt you. I would *never*—"

"No, you just let him do it." I wrapped my arms around my middle as if I could keep myself together and hold it all in, but I was suffocating, disintegrating. "I'm not going back with him. I can't. I won't. I just—" I could step off a cliff and let the waves take me. Would it hurt? Not as much as going home to the colonel. Would Rowan understand if I took that step though? Fuck. I didn't want to become another soul for him to carry, another bundle of bad memory for him to have to suffer.

"I'd rather die." I hadn't meant to say it, but the words were out now. I looked at Mum, holding her gaze long enough for her to know I meant what I'd said.

"Oh God, I'm so sorry, Ash. I'm so, so sorry." Mum pulled me toward her. I resisted at first and then I melted, folding into her arms like a little kid, back when I believed her hugs were the only protection I needed, that her arms alone could keep me safe.

"None of this is your fault. You didn't deserve this. I'm sorry," she said, and I wished I was that little kid again, only needing the armor of my mum's love to shield me from the world, believing everything she said. But I wasn't that kid anymore. That kid had been beaten out of existence.

Rowan

THOUGHTS OF Ash kept sleep at bay.

I relived the memory of our first kiss, their hand at the back of my neck, my frenetic heartbeat. I relived our second kiss shared on the blood-stained earth where I'd died, the press of their body against mine reminding me I was still alive, for now, until the Kilduffs and O'Donnells completed the ritual and ended my life.

They must believe the entity they planned to liberate would grant them power and reassert their dominion over the island. The Kilduffs must believe the prize worth the price to kill one of their own, black sheep though he'd been. I had little doubt Ash's granddad would be the O'Donnell sacrifice. It must be why the murders began when he arrived on the island, why they'd welcomed him back to the fold and wanted him away from Ros Tearmann. It all made perfect, despicable sense, and I despised them more than ever.

Ash. They would lose their granddad unless I could stop the perpetrators. Martha, Orlagh—I doubted two old ladies were capable of shoving Patrick from the cliffs, but Fergus—Fergus had killed before. Last time, we'd failed to prove his guilt; perhaps this time we could. This time, there would be justice. Maybe Ash's mother would be more inclined to seek the truth and not accept the lies served by druid hands.

My sister's candles flickered on my desk, making shadowy swamps of the corners, drawing me deeper into lavender and sandalwood memory, and thoughts of Ash.

I had never wanted to feel, to touch... A deathwalker wasn't entitled to such things, theirs a service to departing souls and those souls alone. Or maybe Ash was right, and it was something else, something there were words for, labels I could pin to my identity if only I could claim them. Demi. Ace. Grey-A. Terms I'd seen before but never truly understood, terms I'd never considered might apply to me. Were they even mine to claim when I was an amalgam, a living history of my ancestors and all the dead I'd ferried beyond the veil?

I'd never felt connected to someone the way I was starting to feel with Ash. Around them I could dream of a different life, more bitter than sweet, an ache severe but savored. The ghosts in my mind responded, offering up their own tender recollections of tongues and fingers, of skin on skin in meadows and hotel beds, of love in all its guises, sparking a desire I couldn't be sure was entirely my own.

Mouth dry and body hot, I picked up my phone, fingers hovering above the keys, wondering exactly what to say and how to say it.

Hey, are you all right? I typed, hating how impersonal my words sounded, hating how I couldn't look into Ash's eyes when they answered and know if they spoke the truth.

Hey! Better now :) Convo with Mum was okay. Think she might actually divorce the bastard.

As long as it lets you be safe and happy, I responded, and slipped from my sheets, careful not to disturb Onyx where she lay curled at the foot of my bed. I threw open the window, letting midnight whisper cool across my shoulders, shoulders marred with black vines. The gashes in my arm were healed, no longer suppurating, the malaise now spooling through my veins and painting my skin. Black butterflies alighted on the window frame, fanning their wings burnished with Otherworld iridescence. If only they could speak. Perhaps they would give me the answers I sought.

Settling at my desk, I pulled out fresh paper and pencils.

What are you doing? Ash texted.

Drawing. You?

Reading. Trying to.

I tried to concentrate on the page, needing to think of something other than Ash and their lips, their sad eyes, their smile—

Wormwood and rue. I drew the symbols from memory, the symbols Gran had shown me in the Grimoire, symbols etched into vellum by the hands of my ancestors. I breathed deeply of the lavender wafting from the candle, once more allowing myself to slip into the ocean of remembrance within me. The ghosts received me gladly, dragging me into memories, this time not of kisses and joy, but of darkness and blood. My thoughts surged with that tide, buoyed through the maelstrom as I searched for something, *anything* to help me gain insight.

My hand moved as I dove into the black waters, pencil scratching at paper as I sifted through fragments, burrowing ever deeper into the annals archived in my mind. Wormwood and rue. I searched for the symbols, for the words, for a whisper of spell or ritual, all the way to the very first rowan.

A boy made of dirt and blood, the blood of berries,

his bones the roots of a rowan ripped from the earth, his flesh from rock melting and flowing to dress the raw bones in meat wrought of magic. A boy fashioned by his sisters' hands, his mother's words. A boy, a spell, made to walk between worlds, to serve the living and the dead as decreed by the gods whose names we'd forgotten and yet in whose shadow we continued to live.

Four trees, four families, four sacred links in the chain that bound.

Wormwood and rue to cage the darkness, a power slithering into the deep beyond.

But chains could be broken, links severed, a prisoner freed.

My phone *pinged* and the pencil in my hand snapped, the candle flames guttering. Onyx meowed in my face and pawed at my chest, her tail twitching across my page, her luminous eyes staring into mine. I blinked away the cobwebs of memory and pulled the cat into my lap. She nestled into the crook of my left arm, her body vibrating with a purr as I picked up my phone.

What are you drawing? Ash asked.

I stared at the page, at what my hand had rendered of its own volition. The symbols repeated, overlaid, inverted and reversed, layer upon layer interweaving, entwining, creating another image, one as surprising as it was undeniable.

Ash O'Donnell stared at me from the page, their eyes a tapestry of rue, their smile a twist of wormwood.

You, I typed and hit send before I realized how strange that might seem. I was already typing up a response to clarify, my thoughts not yet entirely my own when Ash replied.

I'd love to see it. Here's a photo I took of you today. Hope you like it?

I opened the attachment, waiting several minutes for my ancient device to load the image. A boy with red hair and a black butterfly in his hand, my face caught in profile against a backdrop of cave shadow. The breath caught in my lungs, the ghosts whispering again, dark thoughts rising from the void within me.

It's an amazing photo, I replied, which barely began to capture all I wanted to say, all I couldn't say, not without making real the sorrow, the bitterness, the anger, the regret all etched onto the boy's face in the photograph.

You're an excellent subject, Ash replied. *Want to hang out tomorrow? Maybe give me a tour of the crags?*

Absolutely, I responded, agreeing to meet Ash in the morning. They responded with various happy-faced emojis.

I returned to bed, and Onyx curled up on my chest. I lay awake, studying the flickering shadows on my ceiling, trying to understand all that shifted within me, the ebb and flow of memory, the history buried in my bones, the answers flowing through my veins if only I could seize them.

Dawn crept pale fingers through the window, daylight breaking across my bedroom wall, and still I was trying to understand the significance of what I'd drawn, to reassert control over my mind. A familiar nicker sounded from the paddock, a swish of horse tail, a toss of mane and stomp of impatient hooves. I ignored it, dismissing it as usual morning sound, Deirdre no doubt up early and out with Comet. Except—

I rushed to my feet, tugged on a shirt, and raced out of my bedroom, out of the house, passed the ruined stables and into the paddock beyond. Auryn greeted me with a neigh, trotting up and huffing in my face before resting her nose against my chest. Solas greeted me, too, nuzzling my ear with his silver nose.

Keeping my left hand firmly at my side, I rubbed their broad faces with my right, combing my fingers through their manes, still dazed, convinced I must be dreaming until Deirdre, clad only in pajamas, rode toward me on Comet. Flowers bloomed across her nightdress, a veritable garden of pinks and purples as magic brought her happiness to life, blossoms spilling down her arms and curling her hair.

"They're back," she said, a smile splitting her face.

"How is this possible?"

"I told you, they're ours. No one else can have them." She threw her arms around Comet's neck. He nibbled on the green shoots coiling out of her hem, and the morning brightened at the sound of her laughter. The island thrummed with energy today, the sun rising warm and the breeze a caress. The sea glinted gold against a sky bluer than a Kilduff's eye. There was no trace of sorrow in the morning. I'd experienced no call to the Otherworld, so no one could've died, and yet my heart stuttered, my gut tightening, knowing that something was wrong.

Ash

WISH I COULD blame my lack of sleep on the lumpy couch or Granddad's sawing-wood snores reverberating through the entire house, but really it was because I couldn't stop thinking of Rowan. Also, Mum had done an appalling job of creeping out of the house this morning. I'd pretended I was still asleep, not ready to talk to her or even think about everything we'd said last night.

According to my phone, there were three and a half hours until Rowan and I were scheduled to meet up. It was stupidly, painfully early, but I was awake now and might as well make use of the time.

The Brief History of Inisliath, Volume I would've served better as a doorstop. I lugged the hardback into the kitchen and dropped it on the table while I set about getting myself caffeinated.

When I had a steaming mug of coffee in my hand, I cracked open the book's spine, once again assaulted by the must of old paper. This time I noticed a note from Fergus tucked into the jacket.

Thought you might be ready to know more. Now don't be surprised if you can't read it all. None of us can, these days. Hopefully you can make some sense of it.

Right. Last night I'd thought it was just fatigue making the text incomprehensible. Fatigue and distracting thoughts of Rowan. With a gulp of too-hot coffee, I tried to focus on the book. There were no chapters in this volume, just 800 pages of rambling history.

Starting at the beginning again, I studied the weird letters and symbols. Some resembled Rowan's tattoos, others were entirely alien, but two stood out, immediately familiar: the symbols for wormwood and rue I'd seen at his gran's cottage. I flipped through the pages, finding the symbols again and again in the first twenty pages. After that, everything was pretty much hieroglyphics.

It was only on page 135 that the words started to make sense. Vikings, Romans, Normans—seems they'd all tried and failed dismally to claim Inisliath. The book said most of the invaders had suffered a "withering malaise." That certainly didn't sound healthy, but the assholes probably deserved it.

According to Fionnula, some of the invaders were also taken as mates—the book actually used that word as if they were breeding horses, not humans—leaving the islanders with stronger genetics and foreign wealth passed to heirs bearing island names. And this went on for centuries with the O'Donnells apparently running the show, serving as chieftains with Kilduff tanists, which the Internet told me meant a sort of second-in-command.

All very interesting, but none of it particularly useful. Not that I expected to find a chapter titled, *Why people are getting brutally murdered and how to stop it.*

I flipped back to the beginning, staring at the symbols until my eyes hurt and vision turned fuzzy. And through the fuzziness I swear I saw the letters move, wriggles of black slithering into shapes—into words—I could read.

In the beginning was the Dark, and the Dark was Death. A rent, a shadow, a crack in Dark. Roots searching the Dark, branches seeking the Light, and so birthed light and life. Without the Dark, no Light. Without the Light, no Dark. Death in Life, Life in Death. And so, through the breach and onto the skin of the world.

Blah, blah, creation story, blah. I skimmed through a few more pages before the words practically jumped off the page and grabbed my eyeballs.

One wrought of Dark and Light, one with roots in darkness and leaves in Light. One wrought of Dark's earth and Light's breath. One of root and bone, bough and blood, Dark made flesh through Light to be. One to serve the living and the dead, bound by wormwood, rue, and blood. Blood of hawthorn, ash, and oak. By blood, a rowan born.

Holy shit.

One to nourish the bond. One through which all must flow. Life in Death, Death in Life. With souls to reap, the power grows—

One to serve the living and the dead—that sounded an awful lot like a deathwalker.

Bound by wormwood, rue, and blood—the murders must have something to do with this bit.

Blood of hawthorn, ash, and oak. By blood, a rowan born—this was the part I stumbled over. Rowan had been made, killed in a way that was sinister in its similarity to how Andy and Patrick had died. But it didn't make sense. If the ritual had been to bind something—as Rowan said—why did the book talk about *creating* a rowan?

One to nourish the bond. One through which all must flow. Life in Death, Death in Life. With souls to reap, the power grows. Death for Life, Life for Death by pact of blood. Unmade the same for Death and Life to sever, all ebb and cease, the rowan dies.

I read the last part over and over again, refusing to believe what the words could mean. And yet, it sort of made sense. That must've been what Rowan and his gran had been keeping from me. For the ritual to be complete, a Sheehy had to die. It said so right there on the page. I slammed the book shut and closed my eyes.

Fuck that. Fuck this whole damn island. And why the hell had Rowan tried to keep this from me?

I drummed my fist on the table, angry and hurt. Then my phone was in my hands and I was stabbing at the screen asking Rowan if we could meet earlier.

Something's come up. Don't think we can meet today at all, he replied.

This is important, I typed back. *I found something about the ritual. Something about you!*

I waited, seconds ticking by, the screen remaining blank until finally the glorious ellipsis blinked at me as Rowan typed a response.

Meet at the beach where we were collecting sea-glass in an hour?

With my heart beating double time, I agreed and abandoned the book in favor of a quick shower and clean clothes.

For the moment, the sky wasn't leaking, although mist hung like strings of vomit between the twisted trees. Clouds were smeared all over the horizon and chewing up the morning sunshine as I hurried down the path to the beach where I'd first taken photos of Rowan and Deirdre. It felt like a lifetime ago.

A few brave families were scattered across the sand, kids squealing as they braved the cold water, others industriously filling buckets and sculpting castles. I scanned the beach goers, searching for red hair.

Should've known he'd be as far away from the others as possible. He sat perched on a jagged rock where the cliffs jutted out into the sea, hands in his pockets, gaze on the water.

He turned, one eye scrunched against the glare and waved. The skin under his eyes looked bruised and he had a charcoal smudge across his forehead.

"Rough morning?" I asked. "Or rough night?"

"Both," he said, opening his left eye. It was a lot darker now with only the smallest splat of green-brown remaining in his iris. That couldn't be good.

"Want to talk about it?" I asked as he shifted over to make space for me. We sat, thighs touching, and this time Rowan didn't pull away.

"The horses came back," he said with a catch in his throat.

"The guy returned them?"

"Not exactly. I think—" He bit his lower lip. "I think something might've happened to him."

"And somehow the horses came back to you?"

"Aye, not that we can afford them any better now." He sighed and dragged a hand through his hair. His fingers were stained black as well and left sooty streaks through his curls. "Mother is trying to find out what happened, but I'll be needed back at Ros Tearmann soon. I can't stay long."

"That's okay." No, it wasn't. I wanted to spend the entire day with him, here in the sunshine with a sparkling sea and a cool breeze, here where it was easy to forget about asshole fathers and psycho murderers.

His hand moved toward mine, his fingers leaving grey smudges on my skin. With a sigh, I rested my head on his shoulder as close to content as I could be. For just a moment, I could pretend all the shittyness didn't exist.

I felt him shift next to me, his body angling toward mine, and I tilted my head back and caught his eye.

"I'd really like to kiss you," he said.

"Please do."

He smiled and then his smile disappeared as I closed my eyes, waiting for his lips to meet mine. I wasn't disappointed. I tasted salt and copper and honeyed tea. I snaked my good hand up his neck and into his hair, inhaling his spicy scent as his arm wrapped around my back and pulled me closer. His heart was beating so hard, thudding against my ribs—or maybe that was just my own heart doing its best impression of a battering ram.

I might've been about to throw a leg over his lap and slip my hands under his shirt, but the happy screams of kids playing in the waves reminded me to keep things PG. Rowan must've felt the same. He ended the kiss and leaned away, face flushed pink.

He smiled and I could've stared at his face all day. "Hey, you said you found something?" he said, breaking the spell. I wanted so badly to kiss him again, but that was not why I was here, and if our time together was limited, then kissing would have to wait.

"Yeah, it's—look, I don't know if any of this is true or makes sense, but I think I found something in that O'Donnell book." I hauled the tome out of my backpack and opened up to the page where I'd folded down the corner.

Rowan smoothed the crease from the page as he shook his head. "What does it say?"

"Don't you have your specs?"

"Don't think they'd help," he said. "Only a druid could read this." He seemed to choose his words carefully.

"Wait—you think I have magic?"

"Evidently so." A grin tugged at the corner of his mouth. "Guess your island blood is more potent than we thought."

"Should I be worried?"

His grin evaporated at my question, a frown furrowing

his brow. "Honestly, I don't know. I think we should all be worried."

I needed a moment to process what he'd said, a moment to fucking reconfigure my entire identity. Ash O'Donnell, descendant of druids and possibly magical. That was quite different from being Ash Walsh, habitual fuck-up.

"Ash, sorry, but I really will need to get back soon." Rowan shifted, his knee nudging mine and slamming the world back into focus, the world being the page in front of me and what I could magically discern from the scribbles.

"Okay, so here." I tapped the letters as they rearranged themselves. "It says *Bound by wormwood, rue, and blood. Blood of hawthorn, ash, and oak. By blood, a rowan born.* I don't think this ritual is about binding some kind of creature. I think it's about creating the first deathwalker."

Rowan stiffened beside me. "Go on," he said, voice hoarse.

"Then there's this bit: *Unmade the same for Death and Life to sever, all ebb and cease, the rowan dies.* What if—" My mind was racing, leaving me dizzy and nauseated all over again. "What if ... What if that means... Well, I don't think your gran is the target." I struggled to get the words out, hoping he'd understand what I was implying without having to spell it out, because I didn't want to think, never mind say it.

"No, she's not," Rowan said far too calmly.

"You knew." I shut the book, gripping its edges so hard it hurt my fingers.

"We suspected."

"Thanks for the heads up," I said, suddenly furious without really knowing why.

"I didn't want you to worry."

"Worry?" I turned to face him, rock digging painfully

into my backside, but I ignored it so I could stare into his eyes. "Are you fucking kidding me?" I hadn't meant to raise my voice. "I don't think worry even begins to cover how I feel knowing you might be the next to get your throat slit." The last part I'd managed not to shout for the entire beach to hear.

"It won't come to that," Rowan said.

"How can you be so sure?"

"Because I won't let that happen. I'm going to stop the people responsible."

"You keep saying that, but if you've got an actual plan, I'd love to hear it."

He sucked in a breath, his right hand closing around his left biceps where I'd seen the gashes on his arm.

"I want to help," I said. "But I can't if—"

He looked at me, then past me, and the scowl on his face sent a shudder down my spine.

"Ash?"

I closed my eyes at the sound of the familiar voice. Not here. Not now. This couldn't be happening.

"What a pleasant surprise to see you," the colonel said.

I opened my eyes and slowly turned to face my father. His smile was hideous, but his eyes were as hard as ever.

"And with a book," he added. "Didn't think books were really your thing anymore. Who's your friend?"

I hauled open my backpack and dropped the book inside before getting to my feet. Rowan stood beside me.

"I'm Rowan Sheehy," he said.

"Colonel Walsh, Ash's father." He held his hand out for Rowan to shake and, without hesitation, Rowan took it. Now if only my father had a weak heart, he might've done me a favor and dropped dead. Sadly, he survived.

"You're looking well," the colonel continued as his gaze raked over my body. The bruises around my eye were all but gone now, and only the faintest trace of yellow on the bridge of my nose remained. Sometimes I wished the bruises would stay on my skin the same way they stayed on the inside. His gaze dropped to my wrist.

"Surely it's time for that to come off?" he asked.

"Six weeks, the doctor said." I found my voice. "It's only been four."

"How's the collarbone? Back to climbing, yet?" he asked as if we were exchanging some small-talk pleasantries.

"That'll take six *months*," I said.

"So long?" He frowned as if somehow it was my fault my body took so long to heal. "Have you had lunch? Perhaps we could finally have that chat."

"No," I said, straightening my shoulders. Unfortunately, I hadn't inherited my father's height, only his musculature, which meant he'd probably always stand two heads taller than me, always looking down at me. "I'm busy."

"I'm sure your friend won't mind lending you to me for a few hours," he said with a condescending smile.

"We already had plans," Rowan said. "We were just heading off."

"Well, Ash and I really need to talk, so I'm afraid your plans will have to wait," he said, the mask of civility slipping. His words were heavy now, commanding, meant to kick soldiers' asses into gear.

Rowan tightened his grip on my hand but didn't seem intimidated by my father. Seeing Rowan stand his ground ignited my own courage.

"I don't want to talk to you, so you can fuck right off," I said, my insides quivering. Despite the fear, I never seemed able to stop my mouth. Maybe some secret part of me wanted the colonel to hit me, actually did think I deserved it.

"You will not speak to me like that," the colonel said, taking half a step forward. Involuntarily, I leaned back a little, only to press up against the solid warmth of Rowan.

"Or what?" I asked. "You'll break my other arm? Your tactics are getting old, *Dad*." I expected him to close the distance between us, to raise his fists, but instead he sighed and rubbed a hand over his bald patch.

"I apologize for Ash's behavior, Rowan. This isn't how I raised them."

"I know exactly how you raised them," Rowan said, and I wanted to tell him to stop, that it wasn't worth putting himself in my father's cross-hairs, and that provoking the man wouldn't end well. I couldn't get the words out.

The expression on my father's face darkened. "I was hoping we might have a civil conversation, that perhaps you'd grown up a little, but I see, once again, I overestimated your maturity."

His words were bullets all hitting the bullseye.

"I'm seeing your mother later. I was hoping to include you in the decisions we need to make, but—" He shrugged, his look of disappointment like being flayed alive. I felt myself bleeding, dripping from the wounds his words inflicted. "You should know I only have your best interests at heart. Your mother does, too, however misguided she may be. But don't worry, kiddo," he said, ever so patronizing. "This has all been a big misunderstanding. We'll be going home soon."

"I am home," I said, my fingers digging into Rowan's hand, wishing I could tap into the druid magic running through my veins and do something, *anything*, to stop my father. "I'm not going back with you," I added, unable to stop the tears wobbling on my lashes or the crack in my voice. "I'm *never* going back with you."

"Come now, Ash. These histrionics don't become you," he said. "Don't embarrass yourself in front of your friend."

I hated him. Hated him so fucking much.

Rowan pulled me closer, his breath on my neck.

"School starts soon," the colonel continued. "This is your final year, your last chance to make something of yourself." He waved a hand, gesturing to all of me. "I love you too much to see you squander what little potential you have left in some farm school on this antiquated rock."

I love you—I'd never despised three words so much.

"I'm not leaving," I said. "And you can't make me."

"Oh, but I can." He lowered his voice, a blade slipping between my ribs. "You are my child. I'll not have you live in a hovel, in some godforsaken backwater. What your mother did is tantamount to kidnapping. I could have her badge for this. She could go to jail. Is that what you want? Because trust me, if that's what it takes, then so be it. But come back with me willingly, and you'll spare your mother the indignity."

"I think we've heard enough," Rowan said. "Let's go, Ash." He tugged my hand, and I followed, numb and incapable of doing anything else.

"That's okay," the colonel said, miraculously standing aside as we headed for the path leading back up the cliff. "You should make the most of your last day here," he called after us.

I froze. "Last day?"

"We're booked on the ferry home tomorrow morning. This holiday is over and a return to reality is warranted."

His words were anvils in my soul. He was right. This had been some kind of dream, and it was all coming crashing down.

"Ash isn't going anywhere with you," Rowan said.

"Ash will do as they're told," the colonel said, a crack appearing in the veneer of decency he'd so liberally slicked over his face. "The ferry leaves at nine tomorrow. I expect to see Ash there."

"I think you may be disappointed," Rowan said, and

I held my breath, waiting for my father to snap, to lash out, to hurt us both. And he might've done it, might've given us both fresh bruises to wear had a whistle not sounded from the top of the path.

"He's here. We've got him!" A uniformed officer shouted and waved to the people behind them before starting down the path toward us. For a single spectacular moment, I thought maybe they were here to arrest my father. Mum was among the officers, the look of relief on her face quickly replaced by a scowl when she saw me and then the colonel. That was when I knew, it wasn't my father they were after.

Rowan

I KNEW THEY'D come for me, with one excuse or another. I knew they'd come for me with chains and smiles. I only wished this wasn't happening in front of Ash.

"We've got you this time, Sheehy." Claire Kilduff smirked.

"What the hell? What's happening?" Ash's whole body was shaking beside mine.

"It's okay," I said, trying to let go of their hand, but Ash held on tighter.

"Mum, seriously. What's going on?" Ash asked.

"You shouldn't be here," DI Walsh said, her gaze flicking between me and Ash, then Ash and their father. "I told you—I told you I didn't want—" She left the rest unsaid, but I could imagine what she'd told Ash. It would be nothing I hadn't heard before, and maybe she was right. I was dangerous, now more than ever. Ash would be wise to keep their distance.

"Rowan Sheehy, you're under arrest," DI Walsh said,

fumbling with the handcuffs in her hands.

"Arrest? For what?" Ash demanded.

"For the murder of Eamonn Davidson, that's what," Claire said far too gleefully.

Davidson. Murdered. A voice murmured at the back of my mind, a whispered suspicion, treacherous and terrible. I tried to silence it, tried and failed to prevent the suspicion from taking root and sewing tendrils of doubt.

"No, that's impossible," Ash said. "No, no, no." They turned to me, face pale and eyes the turbulent grey of a summer storm.

"Please, you have to let me go." I raised their hand to my lips and kissed their knuckles. Their nails were leaving indentations in my skin.

"You can't let them do this," Ash said.

"Ash, please. You're embarrassing yourself," their mum said, and Ash's face crumpled at the edges, hurt dimming the light in their eyes. "Go home now before you risk becoming an obstruction."

"Come on. That's enough." The colonel stepped forward, his hands stretched toward Ash's shoulders.

"Don't touch them," I said, my voice a growl as something shifted within me. The slithering darkness pulsed in my veins, fire spreading beneath my skin where the vines of magic had left their shadow burned into my flesh. The colonel didn't heed my warning, and the moment before his hand landed on Ash's shoulder, I stepped forward, tugged Ash behind me, and slapped the colonel's hand away.

"He's resisting arrest," Claire said.

Several Kilduffs and O'Donnells sprang forward, their hands wrenching me away from Ash, shoving me to the ground and keeping me pinned with a knee to my back. The insidious magic writhed through my veins as I spat sand from my teeth, but I balled my fists and clenched my jaw, trying to regain control. I didn't need to give them any more reason to believe me capable of murder.

DI Walsh snapped handcuffs around my wrists and hauled me to my feet.

"Mum," Ash said, deflated, face tear-streaked as Claire read me my rights.

"We're going to the station now," DI Walsh said, giving me an ungentle tug up the path.

"But—" Ash started.

"It's okay," I said, trying to take a step forward. DI Walsh jerked me back, her grip on my infected arm sending pain lancing into my shoulder and a black cloud obscuring the vision in my left eye.

"You didn't do this. I know you didn't," Ash said, and I smiled despite the metal biting at my wrists. They believed me innocent—it gave me something to hold onto when the tide of the everyone else's derision threatened to sweep me under.

"Your mom's just doing her job. It'll be fine. You said it, I'm no murderer. This is all a misunderstanding." If only that were true, but I needed Ash to walk away and not risk trading more than words with their father.

Ash hesitated, eyes like chips of granite peering between the fronds of their fringe.

"I promise. I'll be fine," I said.

"Promise?" they asked.

"Aye, I do."

Ash didn't believe me, I could tell from the frown creasing their forehead, by their narrowed gaze and down-turned mouth, but nothing they did would release my shackles now, not when the Kilduffs were out for blood, and DI Walsh had so much to prove to the rest of the O'Donnells.

Ash rushed forward and threw their arms around me despite their parents' protests.

"I'm sorry," they said.

"Don't be," I whispered. Reluctantly, Ash let me go, their gaze following me up the path. At the top of the cliff, DI Walsh deposited me in the waiting cruiser, the locks on the doors slamming home.

"Don't leave Ash alone with him," I said. After a moment, DI Walsh met my gaze in the rearview mirror and ordered Colm O'Donnell to drive Ash home.

Before I could say thanks, the car pulled off, and all I could do was hope Ash would be okay.

I shifted in the seat, trying to get comfortable, but the too-tight cuffs bit into my wrists, and my left arm still ached, the fire reduced from a broil to a simmer. If I was next on the O'Donnells' list, I'd become far easier prey.

Ash

THE STENCH of my father's aftershave made me want to puke. Or maybe it was just his proximity making me sick. They'd taken Rowan, and Mum had let them. I doubled over and threw up, glad when my father backed away, trying to save his shoes from spew.

"Ash, I'm taking you home," he said, placing a hand on my shoulder.

I jerked away and stomped up the path. He said more, but I wasn't listening. He followed, and I ignored him as I pulled out my phone. With trembling fingers, I tapped at the screen until I'd managed to type a message to Teagan. She had to help me. If she didn't, I didn't know what I'd do, but I wasn't going back with my father, and I wasn't going to let Rowan rot in jail.

A cruiser was waiting at the top of the cliff, and one of the younger O'Donnells in their blue uniform stood at the open passenger door.

"I've got orders from your mom to drive you home," they said, voice low and heavy with island drawl.

"Just me?" I inclined my head toward the colonel.

"Just you." The officer gestured for me to get in as they walked around to the driver's side. It was pretty damn satisfying slamming the door in my father's face, and I even managed to give him a wave—instead of the middle finger—as the car pulled off.

Having convinced my cousin Colm to take me to town instead, I spent thirty agonizing minutes waiting for Teagan at the church. My thoughts were a seesaw, slamming back and forth between how to save Rowan and how to escape my father. The book in my hands was useless, unless I planned to use it to bludgeon the colonel. The thought was tempting, but then I really would be the colonel's kid. Not a thought I relished.

A twig snapped, and I looked up to see Teagan stalking between the headstones. She appeared every bit the vampire in torn fishnets, a shredded lace skirt, and black tank top. She'd twisted her hair into a ponytail, leaving two long side pieces trailing her collarbones. Thankfully, her eyes were invisible behind the gigantic sunglasses she wore. I wouldn't be able to take their atomic stare right now.

"You look awful," she said when she met me in the shade of the archway. "Want a smoke?" She tapped a cigarette from the box and lit up, the smell of menthol only making my nausea worse.

"I-I n-need your help," I stammered.

She hopped onto the low wall opposite me and tilted her face toward the clear sky. For once I wished it was raining. Shitty days like this didn't deserve sunshine.

"Hopefully not with that." She pointed a toe at the book in my hands. "Wait, is that Volume One?"

I nodded, and her eyebrows became visible as they

arched up behind the sunglasses.

"You can read it?"

"O'Donnell magic, apparently."

"Huh, that's weird because it doesn't usually—" She snapped her mouth shut and turned away.

"Doesn't usually what?" I asked.

"It's just stronger in girls, is all," she said. "The boys in our family don't usually end up with any magic at all."

I couldn't tell if she was looking at me because of the sunglasses, but I could imagine her giving me that surreptitious sideways glance people did when they thought I wouldn't notice, the glance that was all about trying to figure out whether I had ovaries or testicles. Well, she'd just have to live in wonder.

"I think it's dumb," she said a little too forcefully. "The whole 'only girls get magic' thing."

I kept my teeth gritted together, not wanting to go down this road with her, not now.

"Heard your dad is visiting," she said as if that were a better topic. "Mom says yours isn't too happy about it, though." She blew a delicate smoke ring toward me.

"He's a total asshole," I said. "That's one of the problems I wanted your help with."

"Personality make-overs aren't really within my power," she said as I hauled myself up next to her and jumped onto the wall with my good arm—an easy mantel—and swung my legs around. It was the closest to climbing I'd gotten yet.

"He wants me to leave with him tomorrow."

"You should go," she said.

Her words felt like being slapped. "What? Why?"

"Gods, Ash. Why would you want to stay on this miserable rock?"

"I don't. I mean, I might want to leave one day but right now..." I wasn't leaving Rowan in a jail cell. I wasn't leaving while there were still murderers on the island

267

with an O'Donnell and Sheehy on their hit list. "I'm not going anywhere with my father. Can you help?"

She slid the sunglasses down her nose and looked at me with her too-blue eyes. "And you want me to do what exactly?"

"Your mind-trick thing. Can you make him leave? Can you send him back to the mainland and suck out all his memories of me?"

She slipped her glasses back into position and twirled the cigarette between her long fingers. She took another drag before answering. "It doesn't work like that. We can only absorb emotion directed at us. And even if I could do it, are you sure you really want your dad to forget about you?"

"Yes," I said without hesitation.

"I never knew my dad," she said. "I mean, I know his name. He was a Norwegian exchange student who came to the island for a backpacking holiday and ended up staying three years to impregnate my mom."

"Sounds romantic."

"It's how most of us are conceived, a bunch of island bastards," she said with a short punch of laughter. "Not everyone wants a relationship or romance. I get that."

"Did she eat his emotions, too?"

"Impossible not to when we're that close to a person." She flicked ash from the smoke before continuing. "But once Mom got what she wanted, she sent him back to the mainland. I wasn't even born, yet. I have a photo of him. That's all."

"Maybe you're better off," I said, and she clenched her jaw.

"It's not like I ever got the choice. You don't get it. The way life works here. None of us get any choice in anything. But you do," she said. "You get to choose between staying or leaving. You should leave."

"Not with my father."

"Is he really that bad?" She flicked the cigarette butt onto the ground. "Because unless he's an abusive drunk or something, I kind of think having any father would be better than not having one at all."

"Forget it," I said, the fingers of my right hand involuntarily rubbing at the subluxated nodule of my collarbone.

"Oh." Teagan sucked in a breath. "Oh, Ash. Gods, I'm so sorry. He is an abusive drunk, isn't he?"

"He's not a drunk," I said. I'd already poured my heart out to Rowan. I didn't want to do it again. If she wouldn't help me without me having to spell out the reasons, then so be it, I'd figure out another way.

"I—I wish there was—maybe I could..." She jammed another cigarette between her lips, taking a couple of deep drags before saying, "I'll chat to Lucy. We'll figure something out."

"The ferry leaves at nine tomorrow. He wants me to be on it."

"I work well under pressure. Don't worry. Hey, did you hear they found another body this morning?" she asked.

"Which brings me to problem number two," I said, even as a torrent of gruesome images assaulted my brain. "They arrested Rowan for Davidson's murder."

"Oh, wow. I didn't know. I mean, I knew they were looking for him."

"He didn't do it."

"How can you be so sure? He's already the main suspect for the others."

"Yeah, but Davidson's death doesn't make any sense. It's an O'Donnell and Sheehy they need for the ritual." I paused when Teagan shoved her glasses up onto her head and pinned me with her unnaturally bright stare.

"What would you know about any of that?" she asked. "Did Rowan tell you something?" Her gaze narrowed.

"It's all right here." I tapped the book on my lap. "I know the murders have been some kind of ritual. Rowan thought it was something to do with breaking a binding, but—I think he's wrong."

"Oh you do, do you?" She pursed her lips. "So, what do you think the murders have been about?"

"I'm not sure, but it's connected to Rowan. He'll have to die for the ritual to be complete, and now he's sitting in a jail cell and—"

"Isn't that the safest place for him then?"

"Not if the murderer works in the station."

"You think it's a Kilduff or an O'Donnell," Teagan said, incredulous. "Are you sure that's even what the book says? I mean, it's all just a bunch of squiggles to me, and you're only a quarter islander. Maybe that's not what it says at all."

"An O'Donnell will be next. My *granddad* most likely. And after that, they'll go after Rowan. We have to stop this! And I can't leave the island until we do. I can't go— my father—" I was hyperventilating, blood pounding in my ears, the air too thin even as I desperately tried to suck it into my lungs.

"Calm down." Teagan grabbed my arm and turned me around to stare into her eyes. The familiar, eerie tingle of her mind-trick magic wormed its way into my brain. "Everything is okay," she said. "This has nothing to do with you."

"My granddad."

"It's all right, Ash. He's an old man. He came here to die."

That's what he'd said. He wanted to die here. Not with his throat slit. Not with his blood splashed all over a tree. I tried but couldn't look away, her eyes were mesmerizing, paralyzing, her magic sucking up all my willpower as I gazed into her beautiful face. And not just my willpower, the gratitude I felt towards her and the sliver of fear too.

It streamed out of me, flowing in her direction.

"You don't have to do anything," she continued. "Forget about the murders. Forget about the book." She pried it from my fingers. "Forget about Rowan. He was born to die."

His name was a whip-crack inside my skull.

"No." I fought against her, imagining Rowan's face, his lips on mine, his hands on my neck, the warmth of his body of his smile of his hazel eyes. I blinked and jerked out of her grasp, severing our connection.

"Don't do that," I said. "I'm not a fucking snack."

"I was only trying to help," she said, sucking in deep breaths as if she'd just run a marathon. Her eyes were pale as ice now, her magic clearly spent.

"By telling me to go home and forget about it all? Do you want more people to die?"

She wouldn't look at me.

Shit.

O'Donnells and Kilduffs—that's what Rowan and his gran had said. That the families were in it together. I'd thought Martha and Orlagh maybe, the family elders. Maybe even Fergus, but not—God, I'd been so fucking stupid.

"Was it you?" I asked, aware the book, and my only weapon, was now in Teagan's hands. She didn't appear armed otherwise, but that didn't mean she wasn't hiding a knife somewhere. I risked a glance at the nearest trees. Were they oaks? And if they were, would she risk slitting my throat right here in view of the town? Was I O'Donnell enough for the ritual to work?

"Tell me, was it you?"

"No," she said in a small, mousy voice. "But I think—I think Lucy might be involved."

That made more sense, what with her wanting Cillian and all. And Lucy was vicious with her words. I could imagine her being just as vicious with a knife.

"You're protecting her?"

"She's my sister."

"But she's a murderer."

"I don't know that for sure, yet," she said. "As soon as I have proof. *Irrefutable* proof, I'll go to Claire, and we'll deal with it. As a family. Your mom doesn't need to know anything."

"But Rowan's sitting in jail. They think he did it."

"Lucy wouldn't have had anything to do with Davidson's death," Teagan said, and she was right. Davidson's death made no sense.

"I can't leave Rowan in jail. I have to help him. I need the book," I said.

"You wanted help with your father, right?" Teagan clutched the tome possessively to her chest. "Because I'll help you with that, I'll do whatever you want me to, but you have to promise you won't say anything about Lucy to your mom."

"What about my granddad? What about Rowan?"

"You have a choice," she said. "Say nothing to your mom, leave Rowan where he is, and in exchange I'll get rid of your father."

"Get rid of?" I asked, nervous and hopeful, the hope twisting like a corkscrew through my gut because I knew it was wrong to feel relief imagining my father being the next body they found.

"Whatever you want," she said. "One way or another, I promise he won't be your problem anymore."

A life without fear. A life without my father. A life of freedom for my mum, for me. And all I had to do to get it was nothing.

"I don't want more people to die—not like that. Lucy has to be stopped."

"All the more reason you should go home and be with your grandda. Lucy won't try anything unless he's alone. And she'll have a hard time getting to Rowan while he's in jail."

Not if she had help from the likes of Claire or any one of her cousins. But it was Granddad who was more vulnerable, old and feeble in the cottage all alone.

"Okay," I heard myself say even as the word tore me in two. It was an impossible choice, and one I had no intention of making, but Teagan didn't need to know that. "You deal with my father, and I say nothing."

"You have to swear it," she said. "And swear you won't say something even after you get what you want."

"I promise," I said and extended my hand toward her to shake on it. She gripped my fingers, holding tight.

"But if my granddad—"

"He won't," she said. "I won't let that happen." I believed her. Not sure why—maybe it was the vehemence in her voice or her tightening grip on my fingers. "Everything is going to be okay," she said, and that I believed a whole lot less. "It's sealed in magic. Break your word now, and the consequences will be bad, like cursed-for-life kind of bad. Do you understand?" She glared at me, and I swallowed hard before nodding.

I reached for the book, but Teagan kept it tucked against her chest.

"If what you said is true, I think I should hold onto this. Evidence against my sister, maybe," she said. "I'll ask one of the O'Donnell women to help me with it."

Right, because I was neither O'Donnell nor woman enough to be trusted. Her words scratched beneath my skin, an itch and a sting.

"As soon as I figure it out, I'll let you know." With that, she turned and drifted back through the crumbling cemetery, leaving me feeling cracked and empty, and shitty as hell for being so dishonest. But I needed Teagan to take care of my father, and there was no way I could abandon Rowan.

Rowan

BEFORE, MY prison had been duty, fate, family, and the island. Now my prison came with steel bars and a tiny window giving me barely a glimpse of the darkening sky.

They took my phone and clothes, murmuring and muttering at the marks on my body, at the spreading black weaving what I hoped they'd mistake for fresh ink through old tattoos, coiling around scars. They stripped me of my bracelets and necklaces, leaving me feeling naked in navy sweatpants and a white T-shirt.

They took my fingerprints, scraped beneath my nails, swabbed my mouth, and pulled blood from a vein, collecting evidence as if I hadn't already been convicted and condemned.

"Mr. Sheehy, come with me." DI Walsh unlocked the gate on my cell, and I followed her without complaint to an interrogation room. "Coffee, tea, soda?"

"Just water," I said, my mouth dry and palms sweaty.

She nodded at the uniformed officer, Conall, Claire's younger brother who could've been her identical twin were it not for the stubble on his jaw. We'd been something like friends once, before I'd betrayed his trust. He disappeared and returned a few moments later with a bottle of water, slamming it down onto the table in front of me. DI Walsh sent him out of the room with a dismissive wave of her hand.

I took several swallows then said, "I want you to know I'd never hurt Ash. I know you don't want them around me, and I understand that, but I'd never hurt them. They've been hurt enough." I met her gaze and saw her flinch.

The detective released a whistle of breath as she opened a folder and nudged an evidence bag across the table. "Recognize that?" she asked.

"My bracelet." I picked it up, the plastic crinkling between my fingers. "My sister Deirdre made it for me." The leather was blackened around the knot where it had frayed loose. "You found it on the body," I said.

"Indeed. Care to explain that?" she raised an eyebrow, an expression Ash had inherited.

"I can't," I said. "I lost this bracelet."

"When?"

"I don't know, but I realized I wasn't wearing it yesterday." Perhaps I'd dropped it in the cove, perhaps somewhere along the walk to Gran's cottage. Anyone could've picked it up and used it to frame me—a story I knew DI Walsh wouldn't believe, and I didn't blame her.

"Where were you last night between ten and four?" she asked.

"At home."

"With your sisters?"

"No, I didn't see them." I'd been glad to avoid my family, keeping my door locked. Not even Deirdre had braved my presence.

"No family dinner?" the questions continued.

I shook my head.

"So no one saw you?"

"I don't have an alibi, if that's what you're looking for. After I left your cottage, I went straight home and up to my room. I was alone until this morning. That's the truth."

"We found your bracelet at the crime scene. There was blood on the victim, too, blood I'm pretty sure will match yours. And you've got no way to explain that?"

"You should ask Claire or Martha, I'm sure they'll tell you exactly what happened." I took another swallow of water, trying to wash the vitriol from my tongue.

"I'm asking you. I know you knew the victim. Old friend of your father's. I understand he and your mum were close." She laid a photograph on the table, one of Mother with my father and Eamonn, all wearing smiles on their faces. Mother held my father's hand and kissed Eamonn on the cheek. It had been taken at a music festival on the mainland, the one where Mother had met my father, where she'd gone deliberately seeking a mate and chosen a tall, curly-haired outsider with kind eyes.

"That's your father, isn't it?" Using a pen, DI Walsh tapped the familiar face in the photo, and I nodded. "Your mum's relationship with Davidson must've been difficult, seeing her involved with another man."

I kept my thoughts to myself. I hadn't been allowed an opinion then, and I wasn't sure I had one now. My father had been a biological necessity, unimportant beyond what he could give my mother. Why she'd chosen him and not Eamonn—I didn't understand then, but I think I was starting to now. She may have had genuine feelings for Eamonn and perhaps couldn't bring herself to use and discard him the way she had my father.

"Davidson recently bought your horses," DI Walsh continued. "I understand that was quite upsetting."

"And I know what you're trying to do," I said.

She blinked at me as if I'd caught her off guard.

"You're looking for motive and think you've found it, but you're wrong. I had no resentment toward Davidson. My mother loved him and not my father, it happens. I loved my horse, but she would've starved next winter. She still might." I rubbed my hands over my face at the thought of the three horses back in our paddock, now without even so much as a stable. Whoever had murdered Davidson hadn't done us any favors. "Honestly," I continued. "I'd rather see her sold off the island than dying a slow and painful death. I had no reason to kill Davidson."

"So you say, but the evidence suggests otherwise," DI Walsh said. "Tell us where we can find the murder weapon, and this will go easier for you."

"Easier?"

"If you cooperate, I can put in a good word for lighter sentencing."

I almost laughed then. The Kilduffs and O'Donnells had me where they wanted me. Any one of them could slip into my cell and sink silver into my throat. First an O'Donnell would die and then it would be my turn, with no new rowan to replace me when I was gone.

"What did you use?" DI Walsh continued. "A crowbar, a farrier's hammer, your fists?" She glanced at my hands, but my knuckles were unscathed. I'd never hit anyone and hopefully never would.

"I don't know how he died because he wasn't killed on the island," I said.

She hesitated. Perhaps my words had stoked an ember of doubt in her mind. "What makes you say that?"

I took another sip of water and slowly peeled the label off the bottle, wondering how best to explain what I was to Ash's mum.

"This murder isn't like the others at all," I started, choosing my words carefully. "The others were part of a ritual. I told you before. Someone believes they're performing a spell."

"No tree? No runes?" She peered at me as if her gaze could penetrate my soul and strip away its secrets. "Why not? What was different with Davidson? Was it because he was an outsider?"

"I don't know why he died." Although a suspicion lurked at the back of my mind, one I had no desire to examine in case I found it to be true. "But he wasn't part of the ritual, no. I think—I think whoever killed Andy and Patrick will kill an O'Donnell next."

"You know this with certainty?"

"It's logical," I said.

"Nothing about this is *logical*," she said and again, I couldn't begrudge her scorn. "Whoever killed Andy and Patrick are utterly deranged, and you say they're likely to kill again. Why an O'Donnell?"

"Because the ritual they're performing requires the blood of the four founding families."

"What ritual is this?"

I hesitated. Ash's findings had sewn doubt in my conviction. If the ritual wasn't about binding the creature in the Otherworld, if it was more intimately connected to deathwalkers, I couldn't begin to make sense of it. What were the perpetrators hoping to achieve? Without me, island souls would be left alone in the Otherworld, left to fight their way to the river and fend off the sluagh.

"The spell is ancient; the only reference we have to it isn't very helpful."

"You have this 'spell' in your possession?" she asked, hooking four fingers in the air as she spoke.

"Our copy is incomplete and in the old tongue," I said. "Useless, really. Whoever is doing this, must have their own and better version of the ritual."

"I'll need to see this spell to verify what you're saying is true."

"Speak to my grandmother," I said, though I doubted Gran would cooperate.

"Oh, I will." DI Walsh made a note in her file, and I continued to pry the label from the water bottle. She didn't believe me. Nothing I could say would dissuade her from my guilt. She was like the rest of them; I'd been a fool to think she'd be any different.

Ash's name was on the tip of my tongue. Would their mom believe they could read Fionnula's book? Would she believe the words Ash had discerned and accept their implications? Doubtful. It would only make life more complicated for Ash, and that much I could spare them from.

"What happened, new ink?" She nodded toward my left arm. I had no way of hiding the infection, the black blossoming from the two dark slashes above my elbow, scabbed now and resembling a bumbled attempt at claw marks.

"And those scars. Are they self-inflicted, part of more island rituals?" she asked. "If someone's hurting you, you can tell me." She leaned forward, her tone gentler now, as if inviting me to confide in her. "If you're hurting yourself, I can get you help."

She was trying to be kind, but I didn't even know where to begin. If only I had long sleeves to hide my arms. I traced the scars across my forearm: everything I'd been made, everything I'd given over and over again to make my family what they wanted to be.

"I can't help you if you don't talk to me, Rowan," she said.

"You can't even help yourself." The words erupted as shadows shifted within me, black fingers reaching through flesh and snagging on bone. "If you can't even protect your own, how do you expect to help me? Your father will be next. No one has ever returned from the mainland, and yet they welcomed you and your da with open arms. They're using you, Detective. They have been from the start."

She swallowed hard and snatched back the evidence bags before flipping closed the file.

"Suit yourself. As soon as we match your DNA to the blood on the victim, we'll be charging you with murder. I suspect we'll also match your DNA to samples found at the other crimes scenes, too. Are you ready to spend the rest of your life behind bars?" She stood to leave, looking down at me with the scorn I'd come to expect within these walls.

"Don't believe what the O'Donnells and Kilduffs tell you," I said as she strode toward the door. "Davidson didn't die on the island, nor did he die by my hand. I'm not your murderer, Detective."

She paused at the doorway as if on the precipice of decision, and glanced back at me before she ordered Conall to see me returned to my cell. I stood and exited the room, unsurprised to see Conall pulling on leather gloves. He wasn't as brave as Lucy or willing to touch me skin to skin. I was about to start apologizing, the way I should've that midsummer two years ago, but he spoke first.

"This is for Andy, for *everything*." He shoved me over his outstretched foot, sending me staggering toward the floor. I didn't resist. He grabbed the back of my neck and bounced my face off the wall. Pain and a trickle of warmth down my cheek. My vision blurred. The ghosts clamored within me as the darkness writhed. The foreign magic burned through my veins.

Conall grabbed me again, his hands on my back as he brought his knee up to meet my sternum, obliterating the last traces of our tenuous friendship. A pressure built in my chest, flooding outwards through my arms and into my hands. This time I didn't fight it.

I caught his leg, and he screamed, falling away from me, his trousers scorched, the flesh of his thigh wearing welts in the shape of my fingers.

DI Walsh rushed back into the corridor with a pack of uniforms at her side.

"What the hell happened?" she stared at the whimpering officer and gaped at my hands held up in surrender, fingertips still smoking. I let them haul me back to the cell, using the hem of my T-shirt to staunch the blood dripping from the cut on my eyebrow where my head had met concrete. It was already healing. I ignored their jibes and whispers. They were afraid of me, more than ever before, their hatred unable to mask the stench of their fear as shaking hands locked me in a cell with steel bars, steel that would melt, wrapped in fingers of dark fire.

Ash

NOW GRANDDAD and I were both giving Mum the silent treatment. I would've given her burnt toast and bitter coffee for dinner in case there was any doubt about how I felt, but she'd brought home a casserole courtesy of one of the McNamaras.

She pushed a plateful of something looking suspiciously like it contained beans toward me before she dished up for Granddad. If I'd had a door to slam in Mum's face, I would've done that, but the joys of sleeping on the couch meant I couldn't hide away from her. So now we were all sat at the kitchen table.

Mum stabbed at her food, chewing each mouthful mechanically before washing it down with gulps of red wine. Also a gift—from Martha apparently—a congratulations for apprehending the murderer. I swallowed a mouthful of air so I wouldn't puke at the table.

I promised Teagan I wouldn't say anything, and I wouldn't, not to Mum. Like she'd listen to me anyway. In her mind, Rowan was guilty. Case closed.

Mum's fork grated across her plate, making my teeth grind. The silence was strangulating.

"Ash, be a doll." Mum nodded at the saltshaker on the counter.

I'm not a fucking doll! I wanted to yell, and a whole lot more, but I didn't. Instead, I got up, scraped the uneaten mush into the bin, ignored the saltshaker completely, and escaped all of ten feet to the couch where I'd made up my bed.

Mum sighed and gave me the look usually heralding a lecture, but I popped my headphones on. She got the message and left me alone. Eventually, they finished dinner and retreated to their rooms, leaving me with my thoughts focused solely on Rowan. I wished I could text him but had to make do with rereading all the messages we'd sent.

When that novelty wore off, I picked up my camera, scrolling through the photos I'd taken: shots of Rowan riding Auryn, of him standing on the beach beneath a threatening sky with his back to the pyre. There was a weird shadow around him. Some sort of optical aberration, maybe. I'd be pissed if my camera was damaged with no way to get it fixed here. I went back and looked at the first photos I'd taken of him.

No shadow.

I zoomed in for a better look. There were smudges around Deirdre on the beach, but she hadn't been in focus anyway, so that was normal.

The worst of the aberrations were from the day of Patrick McNamara's funeral. The landscapes I'd taken seemed okay. It was only photos with people in them that were wonky. I studied the series again, wondering how I hadn't noticed the blurriness around Rowan and his sisters before. The smudgy images were all from after he'd been attacked in the Otherworld. Could that be it?

I paused on the photo I'd taken of him holding the butterfly. Those weren't just natural cave shadows and a bad ISO setting. It was like there was something else in the cave with us, a dark presence looming over Rowan's shoulder. And now I couldn't un-see it and couldn't stop imagining some monster escaped from the Otherworld lurking in Rowan's shadow. Thanks, brain.

With a shudder, I ditched the camera and lay with my head angled so I could see through the window. Did Rowan have a window in his cell, and if he did, could he see the same patch of sky as me? I closed my eyes, images of Rowan immediately settling behind my lids, images of him with the sun in his hair and a smile on his lips, of the sun and smile being devoured by black-oozing beasts from the Otherworld.

Rowan

THE CLOCK in the hallway sloughed away the seconds spent waiting for the inevitable.

According to Martha, I had given Conall second-degree burns, so they were charging me with assaulting a police officer. She kept her distance when delivering the news, her eyes cinched tight by the glower on her face.

Claire came to taunt me at dinner time, promising all manner of retribution for what I'd done to her brother. When I didn't respond, or even look at her, she glared at me through the bars as she dropped a large gobbet of saliva into my dinner. She shoved the tray through the gate and told me to enjoy it before sauntering back down the corridor.

Ignoring the food, I waited, letting the minutes trickle into hours as I lay on the hard mattress, straining to hear the other sounds of the station. Boots shuffling along corridors, muted voices from the break room, a cough, a sneeze, someone coming to retrieve the tray, a switch flicking and darkness descending. Finally, all other sounds faded, leaving only the ticking of the clock and the whispers inside my head.

In the dark, I moved from the bed and approached the bars. A light shone dimly at the far end of the corridor—some unlucky rookie left with the unenviable job of watching over me through the night. There were cameras in the corridor, one angled toward my cell, but I didn't care. Let them see the eldritch power slithering through my veins, turning my hands into torches.

The thoughts weren't entirely my own, and I wasn't entirely myself as I closed my fingers around the bars. I shut my eyes and reached for the strange presence infecting my body, hoping to feel the same pressure as before, that explosive sensation emanating from my chest and surging through my hands.

I felt nothing; not the first time I tried it, nor the fiftieth. Whatever power moved through me wasn't mine to summon, reacting only when provoked, it seemed. With this, as with the dead, I was merely a puppet dancing on strings controlled by another.

Soaked in cold sweat, I retreated to the bed. There would be no escaping my fate—whoever delivered it now—I was at the mercy of the O'Donnells and Kilduffs.

Eventually, the ticking of the clock lulled me into a fitful sleep.

At first, I thought I was dreaming when hands gripped my shoulders and a silver blade flashed through the black. Tinkling bells shattered the silence.

Knife at my throat, blood in my mouth, pain roaring through my nerves, and fear gripping my insides.

It took me several moments to realize I was dying.

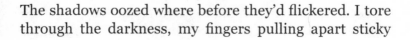

The shadows oozed where before they'd flickered. I tore through the darkness, my fingers pulling apart sticky

286

strands of purple and black as I fought my way along the rocky path.

Above me, the sluagh screamed, their voices adding to the cacophony within my own head. My ghosts sang in sinister symphony as the recently deceased drifted toward me, an indistinct blur of light against the black. Words of warning, of admonition—dread settling heavy in my bones, fear creeping cold fingers through my veins.

The taste of whisky on my tongue, the drink dulling my thoughts and slowing my movements, making it impossible to fend off my assailants. They must've known I'd walk home alone at closing. That, drunk and staggering, I'd make easy prey on the woodland path behind the church.

No, not me—Fergus. Hands on his body, a foot tripping his own. And as he fell, he turned, looking up into the face of one of his attackers.

I squeezed my eyes shut, willing the image to dissipate. It burned in the darkness of my mind, a flaming brand searing into my memory. It couldn't be real. I didn't want it to be true. Iona stared back, hair catching the pale glow of the streetlamp, a curse falling from her lips knowing I'd see her too.

"You witches, you—you *demons*!" Fergus yelled across the Otherworld. "We were right about the bloody lot of you."

He strode toward me, fists beating at the sluagh as their hands plucked like talons at his clothes and hair. It was a battle he couldn't win.

"I shouldn't've stopped with your uncle," Fergus shouted. "I should've blasted every last one of you to the hell you deserve! I should've used that ax on more than just your trees!"

I couldn't move, paralyzed by the memory repeating in my mind: the guilt and regret on her face as another hand drew the blade across Fergus's throat. My knees hit the ground, the crushing weight of the truth bearing down on me.

Fergus screamed as the sluagh tightened their grip. I willed my body to rise, for my feet to gather beneath me and run to his aid, but I couldn't. His words echoed in my mind. Demons, deserving of death, of condemnation. Maybe he was right.

The strange magic unfurling through my flesh reached its roots through rock and soil, anchoring me to the earth. I could've fought it—I should've tried, but I watched as Fergus succumbed to the sluagh.

"Help me, you bastard," he shouted. "Not like this, please. Not like this."

My uncle had pleaded for help. His chest had been riddled with shot, his heart stuttering against the lead puncturing its walls, blood seeping from more than a dozen holes. Fergus had stood over him, watching him die. Just as Iona had watched the blade slice open his throat.

Now it was my turn. Tears clouded my vision as I lifted a feeble hand toward him. I was far too late. The sluagh tugged Fergus from the cliff, shredding his ephemeral form into ribbons of light, dimming and fading as they fled into the nothing beyond. All I could do was watch.

"Death in Life and Life in Death," I whispered, my voice a rasp, my throat dry as bark.

I knelt alone on the cliff, the infection permeating every cell, enveloping me in a pall of velvet. My own sister. She hadn't acted alone. Had it been her idea? Surely not. My tears fell and the cliff disappeared, replaced by the ring of trees I'd seen before. Hawthorn, ash, and oak—each blood-smeared, branches entangled, trunks bending toward each other like grotesque lovers. And me—my legs a tree trunk, shoots and leaves tearing free from the skin of my back and shoulders, berries swelling like beads of blood.

So easy to give in.

So easy to accept my fate.

Beyond the grip of the Otherworld, my body still lay breathing, heart beating—a distant drum rattling the shadows slicking what was left of my skin.

I didn't want to die. Not yet. Not until I'd looked my sister in the eye and asked her why. Not until I understood how she could do it, knowing I felt their deaths. Rage and hatred boiled within me, my ghosts screaming. A deluge of memories lambasted my mind, a war of love and spite, of duty and desire.

Lightning ripped across the night.

The darkness shrieked as if wounded. More light bled through the gash across the sky, the distant drum of my heart settling into the steady tick-tock of a clock on the wall.

Another flash of light, of pain as if my skull were caving in.

I'd tumbled from the bed and cracked my head against the concrete of the cell's floor. My body was soaked in icy sweat, black smoke curling off my shoulders—T-shirt and trousers charred in several places—my skin stinging from a thousand shallow cuts where roots and leaves had opened my flesh.

Still, I was breathing. My heart was beating. The pain splitting my head and burning through my bones told me I was alive.

The lights in the hallway brightened, blinding. Quick footsteps echoed in the early morning quiet.

"What the hell are you doing?" Claire peered through the bars of my cell, her eyes framed by heavy circles of fatigue. She'd probably volunteered to stay on duty. "Saw you on the cameras," she said. "Looked like you were having a fit. Thought you'd do us all a favor and kick the bucket."

"Sorry to disappoint you." I picked myself off the

floor, leaving splatters of blood behind, and rolled back onto the bed, body aching, temples pounding, the ghosts in my head still unsettled.

Iona. Why? Part of me knew exactly why—knew she'd been trying to tell me. I just hadn't believed her capable of it. I'd been so sure of my family's innocence.

"You'll get what's coming to you," Claire said.

"Of that I have no doubt." A Sheehy still needed to die. "You should tell Martha her son is dead," I added.

"What?" Claire's magic crackled through the space between us, its static charge lacing my skin. Perhaps due to some Otherworld residue, her magic guttered before it even reached me.

"Fergus is dead," I said, not bothering to gentle my words. "You'll find him in the oak grove behind the church."

"You filthy, murdering fetch." Claire smashed her night stick against the bars.

"I'm not your murderer," I said softly, easing my tender head onto the standard-issue pillow. I closed my eyes as Claire continued to hurl invective at me through the bars, as she struck the gate three more times with her night stick before turning away, her fury palpable and voice indistinct as she summoned the others.

The O'Donnell was dead, which meant I was next. My blood was all that stood in the way of the spell's completion. And now I had a choice: to let my sister finish what she'd started or reveal her role in the murders and destroy my family.

Ash

MUM'S PHONE was ringing, harsh and shrill, yanking me awake. The ringing stopped, and a few moments later, Mum cursed as she rushed into the bathroom, pulling on clothes as she went.

It wasn't even light out, and I had a major crick in my neck.

"What's wrong?" I asked when she strode through the kitchen and picked up her car keys.

"It's fine," she said. "Everything's fine, go back to sleep."

Yeah right.

"Is it the colonel?" I flopped out of bed onto sleepy legs as she shook her head and zipped up her boots at the door. "Is it Rowan?"

She didn't answer as she tugged on her jacket.

"Mum, what happened? Is he all right? Did the Kilduffs—did they hurt him?" I barely got the words out. My skin turned cold and clammy, a rash of goosebumps erupting all over my arms and my stomach churning on emptiness.

She looked at me, and I hugged my arms around my chest, braced for the worst.

"No, Ash. He's fine, but they did find another body. Just please stay home with your granddad. I'll be back when I can." With that, she made a speedy exit, and less than a minute later, the station wagon's engine grumbled to life. I ran to the bathroom coughing up bile.

Another body. An O'Donnell? I should've asked. If an O'Donnell had been killed, Rowan would definitely be next. At least it wasn't Granddad—he was still sawing wood in his bedroom.

I couldn't do this. I couldn't sit here knowing Rowan was in danger—about to be fucking murdered!—and just do nothing. To hell with Teagan and the consequences of breaking magical deals. How would she even know I'd done anything? If I went to Ros Tearmann, if I asked his sisters for help without mentioning Lucy, then Teagan would take care of my father, and I could still help Rowan.

It was barely a plan, but it was all I had.

"Granddad?" I pushed open his door. He continued doing an impeccable impersonation of a tractor with a clogged engine, so I left him sleeping. He'd be fine. Teagan had promised nothing would happen to him. I had to trust her.

It took me all of a minute to pull on clothes and leave Granddad a note on the kitchen table before I laced up my Docs, tugged on my jacket, and slipped out of the cottage.

Dawn was dribbling yellow across the grey horizon by the time I found my way to Ros Tearmann. I made sure to avoid the hawthorn this time. I didn't want to imagine Rowan ending up like that, but of course the moment

I tried not to think about it, that was all that bloody filled my mind. I started jogging, my body grateful for the exercise even if it grumbled about the lack of coffee and breakfast. I couldn't remember the last time I'd been awake this early. There was a good chance the Sheehys were all still sleeping.

The mansion loomed out of the meadows, upper windows reflecting the ocean behind me. I stopped mid-step at the sight of the stables—what used to be stables, now a wrecked pile of wood. What the hell? Rowan hadn't mentioned anything about that. Not long ago I'd been sitting right there sipping tea while thinking about Rowan's biceps and when I could kiss him again.

Horsey noises drew my attention to the paddock where the three creatures grazed. Deirdre was mucking out a lean-to in the corner of the paddock, singing to herself as she tossed straw about with a pitchfork. She turned at the sound of my footsteps, pitchfork raised.

"What are you doing here?" she asked, tilting the prongs in my direction.

"They found another body. Mum rushed off early this morning, and I think Rowan is in danger. I think he'll be next, because I read this old O'Donnell book, and I know about the ritual, and I think they're going to kill him," I blurted it all in a single breath that left me panting.

Deirdre dropped the pitchfork then wiped her hands on the front of her denim dungarees. The yellow stitching on the seams wiggled about like caterpillars. I blinked and rubbed my eyes, but the caterpillars were still there.

She chewed on her bottom lip before saying, "Let's get Iona." I followed her into the kitchen, which smelled of coffee and fried onions, and I might've been salivating.

"You ready for breakfast?" Iona asked from where she stood at the stove over a giant pan.

"We have a guest," Deirdre said.

Iona turned to face us, the beads and other trinkets

in her dreadlocks clinking together. "Why are you here?" Her gaze narrowed. Considering Mum had arrested their brother, I guess I didn't deserve a warm welcome.

"Ash thinks Rowan is in danger. They found another body this morning." Deirdre poured three mugs of coffee and passed one to me.

Worry cut canyons across Iona's forehead. "Why do you think Rowan is in danger?" She started cracking eggs into the pan. Her fingers trembled. Good. At least I wasn't the only one freaking out about Rowan.

"I know about the ritual," I said. "Your Gran showed us the spell in your family's Grimoire."

"She showed you our Grimoire?" Iona glanced at Deidre, who sat perched on the kitchen table, legs swinging while she slurped her coffee.

"It seemed to explain about the murders," I continued. "At least, Rowan thought he understood what they were about, that someone is trying to undo a binding on some Otherworld creature by murdering members of the founding families."

"I see," Iona said with her back to me as she kept cracking eggs into the pan, fingers turning eggshell into shrapnel.

"But I think he's wrong," I continued, not sure if what I was trying to say would make any sense. "I read this book by Fionnula O'Donnell. I think the ritual isn't about binding some Otherworld creature at all, I think—"

"What book was this?" Deirdre interrupted me.

"*A Brief History of Inisliath: Volume I.*"

"You read that?" Deirdre asked. "All of it?"

"Not at first. I mean, it's not even in English. Or it wasn't when I first started reading, but then the letters rearranged themselves. I don't know, O'Donnell magic."

"You have their magic?" Iona scrutinized me from where she stood at the stove. "I didn't think any O'Donnell power had survived."

"Well, whatever. It doesn't matter," I said. "The point is that I think the ritual is about Rowan, about how the first deathwalker was made."

"You honestly think some O'Donnell knows better than we do about our own history?" Iona pointed at me with the egg-lifter.

"Isn't it everyone's history? The four founding families—this affects all of us. They killed a Kilduff and a McNamara. Rowan said an O'Donnell and Sheehy would be next. Mum said they found another body. That's why we have to do something before they hurt Rowan. He's the last part of the ritual." I took several gulps of coffee, my whole body singing praises as the caffeine hit my stomach.

"He's in jail," Iona said "*Your* mother put him there. How are we supposed to help him now?" She turned back to the stove and savagely scrambled the eggs.

"We have to break him out, obviously," I said. "If the Kilduffs and O'Donnells are behind this—that's what Rowan thought—then he's a sitting duck in that cell. We have to get him out of there."

"And then what?" Deirdre asked as Iona shoveled eggs onto three plates.

"We keep him safe until my mum finds the real murderer," I said.

Deirdre set the plates on the table and gestured for me to sit down. "And if she doesn't find the real murderer?"

"Then he leaves the island, I don't know. But we can't leave him sitting in a jail cell just waiting to get his throat slit," I said.

"Do you really think they'd try something at the station?" Deirdre asked when we'd all started eating. My stomach was still all snarled up in knots, but damn, I was hungry, and the eggs were delicious.

"The Kilduffs and O'Donnells got away with murdering your uncle, didn't they," I said.

295

"Let's not forget it was your cousin Fergus who did that," Iona snapped, taking out her feelings on a mushroom with her fork. "You think we can just waltz into the station and stroll out with Rowan? It's impossible."

"Are you saying it's not even worth trying?" I stabbed a mushroom of my own. "You're okay leaving your brother to get killed by a Kilduff?"

Iona winced and looked away.

"Besides, the station will be empty. Mum said they found a body. Won't they have every cop at the crime scene?"

"They'll leave a couple of people at the station, but one or two we could probably handle," Deirdre said, placing a hand on Iona's arm. "Ash is right. It's time."

"Fine, I'll let the others know." Iona whipped her phone from her pocket.

"Not Neasa," I said, earning frowns from both the girls. "She tells Teagan everything. Maybe better to avoid that right now. Teagan said she thinks—" I stopped myself before I said any more, a moment away from shoving my foot in it.

"What did Teagan say?" Deirdre asked.

"Only that she thinks someone in her family might be responsible," I choked out. "That doesn't matter right now. We just need to get Rowan somewhere safe."

Iona nodded and continued pressing buttons. Her phone didn't even have a touch screen. It was one of those ancient, indestructible models with a rainbow, ruggedized cover.

"We should go," I said, and she put away her phone. "They'll finish processing the crime scene and head back to the station. We don't have much time. We might already be too late." I shoved my plate aside and got to my feet. Deirdre and Iona did the same without argument, and together we tugged on boots and jackets.

"It'll be faster with the horses," Deidre said.

"Can Ash even ride?" Iona asked, picking up tack as we exited the house.

"Definitely not," Deirdre answered for me as she clicked her fingers. The horses all came running toward her, "but you don't have to, just hold on to Auryn's mane, and you'll be fine."

"I—um—okay," I said and suddenly found myself guided to the wooden block. I swung my leg over Auryn's back and knotted my fingers in her hair.

Iona tacked up the big, silver-coated horse and climbed into the saddle. Deidre was already on Comet. Iona rode up beside me and clipped a lead to Auryn's halter.

"Are we doing the right thing?" Iona asked, her question directed at Deidre.

"We're doing what we have to," she answered.

"Hold on tight, Ash," she added before clicking her tongue.

The three horses burst into a run. Trot, canter, gallop, whatever it was it was fast and jolted every bone in my body, rattling my teeth so hard I was sure I was going to lose a few. I might've felt a bit more heroic if I hadn't been so damn scared. Somehow, I managed to hold on as pounding hooves devoured the miles, and black clouds swamped the sky.

Rowan

THE STATION was quiet, manned only by Logan
Kilduff, the newest recruit to the Inisliath police force
and barely old enough to order a beer. His mom had
been an exchange student from China who'd come to the
island on an archaeological tour. She'd ended up living
with James Kilduff for four years before boarding the
ferry one afternoon, either fed up with life on the island
or depleted by James.

Logan shoved a tray of toast, beans, and cold coffee
through the bars of the cell without even looking at me.
I ate mechanically, listening to the ticking clock as I
watched the brightening patch of sky visible through my
window. All I could do was wait: for DI Walsh and others
to return and for the wrath of Martha O'Donnell to be
unleashed. Wait for my sister and those with her to come
and end it. Would Iona even have the courage to do it
herself?

I didn't want to think about Iona's part in all this or
how she needed my blood to complete the ritual. But for

what? This couldn't be about unleashing a creature of the Otherworld. I replayed the memories of our recent conversations, her concern for our family, her desire to change life on the island. The words Ash had deciphered from the book echoed in my thoughts.

Blood of hawthorn, ash, and oak. By blood, a rowan born.

Death in Life, Life in Death...

Unmade the same for Death and Life to sever, all ebb and cease, the rowan dies.

The spell, the binding—maybe Ash was right, and it had all been about me.

"If you're done with breakfast, I think it's time to go."

I turned at the sound of the familiar voice, every fine hair on my body standing up.

"What are you doing?" I asked as Iona unlocked the gate.

"What does it look like?" She wouldn't meet my gaze. "We're busting you out."

"I saw you. When Fergus..." The words stuck in my throat.

"I never wanted to hurt anyone." There were tears in her eyes.

"Not even Fergus?" I asked.

She swallowed hard. "Maybe him just a little."

"You hurt me, too," I said, resentment scrubbing the gentleness from my voice. "You knew I'd feel their deaths."

"There's was no helping that. Sorry."

"You did it anyway." I bit my tongue, trying to swallow the sudden rush of anger. That wasn't me. Was it? I didn't even know anymore. "Why?" My voice quavered.

"We're so tired of this island," she said, tears trailing silver down her cheeks. "All of us. We're tired of being its prisoners, of being dictated to by tradition, of having to choose between family and freedom, of being punished for who we love and for walking away." She hiccoughed and sucked in a breath. "We can't live like this. Who would want to? You understand, don't you?" She looked at me, her gaze pleading, imploring.

I could deny it, I could wield her question as a weapon and hurt her with my answer, pretend I didn't understand why she'd opened three throats with her blade, why she intended to cut mine. But I did understand. I understood so intimately I wanted to wrap my arms around her and tell her everything would be all right.

Death in Life, Life in Death.

Somehow it was my death that would free them, that would sever the connection to the Otherworld and nullify the flow of magic. All this time, it had been me. The rowan was the chain binding the others to Inisliath.

Another part of me wanted to wrap my hand around her throat and unleash the fire burning through my veins. That part of me wanted to hurt her, to make *her* understand what *I'd* be forced to endure. It moved within me, the power uncoiling and spreading through my fingers. My hand twitched at my side, but I ground my teeth together and stifled the urge to end her, shaking as I fought the magic blistering beneath my skin.

"And this frees you?" I asked.

"If our interpretation is correct, it should release us from the hold of the magic. We'll lose our magic, but we'll be free to leave and live as we choose."

I wanted to laugh, to scream.

"Ro, are you okay?" she asked.

"I understand," I said, and she exhaled, her shoulders sagging with relief. "But you'll still have to kill me?" I added, not meaning to make it a question, not wanting to hope for the impossible.

"It's the only way," she said, softly. "Oh Gods, Ro. I'm so sorry." She reached for me, but I pulled back.

Iona would never have taken a life without being sure.

Looking at her clad in tie-dye and rainbows, I couldn't imagine her capable of murder, and yet she'd told me as much that day in the paddock.

"You must've had O'Donnell help," I said.

Iona pressed her lips together.

"Martha? You were supposed to kill Brian, weren't you?"

Iona glanced at me, guilt flickering across her features.

"But you wanted to kill Fergus." Seems I wasn't the only one in my family battling rage and hatred.

"He deserved it," she said. I couldn't argue with that. Maybe he even deserved being taken by the sluagh.

"We should go, the others are waiting," she said. "Ash is here."

"Ash? Why?" The breath rushed out of me as if I'd taken a fist to the gut.

"Rescuing you was their idea."

I gawked at her, dumbfounded. This was hard enough without having to face Ash, to think about their hand in mine, their kisses, and kind words.

"Come on, we need to go."

My feet moved as my mind warred against what was happening. I had a choice.

Did I?

I could run and escape my sister, avoid her blade and the completion of the spell. But for what? For something with Ash I couldn't even name? For a person I'd only just met, and the notion of a life I had no right to long for? My freedom would condemn my family to life on the island, and what of the power in my veins? I stared at my hands. I couldn't escape myself.

Ash paced up and down at the entrance to the station, arms folded, a frown etched deeply across their forehead.

"Oh, thank God you're okay," Ash said when they saw me. I wanted to throw my arms around them. I restrained myself, also not wanting to risk Ash's life, not with the unknown still slithering beneath my skin and remnants of the Otherworld clinging to me. I opened my mouth—shut it. Words failed. How could I explain this to them? How could I explain the choice I was going to make?

"Shit, what happened to your clothes?" Ash asked, their gaze flicking over me.

"No time, let's go," Iona said, heading for the doors. "Where's Deirdre?"

"With Logan. Someone's robbing the Copper Kettle apparently. I promised to stay here until he got back." Ash gave me a careful grin as we walked out of the doors into a morning already drenched by drizzle. Black clouds scudded across the horizon, the wind from the sea sighing a lamentation for Fergus. The rain began to fall harder, the island's tears for yet another loss. Would Inisliath weep for me?

Iona led us across the tiny parking lot to where Solas had been tied to a lamp post. Auryn grazed the sidewalk weeds beside him, then tossed her mane and whickered a greeting to me. My heart ached, pain permeating every cell. It would happen today. It had to. It would only be cruel to let me linger. Perhaps it was a gift. So few people knew they were going to die and never get to say goodbye.

"Could I get a leg up?" Ash asked, looking expectantly at me.

"No, we'll be faster just the two of us," Iona said as she stepped into Solas's saddle. "Ash should stay here. Last thing we need is their mom thinking we're kidnappers, too."

"Right. It's fine," they said, hurt on their face and dripping over their words. "You should go. You need to be somewhere safe."

"Ash, I—" I wanted so badly to touch them, to kiss them again, but I couldn't, not with Iona trotting circles around us and telling me to hurry up. Not with knowing how this ritual ended and the choice I'd already made.

Without saying more, I grabbed a handful of Auryn's mane and swung onto her back.

"I'll see you soon," Ash said, the hope lighting up their eyes and curling their lips into a smile like a knife twist through the heart. Again.

"I hope so," I said.

"Ash?" The colonel approached the police station. He was dressed in a blue rain jacket, wheeling a travel bag behind him. He was tall and heavy-set, balding, with a sharp blue gaze that cut through clothes and skin to rake across bone. The 9AM ferry was leaving in little over an hour.

"Shit." Ash visibly shuddered, their shoulders tightening, their whole body braced.

"Come with me," I said, pulse racing. It would only delay the inevitable, but I needed to know Ash would be safe when I was gone.

"By the gods, we don't have time for this." Iona tugged at the reins to turn Solas in a circle, drawing up beside me. "Come on, Rowan."

"Come with me," I said, and this time extended my hand to Ash, the risk of touching them worth it. Ash looked up at me with island eyes.

"Rowan!" Iona exhaled her exasperation and shook her head at me.

"Ash? Is your mother at work already? I was hoping to speak to her before we left." The colonel smiled, and Ash grabbed my hand. I hauled them up behind me, and they wrapped their arms around my waist, their warmth seeping into my bones.

I nudged Auryn, and she responded instantly. Behind us, the colonel yelled for us to stop. Logan rounded the corner with Deirdre, his eyes wide, mouth hanging slack in astonishment. Deirdre waved to me, her lips trembling.

When we reached the cliff path, Iona clicked her tongue, and Solas burst into a gallop. Ash's grip tightened as Auryn tried to keep up, her hooves pounding the ground. My heart beat in time, the wind screaming in my ears and drowning out the voices in my head. The mist twined around us as if rain and wind weren't enough to convey the island's anguish or hide my own.

We'd barely covered a mile when Iona slowed Solas, allowing us to catch up when visibility became worse. Auryn huffed with the effort of carrying two people at a gallop, grateful for the reduced speed. Iona urged Solas off the path and through the meadow leading to the cliffs.

"Can't see if anyone's following us," Ash said, their head turning against my shoulder.

"The mist will hide us." Iona slowed Solas to a walk.

Carefully, we picked our way along the clifftop, approaching the place where my sisters had ended my life. Ash must've recognized it, too, as their body stiffened against mine.

Iona slid from Solas's back without saying a word. She peered into the mist in the direction of the sea, the wind whipping the dreadlocks about her head, the trinkets knotted in her hair chiming like bells.

"Here?" I asked. "Really?"

"Oh, Ro," she said, my name lost in a sob at the back of her throat.

"Why are we stopping?" Ash asked.

"You shouldn't be here." Iona looked at Ash, not at me, as two figures emerged from the mist. Teagan and Cillian.

"Shit, Rowan. They're here for you," Ash said, their voice spiking with panic, their arms squeezing hard against my ribs.

"I know," I said, only mildly surprised it was Teagan and not Lucy. "You should get down."

"What? No. Ride. Come on. We have to get away. Why are we just sitting here? I don't understand." Ash tightened their fingers in my shirt.

"It's fine, we're here to help." Teagan offered Ash her

hand.

"Go on." I patted their fingers, even though my own were trembling. Ash hesitated before sliding to the ground, immediately flanked by Cillian and Teagan. I dismounted, too, and leaned against Auryn for support as I faced my sister.

"Please don't hurt them," I said softly.

"Ash? Of course not," Iona said.

"And don't let them see," I said, my voice cracking. "They don't deserve that."

She nodded at Teagan and Cillian still standing guard with Ash between them. Ash's face had turned as pale as the mist.

"What's happening?" they asked. "Rowan?" They looked at me but all I could do was shake my head.

"Could someone fucking explain what the hell is going on?" Ash's voice was thick with tears.

"The murders are part of a ritual to release us from the magic," Teagan answered. "Permanently and cleanly. Once it's done, we'll be free."

Martha O'Donnell would never have agreed to that. They must've lied to her.

"Free to live the life we choose away from this damn rock," Cillian added.

"But—but Rowan." Ash's voice cracked and so did something inside me, their pain cleaving my heart in half. I wouldn't get to live at all. My life for theirs. But if not me, then who? Knowing what I did of death, I would never let another Sheehy take my place. And yet, part of me raged against it, a voice screaming *why me?*

"Ash, you should go with Teagan," I managed to say through gritted teeth, my hands clenched into fists.

"Why, so you can die? You're going to let them kill you?" Fury replaced the fear on their face, eyes shining like silver.

"Because I'm what binds them," I said. "And then I'll be free, too."

"You'll be dead. That's not the same," Ash said. "What if the spell isn't what you think it is? What if it doesn't work? It'll have all been for nothing. You'll be dead and—and—"

Feeling numb, I walked on wobbly legs toward Ash. Teagan and Cillian stepped away but didn't go far.

"I'm sorry," I said, then faltered, not knowing what else to say, how to begin explaining any of this or why I knew that as much as I wanted to imagine a life beyond being a deathwalker, a life beyond Inisliath, I was going to lie down on the cliff and let my sister end my life. Again.

"You know I feel their memories. There's so much pain." I pressed my fingers into the scar above my heart, the chorus inside my mind deafening as they continued to assault me with flashes of their recollections. "I could stop it all. I could be the last rowan who has to die, who has to die over and over again. I could end this." Gently, I brushed the hair off Ash's forehead.

"No, not like this. It isn't fair."

"It never has been."

"You can't do this. Please, Rowan. Please don't— you're choosing them? But you could..."

I knew what Ash was going to say, but I didn't want to hear it. I couldn't. I couldn't let them say those words out loud and shake my resolve. Instead, I kissed them, a kiss I hoped conveyed all my longing and regret, guilt and shame, all my hope that Ash would leave this island and live the life I'd never dared to dream of until I met them.

I tasted the salt of our tears as Ash returned my kiss, their arms wrapped around my back, fingernails digging into my skin. When we pulled apart to draw breath, they looked up at me.

"Why are you doing this?" they asked.

"For my sisters," I said, hoping Ash would understand. Their hands left my body and they stepped away, trembling.

"I'm sorry," I said again.

"Fuck you," Ash responded, turning their back on me and taking several steps into the mist. Cillian hung back, keeping his eye on Ash. The mist closed around both of them. At least Ash wouldn't have to see.

The sting of betrayal.

The burn of anger.

The wrench of loss.

The ineffable emptiness of being powerless to change hated circumstances.

I understood it all. The ghosts swarming in my head still hurled memories into my eyes, reminding me Ash's pain was slight compared to the history of anguish endured by the islanders.

Teagan moved forward and tried to take my arm.

I waved her away. "This is between me and my sister."

"But what if—"

"Your presence isn't required." I strode back to Iona, where she waited on the cliff's edge, kneeling where I'd first lost my life.

"I don't think I can do it," she said. "With the others... it wasn't me. You know that, right?"

"It wasn't you who actually cut their throats. I know," I said.

"So how can I do it to you?"

"Do it for Siobhan and Neasa." I had to pause to breathe, to force the words between my teeth. "Do it for Deirdre, for yourself. For everyone." *But me.*

Iona turned toward me, and I folded her in my arms. Thirty generations of rowans gathered like a storm inside me, their presence comforting, their wraiths moving through me, holding Iona, everyone one of them forgiving her, loving her, longing only for the freedom her dagger promised. All were relieved it was nearly over, except me. I, too, had longed for freedom, I just no longer wanted it to be like this.

And yet...my body moved of its own volition, guided by the rowans who came before me as I shed my shirt and pressed my naked back against the skin of the island. I tried to fight it, to push away from the earth and escape the abyss yawning open within me. Inside, I was screaming—a terrified kid again, afraid of the empty darkness waiting for me on the other side of a sharp blade.

The ghosts were stronger and held me down. Perhaps they knew best. The wind moaned around us, sorrow seeping through the fissures in the rock and soaking into the cracks inside me.

"I can't do this," Iona said, her hands shaking as she raised her blade, pressing it against my throat. It had been easier for Mother.

Gently, I wrapped my fingers around Iona's, steadying her hands. Slowly, we lowered the blade together until the sharp tip of silver rested in the hollow of the scar above my heart. It was beating so fast, my fingers slick with sweat where they gripped my sister's.

"Like this, it'll be easier," I said, my voice a stranger's. "It's happened before, remember?" This didn't feel real. It wasn't me lying in the dirt about to die. It felt like I was watching it happen to someone else. The black tendrils spread up my arm. I felt my veins dilate and muscles contract. The vision in my left eye turned purple with shadow.

"Oh Gods, Rowan. I'm so sorry." Her tears spattered my face.

"Take care of Auryn," I said.

"Of course."

"And Ash. Help them."

"I will, Ro. I promise." Iona sobbed, her shoulders heaving as my fingers, moved by other forces, rested at the top of the hilt. I closed my eyes and let the weight of our hands drive the blade into my chest.

Ash

FUCK YOU? What the hell had I been thinking? Those couldn't be my last words to him. I couldn't let them do this. I wouldn't.

I turned, blinking tears from my eyes, just in time to see Rowan's hands clutching the knife.

"No, Ash. Don't!" Teagan grabbed me.

I wrenched away from her and flung myself across the distance, reaching for the blade. Too fucking late, I tried to grab the knife. The blade sliced open my palm as it sank into Rowan's chest, mottled black by the Otherworld.

I reeled back, my blood dripping onto his chest where too much red bubbled up from the wound. Iona bent over him, her sobs tearing out of her in screams that must've left her throat raw. More blood spilled over his ribs, a slow-motion waterfall. Some of it was black and smoking.

It wasn't too late, yet. I could stop the bleeding. We could call an ambulance. We could save his life. I pressed my hands to the wound, my fingers turning wet and hot. His eyes were open, staring past me at the sky, the darkness draining out of the left even as I willed him to blink, to twitch, to breathe.

"No, Rowan. Come on. Please, please." No matter how much pressure I applied to his chest, blood kept welling up between my fingers. My own hand throbbed, but I ignored it, pressing harder against his ribs.

"Come on, Ash." Cillian took my shoulders and hauled me away, pain burning through my collarbone as I fought against the McNamara's grip. Blood-slimed, my hands slipped from Rowan's body. It was too late. I'd been too late.

The ground began to shake. A seismic shudder rumbled through the earth and up my legs, jarring my bones. The horses screamed before bolting away from the cliffs.

The quake continued. Lightning unzipped the cloud-choked sky as the wind tore across the cliffs, ripping at our hair and clothes. Teagan staggered forward, took Iona by the arm, and hauled her away from Rowan's body.

I battered at Cillian, clawing and scratching until he let me go. I ran forward, but the ground rolled beneath me, sending me down hard on my knees. More lightning. Thunder boomed, and the sea thrashed against the cliffs. The wind howled. Literally. It was full of screaming voices. The mist thickened, swallowing Rowan. I crawled toward him, feeling my way across the rock, but all I found was the edge of the cliff.

Then the ground stopped shaking, the mist peeled open, and Rowan was gone.

Gone.

Dead.

I couldn't breathe. Couldn't believe I'd let this happen. I'd stood there while Iona fucking murdered her own brother. She'd pay for this. They all would. I was a witness, and I'd give my testimony, see the lot of them rotting behind bars for what they'd done. They couldn't do this. This couldn't be happening. *Please*—I curled my fingers into a fist, the nails biting into the cut across my palm. I sucked in a breath at the shock of pain.

A little voice inside my skull tried to remind me Rowan had chosen this—his own fucking hands had been on the dagger—but I ignored it. They'd murdered him. And now he was gone.

Voices behind me. Yelling, crying. Hands on my shoulders. Mum asking me if I was all right. I collapsed in her arms, pressing my face into her shoulder, and she held me, rocking me as I tried to reassemble all the shattered parts of myself.

She helped me to my feet, and I wiped my eyes. Mistake. All I'd done was smear blood across my eyelids, making the world look rosy when it had all turned to shit.

Ms. Sheehy stood at the cliff's edge, staring at the sea.

"What the hell did you do!" Martha O'Donnell strode toward Iona. "Fergus is dead! My boy, you killed my boy!"

"He killed our uncle," Iona said, far too calm for all that had happened.

Martha slapped her, the sound echoing across the cliffs, making all of us wince.

"Don't touch her," Ms. Sheehy said, her voice as sharp as her gaze as she turned on Martha, hands raised.

Everyone seemed to suck in a breath. Nothing happened. Rowan's mum stared at her hands, flexing the fingers.

"What...how?" Her face folded into a frown.

"Did it work?" Teagan asked.

"I think so." Iona looked down at her own hands.

"Did what work?" Sile Kilduff asked. I hadn't seen her since the day we arrived on Inisliath, but she faced Teagan now, gripped Teagan's chin and tilted her face up to her own. "What did you do? You will tell me."

Teagan stared into her mom's eyes for a moment before laughing. "It worked!" More laughter bubbled out of her. "Iona, we did it."

At least Rowan's sacrifice hadn't been for nothing, but that didn't stop me from despising each one of them for getting what they wanted when Rowan was dead and my heart—God, the pain in my chest. It was a million times worse than getting punched in the face. Worse than a broken wrist or subluxated collarbone. It went all the way through me, a gigantic bruise wrapping me head to toe.

"You did this?" Ms. Sheehy turned to her daughter, and Iona drew back, huddling into herself. I pressed against my mum, grateful for her arm around my shoulders. I couldn't have stayed standing on my own.

"Our bond to the island," Iona said, her voice barely a whisper. "We severed it. Now none of us have magic anymore."

"You've destroyed us." Martha pointed an accusatory finger at Iona while Mum and I observed. "You lied to me! You said you'd found a way to make us strong again, to give us back our vitality."

"Strong and free and capable of living lives away from this place," Iona said.

"We never wanted the magic." Cillian spoke up for the first time. "We wanted to be rid of it, and now we are."

"But why?" Sile looked to Teagan for answers. "Why would you want to be rid of our power?"

"Is it so hard to understand?" she said. "If there's no magic, there's no reason to stay on this miserable rock! We can love who want to and be who we want to be."

Martha gasped, and was caught by one of the uniformed officers as she staggered. I glanced around for the first time. The whole police force seemed to be out here now—no Logan or Deirdre, though. Lucy was there, too, striding across the grass, making a beeline for Teagan and Cillian.

"This whole time? It was you?" Lucy asked.

"Not only me," Teagan admitted, her gaze flashing to Iona.

"Thank you," Lucy said. "Thank you, thank you." She pulled her sister into a hug with a smile on her ugly, perfect face. Then she turned her attention on Cillian. She caught his hand, and a moment later they were locked together, mouth to mouth, kissing each other as if their lives depended on it. I'd never hated anyone more than I hated Lucy right then.

"And you knew about this?" Sile wheeled on Martha. "You let them kill our Andy? Your Fergus."

"It wasn't meant to be Fergus. Never Fergus. And it was meant to restore us. They told me..." Martha slid to the ground, chest heaving with sobs.

"That's what you get for trusting a filthy Sheehy." Sile spat at Martha's feet.

My gaze was drawn back to the puddle of red on the rocks, his blood slowly seeping into the earth—all that was left of him disappearing even as I watched.

"You." Ms. Sheehy spoke to Iona, breaking the shocked silence. "You are no daughter of mine." She proclaimed it loud enough for everyone to hear. "You have forsaken your Sheehy blood, betrayed your family, this island, your gods. You are dead to me. Do you understand?" She glared at Iona until Iona gave a tiny nod. Ms. Sheehy gathered her skirts, swept away from the cliff's edge, and shoved past Martha and Sile when they tried to stop her.

"Going to disown us, too?" Lucy asked her mum, her hand in Cillian's.

"Don't tempt me," Sile said. "What you've done—" She shook her head then turned away from Lucy and Teagan, and headed back toward the cliff top with Kilduff officers drifting in her wake. They all looked shocked and lost.

"Iona killed Rowan," I said. "She killed them all." Saying it out loud didn't make it any easier to believe. I'd watched him die and still expected him to walk out of the field, to give me his crooked grin and ask me if I was okay.

Mum hugged me tight and kissed my forehead.

"Everyone back to the station, please," Mum shouted, assuming her role as detective again. No one was listening.

Martha was helped to her feet by two O'Donnell officers and all but carried away from the cliff despite Mum barking orders at the cops to get witness statements.

Lucy, Cillian, and Teagan were chatting, the only ones smiling as they began picking their way back toward the path.

Iona remained at the edge of the cliff. I wanted to shove her over the edge and send her face first into the waves. She deserved it. But that was not what Rowan would want. *For my sisters*, he'd said. Fuck, I hated them. They'd taken something beautiful and destroyed it, destroyed it the moment they'd made him a deathwalker and forced him to die over and over again.

I think I hated them even more than I hated my father.

"Who will forgive me?" Iona asked as Mum pulled her away from the edge.

"No one," I said. "Not ever. What you did is unforgivable."

Iona choked up another sob.

"Ash," Mum said in her warning tone, with a shake of her head. But I didn't give a shit. All I wanted was someone to hurt as much as I did while Rowan's blood scabbed my face and hands.

It was late afternoon by the time we got back to the cottage. Mum had taken me to the tiny clinic in town to get my hand patched up after depositing Iona at the station for "safe keeping". I was beyond exhausted. I wanted to sleep for a year, until this was all a distant memory I no longer had to feel anything about. But the universe was its usual uncooperative self and decided to take an extra-large dump on me.

The last person I wanted to see sat waiting in the kitchen, a pot of tea steaming on the table between him and Granddad. Guess Teagan hadn't kept her end of the deal. Yet another reason to detest the lot of them.

"Ash! Dear God, are you all right?" The colonel rushed toward me, and I was too numb to care. He stood frozen as he laid his hands on my shoulders, studying my bandaged hand. "This wouldn't have happened if you'd been on the ferry."

Of course. It was all my fault as usual.

"God, Robert. Could we not do this now please?" Mum collapsed into a chair beside Granddad. He pushed a mug towards her.

"When would you like to do it, then?" The colonel asked. "I've heard all about the goings-on here. A serial killer on the loose? Do you really think this is the place for our child?"

And back and forth it went. The colonel berating Mum, Mum barely defending herself from the barrage of criticism pretending to be concern.

"If you were really that worried about me, maybe you wouldn't have broken my arm," I said, finding my voice.

The colonel turned to me. "Sit down, Ash."

"I'd rather stand." What Rowan had done took a kind of courage I'd probably never have, but standing up to my father, maybe that was something I could do.

"If you insist." My father sipped his tea.

I looked at Mum, and she met my gaze. The bags

under her eyes were puffy and dark, her crow's feet much deeper now.

Don't give in, don't give in. I pleaded with her in my mind, hoping she'd get the message if I stared back hard enough. Her gaze slipped from my face to settle on my wrist, at the cast still there. Her expression changed, her eyes grey as steel as she sat up straighter and cleared her throat.

"I want a divorce," she said, and I held my breath.

The colonel put down his mug, then glanced at me before he turned his full attention on Mum.

"I won't make it easy for you. Divorce me, and you'll lose everything: your career, your home, your child."

"You think I care about a house or career?" She shook her head. "I only care about one thing, and I'll fight you. God help me, I'll fight you with everything I have. If it leaves me destitute, so be it, but I'll not have Ash spend another day under your roof."

"Is that so?" the colonel said, and I recognized the look creeping across his face, the look that usually meant a punch was imminent. If he hit Mum now, I'd kill him. The block of kitchen knives was only three steps away. I'd drive the blade into his heart and twist it for good measure. I almost hoped he'd make a move. I wanted to hurt him, to stop the hurt flooding every inch of me.

Today was not the day to fuck with me.

"If this goes to court, you know I'll win, and I'll make sure you don't even get visitor's rights," the colonel said.

"Why do even want me?" I asked, and his head spun in my direction. "If I'm such a disappointment, why even bother with me? Or do you just miss your punching bag?"

He took a breath as if my words had landed a physical blow. About damn time.

"All I've ever wanted was what's best for you," the colonel said. "All I ever wanted was for you to realize your true potential."

"And how did giving me black eyes help with that, exactly?" I asked, aware of my father's twitching fingers and the muscle ticking in his jaw. It wouldn't be long before he got to his feet and his hands became fists. "Did you think you could beat the failure out of me? Is that what your father did to you?"

Granddad winced, and Mum raised her hands, warning me to stop, but I couldn't. Nothing could hurt me more right now.

"Ash—" My father started.

"Did you think I was becoming my best self when you put your fist in my face? How was that supposed to help me reach my potential? Come on, tell me." I wasn't yelling, I didn't have to. "How about letting me live my life without always being afraid I'll disappoint you and pay for it in black eyes?"

Silence.

Mum gave me a tentative smile, and Granddad gave me a nod.

My father stared at me, eyes wide, mouth opening and closing like a goldfish. He looked down, brushed a crumb from the table and straightened his mug so the handle lined up with the wood grain.

"I—" He coughed and cricked his neck. "You want to stay here?" His voice was soft and civil. He should've been chucking me through tables by now. Maybe Teagan *had* done something to him.

"No, I want to live in the city, but not with you." I couldn't imagine staying on Inisliath now. Not after Rowan. "You say you love me and want the best for me. *That* would be for the best." My words were unlikely to spark some miraculous transformation in him, but they seemed to have shaken him, which was about all I could've hoped for.

"I'm already having divorce papers drawn up," Mum said. "Sign them, and I'll make sure you see Ash as often as possible."

I scowled, but Mum gave me a look that kept my lips sealed.

The colonel seemed on the verge of speaking, but he clenched his jaw, nodded, and stood up from the table. He stepped toward me, perhaps expecting me to flinch, but I stood my ground, and he offered me his hand to shake. Seriously? I offered him a raised eyebrow, and he let his hand drop.

"I do love you, Ash. I'm—I—" Again, he seemed to have a catch in his throat. Was that emotion he was choking on? Could he actually feel something after all? "Have your solicitor send the papers to mine," he said in parting as he headed for the door, and I watched him leave, wondering why the ache in my chest was back with a vengeance. This was what I wanted, and yet watching him leave hurt in ways I didn't understand.

"That didn't go too badly," Granddad said as I staggered my way to the table, managing to land in a chair instead of on the floor.

"Don't be fooled. He's in shock. He'll recover, and then he'll fight us," Mum said. "But this time we'll fight back. This time, we won't let him win."

Rowan

THE ABYSS yawned open, welcoming me with a breath of embers.

The alien presence within me tore apart the threads of my being, unmaking me from the inside out. My skin sheared into bark. My blood turned to berries. My legs twined into roots. My arms stretched toward the bruised sky of the Otherworld.

Hawthorn, Ash, Oak, and Rowan.

Our boughs knotted together, the sacred circle complete. Above us the sluagh wailed, and a thousand butterflies swarmed through the void, shards of iridescence shattering as they fell like stars.

The voices in my head rose in tumult, their cries drowned out by a single, serpent whisper. I let Death take me, break me, consume me in immolating darkness.

Cold.

Cold like knives flaying flesh from bone.

Water lapping at my feet. Water in my chest.

Sand in my eyes. Sand between my fingers.

A scream, not of a spirit in the Otherworld, but of a seagull as it coasted low over the beach. I squinted against the glare and coughed ocean from my lungs, every movement accompanied by jarring pain, every inch of me screaming as skin stretched over bone, as blood pumped thick and hot through shriveled veins.

Gentle hands on the back of my head. Soft wool wrapped around my shoulders.

"There you are," Deirdre said. "We've been waiting for you."
Feeling like a newborn foal, I struggled to my feet, leaning on my sister's shoulder. I tried to speak and only coughed up brine, my lungs on fire as I expelled more water.
"You'll be fine. Gran brought tea. Think you can walk?" Deirdre didn't wait for my answer, instead hauling me by the elbow as we staggered up the beach, pebbles slick beneath my bare feet.
Gran rose on creaking legs to greet me, kissing both cheeks and smoothing the hair from my eyes. She patted the picnic blanket, and I let my knees buckle as I drew

the woolen blanket redolent with sage and lavender tighter around my shoulders while shivers wracked my naked body.

"Here," Deirdre pushed a steaming cup of tea into my hands. Agrimony and burdock with chamomile and basil. It was sickly sweet with honey, but I drank it down and Deirdre poured me more, the warm liquid soothing my salt-raw throat and stilling the queasiness in my belly. Warmed from the inside, I let the blanket slip from my shoulders and tilted my face toward the afternoon sky.

I'd died. I'd been consumed by darkness. And yet...

I felt the sunlight in my marrow, the steady thrum of my heart, the blood singing through my veins.

I was alive.

"You had us worried," Deirdre said, her hands speaking for my gran as well. "We've been out here for days. We thought maybe when Ash—well, an O'Donnell shouldn't have meddled like that, but maybe it was just as well."

"You knew—" My voice cracked and wobbled, my tongue struggling to form words behind my teeth.

"That you'd come back?" Deirdre asked. "No, not for sure. But we hoped. I mean, we were pretty sure that's what the spell meant, weren't we, Gran? We didn't know what Ash's blood getting into the mix might do, but I guess it didn't matter much. You're here." She gave me a smile.

Gran nodded as she touched my face, my shoulder, my wrist. She tapped my skin and I looked down. My skin was smooth and unblemished, marked only by freckles. No ink at my wrists. No scars on my forearms. I pressed a hand to my chest and found no keloid, no trace of death or spell carved into my flesh. The only scars I carried were two silver-pink gashes above my left elbow.

"You've been reborn." Gran signed. "The spell was never about freeing a creature of the Otherworld."

"It was about you," Deirdre said.

My incipient mind struggled to stitch together the truth. Deirdre and my gran. They'd known. They'd allowed Iona to murder. And Ash...

Ash.

"You know, there's a lot we didn't know about this island or our history," Deirdre continued. "All that nonsense about us taming wild gods and claiming their power? Rubbish." She signed while she spoke. "All our ancestors did was make a deal with the feral god of this island. Magic in exchange for the souls of our dead, and a deathwalker to make it so."

"I don't understand." I didn't understand how they'd planned this behind our backs, how they'd let our sister spill innocent blood, how they'd so easily forfeited my life.

"Oh, it's simple, really," Deirdre said. "The old god survives on souls. Long as we kept it fat and happy, it let us have magic in return. But we figured the weak magic was its way of saying it wasn't so happy anymore and wanted more feeding."

"More souls."

"Exactly. More dead people. Or so we thought. And what with most of us hating the magic and wanting off the island anyway, we figured it was about time we renegotiated the deal, only that wasn't really an option." Deirdre ended her sentence with a sigh as I battled to digest the series of revelations.

"The O'Donnells think they're so clever," she continued after a moment. "But they'd forgotten, just like the others. Only the Sheehys remembered about the pact sealed by the blood of the four families. A pact we could unmake the same way," she said, with something like pride limning her words.

It was too much. I couldn't begin to make sense of what she was telling me, and yet the memories of the rowans before me still echoed in my mind, the memory of blood and bark, of a soul wrought from the earth—if only I'd understood my own mind better, not that it would have changed the outcome. I still would have died on the cliffs and been undone. I wrapped my fingers around the scars in my arm. Not the marks of some Otherworld creature, but the fingerprints of a god.

"You killed them?" I asked in disbelief.

"Not me," Deirdre said. "Teagan, mostly. Cillian helped, too."

Deirdre, my baby sister, gentlest of them all, had been the one behind this, the one to order throats cut. It was anathema, a solar flare incinerating my insides. My hands were shaking again as I struggled to fill my lungs, dry lips cracking salt and copper across my teeth.

"How could you?" My voice trembled.

"For you," Deirdre said, lifting my chin with her fingers and forcing my gaze to meet her own. Earnest green eyes, a sad smile on her face. "For our family. For all of us. It was the right thing to do."

I envied her conviction and wished I could be so certain, but doubt clawed through my guts and gnawed at my mind.

"What about Davidson?" I asked, the syllables spit haltingly from my lips.

"A regrettable accident," Deirdre said, her eyes clouding. "I only wanted Comet back. We just meant to talk to him, me and Iona, but then you came to visit Gran, and I thought you'd try to stop us, so when things went wrong with Davidson, we left your bracelet with him. Sorry," she said. "I didn't want you to go to jail, but I knew you'd try to stop us."

"I let Iona—"

"No, I knew you'd die for us." Deirdre tousled my hair. "But I thought you'd try to stop us from the killing Fergus. We couldn't risk it," she said. "We needed to complete this ritual, and thank you, by the way. I was worried Iona wouldn't be able to do it at all."

"I died," I said.

"I thought you'd be used to it." She shrugged with disturbing calm.

I'd died over fifty times, absorbing their deaths, their lives, delivering their souls to a feral creature in some foul bargain we'd all misunderstood.

"By breaking the contract, we've quelled the magic," Gran signed. "And now you're free."

"Free?"

"You're not a deathwalker anymore," Deirdre answered. "You can leave this island, and you'll be fine. You don't even have to be called Rowan if you don't want to. You can go anywhere you want. Siobhan can become a doctor. Neasa will go to college and be with Teagan, eventually. Cillian can be with Lucy, too. Don't you see? It's all grand." She beamed, her laughter peeling like silver bells in the breeze, but the butterflies on her dress remained simple embroidery. The stitching on her seams didn't twine into shoots, or blossom into flowers. The magic was gone, and with it, my duty to the dead. I studied my hands again, tracing the memory of the runes across fresh, clean skin.

"I thought you loved the magic," I signed to Gran.

"I did, but when I lost Brian, when I lost Eileen and Brighid, and knew what became of them. When I saw what ferrying souls did to my brother and son, what it was doing to you. When Siobhan came crying to me after my daughter took away her dreams. It had to end," Gran signed. "The magic was destroying us. Perhaps it always intended to. Who can know the mind of a wild god? But now, perhaps we can live the lives we always wanted."

"Andy, Patrick, Fergus," I said with a shake of my head. Such loss, their lives sacrificed, snatched away so that others might have the freedom they were denied. It wasn't right. It would never be right. I turned away from Deirdre. I couldn't bear to look at her.

"This is why we didn't tell you," Deirdre said. "You're too good, Ro. You feel too much. But it'll be better now without all the dead inside your head." She patted my hand and filled my cup with the last of the tea from the thermos.

"What about Iona?"

"She can't leave the island, house arrest for now," Deirdre said. "Ash's mom hasn't made it easy for Ash either, but they're both leaving soon, and I'm sure Martha and the others will come around and drop the charges against Iona. Anyway, we brought sandwiches. Peanut butter and strawberry jam, your favorite."

Her favorite, but I accepted one anyway and took a bite, the jam far too sweet and peanut butter crunchy. I didn't want Iona to face charges, to end up behind bars like I had, despite what she'd done. I didn't know what to think, suddenly so alone without the ghosts inside my mind. My memories of their memories were all that remained, every thought and feeling entirely my own. But I didn't want these feelings, this heavy hurt grinding against betrayal. My sisters weren't the people I thought they were. There was a darkness in them I'd failed to see, and still struggled to believe when I glanced at Deirdre.

"Oh, you should know," she said. "Ash and their mum are leaving on the six o'clock ferry. They still think you're dead."

Ash.

They'd watched me die. Their last words reverberated inside me, angry, bitter, and justified. I had to see them, to explain, to apologize, to hope they wouldn't hate me.

I had to leave, to be far away from Deirdre, her smile and the blood on her delicate hands. I needed to escape this island, the magic, and what it had wrought, twisting our souls for generations. Gathering the blanket, I stood up, my muscles stronger for the tea and sandwich. My body responded more like it should, no longer operating according to the whims of others.

"Hold on, we brought you clothes." Deirdre handed me jeans and a sweater. She'd brought an old pair of my uncle's boots, too. "Mother is still having a hard time dealing with all this," she said while I dressed. "But Siobhan's with her, don't you worry. Still, seeing you might be a bit too much of a shock." She gave me a knowing look before whistling a loud, high note. A moment later, Auryn and Comet came trotting along the beach. I reached for my horse, wondering if she'd know me, changed as I was.

She lipped my hair and huffed sweet breath in my face.

Perhaps I wasn't as changed as much as I feared, then; perhaps I'd been changed far more than I could know.

I swung onto Auryn's back and surveyed the beach. I'd washed up in the cove where I'd placed pebbles on the eyes of so many of the dead, where I'd endured others' hatred and disdain. I turned Auryn away from the shadow of the pyre and left the cove without looking back.

Ash

OF COURSE the sun fucking shone the day we left, making tinsel out of the waves beneath a disgustingly blue sky without a single damn cloud in it.

Standing on the path overlooking the dock, I watched the ferry approach, snapping photos of the bay.

I wanted to remember this place.

I wanted to forget every fucking thing about it.

It had been a week since Rowan's death. Every time I closed my eyes, I still saw his hands on the hilt, the blade piercing his chest, his blood... Sometimes in my dreams, it wasn't Iona holding the knife, but me. Sometimes it was me on the cliff getting stabbed, the dagger leaving gaping holes all over my body. No wonder I felt so empty, with so much leaking out of me and no way to put a cork in it.

Mum was wrapping up last-minute business at the station, still pissed the charges against Iona and the others weren't likely to hold up. Eye-witness stories were a mess of inconsistencies, and there was a glaring lack of evidence for a conviction. I'd given my statement but couldn't lie about the fact Rowan had wrapped his hands around the dagger and stabbed himself through the chest.

Technically, it had been written off as suicide, and there was very little linking Iona, Teagan, or Cillian to any of the other murders. Mum would've liked to stay and make sure the guilty parties got punished, I think, but I was glad we were leaving. What did it matter? Nothing was going to bring Rowan back.

But Mum was nothing if not a stickler for paperwork. While she shored things up at the station, I had thirty-five minutes to kill before our return journey began. We were going back to the mainland, but not to the colonel. Mum had managed to rent a little apartment from Eileen Sheehy on the outskirts of the city where we'd stay until the divorce was finalized. I'd go back to school, and life would continue as it should've, minus my father. That much Mum had promised me. This time, I believed her.

Granddad had refused to go back, insisting on staying on the island after Rowan's gran paid a visit to our cottage. They'd both acted like love-sick teenagers. It was kind of gross and kind of adorable. I could only hope I didn't have to wait until I was seventy to find true love.

Ash.

The breeze teased my ears. Sometimes I still heard his voice out in the meadows, walking along the cliff tops, down on the beach. I saw his face when I closed my eyes, all the what-ifs playing through my mind. Maybe when I left the island behind, I'd leave Rowan, too. Maybe on the mainland I'd be able to forget his face, his kiss, and how he made me feel.

Ash.

There it was again, his voice on the wind. I closed my eyes. It was torture.

The ferry couldn't come fast enough. The two-hour

trip to the mainland was going to be excruciating but at least—

"Ash," a voice, so real, so close, the breeze like his breath against my neck. A warm hand on my arm.

I stared down at the fingers on my biceps. Freckled fingers leading to a freckled hand, to a wrist without ink, an arm without scars, but when I turned around to face the owner of that hand, it was Rowan staring back at me.

Hazel eyes, the left with a slightly darker band around the iris. His face was so familiar: freckles on his nose spilling across his lips, tumbling down his neck and disappearing beneath the collar of his shirt.

"Am I dreaming?" I asked. Maybe this was some cruel island payback for doing nothing while he died.

"No, it's me," he said. "Death didn't want me." His thumb grazed my cheek, his hand traveling down my arm to find my palm cut by the knife that ended his life. He lifted it, gently, and pressed it to his chest.

Thump-thump. Thump-thump. His heart thudded against my palm.

"But—how?" I held onto his fingers—I'd never let go—and turned his hand over, dragging my fingers across skin that should've been inked and scarred.

"I'm not sure exactly," he said in that broad drawl of his. It kicked up tornadoes of butterflies in my belly. "But what you read in the book was right."

"I think it was the ritual that made the first Rowan," I said, my hand on his shoulder now, squeezing, making sure he was real.

"It *unmade* me, too." He tugged the collar of his T-shirt down far enough to give me a glimpse of his chest. Nothing but smooth skin where there used to be a scar above his heart. "I'm not a deathwalker anymore. I'm—I'm free," he said as if he couldn't quite believe it himself.

"I saw you die. I tried to stop it. I—"

He turned my hand over and kissed the palm, still stitched and wrapped in a thin layer of bandage.

"I'm sorry." He hung his head, looking away. "I'm sorry you saw that. I'm sorry it happened at all."

"You made a choice," I said.

"For my sisters, for my family, and all the islanders." His bottom lip trembled, and I knew he had more to say. "For myself," he added as he looked up, his gaze intense. "I didn't want to die anymore. I needed it to stop. I hope you can understand. I hope you can forgive me."

My hand moved to the back of his neck, his skin hot and hair curling against my fingers. His honesty hurt, but I couldn't hate him for the choice he'd made. He loved his family, and I loved that about him. And how could I blame him for wanting to end all the shit he'd had to deal with carrying the souls of the dead? "There's nothing to forgive," I added, and the suffocating tightness in my chest fell away.

"Thank you, Ash." He exhaled and closed his eyes.

There was so much I wanted to say, but my words failed spectacularly. Kisses, however—

I tilted my head toward him, and our hearts beat, once, twice, before his lips found mine, his hands slipping around my waist, pulling me close. I kissed him back, long and hard, then soft and slow.

"What now?" I asked when we paused to catch our breath, his forehead resting against mine.

"Honestly, I don't know, but I don't want to stay on this island."

There was a backpack behind him and a ferry ticket poking out of his pocket.

"You can leave?"

"Aye, I think I can now," he said. "I have some family in the city, so that seems like a good place to start."

"If you need someone to show you around, teach this island boy how to be a mainlander, I think I might know where you could find them." My cheeks ached from the smile cracking across my face.

"I was hoping you might." His fingers slipped into mine, our palms pressed together like a promise.

Rowan picked up the bag and slung it over his shoulder before we started down the path. The ferry was pulling into port, Mum already down at the dock, scanning the cliff in search of me. She was going to freak out when I showed up with a dead boy by my side, but I didn't care.

Rowan paused on the path, glancing over his shoulder at the town.

"Do you think you'll ever forgive them all?" I asked, trying to keep the bitterness out of my voice. "Because I sure as hell won't."

"They did what they thought they had to," he said. "What they thought was right."

"They would've killed you either way. They weren't actually giving you a choice."

He swallowed and ran his hand through his hair. "It's why I have to leave. I don't—I can't think about it yet. It's complicated." He gritted his teeth hard enough for a muscle to twitch along his jaw. No shit it was complicated, and me giving him the third degree was hardly helping.

"Think you'll miss it?" I asked.

He took a long time to answer, still staring at the town. For several moments I thought maybe he'd change his mind, too afraid to leave what he'd always known, even if life here sucked.

"I'll miss it, parts of it at least," he said, "but I need to do this. I want to be somewhere else."

"To be *someone* else?" I asked.

"Maybe to just be me." He smiled, his hand squeezing mine. Together we continued along the path beneath a blue sky spewing sunshine while a weird bubbly sensation fizzed inside my chest. I think it might've been happiness.

Acknowledgements

THIS NOVEL wouldn't exist were it not for the love and support of so many people, from my earliest beta readers to the team at Skolion who turned a sheaf of papers into a real live book!

In thinking about who needed to be in these acknowledgments, I took a sledgehammer blow to the heart realizing that one of the very first people who believed in this story, back when it was just a 'what if?' and a dream of wild magic on a desolate shore, was Louise Gornall. I cannot put into words how much I miss her, how much I miss our conversations, how often I go to message her and am shocked, yet again, to discover she's no longer there to cheer me up when life and writing gets me down, to rant about plot holes and the vagaries of publishing, to discuss character development and life goals, to gush over travel plans or how good it feels to be alive in an era where adult clothes come bedazzled with sparkly unicorns too. This book is for you, Louise—the book of my heart. I only wish you were still here so I could put a copy in your hands.

I also owe an immense amount of gratitude to Katja for being an early champion of this story, for believing that Ash and Rowan deserved to find their place in the world, and for providing gentle guidance as a sensitivity reader for certain rep in this story.

I'd also like to thank other beta readers for their invaluable feedback: Sara Norja, Cat Hellisen, and Amy Lee Burgess (I hope I haven't forgotten anyone here. Mom? Yes, Mom too!).

332

Huge thanks are owed to my agent, Lindsay, for believing in this story at a time of such tremendous uncertainty as the world slipped sideways into the pandemic. Without Lindsay's encouragement, I might've left this story to wither on a hard drive.

I cannot thank my cover artist enough for creating a design that so perfectly captures the expressions of Ash and Rowan as well as the vibe of the story. Puhnatsson, it's perfect and I love it!

And now onto the Skolion team, without whom, this book would literally not exist: Nerine, Cat, Masha, Tallulah, Yolandie—thank you for making this writerly dream come true.

Lastly, I'd like to thank my family, especially Mark, who not only provides various technical assistance on all projects, puts up with being talked at while I work through a sticky plot point, and is a constant cheerleader for my writing even on the days when I wonder why I do it, but who has also allowed me to figure out who I am, never once leaving me to question his love as I continue to become my full authentic self.

About the Author

CLIMBER, TATTOO-ENTHUSIAST, peanut-butter addict and loyal shibe-minion, Xan van Rooyen is a genderqueer, non-binary storyteller from South Africa, currently living in Finland where the heavy metal is soothing and the cold, dark forests inspiring. Xan has a Master's degree in music, and—when not teaching—enjoys conjuring strange worlds and creating quirky characters. You can find Xan's short stories in the likes of Three-Lobed Burning Eye, Daily Science Fiction, and The Colored Lens among others. Xan hangs out on Instagram, Twitter, and Facebook so feel free to say hi over there.

CPSIA information can be obtained
at www.ICGtesting.com
Printed in the USA
LVHW090323080921
697225LV00004B/145